I0549505

Truth

BE
TOLD

by

Marsha R. West

TRUTH BE TOLD © 2015 Marsha R. West

Cover Art© Charlotte Volnek

Formatting by www.Top-ePublishingServices.com

All rights reserved. No part of this book maybe reproduced or transmitted in any form or by any means, electronic or mechanical, including photocopying, recording, or by any information storage and retrieval system, without permission in writing from the publisher.

The characters and events portrayed in this book are fictitious. Any similarity to real persons, living or dead, or events is coincidental and not intended by the author.

Print version published by MRW Press LLC
Released July 2015
ISBN for print version: 978-0-9961475-2-1

eBook version e-released by MuseItUp Publishing, Quebec, Canada
First eBook Edition May 2014
ISBN for eBook version: 978-1-77127-531-6

Edited by Lady Rosalie Skinner

Line edited by Sharon Pickrel

Layout and Book Production by Lea Schizas

ACKNOWLEDGEMENTS

To my wonderful husband, Bob. You have backed me in everything that I've ever wanted to do. ☺ Thank you for your incredibly fine editing skills and the time you spent to help make TRUTH BE TOLD look as good as it does. I couldn't have done this or any of other endeavors without your love and support.

A tip of the hat to Lea Schizas, MIU publisher, and the other fine folks at MIU who helped birth the e-version of this book: Lady Rosalie Skinner, my content editor, my line editor Sharon Pickrel, and Charlotte Volnek, cover artist for both the e-book and print books.

Excellent critique partners worked with me on TRUTH BE TOLD. Jerrie Alexander and Jeannie Guzman, you brainstormed with me, nagged me, and told me the "truth" about my writing even when I didn't want to hear. (They have had input in six of my books.) Renee Jones was even more of a grammarian than Jerrie and Jeannie. Thanks for loaning me your good eye. Denise Cohen, an on-line CP, gave valuable input, too.

Thanks too for the excellent formatting work of the folks at Top-ePublishing Services.

Margie Lawson, the things I learned from you while working on my first book, I used in this one and in all of my books. You've improved my writing in so many ways. Thanks to my daughters and sons-in-law for their support.

I'm so excited to add this to the acknowledgements. Thanks to my **Readers** who've told me how much they enjoyed the first and third books and wanted to know when TRUTH BE TOLD would be in print. Took me a bit longer than I hoped, but here it is.

You've heard that it takes a village to raise a child. Well, it takes a small town to get a book published. I am indeed fortunate to have such an excellent small town.

CHAPTER ONE

12:30 p.m. Friday, December 18

Meg Bourland jerked to a stop before she reached the bottom of the stairs in her parents' house. Her fingers tightened on the banister. The spit in her mouth dried up like the Texas fields in August. A figure in a long overcoat skulked through the study doorway. Meg reached toward her waist. Damn.

Her weapon lay in the lock box in her Atlanta condominium. Packing it in her bags with the clear marking on the outside, begged someone to steal it. Too great a risk for a flight to Fort Worth for Christmas with her family.

Hindsight was everything.

Meg sucked in a deep breath before she eased her head around the study door. Relief buckled her knees, and she staggered back into the hall. She whooshed out the breath she'd held.

"Stupid. Stupid. Stupid." She slammed her hand on her thigh in time with the whispered words. Damn, the psychologist was right. Meg was close to losing her grip. Not as fine as she claimed, or she wouldn't have over-reacted.

Her father in the shape of the tall dark figure came home earlier than expected and not taken time to remove his coat.

She rubbed a hand over her eyes, sucked in more air then stepped through the doorway into the study.

"I suspected for a moment someone had broken in, Dad. Glad it's just you." Her voice wasn't as strong as she'd intended. Her father didn't respond. Didn't he hear her? He threw a crumpled paper across the room, and then he sank into the chair behind his desk. His head cradled between his hands.

Adrenalin kicked through her system again shooting lightening spikes down her arms. "Dad, is something wrong?" Again no response. Meg moved further into the study. The pipe smoke smell dimly registered. Was he having a heart attack? She stopped in front of his desk. "Dad?" Almost shouted the word.

"What?" He looked up. His gaze lighted on her for a moment before darting around the room.

Didn't he recognize her?

"Meg?" He shoved his hair off his forehead and dragged in a breath. "When did you arrive?" He asked in a voice tight with strain. His gaze never connected with hers.

Not a heart attack. Thank God. She let out a huff of air. "A while ago. Are you all right?"

Her father placed his hands on the desk and straightened into the ramrod posture she'd seen all her life.

"Everything's fine."

He used the same word Meg did when things were the opposite of all right.

"Glad you got home okay." His voice was stronger now. He shuffled through files on his desk. "I…uh…came to pick up this folder." Unusual for her father to stammer. He was always self-assured. He waved the file in the air and shoved others into the center drawer. "I'm heading back to work now."

He threw an arm around her shoulder, hustled them out of his study, and closed the door with a distinct thud.

"But Dad—"

"Don't mention to your mother you saw me."

He glanced toward Meg, but still he made no eye contact. All her cop instincts shouted this was trouble.

"She'll tease me about my memory and try to stick one of her blasted pills down my throat. See you tonight." Her father brushed past her in his rush to get out of the house.

Meg stood for a minute in the open doorway, but then a blast of cold wind skittered in and disturbed the rug lying on the hardwood floor of the entry. She shivered, turned the lock, and straightened the rug before slipping into the living room. She could just make out the taillights of his car as he wheeled down the street.

The flickering flames from the gas fire delivered welcome warmth. She rubbed her hands up and down her arms. What just happened?

The scent of the fresh evergreen enveloped her in the essence of the holidays. As long as they'd lived here, a real tree took center stage in the bay windows of the living room and her father's study. White lights and ornaments bedecked the tall firs. The cheerfulness out of sync with her father's odd behavior.

"Dad," she whispered the word. They hadn't seen each other since the incident resulting in the loss of one her teammates. The incident that almost took her life. Scenes flashed across her consciousness, and her heart pounded faster than a woodpecker's beak against a tree.

Gritting her teeth, she shoved the pictures into the black hole of memory. She clenched her fingers around her forearms and muttered under her breath. "I'm fine, I'm fine. Not my fault." She leaned over with her hands on her knees and drew in big gulps of air. Each breath came out more slowly, her heart rate slowed, until she had herself under control.

Dad had barely hugged her. And don't tell Mom? His words made Meg more determined to speak to her.

On the other hand, she'd suspected her father was a burglar. As much as she resented the psychologist in Atlanta suggesting she go home for two weeks, this may be for the best. She wasn't as fine as she kept telling people. And herself. She headed toward the study to see what the paper was her father threw away.

Loud clumps down the stairs drew her attention, and she returned to the entryway. Sure enough. David. He always rushed to eat their mother's cooking. Meg raised a finger to her lips. At this rate, he'd wake up his partner Scott McClaine who'd come to recuperate with their family.

Her brother slowed his descent. "What?"

"Scott's sleeping."

"And you know that how?" David joined her at the bottom of the stairs.

"Because I peeked in on him before coming down. His

forehead furrowed, and he moaned, not a peaceful sleep at all."

"Personal experience?" David's voice dropped in pitch, and he placed a hand on her shoulder.

"Yeah." She nodded then shoved away her own demons.

Certainly, her brother's partner deserved a happier life after what he'd sacrificed saving David's life. As a cop herself, she understood the risks her brother and Scott took serving and protecting the city of Los Angeles. "Come into the den with me a minute. I'd like to ask you something before we eat lunch."

"Sure. I can survive a few more minutes if you can talk louder than my stomach's growling."

Her brother always the jokester. They reached the TV room, and Meg yanked him down next to her on one of deep leather sofas. "What's going on with Dad?"

"What do you mean?"

Meg told him about the incident in their father's study. David, never one to sit still long, hopped off the sofa and paced in front of the fireplace.

"He didn't give you one of those giant hugs of his, crushing your ribs?"

Meg shook her head. An ache grew in her middle. Did health issues keep her father from lifting her off her feet? Had she somehow disappointed him?

David stopped walking and pinned her with one of his interrogator glares. "He asked how you were doing after Hank's shooting, right?"

She shook her head. A small twinge took up life in her left temple.

"Odd." David shoved his hands in his pockets and returned to crisscrossing the room.

Pain blossomed in both of Meg's temples. She pressed her palms to the sides of her head, hoping to stop its growth to a debilitating level. If the pounding didn't recede, she'd have no choice but to resort to meds, and she hated the way they made her feel.

"Anything else?" Her brother's eyebrows rose in question.

As if with a life of their own, her fingers dropped to her lap and twisted together into a knot about the size of the one in her stomach. "He told me not to tell Mom he'd come home."

"What's with that crap?" David stopped walking. "One of their cardinal rules was always don't keep secrets." He dropped onto the sofa next to her.

"Yeah. They always said if someone tells you not to tell, you probably should. It's the advice I always gave kids I mentored."

David had talked her into volunteering with Big Brothers and Big Sisters in Fort Worth when they'd both lived in town. Her brother mentored a boy now and again in LA. In Atlanta, Meg had dropped the activity. Too many times, she'd had to disappoint her little sister because of spur of the moment assignments.

"What about the paper he crushed and threw away?"

"I didn't have a chance to look. You came down."

"What are we waiting on? Let's go." He rose, grabbed her hand, and strode toward the front of the house.

"Hey, aren't you two hungry?"

Mom. Meg glanced at David. He shrugged and faced their mother.

"You bet. We're heading your way right now." He rubbed his stomach and veered toward the kitchen.

"Great. Everything is ready." Her mother embraced Meg. "I'm glad you're home, dear. You and I will talk later." Mom's shortened "I" sounds and dropped "r's" spoke of her birth in South Carolina, even though she hadn't lived there since college.

She briefly hugged Meg once more. Her heart rated dropped to normal. Guess you never got too old to draw comfort from your mother's embrace.

Meg followed them into the kitchen. David had settled into his spot at the table. Her mother lifted Meg's favorite cobalt blue pottery bowls from the shelf and filled them. "Crackers or rolls?" She set the soup in front of Meg and her brother. Steam carried the mouthwatering aroma to her nose, and apparently, to her brother's, too. His stomach growled louder this time.

"Rolls, if they're yours," Meg said.

David nodded at Meg, and she grinned back. As kids, they'd always fought with their baby sister Kathy over who got the last one.

"Is Scott still resting?" Her mother joined them at the table.

"He's asleep." Meg leaned over and sniffed. She loved her mother's potato soup, always seasoned perfectly, with more than a hint of garlic and onion. Her stomach rumbled.

"Long time since you ate, sis?"

"Yeah. Breakfast bar around six this morning before heading for the airport."

"You know we're happy to open our home to Scott for as long as he needs, son. We'll never be able to repay him for what he did."

David dug into the soup as if he hadn't eaten in days. "I don't know what he'll do without the job. It glued him together." David grabbed a roll.

"Such a shame what happened to him. And he's a great young man." Mom crumbled more crackers into her bowl than usual.

Meg met David's gaze. His eyebrows tipped up to his hairline. Her mother's description of Scott as a "young man" brought a smile to Meg's face. Sweet, but not true. David and Scott were the same age, but right now Scott looked older than her brother who'd celebrated his forty-third birthday several months ago.

Stress and pain had gouged craggy lines in Scott's face after he'd stepped in front of the bullets meant for David. His longer hair had more grey than her brother's did. Pictures taken before his hospital stay showed a strong, well-built man. A sharp contrast to the wiry body of the man she and David had picked up at the airport earlier in the day.

"I hate he's dealing with such a lot right now when we're celebrating." Her mother's chin trembled, but she straightened her back and didn't give in to emotion.

"Scott's strong. I'm concerned about him, but he'll work his way through this." David tipped his bowl to scoop out the last of the thickened liquid.

Had David stated what he believed or only hoped?

"Got any more?" he asked. "Nobody makes this as good as you do, Mom."

"You've got the flattering gene from your father, son. Of course, there's more." Her mother's well-worn, western boots clicked on the tile kitchen floor when she moved to the stove. She ladled the stew-like mixture into his bowl. "What does he do when he's not on duty?"

"Scott? He's all work except when I can drag him to a ball game when I'm taking one of the little brothers. Thanks." David sprinkled cheese in the bowl his mother set in front of him.

The way he went at it, no one would guess he'd polished off one already.

"But you're involved with hobbies, David. You play fantasy football, which I don't guess I'll ever understand, and you follow all the sporting events, plus your mentoring work.

"Not fishing or bowling. But yeah, pretty much everything else."

"All those are important. It's something to take you away from your stress-filled job. Meg, you play volleyball and you've been a Big Sister."

"Yeah, but after Jerry was killed, I didn't do much of anything but work for a couple of years." The pitch of her voice had lowered when she mentioned her fiancé. Her family hadn't cared for him and he'd been a source of contention between them. While they didn't wish him ill, they were glad she and Jerry had never married. Meg tore a roll into pieces and drove the hurtful memories into the dark.

"What family Scott had was connected to the job. And now, no job," David said.

"We'll have to do something about his situation." Her mother rose and retrieved more rolls from the warmer, placing one in front of Meg. "Are you all right, dear? You've got a frown between your eyebrows."

Nothing much got past her mother.

"I'm fine. Only a twinge from a growing headache." The psychologist had indicated they'd be around as long as she buried her feelings about what happened. She also didn't remember her dreams anymore. Another marker of the stress still holding her in its grip.

"He can't be allowed to wallow in self-pity. The man's a hero." Her mother placed her hands on her hips. A sure sign she was about to embark on a campaign. "He needs to be getting on with his life."

Poor Scott. If Mom decided to make him a project…well, no one focused more on getting a job done than Ellie Bourland when she set out to accomplish something.

"Where's Maria?" Their housekeeper had been with them for many years, and Meg hadn't seen her yet. Maybe she could shift her mother's mind off their guest.

"She's gone to the meat market for the steaks for tonight. All she's talked about lately is having all three of you kids home at the same time. She's as excited as I've been. Scott knows Kathy, Ron, and the grands are coming for the holidays?"

Her mother switched the subject back to their guest.

"Yeah. I warned him." David sopped up the last of the soup with one of the rolls. "The rehab center wouldn't let him out to go home by himself, and there wasn't any place else for him to go."

"Well, there couldn't be any better place for Scott than here. He'll eat plenty of nutritious meals, and I'll find a good woman for him. While he's healing, he shouldn't be alone. I bet Joe can help find him a new job."

Her eyes twinkled at the prospect of a project. Mom, never happier than when she had someone or something to fix, wasn't about to drop her rescue mission.

David sighed and looked at Meg, his eyebrows raised. "Help," he mouthed.

She nodded. "Thanks, Mom, great soup. I'll run lunch up to Scott. We shouldn't let him sleep the day away, or he'll be forever adjusting to the new time."

"Good idea." Her brother nodded his encouragement.

"Let me fix a tray for you, dear. Your father may or may not find any whenever he returns from the office."

Her mother rolled her eyes. Meg shoved a piece of roll in her mouth to keep from laughing.

Her parents were movers and shakers in Fort Worth. Her father had held the mayor's position for fourteen years. People had been surprised when she and David left the FWPD and relocated to other parts of the country.

However, the man, who'd filled the seat before her father, had jerked strings for his family, got them into important positions with the city, gave them special grants, let them go on city trips at taxpayers' expense, and set off all sorts of ethics investigations. To remove themselves as possible fodder for those out to make problems for their father, Meg and David had chosen to leave.

She climbed the stairs to the bedrooms. She didn't intend to barge in on something not her business, but she couldn't let her mother blindside Scott when she paraded women in front of him. A gentle warning seemed in order.

She eased open his door with her rear and backed into the room. Turning to face the bed, she studied their guest. Something about him had kicked her libido into high gear. From the moment she'd seen him at the airport, her stomach had turned flip-flops.

Lord, here she stood ogling the man like a voyeur. Her voice came out soft with a breathy quality when she called his name. Better get a grip. She cleared her throat and tried again.

"Scott." Good, more force.

"What?" His eyes popped open.

Meg jerked at his loud voice, and she sloshed the soup. "Wow, do you always yell when you wake up?" Her heart rate kicked into an erratic rhythm. Must be because he startled her.

He struggled to sit up, grabbing his side. "Uh, yeah." He scooted back against the headrest, groaning when he moved.

"We wanted to help you adjust your body clock in tune with local hours, so we couldn't let you to sleep too long. I've brought a bowl of Mom's potato soup, guaranteed to make you feel better."

"It smells great. Thanks." The half-smile didn't reach his eyes.

"Are you comfortable?"

He nodded.

Meg fought the urge to touch Scott's shoulder, and her hand trembled when she placed the tray across his legs. What was the matter with her? She stepped back while he took his first spoonful of the steaming soup.

"Umm, good."

"Mom's a great cook." Meg walked to the window and stared out on the street. Not being a main artery, the road had little through traffic. As kids, she and her siblings had played outside without worrying their parents. Her father made time to pitch to them.

Her stomach tightened like someone had belted her. She and David had to find the paper.

The sound of Scott's spoon hitting the bowl drew her attention back to him. He had a strong face, but with more lines than one expected in a man his age, even a homicide detective.

He'd been patient, not inquiring why she'd stayed.

"This is awkward." Meg eased on to the edge of the bed.

"What is?"

"I need to warn you about my mother."

"Warn? What about?" He frowned, accentuating the creases above his nose.

"She's a nice person, but Mom worries about folks. She works overtime to help them if they're in trouble."

"I'm not following you."

She drew in a deep breath and then let it out, deciding to be straight with him. "Okay, here goes. Mom's concerned you don't have enough outside interests, and she's worried what you'll do without your job. She'll provide opportunities to expand your horizons." Meg paused and cut a sidewise glance at him. "More than activities. She'll introduce you to women she considers appropriate company for you." Meg finger quoted.

"Appropriate, huh?"

Now his smile lit up his eyes, and Meg looked away, afraid he'd see the desire she suspected lingered in hers. Her gaze flitted back to his face. The corners of his mouth twitched. He picked up the roll and sank his teeth into the bread. She cleared her throat before going on. "She's concerned. Mom's grateful for what you did for us and wants to help."

"Why do you think this?" He stirred the still steaming soup.

"Besides her telling me and David? It's what she did when my fiancé was killed."

Scott's spoon stopped halfway to his mouth. "Sorry for your loss, Meg. What happened?"

"Jerry was a cop."

"Oh?"

"He went on a domestic disturbance call and kept the husband from harming the wife, but the bastard shot Jerry." A surge of cold anger still bubbled upward, but she drew in a deep breath and pretended to relax. "A good cop, Jerry didn't deserve what happened."

Even though, he had an affair going with the wife of another officer. Meg didn't find out until after the shooting. Many years ago, but still the shame of the discovery twisted her guts. Why hadn't she seen the signs? Today she still wondered at her blindness. Afterwards, and for several years, she'd doubted her ability to read people.

"Long ago?"

"I'd been on the force here for a couple of years when it happened."

"Rough for you." He spooned soup into his mouth and swallowed before continuing. "Your mother shoved you back into action?"

"Yeah. I had a hard time. At first I felt like a widow without the right to wear black."

He nodded. "A few years ago, I lost my parents and fiancée in a car accident. Drunk driver hit them. People trying to be helpful said to me, 'At least you weren't married.' Like it made a hell of a lot of difference to the pain."

Meg nodded. "You get it." His understanding helped her let go of the death grip she'd taken on her hands. It was long ago and shouldn't still matter, and yet, somehow it did. She forced her hands apart from their unconscious clench.

"Mom decided she'd given me adequate healing time, took matters into her own hands, and started introducing me to likely candidates."

"What'd you do?"

"If they had a dull, safe job—like an accountant, or sales rep—I'd go. If they were in one of the military services, any kind of law enforcement, or medical emergency personnel, I said 'thanks, but I'm busy.'"

His eyebrows rose, and he nodded. "How long did she keep up her matchmaker role?"

"Oh, she's still carrying on. My move to Atlanta didn't stop her, only slowed her down. Anyone she knows who's coming on business or vacation, she's made sure to give them my phone number."

"There's been no one else?"

Meg swallowed loud enough he must've heard. She went with the honest answer, even if it made her out to be a loser.

"Nothing serious." *Pitiful, Meg. Just pitiful.* The idea of Scott feeling sorry for her set the gavel banging in her head again.

"She's still trying to set you up?"

His lips curved into a smile, and he used his roll to sop up the last of the soup the way her brother had.

"Oh, yeah. About four months ago, she sent a racecar driver. After his call, I fell over laughing. Why she thought he'd work out, I'll never know. The addition of the grandkids has been a Godsend. Not only are they cutie pies, but they keep Mom busy. While they don't live here, she and Dad visit them in Oklahoma City, and Kathy brings them down every other month."

Scott placed his napkin on the tray.

"I'm glad you liked the lunch." She stood, picked up his tray, and walked toward the door then turned. "I didn't want to intrude, but I wanted to give you a heads-up on what Mom's up to."

"I appreciate your concern. No harm done. Your mother's right. I probably should be able to move on, but hey…maybe what I've needed was a healthy dose of Ellie Bourland."

Meg's stomach twisted. The pain in her head increased. Did the discomfort relate to the idea of Scott going out with the women her mother set him up with? Stupid of her then. She and Scott had only met today.

In his weakened condition, he still managed to make her hormones stand up and shout. Women must hang all over him. The last time she'd had this reaction to a man…well, no memory jumped to her mind. Scott's scent, the needing-a-shave-look, and his deep brown eyes reached her at a primal level. His effect on her promised an interesting two week holiday.

* * * *

5:45 p.m. Friday, December 18

Meg's father returned from the office shortly after they'd finished the late lunch and holed up in the study, preventing her and David from looking for the paper. Her inability do anything drove her outside to battle the elements. A black cap covered her ears, but her coat lost out to the temperatures in the low thirties. How long had she been gone?

"Hey. Want company?"

Startled, she glanced to her right. David jogged up, wearing a light jacket. A scarf thrown around his neck his only concession to the frigid temperatures.

"Did Dad leave his study? Were you able to go in?" Meg jogged in place.

"No. Mom sent me to remind you to leave time to clean up before supper."

Vapor billowed in front of his mouth. He looked like a cartoon character whose words filled the cloud.

"How late is it?"

"You're okay. She's worried because the temps are low, and because she's Mom."

"And being Mom, she's probably right." Meg kicked up to a faster pace.

"Hey, where're you going?"

"I'm beating you home." She cut across one yard and headed for the next.

"Not fair." Her brother yelled after her.

The thump of her tennis shoes beat a syncopated rhythm to her heartbeat. Then her brother's longer strides ate up the ground, slowly catching up to her. She jumped a low hedge.

At the sound of a crash and yelp, Meg paused and looked behind. David had misjudged the width of the hedge. She smothered a laugh when he got up. He survived. The bush not so much. She flew on, leading all the way to their yard. Breathing hard and laughing, she burst through the front door just ahead of him. They skidded to a halt in front of their mother.

"I considered sending out the bloodhounds to find you two.

Will I hear about any of your shenanigans from the neighbors like I used to?" she teased them.

Meg looked at her brother, shrugged her shoulders, and they both burst out laughing.

"I swear. Put you two together and it's like you're kids all over again." As if remembering those early times, her mother shook her head and sighed, but a smile quirked up the corner of her mouth. "Supper will be ready soon, Get a move on."

"I'm heading up." David headed for the stairs.

"Check on Scott, will you, David? Tell me if he's coming down or needs a tray upstairs. I'm glad he's been able to rest most of the day."

"Will do." With a wink at Meg, David took off up the stairs two at a time.

She stopped to shove the hat in a pocket of her coat and hang it in the closet. "Can I help you, Mom?"

"No, Maria's done the majority of the preparations. I'm cook."

"What are the chances for one of her enchilada dinners while I'm home?"

"I can promise we'll arrange that." Her mother laughed. "Tonight is chicken fried steak, mashed potatoes, and fresh green beans."

"Yum. What a great way to welcome a daughter home."

"I'm proud of you, you know." Her mother kissed Meg on the cheek, took hold of her shoulders, and looked directly into her eyes. "Are you really okay, dear?"

"Sure, Mom." Nothing else to say. No reason to cause her mother more worry.

"The Turners are coming by later for our bridge night. You don't mind?"

"Of course, not. It'll be nice to see them."

"Good." Her mother squeezed her shoulder once and let go. She went through the dining room and pressed open the kitchen door.

"Where's Dad?" Meg asked.

"In the study. He's promised to show up for supper." The steely glint in her mother's eyes trumpeted her expectation he'd better be at the head of the table when they all sat down or she'd know the reason why. The soft swish of the door closing brought comfort. Mom and Maria were cooking. All was right with the world. Or maybe not.

With Dad in his study, Meg couldn't sneak in to look for the paper. She climbed the stairs to freshen up after her run. When she got to her room, she opened the closet door and looked at the possibilities. Her gaze landed on the black cords and her favorite teal and black, scooped neck sweater. They'd work for tonight. She gathered up her clothes and made for the bathroom for a quick sponge off.

When she returned, she grabbed her black western boots standing against the back wall of the closet. She jammed her feet in them and added a silver chain with a turquoise stone around her neck. After brushing, she let her hair fly loose. The more practical ponytail aggravated the headache, which had pounded from the moment she found her father acting oddly in his study.

She'd given in and taken the prescription before she jogged around the neighborhood. The run hadn't brought back the discomfort. The cold air along with the pills helped. Sometimes wearing the ponytail for too long started the drill bit banging against her temples.

Meg took a last look in the mirror. She nodded, then turned and stepped into the hall to see if Scott was ready to go down. Before she rapped the second time, the door swung inward. A God-like specimen stood in front of her. Sick or not, Scott McClaine was the most handsome man Meg had ever seen.

"Supper will be ready soon. How about joining us?" Her voice sounded a bit shaky.

His cheekbones angled sharply above a scruffy beard. She schooled her face to remain passive, but her insides warmed up like the blazing sun. Afraid the desire rushing through her blood would burst from her eyes she cast her gaze toward his chin. Jeez, he had one of those movie star clefts. Her stomach nose-dived to her feet or below.

Scott stepped across the threshold and closed the door behind him. "That's the plan. David's told me these tall Texas tales about a steak the size of a dinner plate. I didn't buy it and bet him he was pulling my leg."

A clean, man scent enveloped Meg when Scott stepped close. She backed away, and forced words from her lips. "You'll lose. Our cook Maria asks the butcher to cut these particularly large for her. Dad and David always eat a whole one, which is what you'll get. You up for it?"

He nodded.

"Mom's determined to help you regain your strength." She smiled at him, hoping the words sounded positive and not critical.

Scott held on to the banister, and she walked in the middle to be in position to assist on his left side if needed. Even though they went slowly, he was a winded when they reached the bottom, and they paused, giving him a chance to catch his breath.

"I hate this shit." The muscle in his jaw jerked. His knuckles whitened where he grasped his cane.

Meg wasn't certain he knew the words had passed his gritted teeth, but she couldn't ignore his pain and laid a hand on his arm. "It's only been a month. It took me a good solid six weeks to recover from a gunshot wound several years ago. Then I worked at about four-fifths of peak. Four weeks more until I got back to a hundred percent."

"But I won't make it back to a hundred percent." He yanked his arm away. "I'm medically retired, and I'll always walk with this god-damned cane." He stabbed the floor accentuating each word.

The anguish in his tone struck Meg like a slap to the face. Heat rushed to her face. How stupid of her. David warned her of Scott's sensitivity to his condition. "I'm sorry. This must hurt like hell."

"No, I apologize. Not your fault." He didn't look at her. "No reason to take your head off. Nobody's fault. It's the way things are." His lips narrowed into a hard line.

Meg stood next to him unsure what to do next. Imagining what he must be experiencing created a giant hole in her middle. The reality for him must be ten times worse. Saving her brother's life had cost Scott his career.

After pulling in a series of long breaths, he met her gaze. "So you telling me these steaks are as big as David claims?" His eyebrows slid upwards.

"How much did you bet?"

"Twenty dollars. Seemed safe enough."

"Well, you can kiss the Andrew Jackson good-by. Right now, it's winging straight to David's pocket."

Scott's deep rumble of laughter surprised her and made her insides go all quivery. Damn, this man knocked the breath out of her. She'd better find a way to keep her distance if she wanted to sail through this holiday unscathed, heart whole, and smelling like a lily.

"Let's go check out these slabs of beef."

His fingers curled around her elbow as if he needed more help than from his cane. Meg wanted to believe he'd wanted to make contact with her. Did the same electricity hit him the way it did her? If so, would the ultimate crash and burn be worth the ride?

CHAPTER TWO

6:50 p.m. Friday, December 18

Scott walked beside Meg into the den. David sat on a dark leather sofa talking with his father. Both men rose when he and Meg entered.

"Good to see you again, son. To say thank you for saving David's life is such an understatement to express how indebted we are to you." Her father's words rumbled out in a deep voice.

It had been several years since they'd seen each other. Joe Bourland's salt and pepper hair had gone entirely white, but his grasp was as strong and vital as before.

"Nice to see you again, Mr. Bourland, and thanks for letting me come."

"I asked you to call me Joe when you were here before. You've always got a home with us here." He clapped Scott on the shoulder. "I'm serious."

Scott forced a laugh. He'd give anything, but David's life, for this not to be a topic of conversation. "If I can't find something to do in LA, I'll consider taking you up on the offer. I like the small town feel of Fort Worth combined with the big city amenities."

"As mayor and on behalf of the city council, I thank you. I'm sure we can find a place for you on our PR staff." The smile on Joe's face grew larger when he faced his daughter. "Meg, I need a hug, darlin'." His arms enveloped her, and he lifted her right off the floor.

He picked up his knife, but Meg's hand on his stopped him. He worked to ignore the jolt, which hit his groin at her touch.

"The knife won't be necessary. The meat's tender enough you'll be able to cut it with a fork."

She smiled, and her blue green eyes sparkled.

"You lying?"

"Nope. Trust me."

Scott glanced around the table again, and everybody seemed to be waiting on him, so he did what Meg said. His fork slid through the funny looking steak like it was a soft banana. Easy.

"Make sure you taste the gravy." Joe's fork poised in mid-air with white sauce dripping from a piece of steak speared on the tines.

"This is good. Chicken fried steak, huh? Why don't we ever eat this in LA, David?"

"I never order it anymore. Got tired of always being disappointed. I come home and have the real thing." David chomped down on a large bite of steak.

"And I thought you came to see us." Ellie mocked him. Everyone joined in her laughter.

Scott got a hand in his pants pocket and slid out his wallet. He handed a twenty across the table to David. "You win, bud, and I always pay my debts."

Ellie brushed David's hand away when he reached out to take the bill. "You are not taking money from this man who saved your life. What are you thinking of? Both of you."

Her gaze swung between Scott and her son, daring them to

continue with the transaction.

"Mom, it's all right. It was a mostly fair wager, and as Scott says, he's an honorable man who pays his debts." Meg winked at her mother. "Let the men play their games."

Scott glanced at the people at the table. Ellie gazed at her son again, Joe ate, and David glared at Meg. Then she shifted toward Scott.

The quirky, half-smile still in place until she met his gaze. The moment she connected with him, electricity zinged through his system. Her pupils dilated, and her lips parted when she took in a quick breath. Heated air sucked them up into a bubble. Everything else faded from Scott's attention. The only two people alive were he and the black haired beauty at his side.

After a moment, she blinked and turned away from him. "What?"

"Meg. Don't hoard the Texas toast."

David's voice filtered through to Scott. *Whoa, buddy. What the hell happened?* Had he imagined her reaction? No way would this gorgeous woman be interested in a washed up cripple.

"Do you like the cream gravy with the steak, Scott?" Ellie stared at him.

"Yeah. It's great." So taken up with her daughter, he'd only had a couple of bites. As soon as they finished the meal, he'd make his excuses and go up to his room. He needed to put distance between him and Meg. Being this close kicked his libido into high gear. On one level, he was glad it still functioned.

He got through the meal focusing on the others at the table.

He'd return to LA to do who the hell knew what, and she'd return to Atlanta at the end of the holiday. End of story.

"Kathy and Ron are driving down Monday, the twenty-first. You'll be amazed at how big Ronny and Katie are now." Ellie turned toward Scott. "If I remember correctly, you don't have any children."

"No, I don't."

"Mom," David protested.

"I'm making conversation, dear. I haven't seen Scott in a number of years, and his not being married doesn't eliminate the possibility of offspring. At least the last time I checked." She raised a hand to smother a chuckle. "It's not like I can count on you sharing, David."

"It's okay." Scott straightened his shoulders, trying to loosen the tension settling in from his imaginative wanderings about Meg. "No kids, Ellie. No wife." He pushed aside memories of Tricia. He met David's gaze, but neither of them said anything.

"So how about them Cowboys?" Joe redirected the conversation and for the rest of the meal, the subject revolved around football teams.

Maria entered the dining room with a tray holding small bowls of dessert. "And in case the hunger bug attacks any of you later, I left sandwiches in the refrigerator."

"Thank you, Maria, but I can't imagine anyone wanting to eat more after this wonderful meal." Ellie finished her glass of wine.

"It's always best to be prepared, Mrs. Ellie."

After dinner, the Turners arrived but without their children.

They'd get in later and stop by then. Ellie, Joe and their guests went to the garden room for bridge. Scott took the opportunity to escape. "If you don't mind, I'll turn in early. Not much stamina yet."

"Best thing for you, man. See you in the morning." David patted Scott on the shoulder.

Scott nodded once toward Meg and shuffled toward the stairs.

* * * *

Meg forced her attention from Scott. If circumstances were different…well, they weren't so she'd be content with following his exit with your eyes. She shoved her hands in the pockets of her cords and focused on David. "I'm glad Jim and Jeff Turner haven't gotten here yet. They'd drag you out for a beer, and we need to search for the paper Dad threw away this morning."

"After you." He held his arm out for her to pass in front of him. "The bridge game will keep Dad and Mom occupied for quite a while."

They hurried toward the study. Meg's stomach tensed worrying about what they'd find. She opened the door and inhaled. The aroma of her father's pipe smoke filled her nose and brought memories of her childhood when he and her grandfather took turns blowing smoke rings for her, David, and Kathy. The kids competed over how many rings each of them caught on their wrist.

This smell, like no other, spoke of the comfort of her childhood, the importance of family, and the group of people who always accepted you. Well, pipe tobacco and the taste of her mother's oatmeal cookies.

"Where was Dad when he threw the paper?" David scanned the room with the air of a detective seeing the place for the first time and not the firstborn son in his family home.

"Behind his desk." Meg took up the position, studying the room. "He threw toward the fireplace then slumped into his chair."

"I don't see anything on the floor. Could the paper have reached the fireplace?"

Meg crossed the rug between the desk and hearth. "Maybe." Thankfully, a fire hadn't been set in a while. She knelt and leaned in. She gasped. A crumpled paper lay in the left corner of the blackened bricks. Snatching it from its hiding place, she stood, and held her breath a moment before forcing air in and out of her lungs. "Okay, let's find out what upset Dad earlier this afternoon." She flicked on the Tiffany light hanging above the desk, unfolded the wad, and smoothed out the wrinkles.

"What's it say, Meg?"

"It appears to be a letter." She read out loud.

> *December 18*
> *Dear Mayor Bourland,*
>
> *David is a handsome man, and Meg is a beautiful woman.*

Her gaze flew to her brother. "What in the world?"

"Keep reading."

She did.

You must be very proud of them.

Before Peggy Coffee died, she left me papers she'd collected over the years about the great Joseph Bourland, current mayor of Fort Worth. I'm Peggy's son, and she was very proud of me.

If you don't want me to share this information with the city council, send $5,000 to PO Box 1340, Fort Worth, TX 76116, by next Monday.

Your friend,
Chuck.

"Oh, my God. Dad's being blackmailed." Shock made her hands shake, and blood drained from her head, making her almost faint. The steak she'd over indulged in rolled up the back of her throat, and she fought the urge to throw up. "Why would someone blackmail him?"

"I don't know, Meg." David rubbed a hand across the back of his neck. His tell when something worried him.

Her hands clenched, and her blood raced at her stupidity. "What was I thinking? I've contaminated the document by not wearing gloves when I picked this up off the floor. The police won't be able to trace any evidence from it." She strode back and forth across the room. Movement helped her think. "Dad couldn't be involved in anything criminal."

"No way."

She held the note up by the corner. "The blackmailer is focused on Dad knowing he or someone is the son of this Peggy Coffee."

"Who is she and why does it matter if she had a son?" David took up his own pacing.

The doorbell sounded its deep, double chime. "Jeez. Hurry up and answer the door." Meg stepped into the front hallway.

The chime rang again, accompanied by snorts and laughter.

"Come on out, David. We heard you were home. Let's grab a brewski."

"Jeff Turner," her brother muttered.

"Get out of here, or their racket will bring Dad to the front, before we've had a chance to discuss this and figure out a game plan. We'll talk when you get home."

"Good." David yanked his jacket out of the closet and opened the front door. "Keep your shirts on guys. I'm coming."

Cold wind drifted in before he closed the door.

A bottle of beer and the calmness of the living room might spark an inspiration about this whole, crazy deal. In the butler's pantry, Meg poured the golden, frothy brew into a tall pilsner, took the paper from her pocket, and read it over again before heading for the front of the house. She went through the kitchen but came to an abrupt stop at the sight of their guest with his head in the refrigerator.

Not upstairs sleeping as she'd presumed.

She'd had no time to deal with the feelings Scott too easily aroused in her. But she couldn't be so impolite as to ignore him.

"Uh, hi." Her voice squeaked like a teenager.

He jerked up. The slam of his head against the top dug at her middle.

"Oh," he moaned and then spun around, one hand rubbed where he'd collided with the metal.

"Sorry if I startled you." She shoved the paper in her pocket. "Can I help you find anything?"

"Yeah. I'm looking for those sandwiches Maria stashed someplace."

"They're in the small fridge in the pantry. I'll get them." Glad for the excuse to put space between her and her brother's too-sexy-for-her-own-good former partner, she escaped. She placed a sandwich on a plate, grabbed a napkin and a bag of chips. When she returned, Scott sat at the table with one leg propped on a chair.

"Sorry." He moved, starting to rise, but a moan snuck past his clenched jaw.

"Don't. Your injury gets you a pass on manners. We're a pretty casual family."

"Care to join me?" He gestured to a chair.

She opened her mouth to refuse, but the man was a guest of her family's. More importantly, he'd saved her brother's life, and at no small cost to himself. "Would you like something to drink?"

"Milk, I think."

She set a tall glass of the white liquid on the table.

"Thanks." Scott took a quick swallow. "So are you making me eat by myself?" One attractive eyebrow rose.

She slid into a chair across from him, hoping the short distance would be enough to alleviate the effect he had on her. "Out of curiosity, where will you put anything else after practically inhaling the steak at supper?"

"Give a guy a break, will you? Protein will improve my health." His teeth sank into the cold steak sandwich.

She forced her gaze away and cleared her throat. "I can warm the plate for you."

"No thanks. Fine this way."

She shoved her hands in her pockets then yanked them out and lightly clasped them on the table to appear at ease. Not sure she was succeeding.

He took another bite and wiped his mouth with a napkin. "I think a paper fell out of your pocket."

Paper? She glanced at the floor. Oh damn. She leaned down and scooped up the escapee, curling her fingers around it. Sipping her beer, she stalled. Maybe she needed the help of an objective third party.

Meg peeled a bit of the label from the bottle and considered her options. She believed in her gut Scott was trustworthy.

"Hey. Did you drift off? I'm not the best of company, but I never had a woman fall asleep on me before."

At his words, Meg's gaze collided with his. Her cheeks heated. "Sorry, guess I'm pre-occupied." She rose and peered out the kitchen window into the back yard. Her fist with the paper tapped on her thigh.

"Well?"

"If you've finished the sandwich, let's move to the living

room." She wanted to put more distance between her and her parents before talking with Scott.

She set his plate in the sink, and dropped her bottle in the recycle bin. In holding Scott's chair for him, their arms brushed together when he stood. Every nerve ending in her body sizzled. What was it with the chemistry they seemed to have?

"Lead on, lady."

Did he feel anything? Apparently, not. They entered the front room and she closed the double glass doors behind them. Both of Scott's eyebrows went up.

"I don't want anyone to hear our conversation."

"Okay." He nodded.

"Are you sure you got enough to eat?" She dithered, but she wanted his opinion.

"Yeah, or I'd still be in the kitchen." He cocked one eyebrow at her.

Did he find her confusion amusing? "My brain's not clicking on all cylinders."

"Meg, what's bothering you?"

The pitch of his voice dropped, welcoming shared secrets.

She released a deep breath in a rush. "It appears my father is being blackmailed." A pain hit her mid-section, nauseating in its intensity. Saying the words out-loud made the situation more real. She dealt with this situation in her job, but this wasn't supposed to affect her family.

"What evidence do you have?"

She retrieved the paper and handed it over. "This."

Scott laid the paper on the coffee table, and lowered himself onto the short sofa. He read the page with care. "Where and when did you get this? What did your father say when you talked with him? Did he call the police?"

Damn, he shot rapid-fire questions at her as if he was working a case or something. "I don't know the answers." She paced the room. "I picked it out of the fireplace in Dad's study this afternoon. I hope he's called the police, but I don't know."

"Have you discussed this with anyone else?"

"David searched with me, but we haven't talked. The Turner twins arrived and dragged him off."

Scott glanced from the paper back to her. "If this were someone else's family, what would you tell them?"

"I'd ask them if they'd gone to the police, and if not, why hadn't they?"

"Perhaps that's what you and David should do."

"Talk to my father, then." She dropped onto a wing back chair and rested her elbows on her knees with her head in her hands. Scott was right.

"One of your options, but you have several. One, talk to your father. Two, talk with Ellie to determine if she knows anything about this."

"What's three?" She raised her head.

"You can ignore what you've discovered. You and David are only here for two weeks. Joe is a smart man. He's not without resources, including the two of you in law enforcement. If he thinks he can't deal with whatever this is on his own, he's got people he can turn to."

Clasping both hands around a knee, Meg rocked back. Finally, she lowered her leg, and glanced in his direction.

"True." She stood and made the rounds of the room, fingering frames on the shelves. She stopped her wanderings and dropped to the edge of the sofa. Closer than she'd intended, and the heat from Scott's body scorched her.

"Ignoring this isn't an option. I'd never recommend not taking action to anyone else. Pretending it doesn't exist, doesn't make this go away. It just gets worse. I guess our first step is talk with Dad." She rested her head against the high back of the sofa. "Don't look forward to the conversation."

He reached out and laid his hand on her thigh. Surely, he meant the gesture in comfort, but one part of her wished he had something else in mind. "Thanks, Scott." She covered his hand with hers. "I'd have figured out those options for myself if my head had been working right. Guess because it's my family, I needed an outside perspective." Meg's fingers tightened on his hand for a moment. "I appreciate your insight."

"No problem."

"Think I'll head up to bed." She rose and walked toward the door then twisted around to him. "My parents and the Turners will play until the wee hours. No telling when David will return from hanging with the twins. We'll talk to Dad tomorrow. Do you need any help with the stairs?"

He rose, using the cane for balance. "No thanks. I'll stay here for a while. It's nice to look at the lights. Later, if I struggle, it'll be good for me."

A gleam flashed at her from the sofa. "Did you drop something?" Scott glanced around, but didn't seem to find what she had. "Here." She held up the shiny metal. "Is this yours?"

"Money clip. It slips out if I don't have it pushed far enough into my pocket."

She placed it in the palm of his hand, careful not to touch his skin.

"Glad you noticed it lying there."

She nodded. "Good night then. See you in the morning." She walked toward the doors, conscious of him behind her. She paused and pivoted toward him. A smile covered his face.

"Thank you again for Dave—"

"Stop." His smile faded. "No more, okay?"

"All right. But we're so—"

"No. More. Am I clear?"

CHAPTER THREE

8:30 a.m. Saturday, December 19

"Meg, tell your sleepyhead brother if he wants pancakes, he'd better kick himself in gear."

Scott smiled at the sparkle in Ellie's eyes. The way she whipped around with ease spoke to her years of cooking for her family.

"I'll be right back." Meg grinned at him before she scooted out of the kitchen.

The door closed sending her scent toward him—clean and fresh, like the outdoors. Last night after she went upstairs, he'd lingered, moving around the room to figure out what had caught Meg's attention. He hadn't noticed them earlier, but pictures of the Bourland family beginning when it consisted of only Joe and Ellie stood on many of the bookshelves. Meg resembled a younger version of her mother.

One showed three kids playing on the backyard swings. Sporting and activity pictures abounded. All three had their favorite. David with football at all ages through college. He'd groused about not being good enough for the pros. Scott figured Kathy had been the one the in dance costumes from around four all the way through college.

Then he'd focused on pictures of Meg. She'd played volleyball from elementary school through college. One of many great shots showed her leaping high to spike a ball over the net. She must've been something on the court. She tipped his world on end, despite his decision last night to crush his reaction to her. Hell.

His mind rejoined his body when Ellie set a huge platter piled with brown, crispy strips on the table. If he'd eaten only moments ago, the aroma would make him hungry.

After sliding three large golden brown discs on his plate, Ellie set a second platter stacked with the giant size pancakes near him.

"How many people are you expecting to feed?"

"When all the kids were here, we easily ate through a pound of bacon in one meal. Now, with Joe and me, we use turkey bacon. I'm splurging today with the real thing. Since Kathy's not here, I won't hear a lecture on how bad it is for us."

"Is Kathy a vegetarian?"

"Yes, since college, primarily from a health standpoint. When you're a dancer, you can never be too thin. She met Ron while she was in the dance performance program at Oklahoma City University."

Right, the dance pictures in the living room.

"Where's Joe this morning?" Scott sipped from a steaming cup of coffee.

"He scheduled an early morning committee meeting on the Saturday before Christmas." Indignation tinged her tone. "What got into him? I told him to make it short, or I'd come down and end the session for him." Ellie set a pitcher of warm syrup by Scott's plate.

He struggled not to laugh at the image of her taking on the

leaders at City Hall including her husband, the mayor.

"Go ahead and eat while it's hot." Ellie urged him.

Scott helped himself to the bacon.

"David's on his way, but I assured him we weren't waiting for him." Meg slid into the chair next to Scott.

"Your brother stayed out late last night." Ellie plated two of the fluffy cakes for her daughter.

Scott's fingers touched Meg's when he handed her the platter of bacon. Her gaze flew to his face. Had the same zing hit her the way it did him? They shared one of those intense looks they had at dinner before she glanced away. Heat, sharp and sweet rushed through his blood.

"This smells wonderful, Mom. You're correct about David. Pass the syrup, please Scott." She smiled her thanks. "He and the Turner twins went out. All this good smelling food will bring him down." She glanced up. "And here he is. More prompt than I gave you credit for."

"Pancakes. Good ol' Mom. My favorites." David put an arm around his mother's waist and kissed her on the cheek.

"No, they're my favorites, and she made them for me." Meg poured syrup on her cakes.

"Leave me some." David snatched it out of her hand, and in the struggle nearly dropped the pitcher.

Scott shook his head at the two siblings' behavior. They were acting more like teenagers than mature adults. He got quite a different picture of his partner from the interactions with his sister. Scott tried to resist, but Meg drew his gaze, the honey to his bear. She'd corralled her thick, black hair in a low ponytail.

Not a young woman anymore but beautiful. The morning light streaming through the kitchen window highlighted the fine lines around her blue-green eyes. Sexy as hell in jeans and a long sleeved t-shirt, which highlighted her generous breasts. Did her looks hinder her doing her job? He bet every man who worked with her fell secretly in love.

Hell. Not a phrase he used any more. Mooning around after Meg all day wasn't on his agenda. He wanted to go to a gym and to schedule a therapy appointment.

He looked away for a moment then found himself staring at her once more. She looked up, and he caught the sudden awareness they'd experienced moments before and last night. His stomach muscles clenched, and he had trouble swallowing. Scary reaction. He couldn't remember this sense of connection, not since his fiancée. Must be only on his side. She was grateful to him for saving her brother's life. That's all.

He'd leave as soon as Christmas was over. None of this staying the extra week David kept insisting on. Being in a perpetual state of arousal around Meg for the duration of his visit wasn't something Scott looked forward to. Not a good situation when he wasn't in a position to carry through. Damn his injuries, and damn David for having such a fascinating sister.

He blindly reached for his mug, and coffee sloshed over the side. "Hell. Uh, sorry, Ellie, both for the language and the mess."

Scott tried to stand. A hand on his shoulder kept him seated.

"No problem. I'll help." Meg grabbed a dishtowel and mopped up the spill.

"Not the first time drinks have spilled at this table, and I don't imagine it'll be the last. Wait until Kathy gets here with her two little ones. They're always knocking over glasses or cups. I'm certain they compete to see who can make the biggest mess." Ellie's eyes twinkled, and her and her lips quirked up in a smile showing her excitement at their coming visit.

David and Meg kept bickering, and Ellie didn't raise an eyebrow. Guess she'd seen everything what with raising the three Bourlands. The grandkids probably loved to hang with her and their granddad.

Scott had been close to his parents as an only child, and the early loss of both sets of his grandparents served to deepen the bond. Damn, he hated to go down this road of memories, because now the face of his fiancée swamped his senses.

Tricia, a teacher he'd met when her roommate was murdered. Tricia, the most down to earth person in the world, who gave him faith being a cop and having a family weren't incompatible. Tricia, who'd died in a fiery crash when a drunk, selfish bastard got behind the wheel and plowed into the car Scott's father drove, killing him, his wife and Tricia. Three lives snuffed out in a heartbeat.

"Scott. Hey, Scott."

He glanced up. David, Meg, and Ellie stared at him.

"Where'd you go, man? Want orange juice?" David raised a

carafe.

"Uh, no." Scott swallowed bile, which had risen in the back of his throat. "No thanks." The best way to deal with their questioning glances was not to respond, and he changed the subject. "I wondered about a place to work out. Got any ideas?"

"Sure. The country club gym isn't far." David glanced at Meg. "You can tag along, Pigtails."

"Because Mother is here, and in deference to our guest, I won't knock your block off for the remark. I'll ask you politely not to call me nicknames when anyone else is around. Got it?"

The muscle in her jaw flexed and released at a rapid rate. He hoped David got the message, because she was steaming.

"Yeah. Sorry."

Scott wouldn't have wanted to step between the two before he became a physical wreck. In his present condition, they'd flatten him. Dammit to hell. This wasn't the picture he wanted to present to anyone, least of all Meg.

So, you coming?" David smiled at his sister.

"Y'all go on. I'll be along later. I'll hang out with Mom for a while, and then I can run to the gym when I'm ready. It'll be a good warm up."

"If you're sure. Let's go, buddy, find out what, if anything, you can do." David stood then walked to where his mother sat finishing her coffee. "Good eatin', Mom. Thanks." He dropped a kiss on her top of her head then moved around the table. He put a hand under Scott's elbow to help him rise.

A groan struggled against his clenched teeth, but Scott stifled it. He didn't want anyone feeling sorry for him. He'd follow the LA therapist's instructions and walk on the treadmill even if the action killed him. He nodded to Meg, "See you later." He shot a smile to his hostess. "Excellent breakfast, Ellie. Thanks."

"You're welcome. David, don't let Scott do too much."

* * * *

Meg released tension with a long sigh after the men left the kitchen. The heightened awareness of her own skin whenever Scott got within three feet of her—well, it was like walking on hot rocks. Not needed or wanted.

Because her father had taken off as early as he did, she and David hadn't talked with him, and they'd been unable to figure out what was what with the blackmail. She stood and picked up their plates.

"You don't need to do that, dear. Maria will be here."

"I'm used to doing this and can give her a head start." She set the dishes in the sink.

"You remember we're having the Christmas party Tuesday, the twenty-second."

"Yes. Cute invitations. Did you design them?" She refilled their coffee cups

"They're from The Letter Store. I couldn't find my usual enthusiasm to work on them, what with everything…you and David…experienced." Ellie's blue eyes deepened to almost navy.

"You can't imagine what went through me when the first phone call came about David. Then two days later to hear about you. I'll never forget the expression on Joe's face."

Meg smiled at her and leaned back against the counter. "We're both fine, Mom. A lot better off than Scott…or Hank." Emotions clogged her throat. Meg dragged in a deep breath. Her stomach cramped with the effort to beat down the guilt and pain. How long before the shooting images stopped plaguing her waking hours? What a wimp. Hank's widow had no one to help raise their two kids. She didn't have the luxury of feeling sorry for herself the way Meg did.

Her brain replayed over and over the incident to find what she could've done differently to guarantee Hank stayed alive. Even if she figured out something, it wouldn't matter. Nothing would bring Hank back to life. She spun into the whirlpool of guilt, anger, and self-loathing, because she breathed, and Hank didn't.

"Meg, honey."

Her mother's voice came to her as if in a fog.

"What?"

"You keep saying you're fine, but are you? Really?"

Meg's legs buckled and she dropped into a kitchen chair. "I don't know, Mom. I don't know." She hated the tremble in her voice. She had to find a way to fill up the empty hole in her center. She clenched her hands on the table.

"Give yourself time, dear."

Her mom's hand on her head reached inside Meg and made tears well. If she let herself cry, she'd never stop.

"I received Julie's RSVP." Her mother seemed to sense Meg

needed a change of subject. "She and her family are coming to the party. You'll find other times to visit, won't you? It'd be good for you."

"Yes. Movie with friends and later a lunch on our own."

"Sounds fun. Sweetie, I need to run a couple of errands—more presents to pick up—then I'll be home later on this afternoon. Come with me. I can I drop you someplace."

"I'll pass, Mom, if you don't mind. I'll probably run up to the club after a while. See you later." Meg hugged her mother then hurried from the kitchen. Did Mom suspect anything with Dad? She didn't seem worried or upset about anything but the dangerous work she and David did.

Meg wandered into the living room. She paced for a while, impatient to resolve this mess. Hard to do with both her father and David gone. She picked up a book she hadn't noticed last night. Must be one of Mom's numerous romance novels, something Meg never took time for in Atlanta. She'd read while she waited for her father to come home.

* * * *

11 a.m. Saturday, December 19

Chuck stood at the back of the aisle in the drugstore. That's her. The one who broke Mama's heart. The woman wrapped in her full-length mink coat smiled as if everything in her life was golden. Not a care in the world. Her words rang clear in the store as she and the other broad yacked about the company catering a party the Bourlands were throwing.

His mother had never owned a long coat, much less one with fur. Joe had a lot to make up for. How come he gave up Mama for this rich bitch? Mama loved Joe with all her heart. So much, over the years she'd clipped every article from the newspaper about him or other members of his family and kept them in a wooden box. Chuck had them now, some yellowed with age.

He picked up a six-pack, following the women's conversation.

"My caterers told me they were so busy for the holiday season, Margie, they needed to hire extra workers."

"Well, I hope they're properly grateful, Ellie." A short, plump old broad said. "Before you used them last year, no one had ever heard of the Out of the Box Caterers."

"If I helped any in their success, I'm pleased." The rich bitch preened herself, her hand actually stroking the long hairs of the mink. They moved down the aisle.

So the caterer needed to hire extra workers, huh? Chuck fingered his beard, pictured walking around in Joe's house, and seeing the family up close and personal. Then leaving the next note. Yeah. Perfect. He'd show Joe Bourland who had the power. Who was in charge.

The money Joe had paid Chuck up to now had come in handy. He'd moved from the rat hole of a motel on Vickery to the cheap rental house about fifteen minutes from the Bourlands' home. No more riding the loser bus, because he'd bought a clunker to drive.

Joe owed him a shit-load more. He owed Chuck for stealing his life and his mom's.

If Joe had married Mama like he'd promised, she'd have lived a pampered life like the woman wrapped in mink.

If Joe had married Mama, she wouldn't have worked herself to the bone every single day of her life.

If Joe had married Mama, maybe she wouldn't have gotten sick, but if she had, she'd have had the best care.

And she wouldn't be dead now.

Chuck breathed fast, the bag of tortilla chips he clasped tore, and chips tumbled to the floor. He dropped the bag and picked up another then followed the Bourland bitch and her friend into another aisle. He smiled at his choice of words. "Bourland Bitch." Afraid she'd detect his hatred, he didn't look directly at her.

Not the time for a confrontation. Yet.

"Look forward to the party, Ellie."

"Glad y'all are coming, dear." The women kissed the air of both cheeks.

He gritted his teeth. She made him sick. He tightened his hold around the packages of beer, tearing the cardboard. A red face stared at him from a mirror above the counter.

He forced himself to calm down before he made his way to the checkout line and paid for the beer, the chips, and a couple of packs of cigarettes. God, these cost a fortune anymore. Another good use of the money he'd collected from Joe.

* * * *

12:15 p.m. Saturday, December 19

Scott attempted to stand when Meg breezed through the

swinging door to the kitchen.

"Hey, slacker. We expected you to work out with us." David teased her.

She waved Scott back down, and since agreeing was easier than arguing, he complied.

"I got busy reading and forgot." Meg dropped a book on the table. "Hey, Maria."

"Want a bowl of soup, *mija*?"

"Sure do." She peeked in the pot. "Yum. I can serve myself."

"No, sit down." Maria guided her toward the table, and Meg slid into the chair next to her brother.

"David." Meg leaned over and sniffed at his cheek. "Did you use products at the gym?"

"Yeah, do I smell good? I'm taking Sally Billings to dinner and a movie this evening. She'll like the aftershave."

"Probably. Be careful big brother. She's recently divorced."

"Well, yeah. I wouldn't be going out with her otherwise."

Maria set a large bowl of chicken tortilla soup in front of Meg.

"You should've made her get her own, Maria, if all she's been doing is lying around the house reading. Scott and I've been working out. We earned this."

"Technically, you've been exercising, David. My paltry fifteen minutes on the treadmill before making use of the steam room and the hot tub hardly counts.

"I bet those helped ease the pain." Meg blew on a spoonful of soup. "Both were great for me when I was wounded a couple of years ago."

Scott experienced another kind of discomfort when Meg met his gaze. Her vanilla scent enveloped him, and he hardened at her nearness.

"Yeah." The one word sounded strangled to him. He'd better be careful. Her brother knew him inside out. Scott didn't want David to suspect a relationship with Meg. Hah. Some "relationship." He lusted after her, pure and simple. Talk about a dog baying at the moon. The postman had a better chance than Scott did. He'd better concentrate on finishing lunch and get upstairs out of her vicinity.

"Dad's still not home."

"Mom will kill him if he does city business all day." David chomped on tortilla chips.

Meg looked at her brother and shrugged.

"TWIN JUSTICE." David picked up the book Meg had been reading. He flipped it over and read the blurb on the back. "FBI agents pursue a vigilante group killing the world's worst criminals while fighting their attraction for each other." He started flipping through the pages. "Any good sex?"

"Give me the book. It's Mom's." She made a grab, but he raised his hand over his head.

"Man. You two read this stuff?"

"David."

Scott got the point she meant business but wasn't sure if David did.

"Uh-oh, she's using her big, bad SWAT voice."

Scott would bet his sing-songy tone was meant to egg her on his sister. Her glare was sharp enough to slice steak.

"I give. I give." David tossed her the book.

The novel bounced off Scott and careened toward Maria who grabbed it, cut around the table, and tapped David on the head with the paperback.

"Behave, Mr. David, or I'll take lunch away."

Scott couldn't stop himself. The laughter rolled out and didn't hurt at all. Not even a twinge. The gym had helped.

"Okay, okay. Can't a guy have fun anymore?" David smiled at Maria.

"You're a grown man, David, and you're acting like a kid. We've got company." Meg frowned at her brother.

"No we don't. This is Scott."

He'd better intervene before the sibling rivalry grew to blows. "The hot tub and steam made me feel a whole lot better, and I made a therapy appointment for Monday."

"Good. Glad to hear it helped." Meg's low throaty voice warmed his insides. Nothing of the SWAT officer in her tones now.

He'd swear she looked at him with gratitude. Not the way he wanted her to look at him. He wanted to see her eyes glaze with desire as she pulled him inside her. He'd been about to gain control, and now here he went thinking about getting into her body. Hell of a note to lust after someone such a long way out of his reach. Of course, pretty much everyone was now. Meg Bourland especially so.

"When are you going in?"

"Eleven."

"If David can't take you, I can. My friend Julie and I are getting together for lunch and shopping Monday. I can easily drop you off before I go."

"Thanks." Not what he needed to hear. He'd be alone in the car with her. How bad was he going to hurt?

* * * *

4:00 p.m. Saturday, December 19

The sound of an engine jerked Meg from the book she'd been lost in. She hadn't expected it to distract her from her mixed up feelings about Scott, worry about her father, and her guilt over Hank's death. Amazingly, it had drawn her into the story. A romance novel. Who knew?

Meg glanced through the window. Sure enough, Dad had returned home. She flew from the living room to the den where Scott and her brother had a movie playing. "David, come now." Her tone must've been serious enough to snare his attention. He bounded off the sofa without asking any questions.

"Dad's home," Meg told him on the way back to the front of the house. "We can grab him when he enters."

Her father opened the door when they stepped into the entryway hall.

"Hi, Dad. Sorry you had to go into the office." Meg helped him off with his coat.

"Thanks, darlin'. Your mom was about to kill me. I promised to be back by three, but I'm late. She here?"

"No. She's been running errands for the party. She's supposed to be back by five at the latest to prepare for the big shindig this evening."

"Good." He reached into in his pocket and shuffled out his pipe.

"You better go into the study before you light up, Dad," David said.

"Yeah, I know. Your mother is amenable about many of my habits, but she's adamant about the pipe in the house. Guess I'm lucky she gives me the study." He moved toward his haven.

"Cost you a pretty penny to install the special air filter, though." David closed the study door behind them.

"Yes, and worth every one of those pennies." Her father sat behind his desk, drew his tobacco pouch toward him, and began packing the bowl.

"You don't mind do you, Meg?" He glanced at her.

"It's your house, and they're your lungs, Dad. Besides, the aroma always reminds me of you and Granddad blowing smoke rings for us kids."

"Your mother didn't like it then either." He laughed and set about getting his pipe lit. "You doing okay, Meg? What you went through had to be horrible, but you're fine, right?"

"Sure, Dad. At least, I will be. The psychologist in Atlanta told me it would take time. She wants me to meet with a colleague of hers a couple of times while I'm in Fort Worth, too. I'll do whatever she says because she has to sign off I'm good for active duty again." She sat on the leather love seat and tugged her legs up underneath her. "Let's do this, David."

He nodded.

"What's going on? Are you two up to your old tricks?" Her father's glance careened off each of them.

"Dad, is everything all right between you and Mom?" Meg didn't detect any particular reaction. He got up and walked around the room, puffing on his pipe as if he'd had trouble getting it lit. But she'd intentionally not rushed him, giving him the opportunity to get the pipe going good and strong.

"Why do you ask? Has she complained about my working long hours again? She knows how involved the job of mayor is."

"No, but—"

"Before I ran this last time, I gave her the opportunity to say no way, Jose, if she wanted out. A disappointment, but I'd have gone along. She can't change her mind midway through the term." He stopped at the end of the sofa, as if he didn't want to move closer to his children.

Her gaze met David's. Damn, guess they needed to be more direct. She moved her legs from under her, leaned forward, and stared up at her father. "Tell us about yesterday's letter."

Her father's gaze darted toward the fireplace.

"Meg and I picked it up." David said in his quiet voice.

"What? You had no right to snoop in my office." He shot a glance at her and her brother,

turned, and stalked away from them. His breath raspy, he stopped beside the Christmas tree standing in the study's bay window and stared outside.

"I told you, Dad. I saw a shadow and initially worried someone had broken in. No thief. Just you, and you were upset about this letter." She held out her hand, and the paper fluttered. He didn't turn from the window. God, this was harder than she'd imagined, and she hadn't looked forward to the confrontation. No mistaking this for anything else.

"Go on, Meg," David encouraged her.

"Dad, you're being blackmailed. Is this the first letter you've received? Did you pay someone money to keep quiet about something? Are you or Mom in danger? Please tell us have you talked to the police?" Her voice rose with each question, despite her efforts to stay calm.

Her father left the window and walked to the chair behind his desk, dropped into it heavily, as if a burden he carried weighed him down. "Let's see if I can answer my oh-so-smart daughter's barrage of questions."

He looked down, put the pipe in his mouth and drew heavily on it, blew the smoke rings she remembered. With a big sigh, he leaned back. He tapped the stem of the pipe on the chair arm in a rapid beat.

David sat, but his crossed leg jiggled to an internal rhythm. Meg forced herself to wait. She fought the nausea building. Her insides clenched tighter than a drum. She wanted to jump up and shake the answers out of her father. Calm, cool, and collected was more her style, but she'd been a bundle of nerves since Hank's murder. Her teeth sank into her lip to keep from asking her father again. Finally, he spoke.

"Yes, I'm being blackmailed."

The indrawn breath evidenced her surprise and pain. David was silent, but the muscle in his jaw twanged with his knee bounce. They waited.

"It's not the first letter."

Her lips thinned when she gritted her teeth. This got worse and worse. She sought David's gaze. New lines seemed to spring into his face.

"Yes, I've paid money."

"Damn." She put a hand in front of her mouth to block the questions, which fought to explode at her father like machine gun fire. Her other hand grasped David's. His grip hurt, but it helped ground her. Agonizing to hear her father confirm her knowledge.

"The writer hasn't threatened to physically hurt me or your mother."

"Thank God. What do the police say?" her brother asked.

"They don't say anything." Dad drew on his pipe and sent blue-grey smoke rings swirling above his head.

"What? Dad, haven't you told them?" Her brother jumped up and paced away, running a hand around his neck, muttering under his breath.

"No." The pipe made its way to her father's mouth. He clamped his teeth and drew in.

"Dad." She walked around the desk to the man who was her

hero. She knelt down, rested a hand on his knee. "What's he threatening that's bad enough you'd pay him?"

"To tell your mother something she knows, but something I won't allow her to be reminded of. He only asked for five thousand dollars the first time. Little enough for Ellie's peace of mind."

"When did you get the first demand?" David stopped pacing and stood behind one of the chairs, his hands clenched on the high back.

"The note came in October. After I paid him, I assumed it was over. Weeks went by, and I heard nothing more. In November, I received the second one. This time he threatened to go to the newspapers."

Meg let out the long breath she'd held. Dealing with this wouldn't be as easy as she'd hoped. She walked back to the leather sofa and sat. She dropped her head into a hand and massaged the ache between her eyes. She straightened, had to ask him.

"So you've paid him, what, ten grand so far?

"Fifteen. I've already sent the money requested in the letter you found."

"What's all this about, Dad? What's he threatening to tell?"

David's voice was deep and low. He must've tapped into his interview persona to keep himself calm. She, on the other hand, had a volcano rumbling around her insides threatening to explode with invectives and accusations.

"None of your business. I appreciate you keeping what we've spoken of in confidence. I'm taking care of the problem, and you don't need to be concerned."

Meg flew off the sofa. "What? You're pretending nothing's going on? Pretending you're not being blackmailed? Pretending won't make this go away, Dad. We've got to go to the police." Her voice screeched on the last word. She dug her nails into her palms. Clearly, she'd lost control.

"No." Her father stood, tapped the pipe into the ashtray, and pinned her with his glare. "No, *we* will do no such thing. *You* will not do anything either, Meg. Nor you, David. It's my business, and I'll handle it the way I see fit."

Without another word for her or David, her father marched from the room and out the front door. He hadn't bothered with his coat.

"Crap." David's only comment.

"You can say that again."

"Crap."

CHAPTER FOUR

7:00 p.m. Saturday, December 19

Scott leaned his cane against the entryway table as Joe in a tuxedo and Ellie in a long, purple gown descended the stairs. Joe's head tipped toward his wife as if he didn't want to miss what she had to say. When Meg, David, and Maria broke out in applause, the couple paused. Scott joined in the tribute.

Ellie smiled up at Joe. "I guess we ended up all right."

"I told you. Belle-of-the-ball. Give me her coat, son."

David handed it to Joe, and he helped Ellie into her full-length fur.

"Good night for the mink, Mom. It's freezing out." Meg assisted her father into his overcoat.

"You make a handsome couple." Scott shook hands with Joe and kissed Ellie on the cheek. She blushed. "Have a good time."

"David's going out with Sally Billings." Meg notched her chin toward Scott. "We'll hang out with the TV. Here, we need a picture." She aimed her cell phone.

Ellie leaned against Joe and flashed her dynamite smile, reminding Scott of Meg's. Joe's was strained probably from worry about the blackmailer and putting on a good show for his kids.

"Go home, Maria," Ellie said.

"I will as soon as I put food in the butler's pantry."

Ellie laid her hand on David's arm. "Now, son, be careful what you say to Sally. Unless you're interested in getting *hitched*." She finger quoted. "Sally gets in and out of marriages faster than any woman I know. My last word on the subject. Breakfast at nine. Church at eleven. See you all in the morning." She smiled at Joe. "Let's go, dear."

Joe ushered Ellie out. Cold, blustery wind blew into the entryway before Meg shoved the door closed. "Brr. Good idea to warm up the car for them, David."

"Yeah." He tapped his fingers against his thigh. "How serious was she with the comment about Sally?"

Scott detected a hint of apprehension in David's voice, and the creases between his eyes had become more pronounced.

"She doesn't make negative comments about people, David." Meg linked her arm through her brother's and started toward the kitchen.

Scott brought up the rear. His cane made a tapping noise on the hardwoods, a constant reminder of his physical limitations.

"Mom must be concerned to warn me," David said. His gaze slid to Scott, who grinned at his former partner.

"Maria, I can take it from here" Meg patted the woman on the back after they entered the kitchen. "You head home. Enjoy the rest of the weekend. Tell your grandkids I'll stop by for a visit while I'm in town."

"They'll be happy to hear the news." Maria slipped off her apron, grabbed her coat and purse from a kitchen closet. "They missed you when you were here last. See you Monday morning."

Maria headed for the front to her car parked on the street.

"I'm not quite as excited about this evening." David leaned against the kitchen counter, both hands braced behind him.

"It's too late to renege on the date now, David. Go to dinner and be your charming self. You can pretend a headache, and take her home early," Meg advised.

"If it appears you're getting into hot water, call us. We'll rescue you, okay?" Scott lowered into a chair at the table.

"Right." David slugged Scott a solid hit on his good arm then dropped a kiss on Meg's head. "I can handle this."

"Don't forget a coat."

"Yes, Mama, and you two stay out of trouble." David waved over his shoulder as he made his way toward the front of the house and the rental he'd parked at the curb.

Scott drummed his fingers on the tabletop. What had David meant by his last comment?

"In here or back in the den with the TV?" Meg asked.

Had he somehow picked up Scott's delusions about Meg? Meg stared at him, her eyebrows arched in question. "Happy to stay here for a while." He needed to keep his head in the game, or she'd wonder what was going on with him.

"How about a beer, sweet tea, or cola?"

He cleared his throat before answering. "Water's fine, thanks. A couple more days, and I'll take you up on the offer of a beer."

Meg set a glass in front of him and got a beer for herself then retrieved the salsa from the refrigerator and filled a basket with chips.

Scott wasted no time, plunged a chip into the chunky, red sauce, and gobbled it down. "Whoa!" He reached for the water.

"Sorry. I should've warned you. Maria makes the recipe especially hot for us. Are you okay?"

Scott nodded, but couldn't make any sound. Tears filled his eyes. He swallowed more water.

"Chips will help." Meg shoved the basket closer to him. "Milk's best."

She poured him a glass, and he gulped. "Good stuff," he said in a strangled voice.

Meg laughed at him and pushed more chips his direction.

After a bit, Scott managed a hoarse chuckle. "How long has Maria worked for you? She seems like family."

"She is family. Maria was a young girl, sixteen or seventeen when she came to this country for a new life. Mom struggled a bit with the three of us, and Dad knew someone who knew Maria's brother. They were illegals and needed work. She started coming three times a week and over the years became our full time housekeeper."

"Has the illegal business caused any problems for Joe politically?"

"I suppose it might've if she'd started anytime in the last fifteen years or so. Lots of candidates and elected officials got into trouble back then for not paying employment taxes for all of their employees."

"Did Maria ever become a citizen?"

"Yeah, and Dad always paid social security taxes for her, so she's in pretty good shape. I was still in middle school, but I remember us going down to the Tarrant County Courthouse for the swearing of her oath. Powerful, let me tell you. All those people came to this country for a new life. Ordinary men and women had worked hard to learn our history, government, and language. Saying the Pledge of Allegiance with Maria and the others, well…."

He reached across and brushed at a tear sliding down her cheek. A small gasp passed her lips, and she leaned away.

"Sorry. I'm more emotional than before…than I ever used to be."

"Understandable. I still jump at loud noises. My shrink say the reaction will eventually go away. God, I hope so. I've spilled a lot of coffee lately."

Meg laughed, which had been his intention. "So, did you or David ever manage to talk with Joe today?"

"Yes." She took a long pull from her beer. She set the bottle on the table and nodded. "We did." She didn't say anything else.

Scott rose and carried the glass to the sink. He pivoted to lean against the counter, resting his leg, arms folded over his chest.

"I'm here to listen, if you want to talk."

"Scott, it's worse than I first imagined."

She bolted from her chair and made a circuit of the large kitchen. She yanked a paper from her jeans pocket. "Dad's received three of these letters in as many months. He paid the man five thousand dollars after each one." Her voice cracked.

"So if the pattern continues, your father can expect another one about the middle of January."

"And we won't be here. I'm scheduled to return to Atlanta right after the first of the year and David earlier. How do we leave with whatever's going on here?"

Scott grabbed her arm on one of her trips past, stopped her, and made her face him.

"Meg, you're working yourself up. Not a good place to make decisions." At first, she held herself stiffly. It took every ounce of willpower not to pull her into his arms. He wanted to show her she wasn't alone.

She met his gaze, and after a moment, the starch went out. She dropped her head, heaved a sigh, followed by several deep breaths.

"Thanks." Meg stepped back. "Must be what thinking about jumping from top of a tall building feels like." She rubbed her hands down her legs. "Never been this uptight." She tossed her empty into the recycling bin. "Can we sit by the fire?"

"Sure."

"Want anything else to drink?" She helped herself to another bottle.

"I'll try Maria's sweet tea."

"Mom's specialty, not Maria's." After Meg fixed his glass, they made their way to the den.

Scott sat on one end of the sofa. Meg sat on the other end, scratching at the label on the bottle.

"How do we do this? I ask you questions, or you tell me in your own way what the two of you found out?" The clanking of his glass against the metal coaster broke through her reserve. She jerked once then explained what had happened when she and David talked with their father.

The situation stunk. He couldn't imagine how he'd react if his parents had ever been involved in anything this bizarre. It must be eating at Meg and probably accounted for the strain he'd noticed around David's mouth. When she stopped talking, Scott asked, "What will you do next? Or did you and David decide to ignore the whole incident?"

"This isn't something we can ignore. Would you if this were happening to your family?"

He shook his head.

"I mean, maybe the blackmailer's not violent now, but what if he asks for a lot more money, Dad decides he can't or won't pay it, and the guy goes after one of them. I can't walk away, but Dad was adamant. This is not our business." Meg gulped more of her beer.

Her throat muscles moved with each swallow, and Scott squeezed his hands together to keep from reaching out to caress her neck. Not what she needed or wanted from him. He focused on the orange and red flames leaping in the fireplace, not unlike what went on inside his body. They must put something in the gas fire to make it pop and smell like real wood burning. The aroma reminiscent of an easier time contrasted with the seriousness of their discussion.

"He insisted we not say anything to Mother. Do we chance ignoring Dad and talk with her anyway?"

Meg looked at him with those blue green eyes filled with confusion, probably not a place she found herself in often. He took a moment before speaking. "Joe's goal seems focused on not bothering Ellie with any of this. If you can respect his wishes, he'll be more willing to work with you and David."

She nodded. "You're right. If David's not late coming in tonight, we'll talk with Dad again after Mom goes to bed." Her laugh held a rueful note. "For David's sake, I hope he's early. Mom has Sally's number."

"I'd put my money on David. He can handle himself pretty well. A number of women have gone after him in LA. He's always walked away smelling like a rose, and they still like him. He's something of a legend." Scott chuckled at the expression on Meg's face. She didn't seem to be able to decide whether to be proud of her brother or appalled at his behavior. Scott picked up the TV remote. "Movie or sports?" He flicked through a couple of stations. God knew he needed something to distract from the beautiful woman sitting near.

* * * *

10 p.m. Saturday, December 19

The movie ended and Scott stretched. Sitting companionably with Meg left him yearning for something he couldn't quite name.

The chime from the front door opening sounded, and she jumped and slapped her palm against the side of her head. "Damn, how stupid. Dad's being black-mailed, and I didn't make sure to put the alarm on." She sprang off the sofa, taking something of a defensive stance.

Scott winced at the knowledge she'd be the one defending him in a crisis. He couldn't protect her. Not now, maybe never. White hot shame rolled through his body. The body, which betrayed him. The body he couldn't count on.

She glanced in his direction and let out a long breath. "Whoever, they're setting the alarm. Must be David. It's too early for my parents."

"Hey, guys." Her brother walked into the den. "You're still up."

"Well, yeah. It's ten," his sister answered.

"But Scotty boy's been hitting the bed by nine ever since he got out of the hospital."

"You should've told me, Scott."

She looked at him as if at any moment she expected him to collapse in a heap. "No sweat. I'm fine. Drop it, David." His words were another slap at Scott's battered self-esteem

"How'd your date go?" Meg scooted over on the sofa closer to Scott to make space for her brother.

Despite his intentions to ignore his reactions to Meg, Scott extended his arm along the back, close, but not touching. If David weren't in here now, and he was his old self...maybe then she—

"A tiger. If Mom hadn't warned me, I might've fallen for Sally's line. It's too bad. She's a real beauty, and she has a sweet name. Who'd-a-thought it?"

Scott slipped his hand down to Meg's shoulder and squeezed

briefly before letting go. She jerked and looked around. He cocked his head at her and then toward her brother. Her lips thinned into a straight line, and she squared her shoulders.

"David, we need to talk more."

"Sure. You give anymore thought to this situation with Dad?" He frowned at her.

"How we can ignore the situation? It's not only the fifteen thousand dollars he's paid. It's the safety issue. And the legal issue."

"You don't have any of the other letters, do you?" David asked.

"No. Only the one I showed you."

David got up and set off for the double doors.

"Where are you going?" Meg asked.

"To look for the others." He stopped and turned back to them. "You staying here or helping?"

Meg got up and reached out to assist Scott. "We're coming."

Electricity zinged through Scott's body from the point they touched. He willed himself to let go when she did. She angled away toward the study. Scott rubbed the fingers of his left hand together. The connection remained.

David walked directly to his father's desk. "Start hunting, don't just stand around." He yanked at a drawer, but nothing happened.

"Open the middle first then the others should release." Meg instructed her brother in a low tone. A tone Scott wanted to listen to for a long time. The tone warmed a place in his gut.

She glanced at him and away. "I'm sorry to drag you into this. You don't have to stay."

"Of course he does." David never raised his head. "He's got great eyes, and he's more objective than either of us right now." David continued going through the desk.

"I've got these shelves." A glimmer of hope took root at his partner's faith in him. "You start over against the other wall," Scott nodded to Meg. She moved to follow his suggestion.

* * * *

11:50 p.m. Saturday, December 19

"Oh, God, my back is killing me." Meg slumped to the floor with her legs stretched out in front of her and leaned against the shelves. She rubbed at the ache threatening to split her head. "David, we have to stop. It's nearly midnight. Mom and Dad will be coming back anytime now. Poor Scott. You must be dying."

"I'm fine, Meg. Wherever Joe hid the other letters, they're not in here."

"You're right. Where else would he put them, sis? Up in their room?"

"Maybe, but seems kind of risky if the whole deal is to keep Mom in the dark. For now, let's make sure they can't tell we've been through here like a tornado." Meg picked up a book from the floor and replaced it on the shelf. "I don't look forward to explaining our presence in here if they come back and find us. Not the way to keep Mom out of this."

"When's the next opportunity to search?" Scott asked.

They swept the study, getting everything back in its place. "Not tomorrow morning. We'd disappoint Mom if we all didn't all go to church with them. She likes to show us off." Meg led them into the hallway and by mutual consent toward the den.

"I need a beer." David stopped in the kitchen. "Anyone else interested?"

Scott shook his head.

Meg took the one her brother handed her, held it to her forehead for a moment before moving into the den. She took several swallows from the bottle. Damn, what an unbelievable situation.

"So, the morning is out of the question, and lunch may take us through the afternoon." Her brother paced the confines of the den, first one way then the other.

"Let's be clear about our plans." Meg sat on the sofa next to Scott while David wore a path in the rug. She gulped the cold liquid. "Number one, we don't talk to Mom. Number two, we convince Dad to go to the police."

David stopped, ran his hand over his face then looked at Scott. "What do you think? Meg and I aren't making the best decisions right now. Sorry." He nodded at her.

She shrugged her shoulders. "Can't take exception with what you said. I haven't known you long, Scott, but I told you when I first brought you into this I trust you. You saved David's life."

"Will I have to listen to this forever? Big bad Scott saved my life?" David scowled.

Meg hopped up and threw her arms around her brother, going up on tiptoe to rub the top of his head. "Yeah, probably so," then stopped in front Scott. Anything he ever needed or wanted was his because of the huge debt the family owed him. "Thank you." She leaned in and kissed him on the cheek. The stubble distinctly unsettling, stirred feelings way out of line for what she'd tried to do. Her heart rate skyrocketed, sending her into full retreat from the man.

The entry alarm sounded. Must be her parents.

* * * *

5:30 a.m. Sunday, December 20

Meg wandered into the kitchen. For the first time since the shootout resulting in Hank's death, she remembered what she'd dreamed. Last night her brother's sexy partner had kept her from sleeping well. She and Scott participated in highly sensual activities while the whole family looked on. Then a faceless person stalked her mother and father, money rained from the heavens, and she blew a man away. An action she repeated over and over and over until morning. The gun grew larger with each replay of the scene, No wonder she'd risen at such an ungodly hour.

Maria, who didn't come in on Sunday, had left the coffee pot ready, and all Meg had to do was plug the cord in the socket. Thank God, this wouldn't take long. Meg stood at the kitchen sink staring out into the bleak back yard. December in Texas. Everything painted in shades of gray or brown. Some years you'd find temperatures in the seventies, and others the wind chill made you swear the mercury sat at zero like today.

What had she been thinking to kiss Scott? No one could misinterpret it as something other than a thank you, could they? It was only on the cheek and right in front of David. Had she subconsciously intended something else?

She filled a mug to the brim. If she drank enough of the hot, black backbone, she'd have the strength to press through however long she'd be here. She'd be able to deal with the crazy blackmailer and not react like a stupid person because she slept in the same house as Scott McClaine.

Face it, gal. This attraction to your brother's former partner doesn't mean anything, except you're alive. And thank God for the feelings. For years, she'd sworn that part of her had died with Jerry. The loss of her fiancé and his betrayal had killed her libido. She'd thrown herself into her career. Romance wasn't for her.

She shut off the security system and hurried down the front walk to pick up the Sunday newspaper. Should've thrown on a coat. Her robe wasn't near warm enough. Chill bumps ran across her shoulders, and her nipples perked up like they'd been touched. Jeez, the paper froze her fingers. She swirled toward the house. The sound of an engine caught her attention and brought her to an abrupt stop. Who else rose this early? She scanned the area and caught a glimpse of what looked like an older model maroon sedan driving away from the house next door. The Jenson's visitor had gotten an early start on his day

She carried the paper and her mug into the den, started the fire, and settled on the sofa. *What's happening in Fort Worth these days?* She flipped the pages with one hand and sipped at the cup in the other. At a sound, she sprang from the sofa, nearly spilling the hot liquid. She set the cup on an end table, her unusually jumpy persona taking control. She tiptoed toward the kitchen. It had to be a member of the family.

Not quite. Scott stood in front of the counter, wearing low riding jeans and a long sleeved T-shirt, pouring a mug of coffee, barefoot. What about being barefoot made he seem sexy? "Good morning." She forced the words from her mouth. Wouldn't do for him to catch her staring.

* * * *

Scott turned around and smiled. She was beautiful even this early in the morning. Her loose hair flowed around her shoulders. He liked it better than in the ponytail. Wearing blue plaid pajamas and a bathrobe, she was drop dead gorgeous. Before Scott got his mouth in gear, David wandered into the kitchen.

"Good morning, good morning. Let me at the coffee. I see we're all up and at'em."

Meg slipped into the den then returned with her mug.

David gulped the coffee.

After topping off his cup, he finally yanked his attention from the all-important pot and studied them. "Y'all are awfully quiet? Not enough caffeine, yet?"

"I'm taking mine upstairs. I'll be back after I'm dressed to help Mom with breakfast." Without making eye contact with either man, she hurried from the room.

David took a couple more swallows. "My sister's acting a bit odd. Pulling her away from the newspaper is tough until she's touched every page. She mention anything to you?"

Scott met his partner's gaze for a moment before glancing away worried. Could David somehow read his mind? "No." He held the cup to his mouth.

"Man, Meg and I appreciate your help on this situation with Dad."

"Sure, no problem." Scott grabbed his cane where he'd leaned it against the corner of the counter and followed David into the den.

"Here's the paper. She's always the first one to bring it in. I start with the Sunday funnies." He separated the colored pages he wanted. "You want the sports?"

"Yeah." Scott took the section and read for a while. He put it down and picked up another. Reading about the physically fit players on the Cowboys football team caused his stomach to pitch. Occasionally, David chuckled. Scott sipped his coffee, and after a time, he folded the paper back together. "I'm gonna head up and dress, too. Wouldn't do to keep Ellie waiting, and I'm still slow."

"No sweat. Yell if you need anything. I'll be along after a while." David went back to his comics.

Scott stood and walked toward the kitchen. He set his cup in the sink before starting for the stairs. He'd reached the top when the bathroom door opened, and Meg stepped into the hall. She'd caught up her hair on top of her head, but a few wisps fell around her ears. *Dear God.*

She clutched the white bathrobe with one hand and carried a small caddy in her other. Did she wear anything underneath? He slammed one hand into his jeans pocket, and with the other, he clenched his cane, resisting the desire to reach for her. He stared and filled his mind with the image of this woman. An image he'd take with him back to LA.

"Oh." Her tongue slipped out then her teeth nibbled on the lower lip. "The bathroom's all yours." Her voice had a husky sound.

A slight flush spread across her cheeks before she veered away and dashed toward her room. Why the blush? She was more covered up than if she'd been in a bathing suit. In the old days before the shooting, Scott wouldn't have hesitated to make a play for her. Not now. Not with Meg. Not with anyone. Scott went to his room grabbed his travel kit and clean clothes. If he got a hard on every time he got close to David's sister, this promised to be a tough holiday. Yeah, a long two weeks.

CHAPTER FIVE

8:30 p.m. Sunday, December 20

Chuck shut out the smells of the pizza baking and the sounds of the manager shouting orders to the cooks slopping together the dough and ingredients. He leaned back in the booth, swallowed beer from the frosty mug, and studied the females in the corner. Meg, the beautiful, sat in the middle.

He'd kept an eye on the Bourlands in the afternoon. The two men had gone to the club judging from the way they were dressed and the bags they carried with them when they left. Chuck had followed Meg when she drove off in her mother's car. She made one stop to pick up another woman then drove to the movies. A patient man. He'd sat and waited outside the theatre.

Because she'd come along in the family after David, Chuck didn't hold her responsible for what had happened to him. Joe, David, and Ellie? They were different. Especially Ellie. She had to pay. He raised the beer mug, drank, and focused on the black-haired woman.

Meg had captivated his attention since she first arrived home. His blood raced when he saw her. He imagined nailing her. His cock twitched. She wouldn't stop him from accomplishing his primary goal, but screwing her? Yeah. He reached one hand under the table. With the other he raised the mug and gulped the beer, trying to quench the fire she lit inside him. Despite the hard on he had for her, she wouldn't wreck his plans.

Right after overhearing the bitch Ellie telling her friend in the drugstore the caterers needed help, Chuck had gone straight to the business. Because he already had a food handler's license, he'd had no problem getting a job. He'd be the muscle carrying supplies and food in and out, moving items around, and he'd be inside for their fancy holiday party. Then he'd serve. He had a catering job to work Monday, so keeping an eye on the family then was out. He'd especially miss watching Meg.

She looked up and right at him. Did she really see him? Had the intensity of his gaze drawn her? He didn't turn away. He was the stronger one. Tuesday he'd show them all when he walked right into their home. Like it was his. He raised his beer mug and swallowed, never looking away. Yeah. He had the power.

* * * *

Meg shivered. Damn, what was the matter with her? Imagining things now?

"You cold, Meg? Let's switch to a booth closer to the fire." Mary Ann pointed to the old fashioned black gas stove across the room from where they sat.

"No, it's…the guy in the back has been staring at us for a while."

"Which one?" Mary Anne asked in a husky whisper.

"With the beard and long hair, sitting at the back booth. Don't look." Meg might as well have saved her breath. All the women ignored her request anyway.

"Well, of course he's ogling us, silly. We're a bunch of hot broads." Julie reached for another slice of pizza, the cheese stretching from the pan to her plate. "Third piece. Extra mile on the treadmill tomorrow." Her laughter bubbled out before biting into the dough.

Meg smiled her best attempt to join in her friends' banter. She buried her concern and contributed to the discussion of which of several actors was sexier and what they'd like to do with the men in question. They agreed to take in another movie during the holidays and to continue to debate the merits of the hunks then. Around nine-thirty, the group split up.

"Is Meredith's school still in session, Julie?" Meg maneuvered through the traffic after supper.

"No. She's out for the next two weeks. Mom's keeping her a couple of days and thrilled to do so. They're going shopping for her gifts for Tim and me."

"Some drivers are dammed inconsiderate."

"What's the matter?"

"Oh, this guy behind me has his bright lights on and is following way too close."

"Pull over and let him go by. We're not in a hurry." Julie said.

"Okay." Before she acted on Julie's suggestion, the bright lights blinded her as the vehicle rushed their bumper and again flashed its lights a couple of times. Tires squealed when the driver tore around them and flew by.

"Must be a teenager." Julie let out a long sigh. "Hope he gets home in one piece."

"You're way more understanding than I am. I hope a cop pulls the asshole over. Wish I'd been able to see his license plate." Meg rubbed a hand over her eyes where white spots flashed. She drove in silence for a while then when the car didn't show back up, she asked, "What are you getting Meredith for Christmas?" For the next couple of blocks they exhausted the subject of kids' toys.

"Meg, what are you doing? You keep speeding up and slowing down. We're not in a hurry, but really."

"Think we may have picked up a tail." Her voice held little of the emotion churning in her chest as she went into work mode.

"The car from earlier?" Julie craned her neck, angling for a clear look.

"Don't know. We'll find out. Hold tight."

"Damn. You gonna out run him?" Julie's eyebrows skirted her hairline.

"Sure. You're not too old for this, are you?"

"No. But Tim needs me home in one piece. I trust you're as good as you used to be." Julie grabbed hold of the "Oh, shit" handle above her door.

"Believe so." Meg executed a few quick turns. At first, her rear view mirror was clear, but after three blocks, the smaller car came into view. "Damn. Spot it?"

"Yup," Julie said. "But I can't make out the plates. It looks like a dark colored sedan."

They came to another corner where the traffic had picked up. "Okay, let's find out how good you are, bud. Hang on, Julie." She floored her mother's red Infinity, wishing for a less noticeable color.

Her heartbeat accelerated with the car's speed. Several quick turns, a cut in front of someone stopping at a light, a squeal of breaks, a mad dash through another intersection, and they were on the freeway. Her pursuer stopped at the red light she'd sped through. Not recommended driving for a civilian or a cop.

"Whew." She slowly lifted her fingers one at a time from the steering wheel, flexed her shoulders, and slowed down.

"Way to go, Meg. You lost him. Damn." Julie patted Meg's arm then fanned her face. "I'd forgotten how exciting a chase was. Wow."

"Right. Let me get you home, Julie, before Tim decides we can't be alone together." Meg took the next exit leading back toward their neighborhood, her heart rate slowing down.

"Like our mothers did when we were little, and we spread bath powder all over your bedroom? They kept us apart for a week."

"As I recall we were into the third incident in row." Meg chuckled, releasing more tension.

"I had more fun than in a long time." Julie laughed. "You need to include a heart healthy warning for your regular friends who ride along with you on a movie and pizza invite." Her laughter petered out. "On a more serious note, any idea who'd follow you?"

"Probably a jerk after something he calls fun." Meg stopped the car in front of Julie's two-story Tudor. "I've got you safely home, now. Tim can't ground us."

"I can't wait to tell him about our ride." She climbed out. "Thanks. It's only a couple of blocks but keep your cell handy on the way back to your folks."

"Will do. See you in the morning." Contrary to Julie, Meg didn't look forward to telling David and Scott about this, but she couldn't avoid updating them.

In less than five minutes, Meg reached the driveway of her parents' house. She glanced around but saw nothing, steered into the garage, and then closed the door. The alarm chimed when she let herself into the mudroom. A clock struck ten. "Hey, anyone home?"

"We're in the den, dear."

Meg followed the sound of her mother's voice. Her father, brother, and Scott sat amidst the litter of pizza boxes on the coffee table and beer bottles on the floor.

"How were the girls? Did you enjoy the movie?" Her mother took a sip from her glass of red wine. Everyone else drank beer with pizza, but her mother insisted on the juice from the vine as she sometimes called it.

Meg smiled. "Fine, good to catch up." She dropped onto the arm of her mother's chair. "The movie was funny. You guys have a good evening?" She aimed her question at anyone who chose to answer.

"We'll talk when this movie is over." David said.

He didn't look up at her. Meg shrugged and raised her eyebrows at her mother who patted Meg on the knee and winked. Like old times when all the females in the family made a connection against the men. With a long breath, she released the last of the tension from the drive. Nice to be home.

* * * *

9:40 p.m. Sunday, December 20

Shit. He lost her, but he probably scared the pee out of her. A smile lifted one corner of his mouth. Yeah, bet he got her heart rate up. Give her a taste of what was ahead.

Where she'd end up wasn't a secret. Chuck reversed directions, drove the speed limit, and made his way to the connecting street where the Bourlands lived. With only two directions to the house, he'd see her, whichever she chose. He smoked a cigarette, cracking the window to let out the smoke. He waited. Lit a second smoke, drew the nicotine deep into his lungs. The fingers of one hand tapped an idol beat on the steering wheel.

Halfway through the third cigarette, the sight of the red Infinity rewarded his patience. About freaking time. She drove into the driveway, paused before pulling into the garage. After a moment, the door went down. He missed seeing her climb out. Damn, he wanted a longer look.

Someday, he'd drive a sports car, maybe a Corvette. Yeah, something fast and hot to attract the women. Before long, he'd have enough money to buy any kind of car or woman he wanted. He'd get him a piece of the black-haired beauty before he got started on the others. As he drove by, he glanced at the white house with the Christmas decorations outside, the trees, and the lights in the windows. The house, which should be his.

He directed the car toward his small rental near the park. Close to his target. As soon as he finished his next letter, he'd go to bed.

He'd start his new job tomorrow and didn't want to be late. Everything he learned Monday he'd apply to make a smooth entrance to the Bourland's party when he'd walk into the home where he belonged. His mother would be proud.

* * * *

10:30 p.m. Sunday, December 20

"You can't drop information and then not expect to explain." Scott's words came out harsher than he'd intended, and he stood with both arms crossed over his chest to keep from reaching for her. Not an accommodating stance, but what the hell had she been thinking anyway?

"What do you mean you were followed?" David repeated.

Meg executed a one-eighty, crossed on the other side the table and made for the kitchen door. Scott moved into her space and stopped her escape.

"I don't have to explain anything to anyone, least of all you." She brushed by him, and he staggered and groaned. She stopped in the doorway, drew in a quick breath, and faced them with both fists planted firmly at her waist. "I appreciate your concern. It shouldn't surprise me you two macho types overreacted. A guy followed me. I lost him. End of story. Do I need to remind you I'm a SWAT officer? I can take care of myself." Her tone said she thought they were morons or something worse.

David surrendered with hands up in front of his body. "Nope. I know exactly how competent you are. I'm out of line."

She about faced and stomped from the kitchen.

"Sorry," David hollered after her then grabbed on to Scott's arm when he went to follow her. "You'll lose this one. Let it go." David dropped on to a chair. "She's always had a short fuse when it comes to doubts about her competency."

"I don't doubt her, man. My God, the woman took out her team member's killers in a dangerous situation and got out without being injured. No one can doubt her abilities."

"You know how it is, Scott. When a woman's in police work, someone always questions whether she can be trusted to carry the load. Meg proves her value, not for herself alone, but for the other females in law enforcement."

"Okay, okay." Scott nodded his understanding. "Do you think her tail had anything to do with Joe's situation or was it a random coincidence? A guy liked what he saw of Meg and followed her. Probably happens a lot." Damn, he didn't like how his gut clutched. He had no right to feel in the least possessive of the woman. Yet, he did. David's crossed leg jiggled in time with his thought process.

"I don't know, Scott, but I wouldn't bet against the house on a possible connection." David crossed his other leg and continued the movement. "We're about to run out of opportunities to look for the other letters. Tomorrow after lunch may be our best time. Dad will go to the office again, and Mom's having a final meeting with the caterers about the party. Kathy, Ron and the kids arrive later in the afternoon. It'll be a zoo around here from then on."

"How about after I finish with the therapist?"

"Yeah. I'll ask Meg if you can ride to your appointment with her in the morning. I've got a couple of errands to do before the little tornadoes arrive. After I pick you up, we'll stop at the car rental and set you up in your own wheels. With a house key, you can come and go at will."

"No problem." Getting the car was a good plan, but damn, riding with Meg wouldn't be fun. He was as horny as a teenager around her. Not a time he remembered fondly. Sleeping in the room next to hers would lead to more of the erotic dreams from the last two nights. Frustrating as all hell.

* * * *

10:45 a.m. Monday, December 21

"Listen, I need to apologize for last night."

Meg shot a glance at Scott in her passenger seat. "What about?" If anyone needed to apologize, she probably did for acting high and mighty.

"I wasn't implying you're not up for a tight situation. I respect what you do and what you've accomplished."

"Thank you." She yanked her gaze away from him. "I'm sorry I practically snapped your collective heads off."

After she steered the car to the curb in front of his therapist's offices on Bryant Irvin, he held his hand out. "Truce?"

"Truce." She met his grip firmly. "I hope the session goes well," Meg said. "When do you want me to pick you up?"

"David's coming. I'll be finished in about an hour, and you'll still be having lunch with your friend."

"Okay, see you later then." He walked into the building, and she squashed a stupid desire to see him with fewer clothes on. Yeah, he was on the thin side, but something about him lit her fires. "Don't be stupid." The sound of her voice surprised her. She rubbed at a pinprick of pain in her temple before pulling into traffic.

Scott turned her inside out despite his appearing not to be the least interested in her.

Yeah, they lived across the country from each other. They were both coming off highly emotional experiences. And she recognized a kindred spirit in him.

Maybe that's all this was. But she'd met men in Atlanta in the same situation. None of them had the effect on her Scott did. Maybe Julie could help. Meg had to talk with someone before she lost her ever-loving mind, attacked him in the middle of the night, and dragged him into her bed.

"Jeez."

She parked in the lot of the Village at Camp Bowie, an upscale shopping center on the westside with a great little restaurant. Meg wasn't normally the tearoom type, but The Lunch Box had been a part of her whole life. Her mother and grandmother brought her and Kathy here when they were young children. The servers had always treated them like they were adults. The memories made her smile.

Julie Smith's car took the space next to Meg as she climbed out. "Hey, Julie." They had joined the Fort Worth PD at the same time. Years after Meg moved away, Julie left the force to stay home with her and Tim's baby.

They walked in, and Meg stopped, glanced around and smiled.

The smaller white wrought iron tables took the upper level, and larger ones for groups of more than four covered the lower section. Daisies, even in December, filled white milk glass vases in the center of the tables. Just as she remembered. They gave their orders quickly.

"It's nice your mother doesn't mind keeping Meredith," Meg said, after their food arrived.

Julie nodded. "Between the two grandmas, they'd provide full-time babysitting if we wanted." She took a bite of her egg salad on rye.

"Do you ever imagine returning to the force?"

"Occasionally. Last night certainly made the juices flow, but I couldn't be a beat cop again. I can't take a chance of leaving Meredith an orphan if something happened to both Tim and me. Sure, tragedy strikes regular folks too, but I can't compartmentalize enough to do the job safely and well."

Meg wasn't sure why she'd asked the question. She wasn't thinking of quitting. She drummed those thoughts from her mind and bit into her chicken salad sandwich. "Um. This is so good."

"Might account for why they've been around for close on forty years, huh?" Julie raised one eyebrow.

"Well, maybe." Meg laughed.

"Enough of the chit chat, tell, me how you're doing for real?"

"Hanging in." Meg picked up her napkin and dabbed at her mouth to give her hands something to do. As good a friend as Julie was, Meg wasn't about to discuss her father's situation with her.

"You mentioned since the incident you'd stopped recalling

your dreams. Do you remember them now?"

"Yeah. Started after I came home. My Atlanta psychologist set me up with one here and wants me to see her twice before I go back to Georgia."

"Sounds wise. You need to give yourself time, too." Julie took a couple of bites of her fruit salad. "You seeing anyone in Atlanta? A Southern boy catch your fancy?"

Meg grabbed for her iced tea and gulped to keep the heat from flaring in her cheeks. The glass, held against the side of her face, added a touch of relief. She wasn't a young woman, and this wasn't her first rodeo, as the saying went. She was a mature forty-year-old. Secure in who she was. She didn't need a man to make her whole. "No Southern guy." The words came out softer than she intended.

"But someone, if I'm not mistaken. Give." Julie leaned across the table. "Who is it? Have you slept with him?" Julie lowered her voice. "Was it great? You'll follow him to Timbuktu? Tell the truth."

"Well." Damn. She had no guy, Southern or otherwise. Her fingers tapped her glass, and she looked across the room. Anywhere but Julie's too perceptive eyes. Meg couldn't remember when she'd last slept with anyone. Did she want to sleep with someone? A different question indeed.

"Too much wait time, girlfriend. Come on. I can keep a secret. You can trust me."

That was a fact. Meg and Julie had formed a bond when they joined the force together and even after years apart, it remained strong. Meg gripped the napkin in her lap.

"My brother's partner—"

"The one who saved his life? Scott something?"

"Yeah. Scott McClaine."

"What about him?"

Meg looked down then out the window again avoiding Julie's gaze.

"Oh, my God. You've got the hots for your brother's partner?" Julie clapped her hands.

Meg wanted to shake her head but couldn't quite pull off the denial of the emotional pull the man had on her. Not and be truthful.

"And he's staying at Joe and Ellie's, right? Where's he sleeping?" Julie scooted to the edge of her chair as if she feared missing a word of what Meg had to say.

"Next door to me."

"Oh, my. So have you done it in your parents' house?"

"God, no, Julie. We haven't 'done it' anywhere." Her heart rate jacked up at Julie's suggestion. Meg thrust images from her mind too easily formed of her and Scott rolling around on her bed.

"Please tell me you've at least kissed."

"No. I mean, I kissed him on the cheek as a thank you for taking care of David. I'm not sure he's interested."

"Not interested? What's the matter with the guy? Is he gay?"

"He was badly injured saving David's life. To the extent, he's been forced into taking a medical retirement." God, sitting here and discussing this drove her crazy like little wires were sticking out all over her head. Meg wanted nothing more than to run out of the tearoom.

"What a crying shame."

They ate in silence for a while, and Meg took a relieved breath. Julie had dropped the subject.

"Do you mean he's physically incapable of the act?"

"No." Meg sloshed her tea. "I mean." She toyed with her food. "I don't think so." She dropped her fork on the table and fidgeted in her chair. "I mean, obviously, I haven't asked, but David never mentioned anything specific. Scott told me he'd always walk with a cane."

"Do you find his disability a turn off?" Julie's eyebrows drew down in a frown, waiting for Meg's response.

"No. Would you if all of a sudden Tim had to use a cane?"

"Of course, not, but we're in love. It's the *for better or worse* part." She stopped eating and stared at Meg. "Jeez Louise, lady."

"What?"

"Have you fallen for him?"

"No. No. Of course not. I…I couldn't have. We've only just met."

"What, you've never heard of love at first sight?" Julie's soft chuckle and smile said she knew it all.

"Yeah, Julie, but isn't it usually mutual?" Damn, she wished her heart would slow down. Its flutter at the center of her neck made her lightheaded.

"Are you sure he doesn't feel something for you? Think," Julie insisted.

"Well, twice, or three times when our gazes met—"

"Yes?"

"I would've sworn something happened between us. But he's never made anything like a pass." Meg rubbed her temples with both hands, the earlier tapping increasing to loud bangs. "I've never been in the position of lusting after a guy who didn't reciprocate my feelings. Not since middle school when I had a mouth-full of braces, anyway. This is embarrassing." She raised her tea glass to her cheeks again, one side and then the other, hoping to cool the warmth.

"What…what should I do?" The "poor pitiful me" sound to her voice increased Meg's discomfort as she waited for Julie's answer.

"Well, you're an adult with adult needs. Neither of you is married or involved, I presume. Go after what you want. If you need a place, you can use our guesthouse. Give me a heads up on the timing." She sat back with her arms across her chest, as if she'd solved all the problems of the world.

"God, I can't believe I'm listening to this suggestion." Meg fanned her napkin at her face to cool off. She wanted to jump up and run. Her leg bounced up and down under the table.

"Meg."

She stopped fanning, took several swallows from her glass, and studied Julie's face.

"More important than what I think, is the small matter of what you want to do."

Julie gave Meg the hard cop stare mastered in the early years. When Julie gave someone the eye, the truth generally popped out of the subject's mouth. In this situation, what was the truth?

"I've never done one night stands. I'm afraid this couldn't be anything more. I mean, what else? He lives in LA. I live in Atlanta. He's my brother's best friend and former partner. I worry about the impact on their relationship when we'd brake up. I'm not completely certain he's interested. Except for those times…."

Meg nibbled her sandwich. Another of Julie's many good qualities was her ability to be quiet. Within the silence, Meg found her answers. She washed the last of the sandwich down and slid the plate away from her. She'd reached a decision.

"More important than all of those reasons is my choice not to risk my heart with a law enforcement type. What's the old cliché? *Once bitten twice shy?* Or, *'Been-there-done-that.* Or maybe it's *I'm not taking a second turn on the merry-go-round.* Obviously, lots of common sense advice telling me to walk away."

"Your final answer?" Julie was a game show fanatic.

"Yes, my final answer." Meg exhaled a long sign. "Thanks. I needed to work through the repercussions of a relationship. As always, you're a big help."

"Didn't seem like I helped much." Julie's mouth turned down like she was disappointed.

"You and Tim are bringing Meredith tomorrow evening to the party, aren't you? Mom will be miffed if you don't."

"Way to change the subject, Meg."

"The subject is dead." What happened to the heat earlier searing her middle? Now cold engulfed her all the way to her toes.

* * * *

2:00 p.m. Monday, December 21

As soon as she'd returned home, Meg, David, and Scott went upstairs to her parents' room. Again, she took pictures with her phone of what everything looked like before they started their search. They skipped over anything of Mom's on the theory Dad wouldn't take a chance of hiding something among her belongings. If the whole point of the exercise was to keep her in the dark, any other action didn't make sense.

Her brother drove her nuts, fussing and fuming. Snooping through a parent's personal belongings was damned unsettling. In an hour's search, they'd found nothing.

"He must carry them with him all of the time." David slammed his fist on his thigh in frustration.

"In a pocket of his pants, maybe, or jacket. This is my fault. I should've searched first before saying anything to him." She ran her fingers up under her ponytail to release tension clawing at her head.

"Cut yourself some slack, Meg," Scott said. "You didn't know other letters existed then."

She cast her gaze in his direction for a moment. "Guess I'm not thinking clearly right now. What if he burned the others? He threw the one I found toward the fireplace. If he'd lit a fire—"

"We'd be nowhere," David said.

Twenty minutes later, David ran a hand across his face and let out a gusty sigh. "Listen, we're finished here. Let's see how we've done."

Meg held out her phone, and they checked they'd returned everything to its proper place. They trooped down the stairs and none-to-soon. They walked into the kitchen to the sound of a car pulling into the garage.

"Crap. Way too close," David muttered.

Meg put a large pot on top of the stove, clanging it in her hurry. She reached for oil. "We're watching a movie. Go find one, Scott. David, take down the bowls." Meg shot out orders, and everyone did as she intended. The corn popped to the sound of the door-opening chime.

"What a good idea, Meg." Her mother came in sniffing the air. "Nothing smells better than corn popping. Is your father home?"

"Uh, no." Meg cast a quick glance at her brother who shrugged his shoulders. "Scott's picking out a movie. Join us?"

"Love to if you're sure you have enough."

"I remember how this family eats popcorn. I made plenty. David, find Mom a bowl, please."

"Sure, but hey, Meg, you're spilling on the floor," David ragged on her

In no time, the four had gathered in the den. She, her brother, and Scott acted as if everything was fine. Just fine.

"Can we talk through the previews?" Ellie passed napkins to everyone.

"No problem for me." Scott threw a handful of the white kernels in his mouth.

Meg's gaze riveted on his throat when he swallowed. Might

take her mind off the mess, but not good timing. She studied her popcorn bowl before selecting a couple of kernels. Normally, nothing tasted better than the salty, buttery flavor of fresh popped corn. This afternoon she might throw up if she ate much.

"Good. Then we can catch up before the movie starts."

Meg pretended a normalcy she didn't feel. What was normal now, anyway? Would her family find that again? Scott's hand slide down to rub his leg. Did it hurt him? Her stomach clenched, and she ached for the man and what he'd been through.

Her mother chatted, while Meg considered the uncomfortable situation she found herself in with Scott. Her skin sizzled when he looked at her. His gaze left a physical caress every place it touched, and yet he seemed completely unaware of his effect on her.

Mom kept going on about the food for the party. Normally, Meg would've joined in. Damn, normally, she'd be fighting her mother and the guys for the popcorn, but now her stomach roiled from the one handful she'd eaten. Her nerves stretched thin. Her libido hadn't gotten the message from her brain about having nothing to do with her brother's former partner. Incredible she'd allowed a hint of her reaction for Scott to creep into her conscience when everything hung in flux with her father and the letters. She was more screwed up than she'd realized. Maybe the psychologist could help.

She straightened in the chair and tuned back in to the conversation.

"Scott, how did therapy go?" her mother asked.

"It was rougher than I expected. The therapist liked what I did at the club, and he wants me to go every day. I've got appointments to see him a couple of times during the two weeks."

"I'm sure he'll help. Meg, dear, is Julie bringing Meredith tomorrow night?"

"Yes, I told her you'd be disappointed if she didn't."

"Good. She's always been one of my favorites of your friends."

Right before the movie began, her mother rose and picked up her bowl of popcorn. "As much as I've enjoyed the chat, my book is calling from the living room. See y'all later."

Meg stifled a laugh when they all three heaved sighs like smoke stacks belching after her mother's exit. "What fun. Our next foray into the acting field will be when Dad gets home. This is harder than I imagined. It's like I'm being sneaky or deceitful." She rubbed her hands down her jeans.

"Do you wonder if they've always been straight with us?" David leaned forward and took a swallow from his cola.

"What are you talking about? Besides, Dad's not lying. He's just not doing what we think he should." She sounded as enabling as all the families she ran into at work, making excuses for men's inexplicable behaviors.

"I bet plenty of times our parents don't tell us personal, private stuff about their lives, which happened before we came along," Scott said.

"Well, sure." She dragged herself from the trashcan of remorse and tried for a lighter view. "I remember a lot of Kathy's exploits she needs never to tell her kids. You don't even want to know, David."

"Scary. You could've gone a long while without saying so." David rolled his eyes.

She forced out a laugh, hoping it didn't sound fake. Her laughter stopped abruptly when she heard the familiar whirring sound of the garage door opening. "Dad."

"Must be." Scott stood. "I'll go hang out with Ellie."

"Text me if she makes a move to come back here." David's lips thinned in what Meg recognized as his "Don't-mess-with-me-or-I'll-kick-the-crap-out-of-you" look. He was primed to take on their father.

Scott nodded, took his cane, and lumbered out of the den. David stood, his feet spread.

Did the position give him the illusion of control. They didn't have any amount of control over this situation in Meg's opinion. But that was about to stop. Three smart, capable people were sure to figure out something. Letting Dad continue to pay the blackmailer was out of the question. Her hands balled into fists of determination.

The door between the mudroom and the den opened and closed. Her father walked in and stopped when he saw them. "How's everyone this afternoon?"

"We're okay," Meg answered for them. She muted the TV.

He laid his coat on the back of one of the chairs. "Where's your mother?"

"In the front room with Scott." Her hands, of their own accord, gripped each other. She stood and forced them to hang limply at her side. "Dad, David and I'd like to talk with you before you go see her.

Can you give us a minute?"

Her father's brows drew together. "What's this about?"

Meg met her brother's gaze and struggled not to roll her eyes. "The blackmail."

"Dammit, Meg. I told you and David I'd handle this situation."

"Situation? My God, Dad, you're being blackmailed. This is a hell of a lot more than a situation." The disappointment in her father's eyes made Meg's stomach clench. She'd never wanted to let him down and to her knowledge, never had. Somehow, she had now.

"I'll take care of this." He spit the words through gritted teeth. "I do not want either of you involved. I do not want your mother bothered in the least by anything." He turned and stormed toward the kitchen.

"Dad." David moved between his father and the doorway.

Their father glared at him. The silence scratched on her nerves.

"Step aside, son."

The two men, the same height, stood toe to toe. Anger reddened her father's face.

God, she hoped he didn't have a heart attack.

"Report this to the police, Dad."

"No, I will not. Now get out of my way."

After what seemed forever, David moved aside.

"I'll see you at supper." Breathing hard, her father raised his voice as he went in search of his wife. "Ellie."

* * * *

11:30 p.m. Monday, December 21

Scott sat with the David and Meg in the den. Ellie and Joe had gone upstairs an hour ago. Sudden silences had strained the evening meal. Ellie asked Scott if he hadn't liked what Maria cooked. He'd assured her he loved the roast beef, but therapy had messed with his appetite.

How were David and Meg managing? This wasn't Scott's family, and yet his stomach had tied into knots. Easier to deal with the viciousness in the world when you weren't personally touched. While technically, not Scott's family, they came as close as anything else did these days.

"This sucks," David exploded into the quiet of the den.

Meg tapped her fingers on the chair arms and jiggled her crossed leg.

"Well, you're right, partner." Other things sucked, too. Like not being able to go back to full active duty. Hell of a kick in the ass when his doctors in LA told him. He'd hardly processed the reality of his medical retirement to this day. Hellfire. He was too young to be a washed-up-has-been. But he was. Pain twisted his insides into sharp blades, tearing him in two. He clenched his fingers around his cane, determined not to bolt from the chair and cause a scene. Sucked is right.

"Should we go to the cops without him?" Meg's foot stopped its frenzied movement for a moment then kicked back into motion. "We both know people from when we worked with the department who'd be discreet."

"I can't bring myself to disrespect Dad by ignoring his request.

At least, not yet. However, if you come across any more tails, I might."

"What if I stake out the P.O. box?" Scott leaned forward and rested his elbows on his knees. "Regardless of whether or not our blackmailer has watched the house, he probably wouldn't recognize me." He stared at Meg. "I'm not about to assume the tail wasn't somehow connected. The blackmailer zeroed in on you two. The note suggests as much."

"Sounds logical." Meg sprang from her chair and paced in front of the TV screen no one paid attention to. "You and I aren't thinking too clearly, David, or we'd have come up with such an obvious idea."

"Are you sure you're up to it?" Worry lines puckered David's forehead. "Your focus has to be on getting well."

"A few hours surveilling won't kill me, David. With the rental you and I picked up today, I can come and go as needed. You won't have to drop whatever you're doing to take me if I pick up an extra therapy session when someone cancels."

"We don't mind driving." Meg stopped pacing. "It's the least we can do."

Those blue-green eyes in the fair face surrounded by the black hair kicked him right in the gut. He couldn't remember a woman affecting him so. Never one he couldn't have, at any rate. They had to solve the mystery, because he had to get out of this house and away from Meg. The torture of being around her and not having a snowball's chance in hell with her, made the loss of his career a small hill to scale. He'd find something else to do with his life, but Meg wouldn't be included. A barren desert came to mind.

David got up and aimed for the kitchen. "I'm getting a beer then turning in. See y'all in the morning."

"We probably should, too. When Kathy and her kids arrive…well, our lives will not be our own." Meg followed her brother.

Scott stepped in front of her. He'd gotten better with his cane, and he moved easier.

"What's the matter?" She tilted her head up toward him.

"You promise me you'll be alert. There's no telling what the deal is with this guy."

"Yeah, I know. Thanks."

She laid her hand on his arm. His stomach clenched.

"I'll be careful. Do you want any help getting up the stairs?"

There were activities he wanted her help with. None of them involved the stairs. "No. I've gotten where I can manage them on my own using the cane. Takes me a while. You go on." Hell. He hated her seeing him as needy.

CHAPTER SIX

3:30 p.m. Tuesday, December 22

After his therapy session, Scott drove to the newly built post office with lots of glass across the front. When he arrived, he went inside, identified the location of box 1340, and hung around for a while, getting a sense for the flow of foot traffic. He didn't stay long enough to cause the employees to notice him. When a parking space with a direct view of the box opened up, he moved the car.

Stiffness from a couple hours sitting forced him to walk to the convenience store across the street. A steaming cup of coffee in hand, made the cold temperatures bearable. Scott kept his eye on the post office. Nobody attempted to open 1340.

Joe needed to receive another letter and send in a payment to increase the chances of catching the blackmailer. For all they knew, the man never used the box except to collect the dollars Joe sent him. Scott figured to stay until five-forty-five in case the suspect checked his mail on his way home from a job.

Between the cold and getting in and out of the car, Scott's body ached. Too bad. No time to stop by the gym to use the whirlpool before the party. He'd be stiff tonight. He walked in front of the building a couple more times, never losing site of the box. How long before they'd find this dude? When he did show up, Scott planned to take pictures then follow him. Meg and David still had to convince Joe to go to the police. A tough sell.

* * * *

6:15 p.m. Tuesday, December 22

Scott made the turn onto the Bourland's street, slowing way down because of the traffic. He slid to the curb in front of a neighbor's house, but a young man in a purple jacket got to Scott before he climbed out. David had told him about the valet service his family hired whenever they had one of these bashes where they expected several hundred people. The street wasn't wide enough for everyone to park on both sides and still let cars pass. Scott took the ticket and handed over his keys.

Kathy, Ron, and the kids had been scheduled to arrive in the afternoon. Scott didn't see anything with an Oklahoma license, but their car had probably been moved, too. Couple of caterer's vans had backed into the driveway right up to the open garage doors. This was one big shindig. Scott made his way toward the porch and ambled through the front door.

The aroma of cinnamon and roasting turkey greeted him and made his stomach growl. Guess the eating would be even better than he'd experienced in his stay so far. Ellie had told him not to expect a sit down family supper tonight because of the party. While some guests would be decked out in black tie, Scott's dark suit would be fine. Good thing. Not like he owned a tux. No use for one in his line of work. Former line of work. That sucked.

Shoving questions of what he'd do next from his mind, he wandered toward the kitchen. Ellie and Maria were giving last minute directions to the catering staff all dressed in black slacks, long sleeved white shirts with black cummerbunds, and bow ties.

"Hey, Scott. How'd you do today?"

Before he answered, Ellie went on.

"Probably a less hectic day than ours. Kathy, Ron, and the grands arrived. I hope you had a late lunch." Her energy and fast deliver of words tinged with its hint of Southern accent always surprised Scott.

"Yes, but I had to come see what smelled good and see how you and Maria marshaled the troupes."

Ellie looked at the housekeeper, and they both laughed.

"He's right, Miss Ellie, it's like a battle plan." Maria laughed. "And you're '*la jefe*.'"

"Well, you must be my adjutant, and the Out of the Box Catering folks are our soldiers." She glanced at a server walking by. "One minute, young man."

The tall, slender staff member stopped. His eyes grew wide, and his hand reached up as if to assure himself his ponytail hadn't come loose. A bushy mustache obscured his mouth.

"It's all right." She smiled. "You haven't done anything wrong. I need to fix your tie. It's crooked, and I'm guessing uncomfortable." She reached way up, and he leaned down. Ellie adjusted the bow. "Now, much improved. Feels better, too, I guess."

He nodded. "Yes, ma'am."

"Well, don't let me keep you from whatever you need to be doing."

"Thanks," the man mumbled and went around toward the

garage.

"Everything looks in good shape." Ellie glanced around one last time. "I'm going up to finish getting ready. See you later, Scott. If you need me for anything, Maria—"

"Call. I know. We should be fine. You go on."

Ellie smiled and breezed out.

"She doesn't need to worry. We've done this many times, and everything runs good."

Maria turned briefly to the counter then back to Scott.

"You want a sample?" She held out a green napkin with two small white triangles with cheese dripping along the side. "Turkey *quesadillas.* Don't tell her I gave you anything."

A twinkle in Maria's eye brought an answering smile from Scott.

"She won't hear it from me. Thanks, Maria. Guess I'd better head up. See you later." Scott bit into one of the *quesadillas.* Yeah. Good eating tonight. He inhaled the second one while he made his way past a couple of the staff members.

When he'd arrived at the Bourland's several days ago, Ellie had already decorated for Christmas, but the workers added more flower arrangements and lit candles. He stopped on the stairs, glancing back over his shoulder. Huh. So this is how the other half lives. Something else. Would anyone here tonight detect the family's strain because someone was blackmailing Joe Bourland?

Squeals made him look up. "Whoa. Hey there, little buddy." Scott reached one hand for the banister, dropped his cane, and grabbed for the pint-sized fireball bouncing down the stairs. Straining his muscles, Scott struggled to stay on his feet and not let go of the small human.

"Sorry about him. He got away from me. Not fond of baths." The attractive woman in jeans and sweater scooped up the small boy with one arm. Black hair piled on top of her head made her resemblance to Meg unmistakable.

"You must be Kathy, and he must be the Ronny I've heard about."

She nodded and hefted the urchin, who continued to squirm, higher on her hip. "And you're Scott, our special Christmas angel, who saved David's life. I'm glad to meet you. Sorry about the cane. Let me grab it for you." She started down the stairs.

He stopped her with a hand on her arm. "I can manage. You've got a lot to deal with."

"Not for long. Ron," she hollered over the boy's giggles. "Come get your son." She continued to stand with Scott. "Ronny is always my husband's son when he's acting up."

Her grin and raised eyebrows indicated this happened often, and she loved them both anyway. A stout man with the build of a construction worker started down the stairs.

"Ron, take him. Ronny nearly knocked Scott down. How would you like that on your conscience? Scott, this is Ron, the father of our little terror." She handed the boy to his dad.

"Nice to meet you, Scott. You shouldn't have waited this long for his bath, Kathy." He draped Ronny over his shoulder like a sack of potatoes, the boy's legs kicking, and Ron took the stairs two at a time.

"Well, I hoped to keep him clean until at least the first guest arrived," she said to his retreating figure. She sprinted down, retrieved Scott's cane, and then returned. "We can't thank—"

"Enough already. I've threatened to leave if I hear any more words of gratitude. David would've done the same." Together they continued up to the second floor. "Thought Ron took your son for the dreaded bath." Scott gestured toward the open bathroom door.

"He is. We're up on the third floor. Mom and Dad redid the attic when we were in our teens to make more room for sleepovers. We've got several beds, a full bathroom and space to play games."

"Wow."

"Yeah. It's not used much when none of us is here, but because of it, holidays are easier when we all invade the old homestead. If you're all right, I'll rescue Ron and finish getting Katie and me ready for the festivities. Glad you're here, Scott."

* * * *

9:00 p.m. Tuesday, December 22

Meg had kept her distance from Scott throughout the night. Easy to do with a large number of people milling around. The catering staff had been kept hopping with the food and beverage service. Several times, she'd glanced around to find the same server staring at her. The slender man wore his longish brown hair in a ponytail. Something about his bushy eyebrows and mustache reminded her of the guy at the pizza joint. Except that man had a full beard. Who knew what his features were?

"Another glass of wine?" He offered her a tray, which held glasses.

"Thank you." She stated to ask him if he'd been at the restaurant, but before she had a chance, he moved off to serve other guests.

"The party is wonderful." Julie, in a black dress with green bead accents, took Meg's arm and walked her into the library. "Your mother swooped up Meredith, and she's been passed around to others who nicely oohed and aahed over her."

"Well, of course, they did. She's a little charmer."

Julie's gaze traveled from the ridiculously high heels Meg had on to the dangerously low- cut gown. Her friend's lips shifted into a lopsided grin.

"What?" Meg tugged her hair behind one ear. She shouldn't have worn it down or at least she should've used two rhinestone clips instead of one.

"The dress is awesome with your hair and coloring."

"I shouldn't have let you talk me into buying this rig. I'll never wear this in Atlanta." She tugged self-consciously at the opening, trying to bring the swaths of material closer. What had she been thinking? More than modestly endowed, she'd always downplayed the attribute, from the first moment she pinned on a badge.

"Has Scott seen you?"

"I don't know. I haven't noticed him."

"You haven't? How did you miss him? He and David have

been everywhere. Unless you were deliberately avoiding him—oh, you were, weren't you?"

"No." Meg denied, hoping no shade of pink stained her cheeks.

"David introduced Tim and me earlier. Scott's on the thin side, but still quite something. The cane adds a mystique of romanticism. He's pretty much to die for now. When he's recovered, wow. You need to re-consider having a go with him."

"Julie." Meg's stomach flipped. Her heart sputtered as pictures of Scott filled her mind.

"The eye-rolling doesn't become you, but the blush is a nice accent to the red dress. I have your best interests at heart, girlfriend. It's been years. Past time for you to move on. If he's so inclined, you owe yourself the opportunity to investigate the relationship."

"But he's a cop."

"Not anymore. Besides, who better to tolerate the life style? It's like two actors getting together. Nobody understands the strain of the business better than a person living the same kinds of experiences." She paused as if waiting for Meg to say something. "Sweetie, a great love affair is awaiting you—okay, at least great sex."

"Julie Smith, you are absolutely too much. I'm visiting—"

"With Scott?"

"No. The other guests. Try to stay out of trouble."

As she walked off, Julie whispered, "Try getting into trouble with the handsome cop."

Meg shook her head once, wandered toward the living room, and made small talk with the guests there. Unfortunately, many of them commented on meeting Scott and how wonderful he'd saved David's life. Two of the younger women Meg's mother had introduced to Scott, were literally drooling as they spoke of him. All of which made a counterpoint to Julie's words replaying in her head. Should she? No. Absolutely not...well, maybe.

"Would you like another glass of wine, miss?"

She glanced around, surprised to find the same mustached server she'd noticed earlier. She didn't remember putting down her glass, but she didn't hold one in her hand now. She'd been preoccupied with Julie's conversation.

"Nice party." He continued to stare at her.

"Yes." She reached for the glass. Did he pull the tray away from her?

Laughter and chatter flowed around them, but the hairs on the back of her neck stood on end. Meg extended her hand for the glass again, never taking her gaze from his.

"I hope you have a good evening." His tone implied the exact opposite.

He sauntered away. A chill slid along Meg's spine. Most servers didn't make conversations with the guests.

"Oh, Meg, you look lovely."

Meg focused her attention on a woman dressed all in gold, a member of her mother's bridge club.

"Thanks, Miriam."

"So glad you got home for the holidays. Joe and Ellie's party is delightful as always. I must get her recipe for the shrimp dip." The woman sailed off in search of her hostess.

Pivoting, Meg searched for the bearded server, but he was nowhere in sight.

She took a swallow of wine. How much more alcohol before she got up the Dutch courage to act on Julie's advice? Maybe this last glass was enough. She set off in search of her brother's partner. After avoiding them all evening, now she'd need an excuse. She'd share her misgivings about the server. Sounded like a plan.

But almost an hour later, she'd not found him or her brother. Despite the hour, Meg saw no signs of it closing down. A few of the older crowd had left, but many others still partied, ate, and drank.

Well, wouldn't you know. After consciously avoiding Scott all evening, now when she wanted to find him, she couldn't. Maybe he didn't want to see her either. She set her glass on a table. A woman server came around the corner and picked it up. Meg smiled her thanks at the efficient staff member.

"You look dazzling in the red dress," another one of the women in her mother's bridge club hugged Meg.

"Thank you, Melba." Before Meg got out another word, the woman went on her way into a throng of guests. Meg shrugged and continued her search. Had the guys hidden themselves away somewhere?

Julie and Tim, with Meredith asleep on her father's shoulder, stopped in the hall for their coats and said their thanks to Meg's parents. Julie drew Meg aside, hugged her, and whispered in her ear, "Go find him."

Barely containing an eye roll at her friend, Meg meandered through the rooms where she discovered Kathy with Katie, also asleep.

"Looks like she's done in." Meg brushed a hand across her niece's dark curls.

"Oh, yeah, and we'll probably pay for the late evening tomorrow. She'll be overly tired and grumpy."

"Little Ronny will be worse than usual?"

"Afraid so. Ron took him up a while ago."

"Have you seen David lately?"

"He and Scott headed for the garden room in the back. You know how it's always cooler in the winter, so fewer people gather there. Poor David had the strangled look he gets when he's partied out. One too many of Mom and Dad's friends going on about what he does and how glad they are he's okay, while stopping to throw appreciation Scott's way." She studied Meg for a moment. "Is everything okay?"

"Sure, haven't seen either of them this evening."

"Well, they couldn't have missed you. You're absolutely gorgeous. Tell Julie I approve, and next time I want to go shopping with her. Mom's want to look sexy too." Katie stirred on her mother's shoulder, making little mewling sounds. "Okay, we're outta here. See you tomorrow." She kissed Meg on the cheek and hurried toward the stairs.

Sexy? Did she want Scott to see her as sexy? Damn right. Garden room, huh? Before she could get out of the entrance another couple stopped her.

"Good bye, Mr. Franklin. Mrs. Franklin. I enjoyed catching up on your family." Meg gave the couple a quick hug and moved on.

Thank heavens the party was beginning to break up. Heels were not regulation wear, and her feet were making their displeasure known with sharp, shooting pains. She'd kick them off in a heartbeat if not too many guests had congregated in the back of the house.

What a relief. Nobody here except for her brother and his partner. She reached down and yanked the offenders off, walked barefoot to one of the wingbacks, and leaned across it, the shoes dangling from one hand. "This is where you two are hiding out." The chair provided a shield against Scott's sharp eyes, which never seemed to miss anything. Second thoughts about how 'sexy' she wanted to appear to him flowed through her like the chocolate from the fountain in the dining room.

"We had a ton of people here tonight, Meg. I'd forgotten how long this party went, with all the blue hairs going on about how cool my job is. I'm sorry, man." David elbowed Scott. "Not much of a restful evening for you."

"No sweat. Everyone was friendly and not too pushy about details. They seemed to care about your parents and you guys. Despite the warning, Meg, Ellie surprised the hell out of me when she tried to hook me up with a couple of younger women. Beats me why they'd be interested."

"Did you ask any of them out?" Meg held her breath, dreading the answer.

"No." His gaze connected with hers.

She forced out a laugh. "Mom can be a demon on wheels when she gets fixated on an idea. You'd do better to give in and ask someone." Damn, her stomach pitched as the words left her lips.

David stood and stretched. "Do what you want to with the ladies, man. I've had it, and I'm calling it a day. See you two in the morning." He moseyed out.

Well, now she was alone with Scott. If that's what she wanted, how come sweat popped out on her palms?

* * * *

10:30 p.m. Tuesday, December 22

People had overflowed the house. Chuck had never attended a party like this one. In the kitchen, he dried platters when David came in and helped himself to quesadillas. He scooped them onto a glass plate and popped them in the microwave. People scurried around him. Did he expect them to make room for him? Of course, he did. He was the prince after all. At the ding, David grabbed a napkin and removed the plate.

Chuck's mouth watered at the hot, tangy aroma. Mexican food, his favorite. He'd snatched samples earlier when no one was around to catch him. While David grabbed a beer, Chuck stepped into the doorway, blocking his exit. Chuck stared at the prince.

"Excuse me." David maneuvered around him toward the stairs.

Should've been me in the nice suit.

Should've been me getting to visit with the guests.

Should've been me the pretty women flirted with.

Chuck set down the tray and walked with determined steps toward the front of the house. The heir climbed the stairs. At the top, David turned and for a moment seemed to stare at Chuck before heading off. Chuck's fingers played with the letter in his pocket. Anticipation for what lay ahead spiked his heart rate.

He found Mr. and Mrs. Bourland in the entrance hall, accepting the thanks of their departing guests. Chuck's jaw clenched to keep the scream inside. *Look at me.* His teeth ground together. Not the right moment yet. Steps remained to be taken.

Chuck moved up behind Bourland. Finally, he'd be face to face with him. Catching a breath became difficult. Would he say anything right off? Chuck's hand trembled when he reached out and touched the mayor on his shoulder. The man jerked around. Surprise raised his eyebrows.

"I'm sorry to bother, sir. Here's a letter for you." Chuck struggled to conceal the smile pushing against his lips at the look of shock in Joe's eyes. His face whitened. His gaze glued to the white envelope in Chuck's hand.

"What is it, dear?" Ellie glanced at her husband.

"Nothing. Excuse me." He spoke to the departing guests. "We're pleased you came tonight. Merry Christmas." Joe took Chuck by the arm and dragged him toward the study.

Even here, drink glasses and plates littered tables and the bookshelves. Chuck would see to it they got picked up, but thank God, he only had to do this kind of work for a while longer. Soon now, very soon, his plan would reach its climax. He held the envelope out to Joe.

"Who gave this to you?"

"Sorry, sir. I don't know."

"Well, what did he say?"

"Not much. I served drinks. A man took a glass, and laid this envelope on the tray. Winked at me and said, *Make sure Joe gets this before the party's over.*"

"What did he look like?"

"I'm sorry, I didn't pay attention. I figured a Christmas card. Isn't it?" When had he had more fun? Excitement charged through his system, making it difficult to stand still. To be talking with the man this way.

Finally, Joe took the envelope and ripped open the envelope, yanked out the paper and quickly read the words.

Chuck bit his cheek to keep from smiling. This evening was about to provide a few thrills.

One hand went to his chest. Joe staggered back, leaned against the desk. "Oh, my God. This can't be."

Bourland's face turned red, his breath came in short pants. One hand rubbed his chest.

"Is something wrong, sir?" Was the old man having a heart attack? Not what Chuck wanted. At least not yet. "Should I find Mrs. Bourland?"

"What?" Joe looked up, as if shocked to find he wasn't alone. "No. No. Do not go for my wife. Thank you. I'm sure you have duties. Go." He staggered around his desk and slouched into his chair.

"You're sure there's nothing I can do?"

"Get out. Didn't you hear me? Get out." His voice rose and cracked.

"Of course, sir." Chuck sauntered from the study. Ellie stood in the hall sending her guests on their way. What a successful evening. He'd walked around the house in every room on the ground floor, taken a few pictures. Afraid of someone catching him, he hadn't attempted the upstairs area. Someday, he'd not worry about where he roamed in this house.

Chuck went back to the kitchen, and continued drying the company's trays. Take about an hour to pack everything away. He'd stay as long as he didn't detect any danger. Joe would probably hide out in his office until everyone was gone. He seemed to be under something of a strain. Chuck didn't stop the smile at what he'd accomplished.

* * * *

10:30 p.m. Tuesday, December 22

Scott studied Meg's face with its high cheekbones. Late at night after a long day, and she was still gorgeous. She'd stolen from behind the chair and perched on the edge. Like she'd fly away if the least movement startled her. The sound of his fingers rubbing his pant leg reverberated in the room. Did she hear? He resisted reaching out to her. Clearly, he'd lost his mind.

After one glimpse of her in the red outfit, Scott had deliberately avoided running into her during the party. Oh, he'd looked his fill from a distance. The dress showed up her curves and displayed her breasts. He wanted to touch, caress, sooth, tickle, arouse.

Still, he sat quietly, because his desires were a fantasy. She didn't need anything from him. She deserved a strong man. A man to match her in strength and power. He wasn't that man anymore. The idea of her being with someone else made his gut twist. On the other hand, he wanted her to be happy. No way to stop wanting this woman, but he couldn't have her.

"Are you enjoying the party? Mom always plans for more people than those who RSVP, and she's always right. More come than say they'll be here. The opposite of most gatherings."

"Rules of some sort, huh? Someone studies this?" He'd talk about anything she wanted as long as she wore the silk, which caressed her breasts as she breathed and spoke.

"Caterers tell you to plan for a quarter of the people you invite to show up. For this party, half the invited guests always attend. My parents have lived here all their lives, and with Dad in politics for twenty years…throw in work and social contacts and you've got a large number. In the past, she's sent out five hundred invitations. I can't imagine this year is any different.

"I'd estimate you had between two-hundred fifty to three hundred people in and out all evening. Your percentages work out." He continued the odd topic of conversation.

"Were you counting?"

She smiled, and he swore if he hadn't been sitting, his legs would've buckled. "Got an eye for numbers. Did you notice anyone or anything unusual?" His voice had a strangled sound, and he swallowed a couple of times. He leaned forward, but couldn't reach the beer bottle.

"Let me." She stood, took a couple of steps, smothering a groan as she moved. Leaning over she stretched her arm for the brew.

His gaze riveted on the curve of her breast. He hardened. His fingers curved around the bottle when she extended her hand, and he took a hasty swig. Pulling his mind together, he remembered her expression of pain. "What's the matter? Are you hurt?" He reached for her hand, tugged gently, and she settled down beside him. Her scent, a mix of vanilla and something he didn't recognize, washed around him. Reluctantly, he released his hold.

"I'm ashamed to confess, it's vanity, pure and simple. Julie insisted with this dress I had to wear these shoes." She held them in the air by a slim strap. "I seldom wear heels, and never this high." Then she dropped them on the floor like she never wanted to put them on again and swung her feet up on the small table in front of them. "Oh, better. What a relief to pull them off when I came in here."

She wiggled her red tipped toes, and he grew harder. Never getting this woman into a bed might kill him. He gulped in air. For now, he needed to concentrate on something else. When she finally seemed relaxed, Scott hated to raise the issue with her, but blackmail would do the trick. During the evening when Scott had caught sight of her, she had a shoulder hiked up or fingers rubbed her neck, sure signs of stress. Before he spoke, she did.

"You asked if I'd seen anyone unusual. I recognized almost everyone here except for a half a dozen newcomers. But one man was kind of odd—"

"What'd he look like?" His mind split in two pieces. Half considered what she said. With the other, he imagined his life with her if he hadn't been injured.

"He wasn't a guest." She flipped long dark strands over one shoulder.

"No?" What this woman did to a man. His fingers twitched with the need to run through the black mane and over her whole body.

"Meg. Meg, are you back here?"

Ellie's voice held a sharpness he hadn't heard before.

"I'm worried about your father."

Meg hopped up. He rose more slowly. The bulge in his pants forced him behind a chair. Her gaze locked with his. Fear sparked then disappeared before she shifted her attention back to her mother.

"What's the matter with Dad?"

"He went into the study earlier, but I can't open the door, and he won't answer me." Meg's mother's hands twisted together.

"He's probably fallen asleep, because this is past his bedtime." Meg teased trying to lower the tension.

She slid her feet into the sexy slings and rushed through the door as if she had on tennis shoes. He put his arm around Ellie's shoulders, and they followed behind. "Tell me what happened?"

"One of the catering staff wanted to check the room. He'd

heard guests had left plates and glass in there, but he couldn't open the door. I couldn't either." Ellie's hand gripped his arm. "He's okay, isn't he?"

She looked at him for reassurance, and Scott did what he always did in a situation like this. He spoke as hopefully as possible. "I'm sure it's nothing, but we'll handle whatever it is."

The sounds of pounding caught his attention as they approached the front hall. Meg beat her palms on the door of her father's study, each blow harder than the last.

"Dad. Dad, open the door." She glanced over her shoulder at Scott. Her brows shifted together in concern while she chewed her lower lip.

"What's the matter with him, Meg? Why doesn't he answer?" Ellie's face had gotten paler by the moment.

"Whoa there. Hold on, Ellie." Fortunately, Scott had kept an arm around her, and the moment her legs gave-out he added his extra support.

He half-carried her to a bench in the entryway. Fire burned in his side, and shot from the wound in his leg, but he wouldn't let the pain defeat him. "Put you head down a moment."

"Call David and get him down here, please." Meg knelt by her mother.

Scott used his cell, but kept one ear cocked to catch Meg's words.

"I'm sure Dad's fine. You'll see he's fallen asleep." She met Scott's gaze, hope reflected in her eyes.

"Want to try busting in the door with me or wait for David?" Scott asked. "I'm still not strong, but can we wait?" The admission of his weakness to this woman he admired, made him more determined than ever to reclaim as much of his pre-shooting strength as he could. Regardless of what the doctors and the therapists predicted.

"I hate to be the cause of us hurting you more, but I'm afraid to wait." She gulped in a shaky breath. "If you're sure, let's try." They backed up, but before they moved forward, clumping noises jerked them both around.

"What's going on?" David had un-tucked his shirt and taken off his tie.

"Oh, David. I'm glad you're here," Ellie's fingers were white where she grasped the seat cushion.

"Door's locked. Dad won't answer." Meg spit the words from her mouth.

David nodded. "Okay, give me space." David stepped back then slammed his shoulder into the door. The second time, the splintering sound exploded in the quiet house.

He raced into the room. "Crap."

Joe Bourland sat slumped over his desk.

CHAPTER SEVEN

11:15 p.m. Tuesday, December 22

"Joe." Ellie's voice cracked on his name, kicking Meg in the gut.

David placed two fingers on his father's neck. "He's breathing."

"Thank you, God." Meg whispered the low prayer. She wanted to rush to his side, but she stayed by her mother, supporting her.

"Didn't you say he doesn't drink much?" Scott held up a half-empty bottle of whiskey and waved a hand at the alcohol fumes.

"Oh, my goodness." Her mother sagged against Meg.

The alcohol smell swirled toward the doorway. "I've never known of him getting drunk, have you, Mom?" she asked.

"Once when we were young and the business was struggling. Never since."

"This is beyond weird." Meg's stomach clenched. Before they did more investigating, she needed to steer her mother upstairs.

"So, Mom, we've solved the mystery." Meg squeezed her mother's hand. "Too much liquor and the late hours put Dad out. We'll settle him down here on the couch. You go on up to bed now."

"He'll have a terrible hangover tomorrow," David said.

"You can give him heck then." Meg patted her mother's shoulder and forced a smile.

"If you say so. Are you sure he'll be all right down here?"

"Absolutely, Mom. Scott or I can stay with him, if you'll be more comfortable." David added his persuasive words.

"Thank you, son, I'll go on up. Good night, Scott. Good night, dear." She kissed Meg on the cheek and proceeded toward the stairs, shaking her head as if she couldn't make sense of her husband's behavior.

Silence prevailed. Meg stared at her brother and Scott. "What's going on?" She spread her open hands in front.

"Could someone have drugged him?" David shifted his father into an upright position against the chair, and he let out a loud snore.

"Possibly." Scott nodded his head.

Meg picked up the papers her father had lain on top of and glanced at them. "Oh, my God. Guys, look. It's the letters we've been searching for. Plus a new one."

"Read." David clenched teeth making the muscle bulge and release, bulge and release.

Meg glanced at Scott and her brother then looked back at the papers and quickly put them in date order. She tried to read, but her voice shook, and she couldn't put the words together. She was a cop. A damn good cop. She'd deal. She stiffened her spine, drew in the deepest breath possible, and tried again:

October 27
Dear Mayor Bourland,

I have information you should be willing to pay me a substantial amount for. Does the name Peggy Coffey mean anything to you? It's been over forty years ago, but I bet if you try hard you'll remember the pretty brunette.

Unless you want me to bring her name to your wife's attention, send $5,000 to PO Box 1340, Fort Worth, TX 76107, by next Monday.

Your friend,
Chuck

"Damn. It's the first letter." David ran a hand through his hair, leaving it sticking on end. "Though Dad told us, hearing the words increases the starkness of the reality."

"What else do you have, Meg?" Scott asked.

"Here. You read." She handed him the paper.

Scott's low voice rumbled out the message.

November 24
Dear Mayor Bourland,

Thanks for the dollars, but I've realized I will need more if you don't want me to share this story with the newspaper.

Send another $5,000 to PO Box 1340, Fort Worth, TX 76107, by next Monday or your family will be reading about your affairs with their morning coffee.

Your friend,

Chuck

She handed a letter to David. "This is the one we found the other day."

> *December 18*
> *Dear Mayor Bourland,*
>
> *David is a handsome man, and Meg is a beautiful woman. You must be very proud of them.*
>
> *My mother was proud of me. Before she died she left me papers she collected over the years about the great Joseph Bourland, current mayor of Fort Worth.*
>
> *Did I tell you Peggy had a son?*
>
> *If you don't want me to share this information with the city council, send $5000 to PO Box 1340, Fort Worth, TX 76116, by next Monday.*
>
> *Your friend,*
> *Chuck*

Meg flipped the next page once, the crinkle loud in the silent room, then she began.

> *December 22*
> *Dear Joe,*
>
> *We know each other well enough now to be on a first name basis. Thanks for the money. You've got big*

doings going on in your home this evening. Nice party.

I forgot to tell you what name Peggy's son goes by. It's Coffey. But not what his name should be. Can you guess what his last name should be, Joe?

If you don't want me to share what his last name should be with your family, send $10,000 to PO Box 1340, Fort Worth, TX 76107, by next Monday.

Merry Christmas.
Your friend,
Chuck

There's a handwritten line:
P.S. Meg is a real babe in the red dress.

A shiver shook Meg from her head to her toes. "Oh, my God. This…this sounds like he was in the house tonight." She had trouble catching a breath. "He's been in our home." Her voice rose in pitch. Fear for her family exploded quickly into rage and shot fire through her veins. She glanced toward the entryway. *Could he still be here?* Ice followed the fire, and she shivered again.

"Here, take this." Scott slid out of his jacket and helped her slide her arms into the sleeves. For a brief moment, he held her close. His warmth comforted and strengthened her as she sank against him. She hated to admit the sense of loss when he let go.

"You stay here with Joe in case he wakes up. David and I will make a quick tour and make sure everything is clear and locked up."

"But—"

"Meg." Her brother's face looked haggard with lines she'd never noticed before. "You'd do me a big favor if you'd stay here when we leave. I wish the door lock worked."

"I can—"

His hands came up in front as if to stop her from protesting more, and Meg saw the slight tremble before he dropped them.

"I know how capable you are, Meg, but I'm not sure about Dad right now. What if he wakes up and wanders out into the house? What if the guy is still here?"

"Shove one of these large chairs against the door, Meg to give you warning if someone tries to force his way inside," Scott said.

"Please, Meg." Her brother's voice held a hint of desperation.

"Okay, okay. I hear you. Before you leave, let's settle Dad on the couch. He can sleep off his drunk here."

"Yeah, it'd be a tough job getting him upstairs in his present condition." David slid one arm under one of his father's. "Can you manage, Scott?"

"Yeah, give me a minute."

Meg picked up the throw from the back of the sofa, and after the men lowered her father on to the leather cushions, she draped it over him. Her hand brushed at his hair. "I wonder how he'll explain this to Mom."

"Let's move, David. We need to make certain the house is secure."

"We can talk about what to do next when you guys return.

Maybe Dad will be awake by then. Hurry now, but be careful." After they left, she dragged the heavy leather chair up against the splintered door as Scott asked. She glanced at her father, but he didn't budge. She paced the room, her hands tapping her thighs. How were they doing in the rest of the house?

Hard to believe the blackmailer had been brazen enough to enter their home. On the one hand, she was grateful no one had been hurt. On the other, maintaining some kind of control if she got her hands on the guy would be damn difficult.

She stopped in front of the paneled bookcase. She gave herself a mental head slap, because her brain had ceased to function. Her father used to keep a gun in here. When they searched the study before, neither she nor David had remembered the hidden space with its disguised key hole. Now if he kept the key in his old tobacco pouch the way he used to. She opened the center drawer of the desk and slid her hand to the back.

She pulled out the pouch, the pungent odor hitting her. Her finger swept through the tobacco. *Yes, here it is.* Great. She glanced at her father before walking back to the shelves. After a little finagling, the lock clicked, and she opened the door. A wooden cigar box sat on a high shelf. Inside lay her father's .38 Smith and Wesson. Loaded. She heaved a sigh of relief. Wished she'd remembered this earlier to give to David and Scott, but at least she had the gun now, and she'd take care of whoever came through the door.

After making her way back to her father's desk, Meg slumped into his chair. The notes practically jumped off the desk at her. Each one a live grenade threatening her family.

She slid the one with today's date around with the eraser end of a pencil. She looked at the words again. Had she missed anything? Damn. Scott got that right. The person did seem focused on her and her brother. He mentioned both of them in all the letters. She dropped her head onto her left arm, but clutched the gun tightly in her right hand. "Oh, Daddy. Daddy, what did you do?" A tear dropped on the blotter. Her heart ached. They had to resolve this mess. But how?

* * * *

12:30 a.m. Wednesday, December 23

Meg jumped at the knock on the door. When she recognized her brother's voice, she loosened her grip on the butt of the gun, and slid it into the pocket of Scott's jacket. "I'm coming." She shoved the chair aside enough for them to squeeze in. "Everything okay?"

"Yeah. The last of the catering staff had just left when we reached the kitchen. David glanced at his father. "He hasn't moved?"

"A couple of snores is all."

Her brother's normally smooth forehead furrowed into wrinkles. "I don't want to be around when he tries to explain this." David gave a short laugh and glanced at Scott who shook his head.

"He'll be out the rest of the night. Go on to bed. I can sit up with him." Scott volunteered.

"We need to talk through the issues first. We can check on Dad after a while." She glanced at Scott and her brother. "Coffee first." She led the way, and the two men followed. "Oh, I remembered where Dad hides his gun." She patted Scott's jacket pocket.

"He still has one? Good." David strode toward the kitchen.

When they arrived, Meg rolled up the jacket sleeves to keep from getting them wet while she filled the carafe before she flipped the button for a fresh pot. While it perked, she found clean cups. She'd expected to wash some, but the caterers did a good job putting the kitchen back in order.

Meg filled their cups then then picked up hers. "I need the fire in the den for this."

"I'll check on Dad then join you." David made a bee-line in the other direction.

Meg headed out with Scott following close behind, his cane tap-tapping on the wood floors. She sank into the big chair she'd hidden behind earlier, kicked off the fricking high heels, and rubbed her aching feet. "I'll be damned if I ever wear those again." She glanced at Scott and away. "I appreciate your help."

"No sweat. Whatever you need."

David joined them and Meg went right to the point. "Okay. Where are we, and where do we go from here?"

"Number one, your father is being blackmailed. Number two, he's made at least two maybe three payments already." Scott ticked off the points on his fingers.

"Number three." David took over the count. "Dad's trying to keep Mom in the dark about   whatever this is, and he's willing to do anything to keep her unaffected." David set his cup on the small table to the right of the sofa.

Meg withdrew the three letters from Scott's jacket pocket.

"Number four. It's safe to assume Dad will want to pay the latest demand."

"Which may be our best opportunity to catch the bastard." Scott's cup banged on the table.

He'd been David's partner for eleven years. Still the vehement tone of Scott's voice both startled her and displayed his caring for them—a warm blanket thrown around her shoulders like his jacket.

Scott went on. "I can keep up the surveillance at the P.O. drop after Joe sends in the next payment."

"This guy seems to have a special interest in me, unless he mentioned the dress to establish his presence inside our house?" Meg ground her teeth at the idea he'd been here. "If he is, maybe I can draw him out."

"No."

"Hell, no," Scott echoed David's words.

She dropped her head in her hand. Would they never realize she could take care of herself?

"What I meant to say, Meg, is let's try Scott's way at the post office first."

Her brother seemed to catch on to his error faster than Scott. "If we miss him there, yeah, then we need to consider your idea, Meg."

Scott shot up from the sofa. "What's the matter with you? You're talking about using her as bait?"

Her brother waved his arms in front of Scott, trying to back him off. Meg fought a chuckle at David's actions. Wouldn't do to appear amused.

"That's a stupid idea." Scott stormed around the back of the sofa as fast as his cane clicking on the wood floor allowed. "I refuse to let you, Meg."

Anger threw Meg out of the chair. She marched up to him and stood toe to toe. "What do you mean you refuse?" Her fists planted at her waist. "You have no say in the matter."

Scott's nostrils flared. His hand balled into a fist, and from his breathing, you'd guess he'd been running. Meg knew he'd never hit her, or she would've stepped back. Not that she moved away from a fight. She'd learned early on, the only way to earn the respect of the men in the department was to show no fear and to stand her ground. Both literally and figuratively.

"Knock it off," David said. "We've got enough problems without you two going at each other."

* * * *

Scott paused and drew in a deep breath before he made a complete fool of himself. David's words had broken through Scott's haze of desire for and worry about the black haired beauty. Yeah, guess kissing Meg the way he wanted with her brother standing right here wasn't the best of ideas. As if she'd welcome his advances anyway. Right. With great strength of will, he forced his feet to step back, relaxed his fist, turned, and tapped his way around to the front of the couch.

"David's right, we need to stay focused. Where were we?" Scott rubbed the back of his neck. He'd been—about to kiss Meg until he drove her out of her mind with need for him. *Not happening, bud.* He had to be losing his grip on reality. She might've given him a second glance before the shooting, but now? A capable woman, Meg didn't need to saddle herself with someone who wasn't equally so. She deserved a man able to keep up with her.

"We're trying to catch our blackmailer." Meg walked around to her chair, stuck her feet in the sexy shoes and sat with one knee over the other, swinging her foot.

Probably shouldn't kiss her, but he'd love—no, not love, lust. He lusted after her. He wrenched his attention away from her and focused on their problem, picked up one of the letters, studying every word. No one spoke for a moment.

"What if, instead of sending the money in his response, Joe asks for a meeting?"

"Go on." David leaned across the back of the chair.

"We all agree the guy seems fixated on the family. He mentions one or both of you in most of the letters. In the December 18th letter he talked about David being handsome and Meg being a beautiful woman and how proud your father must be of you." Scott picked up another. "And then in tonight's letter it's family."

"Why does Dad care about what this guy's last name is? Why would it matter to us? What secret is important enough to Dad to make him pay the blackmailer?" David asked.

Scott studied David and Meg. They weren't going to like what he had to say. But his theory made sense. He heard the wheels whirring as they tried to come up with a plausible explanation.

"What if he's claiming to belong to this family? What if he's claiming to be your father's son?"

The pain in both the sibling's eyes made Scott regret bringing up the idea, but to solve a problem you had to look it square in the face. Meg's normally blue-green bordered on navy. David's lips disappeared, and he had noticeable difficulty swallowing. Then they both spoke at once.

"Man, are you crazy?" David's face grew red.

"No. No." Meg jumped to her feet.

"Can we agree to the blackmailer it's true?"

The brother and sister looked at each other then faced him. After a moment, they nodded. "Now, I'm not saying for certain he is, because right now we don't know, but it's a possibility. You're probably not comfortable thinking about—much less talking about it—with your parents. For now, we're still in agreement to keep Ellie out of this, right?"

"Yeah. As long as we can." David's words crept through tight lips.

"It's what Dad wants," Meg added. "Of course, he's not thinking clearly right now."

"Want me to do my deal, David?"

"Yeah." David nodded, heaved a gust of air, and dropped into the chair. He slanted a glance in Meg's direction. "Scott considers the worst case scenario and then eases off. He says his strategy frees you to imagine the worst and then to realize you'd survive."

"What is it for our situation?" Meg eyes had returned to their normal turquoise.

"Your Dad stops paying, and the blackmailer goes public with his information. He's able to prove he's your father's son."

The indrawn breaths of Meg and David told Scott how this hurt them to hear.

"The papers carry the story. Joe is forced from his position as mayor, because the *holier than thou* folks make his early indiscretion an issue. Your mother is embarrassed."

"He'd hate that," Meg murmured.

Relentless in his determination to make them look at how bad this could become if they pursued the blackmailer, Scott said, "Your mother leaves Joe."

"Damn, man. It might kill Dad." David rubbed both hands down his face.

"You got anything more in your crystal ball?" Meg seemed stunned, but determined to look the worst-case scenario in the face.

"Afraid so." Scott tightened his hands on his cane. The rest of what he'd considered was worse, but they needed to hear him out. "After ruining his reputation, this guy kills your father, mother, and one or all of you. And for good measure, maybe me or Kathy's family. Say he kills all of us. And he goes free."

"No," Meg shouted the word as she bolted from the chair. She took two turns around the room then stopped in front of Scott. "I'll kill him myself before I let that happen."

* * * *

10:00 a.m. Wednesday, December 23

Dreams troubled Meg's rest. She'd alternated between erotic

activities with Scott, which left her wet, wanting, and wretched, to ones about the blackmail. In one, she became her father, and the bearded guy chased her and hollered, "Dad. Dad. Don't leave me." Waking from the dream drenched in sweat, she lay staring at the ceiling for what seemed hours before she must've fallen asleep again. She'd slept way past her normal get up time and was late going downstairs.

Her mother sat alone in the dining room with the paper and coffee in front of her.

"Morning, Mom." Meg kissed her on the cheek.

"Thanks for all the help last night, dear. I'll keep a closer eye on what your father drinks next year. I can't believe he passed out." She shook her head a slight smile playing around her mouth. "Can I get you anything?" Her mother got up.

"No, no." Meg placed a hand on her mother's shoulder to settle her down. "I can help myself from the sideboard here." She poured from the pot. The steam spiraled up and warmed her face. "Still hot. Since I've been such a sleepy head, wasn't sure what I'd find."

"Maria refilled it just before you walked in." Her mom took one of the newspaper sections and handed it to Meg.

Scary. The quiet in the house. Meg had mentally been prepared to face chaos with the kids running around crazy like they did when they were short of sleep. The lack of sounds but for the occasional rustle of a page turning and a cup clinking against the saucer unnerved her. Where had everyone gone? Damn, she should be comfortable asking directly about Scott. Then why were her hands sweaty?

"Where is everyone? I expected to see the whole crew down here and moving slowly after last night."

"Kathy and the kids were up at the crack of dawn. She and Ron took them to the mall to see Santa and ride the train."

"Sounds like fun." If memory served, they'd be in something like a zoo, but fortunately for her the kids were not here. Meg loved her niece and nephew, but they were quite a handful. Frankly, her emotional reserves had dropped too low to deal with them.

"And the guys?" Way to wimp out.

"Scott had a therapy session early this morning then planned to hit the gym. Your brother went Christmas shopping but he planned to join Scott there afterwards. You hungry, Meg? Let me at least give you a piece of toast."

"No thanks. I'll find something later."

Her mother rose and refilled her cup. "If you're sure you don't need anything, then I'll read my paper and visit with you." She returned to her seat. "Maria's making sure everything got put back in its original place and taking care of those dishes left in Dad's study. I still haven't recovered from the shock of Joe's behavior and what David did to the door."

"We had to get to him, Mom."

She chuckled. "Of course you did, dear. I wasn't scolding, but now the carpenter has to come. Joe found someone who will start this afternoon. I'm sure he considered quick action important given the little ones in the house."

"Yeah." Meg swallowed a sip of coffee. "Uh...where's Dad now?"

"Since he couldn't work in the house without being disturbed, he's gone into the office, feeling considerable pain, I might add."

A smile played around her mother's mouth, and her eyes twinkled. Almost like she thought her father was getting what he deserved for scaring them all the way he did.

"That man. I keep telling him it's the holidays. He says the staff isn't let off until Christmas Eve."

"You reminded him he's not staff like I've heard you do?"

Her mother laughed. "I guess when you've been married as long as we have you learn how the other person thinks."

"Yeah, I guess so." Since she couldn't talk with David, Scott, or her father, Meg needed out of the house, or she'd go crazy worrying about everything she couldn't fix. "Mom, I'm going on a run. I can finish my shopping this afternoon. You okay with my plan?"

"Of course, dear, this is your vacation, too. While I love having all of you home I don't expect you to hang out with me all the time."

Meg leaned over and kissed her mother. "Thanks. One of the reasons we come as often as we can is you don't cling." She started for the door.

"Meg, have you made an appointment with the psychologist here?"

"Yes. I'm seeing her early tomorrow."

"Christmas Eve morning? My goodness."

"She's a friend of my Atlanta psychologist. It's the only spot she had open. Then I'll see her once next week."

"I'm glad. If you ever need to talk to a non-professional, I'll listen. I promise not to offer advice. I really can keep my mouth shut."

Her smile, tinged with sadness, yanked at Meg's heart. "Well, Mom. Yeah, maybe." Meg paced around the table. Should she talk to her mother about this?

"What is it, dear?" She laid her folded paper on a placemat.

"It's about Scott."

"He's such a nice man. If he hadn't saved your brother's life, I'd still want him in our family."

"Well…how about not marching out potential girlfriend candidates for him, like you did last night?"

"Why? Did he find someone on his own? I hadn't heard."

"Mom." She sounded like a thirteen-year-old version of herself.

"What, dear? I'm sorry if I'm being dense, but I fail to see why you'd care if I help Scott find—Oh." Her mother's eyebrows shot up, she stood, and took hold of Meg's arm to stop her pacing.

She couldn't meet her mother's gaze, but then she put her finger under Meg's chin and tipped it up. Warmth rushed across her face, and she nibbled on her lower lip.

"Oh, my dear. *You're* interested in Scott."

"Well, I—"

"Wonderful, Meg. I'm happy for you. Of course, I'll stop match making. Am I the only one who knows about the relationship?"

"It's not exactly a relationship, or at least at this point it's all one-sided, but I'd like a chance to see if our being thrown together doesn't lead to something."

"I'll keep my fingers crossed for you." She leaned in and kissed Meg's cheek. "If I were a betting woman, I'd put my money on you."

* * * *

Meg ran down the sidewalk about mid-morning, enjoying the neighborhood. The giant, live oaks with their leaves still on them. The red oaks with their bare branches reaching to the sky. The friendly neighbors who waved when she passed. The cold didn't stop people from pushing strollers, or walking dogs. The distinctive scent from the fireplaces tickled her nose. For the most part the cars kept to the speed limit or under.

At one time, she knew every family on the street and the surrounding ones. Julie grew up in a house a block away—the same one she now shared with her husband and child. A super location. If Meg had kids, she'd like to raise them in a place like this. In fact, she'd want to raise them in Fort Worth.

However, at forty and with no one to share the responsibility with, she wasn't likely to give her parents more grandchildren. A laugh burst out on puffs of vapor when Ronny flashed in her mind. Ronny, the small tank who ran full out at everything he tried to do. Good luck to anyone who got in his way. Maybe her lack of progeny was a good thing. How could they manage with two little ones like Ronny around? Kathy wished they lived in Fort Worth to be closer to the folks, but with Ron's company based in Oklahoma City, they wouldn't be moving.

Jogging in place, Meg paused at a street corner to let a car pass. Despite all the activity, a chill ran down her arms and legs. She should've put on long pants along with the shorts for the run. Then she stopped all together for a moment. She must be losing her mind. Her heart rocketed to her throat. The driver reminded her of the man at the pizza restaurant. She jogged in place while the car continued down the street. Coincidence? Over active imagination? Had seeing Hank killed made her lose her nerve, made her jump at nothing, made her a poor cop?

A shiver spread across her shoulders having nothing to do with the temperature. Overreacting. Yeah, must be it. Getting her feet moving in place again, she stayed on the corner until the car drove out of sight. The driver had watched her in his rearview mirror. One man or more? The pizza man had a full beard. The server last night had a mustache, but not a beard. The driver had the same bushy eyebrows, mustache, and the same long hair, but no beard. Weird.

She'd intended to talk with David and Scott about the server last night, but then they'd found Dad in the study, and the new note. She'd forgotten how odd the behavior of the server was until right this minute. Her brother and Scott had to know. She glanced at her watch. They should be at the gym by now. Shifting directions, she altered course toward the club to catch them before they left.

Fifteen minutes later, Meg ran up to the entrance. She keyed in the family's code and plowed through the door. Lunchtime and the gym had only two other people working out besides the ones she looked for. An occasional "huh" when a younger man heaved bar bells over his head, disrupted the quiet. Her brother used one of the upper body weight machines, and Scott walked on a treadmill.

"Hey. You nearly finished?" she asked.

"What've you been doing, Meg. Sweat is dripping off you."

"Look who's talking?" She grabbed a towel from the floor at David's feet and flicked it at his rear. He yanked it from her and popped her back.

"Hey, boys and girls, I don't want to get kicked out. I need this workout."

Scott's voice held a note of teasing, and his eyes twinkled.

She and David laughed. Concerns about their father forgotten for the moment. But the fun times didn't last. "Listen. We've got to talk."

"I've got this one last repetition to finish," her brother said.

Scott slowed the walker, but didn't step off until it came to a complete stop. "Been running far?" He wiped her eyes with the edge of his shirt.

Her breath hitched at the brief sight of an ugly red scar on his abs. No wonder a moan sometimes escaped his gritted teeth. "In the neighborhood, but at a pretty good clip. I remembered something I'd meant to talk with you about last night, but all the business with Dad made me forget."

"Understandable. Can we sit down?"

"Sure."

Scott grabbed his cane then limped over to one of the benches and dropped down.

"Rough therapy session?" she sat next to him.

"Yeah." He grimaced. "I can't wait to get in the steam room and whirl pool."

"Did you see Mom before you left this morning?" David settled on the floor in front of them rubbing his towel over his head and neck.

"She seemed amused about Dad drinking too much last night and plans to keep an eye on him in the future. She figures the charge for the new door will also be an effective deterrent."

"What'cha got, Meg?"

Scott's smile warmed her insides. He should use it more. "Okay." *Breathe, woman. Focus on the problem, not your brother's sexy former partner.* "Well, I wondered—"

"Spit out whatever is on your mind, sis, if it's important. I've got more to do here." His impatience spiked his tone of voice, probably a result of stress.

"Sorry. I lost focus for a moment." She raised one knee and wrapped her arms around it to balance. "One of the servers last night kept appearing with an odd frequency. He must've been paying close attention to me or he intended to get me drunk, because whenever I got close to finishing a glass of wine, he'd show up with another."

* * * *

"Describe him?" Scott shifted toward her brushing his bare knee against her equally bare thigh, and heat built in his groin. He should move away, but no. Sweet torture.

"Probably as tall as Dad and David, dressed like all the other servers, but with a bushy mustache and eyebrows. He had longish brown hair he wore in a ponytail. He's not as broadly built as you, David."

"Thinner, like Dad?"

She nodded.

"Interesting. I remember the guy." Her brother's forehead crinkled.

"Did you talk with him?" Scott asked.

"A few words. Toward the end of the evening, I'd scavenged goodies from the kitchen and headed toward my room. He blocked my path through the doorway. Kind of strange. When I got to the top of the stairs, I looked down. He'd come into the hallway and stared up at me. Odd, you know."

"What made you think of him while you were running, Meg?" Scott fought the urge to drop a hand on her leg. He had to be satisfied with the slight brushing of her skin against his. What a jerk.

"I saw him again—or at least I think I did. I stopped at a corner to let a car go by. I'd swear the driver was the same man. Mustache, longish hair. He drove slower through the intersection than necessary and focused on me the whole way in the in the rearview mirror. He reminded me of a man I noticed at the pizza joint where I ate with the girls. He had a beard but the same bushy eyebrows and long hair."

"Did you notice what kind of car?"

"Of course I did, brother of mine. What do you take me for…a ditz? The vehicle was an older, maroon-colored sedan. The tags were so mud spattered, I couldn't read the number."

"Possibly our suspect." Scott worried more than he liked to let on about the dude who kept turning up around Meg. "Or suspects, plural, if it's more than one guy." Maybe one of them tailed her the other evening.

"The beard, no beard description is confusing. How many are we dealing with? Their build is similar, like Dad's," Meg said.

"Yeah, I've been wondering, too. Man, I'm being stupid, but I just don't want to imagine our parents doing it, and certainly not with other people. If one of the guys is Dad's son, when do you think…?"

"When did it happen? Hard to tell, but I'd say he's around your age, give or take a year either way. One of the letters mentioned 44 years ago. That'd be about right." Meg reached across for her brother's hand. "David, this doesn't affect you or me. Let's tell Dad what we're speculating. Lay it right out there in the open."

"She's nailed it, David. You only give power to a blackmailer if you keep the story secret. If you say, so what? He loses his influence over you." Meg's maturity in dealing with all this impressed Scott. Their gazes locked. Could she read his mind?

He turned back to David. "What's the back-up plan in case Joe doesn't agree with you about going public?" Scott hated to push them, but they had to face the possibilities.

Silence dragged on, punctuated by the grunts from the young weightlifter. Scott waited for Meg or David to offer an idea.

Meg's put her foot on the floor and straightened her back. "First we have to find out who the guy is before we can convince him to stop harassing the family." Meg leaned toward Scott. "You have an idea how we can do that?"

He loved the directness of her eyes. She gave you her full attention, good or bad. With effort, he focused his mind back to their problem and not the depth of her gorgeous aquamarines. "Let's check with the catering service. I bet they don't have too many long haired guys with mustaches working for them," he suggested.

"None of us has any authority here," David reminded them. "What if they give us his name and address—and I'm pretty certain they won't—what do we do? Knock on his door and say, 'Hey, buddy, we suspect you're blackmailing our father, and we demand you stop.'" He snorted. "Probably won't fly."

Meg's smile hooked up on one corner in a rueful grin. The dimple that occasionally popped out, winking at him. "Okay, David, but if we had a name and where he lived, we could follow him."

"Last night, I suggested we convince your father to call the guy's bluff and set up a meeting. If the man won't agree to meet then Joe makes this last payment, and we catch him picking up marked bills."

"But—" Meg began.

"Your father doesn't want police involvement, because then the whole story comes out. But we can mark the bills and threaten our blackmailer with prison if he doesn't quit."

"Okay." Meg stood up.

"Okay, what?" Her brother looked at her from the floor.

Meg leaned a hand down to him, David took it, and she lugged him off the floor. "Let's clean up. We've got to talk with Dad again. Scott, we need you to be in on the discussion. Maybe he'll listen more to someone who's not his child."

CHAPTER EIGHT

4:00 p.m. Wednesday, December 23

"He's cagey, Joe is." Scott pried off the top of a beer and handed one each to David and Meg.

His fingers tingled where hers brushed his. He had to batten down his reactions to the woman. He took a healthy swallow then continued. "When we try to tie him down, he's got an excuse—work, the grandkids, your mother needs him to do something." He ticked them off the fingers of one hand.

"Now he and Mom have taken the kids to see the latest animated flick." David lifted a Lucite container out of the cupboard and poured cashews in the bowl. He threw a few in his mouth before shoving the dish in their direction. "Have some."

"Let's try the caterers." Meg took a pull from the long neck.

Scott reached for the cashews, but he had a great deal of trouble concentrating, his gaze glued to her lips on the tip of the bottle. He dragged his attention back to the problem at hand. "What do you mean?"

"We wanted to talk with Dad first. If we can't, let's follow up on plan B–check with the caterers. We gotta find this guy." She slammed her bottle on the counter, sloshing her beer. "Sorry. Guess I'm more uptight than I'd like to admit." She grabbed a sponge and cleanser bottle from under the sink and wiped up her mess.

Responsible and conscientious Meg was. Scott admired

everything about her, and all of the many ways to show her flooded his mind. Would David be okay with Scott's interest in Meg? Of course, he wasn't going make any moves on her. Frankly, he didn't know how he'd deal with rejection these days. He wouldn't pursue her, and whether or not David had an issue with them was a moot point.

"We can go now if you want." God, what a glutton for punishment. Scott swallowed the last of his beer.

"Okay. At least we'll be doing something." Meg took a final sip before she put the bottle in the recycling bin. "You coming, David?"

"You two take care of the catering connection. I'll hang here on the off chance of catching Dad."

"Sounds good. If he shows up, call, and we'll head back. Let's go, Scott. I'll drive. I know my way around town in case we pick up my tail again." She grinned.

Scott couldn't argue with the fact she knew the area better but hated she relegated him to shotgun. Well, nothing for it now. He'd enjoy being alone with Meg, without all of the troops gathered under the Bourland roof. She'd been right when she'd predicted the house would be zoo-like when everyone arrived home.

"Do we have a game plan?" Scott asked as Meg maneuvered through one-way streets.

She chewed on her lower lip. Scott coughed to squash down his smoldering desire. She made him nuts.

"How about this? Mother appreciated what a great job all the workers did, but she'd noticed a particular man and wanted to send him special thanks."

"Won't they say deliver the note to the business?"

"Probably, but I bet they'll at least give us his name."

"It's worth a shot."

She capably maneuvered the car in and out of the traffic. Like she did everything. Capably. He used to do everything capably. He sidestepped the thought. Don't go there. She parked in front of the Out of the Box Caterers, located in a nondescript strip shopping center.

Scott held open the door of the business. The brush of Meg's body as she moved past him sent heat straight to his groin. The shooting hadn't affected his sex drive, at least not where she was concerned.

The warm room contrasted sharply with the temperature outside, and he and Meg unbuttoned their coats. A middle-aged woman with platinum blonde hair sat behind a white desk, but she rose when they entered.

"I'm Sarah Dalrymple, the owner. I'm glad to see you. You're a smidge early, but no problem." Her mouth took off like a train trying to make up for lost time. "We'll have more time to work on the wedding buffet. We have quite a variety of offerings from simple backyard BBQ's to full sit-down meals." The woman walked around to the front of the desk and held out her hand.

Meg, with a perplexed expression, automatically extended hers.

A steady stream of words cascaded from the woman's mouth.

"I'm happy you came in. February is pretty fast turn-around for us."
Next, she shook Scott's hand. "You're lucky we had a cancellation.
Why don't we sit over here? I'm sure we'll be able to provide what
you need."

She indicated a small round table with four chairs. The ones
with material draped over the entire chair with a large bow tied
around the back. Scott eyed them. Not comfortable he bet.

The owner continued, "I've got books I can show you with
pictures and menus."

He made a pretense of studying the room to hide a smile when
Meg's face morphed into further confusion. Her mouth fell open, and
her face deepened into a pink tone. She moved only when the woman
literally herded them in the direction she wanted them to go. He
chanced resting his hand on the small of Meg's back. Better than
nothing.

"I'm sorry." Meg shook her head as if she were coming back
from somewhere other than this showroom. "Ms. Dalrymple, did you
say? I'm sorry, but you confused us with another couple. I mean
people." She glanced at Scott and away. "We're not a couple." Her
hand flapped between them. The pink now blossomed into true red
and covered her face and neck.

"Oh, but you must be. You're perfect together." Sarah clapped
her hands and smiled.

* * * *

"Well, uh, we're not." Meg stood straight and shoved her hands
in her coat pockets. Good lord, what must Scott think? She'd

colluded with the owner of the business to put ideas in his head? She should step away from the warmth his hand brought to her lower back, but her feet had a mind of their own. What did his hand mean? Was he the teeniest bit interested? She'd never seen any earlier indication.

"Give it time, dear. I'm sure something will work out."

Meg opened her mouth to deny the speculation, but words failed her. She hoped the woman's suggestion didn't embarrass Scott. Embarrassed enough for both of them, she took a deep breath and decided to muddle through. "Ms. Dalrymple, I'm Ellie Bourland's daughter, Meg."

"Oh, we catered your family's traditional holiday party. I must say, since Mrs. Bourland hired us last year, our business has taken right off. I can't begin to thank her enough." She stopped and studied them both. "You're sure you aren't a couple?"

"No, ma'am."

"No, you're not a couple, or no, you're not sure?

"Let's leave the couple idea alone and focus on the reason we stopped by." Better not to respond to Dalrymple's implication. Because Meg wanted something to be going on between them, didn't make them a couple.

"Well, what can I do for you then?" She sat at the small table and waved them down before glancing at her watch. "I only have a few minutes before my real February couple arrives."

Meg gave in and Scott held the chair for her, evidence of how much his health had improved since he arrived. Of course, this chair wasn't as heavy as the ones at their dining room table, which he'd struggled with his first night at their house. She hoped, for his sake, his actions marked real progress. She sat next to Sarah. He sat on Meg's other side, so close their knees brushed. *Pitiful, Meg, to find such pleasure from a small touch.* She didn't dare make eye contact with him, afraid he'd read her desire.

"Okay, Ms. Dalrymple—"

"Sarah, please, dear."

"Sarah. My mother was happy with how well your staff worked at her party. She wanted to contact one man in particular."

"I hope you had no trouble. We've been busy, for which we're grateful, as I said, given the way the economy is right now, but I've had to hire extra staff. Did you encounter a problem with someone?" The woman's eyebrows drew together with concern.

'No, no. Mother wanted to write a thank you note particularly to him and needed his name and address." Wow, the lie fell from her lips with no effort.

"Well, she can use our address, and I'll make sure he gets her letter. Very kind of her, but I can't give out home addresses for our staff."

Meg raised her eyebrows, giving credit to Scott and David. "Sarah, if you'd give us his name, Mother plans to personalize the note. She'd appreciate the kindness. He had a moustache and wore his hair in a pony-tail."

"Oh, well, of course. Chuck Coffee. He's new."

"Coffee?" Meg's palms dampened. This couldn't be a

coincidence.

"Yes, I hope all the hair wasn't a problem. He told me he wore it long for religious reasons, and the laws these days—Well, you can hardly make employees do anything they don't wish to especially if they say they're doing whatever because of their religion."

"No, Sarah. No problem with his hair. Mother wanted to thank him for helping out with a guest who became ill." The front door blew open with a cold burst of air and a young couple, who looked to be in their early twenties entered. Chuckling and cuddling with their arms wrapped around each other they never looked up.

"I bet this is the couple you were expecting." Scott spoke for the first time. He stood and held Meg's chair. "Let's move."

"Yes, of course. I'm glad you stopped by, and I'll make sure he gets the note when you bring it in."

"Thank you, Sarah." She and Scott both shook hands with the owner.

"Don't forget us if you find you are after all a couple." A smile engulfed her face, matching the life-is-wonderful-tone of her voice. Then the owner welcomed her guests, and Meg and Scott scooted outside.

"I'm sorry. I hope you weren't too embarrassed by her ramblings." Meg welcomed the cold wind to help cool her cheeks, which she suspected had more than a healthy glow.

"Don't give it a thought, Meg. No one would credit for a minute you'd end up with someone like me."

"Clearly, Sarah made that assumption," she muttered under her breath. What reality did he live in? Didn't he realize despite his present condition and walking with a cane, he was twice the man most were?

Scott stopped on the sidewalk and stared at her.

Damn. Had he heard her? Pretending she didn't say anything and ignoring his reaction was her best bet under the circumstances.

* * * *

4:20 p.m. Wednesday, December 23

Chuck jerked open the door to the Out of the Box Caterers. He'd grab his check and tell the boss he wasn't available for the party tonight. He'd never planned to keep working. He just needed the job to allow him into Bourland's house, and he liked the extra dollars. Better to get money without being tied down by continuing to work here, but for now, he'd put up with this.

"Oh, hello, Chuck."

His boss sat at the small front table with a couple. "Why don't you two continue through these books to see if you find a cake you like for the kind of wedding you're planning? I'll be back in a moment." She stood and walked over to him.

"Ms. Dalrymple, I came for my check. And I can't work the party this evening."

"In this job, Chuck, it's important to be responsible. As it turns out, one of my former employees stopped by this morning and wanted occasional work. If Benny hadn't, I'd definitely be miffed with you." She stepped behind her desk, ruffled through some papers then handed an envelope to him. "Oh, if you'd stopped by earlier you'd have run into Meg Bourland from the party last night. Her mother sent her in to find out your name and address."

Chuck reached out, but stopped himself before he grabbed Dalrymple's wrist. "You didn't tell her, did you?"

Her eyebrows drew together. "Only your name, not where you live. Her mother wanted to personalize a note to you to say how much she appreciated your help."

"Yeah? Meg by herself?"

"Oh, my no." A grin spread across the women's entire face, putting lines where none had previously been and lighting up her eyes. She leaned closer to him and whispered. "I thought they were a couple. They denied it, but I saw sparks fly between the two." She glanced at the booking calendar on the top of her desk. "Can I put you on the schedule for later this week? I've got two parties on the day after Christmas. I'll need everyone in."

"Sure." He wanted to leave and find where Meg and the guy with had gone. Damn, it's good he hadn't been earlier. They'd have run into each other, and Chuck only wanted to do that on his terms.

"I'll give you the details later. The Hankings-Holt couple waits for me." She smiled and moved away.

His boss returned to the couple, and Chuck walked out the door. He lit a cigarette, inhaled the nicotine deep into his lungs, enjoying the pop then dropped the match on the ground. He crawled into his old maroon car. The piece of junk got him around. All he needed. For now. Finding Meg became a priority. Because of the party, he had connected everyone to their wheels. Sometimes they drove each other's cars, but he recognized them all now and had jotted down the tag numbers. They could be anywhere, but he'd start at the Bourland house and circle outwards from there.

An hour later, Chuck admitted he was shit-out-of-luck. Where had they gone? He circled around toward the ancestral home, the three story white house with the Christmas trees in the front windows, and parked down the street to watch the goings and comings. They'd turn up here.

* * * *

6:30 p.m. Wednesday, December 23

The warm water sluicing down her body brought comfort, but she couldn't stay in the shower forever. The family gathered downstairs and waited for her. After drying her hair, she dabbed on a minimum of make-up, threw on pants with a matching sweater set, and stepped into low-heeled boots. She glanced in the mirror one last time, shook her head. The strain definitely showed. She didn't look particularly festive. Her niece and nephew would provide be a nice diversion.

Meg hurried down the stairs toward the noise coming from the dining room.

"Hey, sweetie. Thought about sending up scouts for you." Her mother kissed her on the cheek as soon as Meg stepped through the door. "I'm glad you're home."

"Yes, me too. Can I do anything for you?"

"No thanks. Dinner is ready, and there's nothing worse than cold Mexican food." Her mother picked up her knife and tapped on her water glass. "Instruction time, everyone. Kathy and Ron, go first and fix the kids' plates. The rest of us are on urchin duty until their parents can join the little guys then we can follow along." She rubbed her hand through the curly hair on each of their heads before continuing. "Serve yourself from the buffet. Maria made us enchiladas and tacos. Just as you'd requested, Meg."

"Yea. And guacamole, too." David hopped in front of his brother-in-law and stabbed a chip in the green dip.

"Watch it there." Ron tried to knock David's hand away.

"He never changes, does he, Kathy?" Meg laughed at her brother's antics, and everyone joined in.

"Our parents spoiled him. The first born, only son." Kathy's voice sailed over the chuckles.

David, Scott, and Meg's laughter stopped then stuttered on.

"Hey, what's the matter? I was teasing." Kathy poked David in the side. "You've always been such a good sport. You getting prickly in your old age?"

Meg's gut clenched, her breathing stopped, and her gaze sought Scott and David.

Then the kids banged on the table and everyone spoke at once. Thank heavens. She let out the breath she'd been holding. They had to talk with her father, but not this way. Not in front of Mom and Kathy's family, especially the kids.

"What are you all doing tomorrow?" Ellie asked, after everyone had served their plates and taken a place at the table.

"I've got an appointment with a psychologist at ten." Meg took a bite of the baked tortilla stuffed with cheese and onions. "Umm. Yum."

"I've got a therapy session." Scott said.

"Then we're both hitting the gym after." David bit into the enchiladas. "Wow. You called it, Meg." Everyone nodded in agreement.

"No one makes them as good as Maria," Ellie said.

"If the sun stays out, Ron and I are taking the little ones to the Zoo. Probably won't be back until after lunch."

"You'll have to bundle them up plenty, Kathy." Ellie, sitting next to her granddaughter, wiped guacamole from her chin.

"Yeah, we will, but they're tough. The plan is to wear them out so they take a big nap in the afternoon."

"Good, because I only ask of you to be ready to leave for church no later than seven tomorrow evening."

Meg nodded along with everyone else.

"Joe, where did you find a carpenter to come in so quick to fix the door?" her mother asked.

"We use Pete for some repairs downtown. He's not a regular employee of the city, and he had free time. I paid him extra, because of the short notice." His voice held a strained quality like he'd eaten something with too much vinegar.

Her father, under the spotlight of her mother's interest, squirmed in his chair, and fiddled with his water glass, turning it around and around on the place mat. He looked guilty as hell, but Ellie went on as if she saw no problems.

"Well, I'll want his name and number. My friends are always on the hunt for someone good, quick, and who cleans up after himself."

"I'll give you his contact information."

"Thanks. Plans, Joe?" Ellie took a sip of her wine.

"I'm meeting friends at the club for lunch."

"Looks like you've got the house to yourself, Mom, at least in the morning." Meg took a sip from the frosty beer mug with circles her niece Katie had drawn on the glass.

"I know." She smiled and her eyebrows canted upward. "I have an appointment with the den fireplace and my book. It will be delightful."

* * * *

10:05 a.m. Thursday, December 24

Meg rearranged her legs in the chair across from the counselor. How did she answer the question?

"I merely asked how you were doing," Grace Patterson, a tall, slender woman with long brown, straight hair stared at Meg after she'd let too much time pass before responding. Perhaps a few years older than Meg, but her face didn't give much away. The long swirling skirt, tunic and full-sleeved, colorful blouse reminded Meg of a carnival gypsy's attire.

"It wasn't a trick, only a way to begin a conversation." Her smile, big and wide made Meg relax.

"Then the answer is, I'm doing fine, just fine, thank you. How do you know Susan Culver? She didn't explain what connection y'all had when she recommended I come see you after I got home."

"Susan and I were in school together Dallas. She went back to her home in Atlanta. I stayed in Dallas. When I married a Fort Worth man, I set up practice here to avoid commuting. I know folks who make the run every morning and evening. I didn't choose to be one of them."

"No, not my choice either. My condo's in downtown Atlanta. It's small, but handy to work. The traffic in both cities is pretty grim."

"What do you do when you're not working, Meg?"

"I play on a volleyball team, and I like to travel."

"Good. Where have you gone this year?"

"Last February, I went skiing with friends in Copper Mountain, Colorado." Meg thought, but came up with no other trips. "And I came home for the holidays." She twirled the end of her ponytail around a finger. "Busier than usual at work this year."

"What about little weekend get-a-ways with a cute guy in Atlanta?"

"No. None of those." Meg couldn't meet Grace's gaze, because Meg felt the heat of a blush rising in her cheeks. Scott didn't qualify as a weekend get-away, just because she wanted to go away with him. Nor did he live in Georgia.

"What's the status now with your dreams? Remember any yet?"

"God, yes. They're dreadful, scary, erotic, and I wake up drenched in sweat." She'd decided to be honest. They wouldn't let her return to work until she was okay. While she ached to return to the job, if she returned before she was ready, she'd be a liability to the team. She'd do whatever work the counselor required.

"Good." Grace made notes in the folder in her lap.

"Good?" Meg sat forward in the chair.

"Yes, you're beginning to come to terms with what happened."

"They are so not fun. Can you tell me what they mean?"

"You're the best person to figure the symbolism. As soon as you wake up in the morning, jot down everything you can remember in a journal. After several days, look at the notes, and see if you recognize a pattern. Remember what happened on a particular day, and see what, if anything, you can connect to those dreams."

"Sounds easy."

"Well, takes commitment and being able to look objectively at your own life. Susan assured me you were capable of the action. Is she right?"

Meg shifted one crossed leg for the other. "Yes. Yes, I am."

"Good. What are you happiest about in your life right now?

Meg's brain shot off in all directions. Her brother survived. She'd met Scott. Everyone had been able to come home for the holidays.

"If you can't decide on one, you can list several."

"My brother is alive and well."

"Has he been ill?" The psychologist paused in her writing, her pen lifted from the page.

Meg briefly explained what had happened. "If not for Scott

McClaine's quick actions, my brother would be dead."

"Was this a recent occurrence?"

"It happened right before Thanksgiving."

"Goodness, the same time—"

Meg nodded. "When I shot the drug dealer who ambushed my team member. A near miss for me. Rough month for my parents. They got the calls about us days apart." She worked to keep her hands and her crossed leg still. Somewhere she'd heard if you pretended a calmness you didn't feel, it would become real after a time. She wanted to convince Grace she was cool with everything.

In reality, Meg's muscles spasmed with the effort not to eject her body from the chair to pace the confines of the woman's office. Meg needed a good run. Sometime before they went to church in the evening, she'd head out. She'd been missing the daily routine of running to burn off excess energy. She sighed. Nice to figure out what was wrong with her.

Grace appeared to be staring at her. "I'm sorry, did you say something?" Way to make the "fine, just fine" argument solid.

"Has dealing with both of you in dangerous jobs been difficult for your parents?"

"They seemed to have handled their concern all these years. I've been injured once before and so has David. I'm afraid this happening to both of us at the same time was wake-up call and troubled them more than they've let on."

"I don't imagine they appreciated being reminded of how close they came to losing you."

"No, but they've adopted Scott." Meg forced out a chuckle. "He's an additional member of the family now."

"So, a second brother?"

Grace's question unsettled Meg on a couple of levels. She certainly didn't connect to Scott in a brotherly way. What about Chuck who possibly thought of himself as a half-brother?

"Let's say it's been a particularly interesting homecoming."

They talked for a while longer, and finally Grace closed her notebook.

"So, the assignment between now and when I see you next week is to write down the particulars and figure out what they're telling you."

Meg drew in a deep breath. Was Grace springing her for the day? A surreptitious glance at her watch showed Meg fifty minutes had passed. Amazing. She promised to bring notes next time, wished the psychologist Merry Christmas, and hurried out of the building to the blustery, gray day. She hugged her coat closer around her, ducked her head, and dashed for her mother's car. The skies opened up and rain pelted her like sharp bee stings. Depending on how long this lasted, she stood to lose her much-needed run.

The snap of the seat belt coincided with a loud noise. She jumped. Glanced through her side window. Damn. The outline of a man, his face pressed to the glass stared at her. He stepped back then splayed his hand on her window. She struggled to unhook her seat belt, without taking her eyes off the man. The man from the party? The blackmailer?

He backed away, waving the whole time. She was damn sure talking to him. Stop this crazy business right now. Still her fingers fumbled. She gave in and fixed her gaze on the belt to unhook the catch.

Meg jostled open the door, stepped into the deluge. Her gaze darted around the parking lot. Gone. She circled three hundred and sixty degrees. No Chuck. He flat disappeared. She clicked the car lock, and set out on foot to double check the area. Only three other vehicles in the lot and no one sat in any of them.

Well, hell. Meg swiped her drenched hair from her eyes, made her way back to her car, and climbed in. A chill racked her body and not from the rain and wind. She jacked up the temperature full blast. Despite the heater, by the time she got home, she still shook like the proverbial leaf in the wind.

"Meg, that you?" Her mother's voice stopped her before she got to the stairs.

"My heavens, honey. You're dripping wet. What happened?"

No way she'd say anything about seeing Chuck. "I didn't take an umbrella and got caught in the rain going from the doctor's office to the car."

"Well, climb out of those wet clothes and into a hot shower before you catch a cold. Can I do anything for you?"

"No, I'll follow your suggestions, plus take a handful of vitamin C. I didn't see Kathy and Ron's car. They're not back yet?"

"No, and I can't imagine how they're handling the zoo with the rain. Can you grab a short nap?"

"Good idea, Mom, and don't worry. I'll be fine." That word again. "Go back to your book." God, Meg hoped she'd sleep, but was afraid if she did, her dreams wouldn't be happy ones.

* * * *

12:00 noon, Thursday, December 24

"Must've rained while we were working out." Scott stepped around puddles before he climbed into David's car.

"Yeah. Hope this dries before the temperature drops more." David steered out of the country club parking lot and made for the house.

David had introduced Scott to a buddy of his, Marty Smith, a former cop hurt in the line of duty. He now ran a company specializing in security. Judging from his membership at the country club, he did all right.

Scott was frankly amazed at how much easier he moved since going to the gym. The steam, whirlpool, and walking were having a positive effect. His left leg might always be stiff, the cane a constant companion, and he'd never run as fast as a locomotive or leap tall buildings, but then he hadn't been able to before the shooting. A chuckle escaped.

"Going to share the joke?"

For the first time since the shooting, a small seed of optimism took root and grew, though not breaking out of the topsoil yet. Maybe finding valuable work wasn't an impossibility.

"Hey, man. You okay? Too much steam's made a mush of your brain?"

"That's about it, and you know what?"

"What?" David angled into his parent's driveway.

"I'm starving." Then Scott laughed out right.

David joined him. "Yeah, well, we worked up a sweat." He opened the front door and hollered, "Hey, Mom. You home?"

"Yes, dear, and my hearing is quite adequate. No need to yell." She came from the back of the house, a smile on her face, a book in one hand, and her finger between the pages where she'd stopped reading.

"Sorry. Where is everybody?"

"Your Dad's gone and come and gone again. Kathy, Ron and the kids are still at the zoo. I'm guessing they got wet, but I haven't heard from them. Meg is upstairs sleeping."

"I'll go roust her out." David swung toward the stairs.

"You will not." His mother grabbed her son's arm. "She got soaked during the storm. I guess she stood outside during the worst of the downpour. If she'd made a dash for the car, surely she wouldn't have been dripping wet."

"She had an appointment with the psychologist this morning, didn't she?" Scott hung his jacket in the front hall closet.

"Yes, she did. When she got in, I sent her for a hot shower and a nap. Are you boys hungry? I presume that's why you were yelling."

"Ah, Mom." David threw an arm around her shoulders. "You know me well. Wha'cha got to fill my belly?"

"Maria left fixings for sandwiches for lunch. I told you we're having soup and cornbread for supper tonight before church. The big

Christmas dinner is planned for the middle of the day tomorrow."

Scott couldn't keep a smile from spreading. "I applaud you, Ellie. You've got feeding this family down to a science. I can't remember when I've eaten this well."

She patted him on the shoulder. "Glad you're enjoying the visit with us, Scott. Y'all need any help with the sandwiches?"

"No, we're good. Enjoy reading." David teased.

"I will." She ambled several steps then stopped, and circled back to them. "Seriously, if you need anything, I'm a holler," she winked at them. "away." She proceeded toward the den, escaping with her book.

Scott smiled and followed David to the kitchen. "Your mother is…she's special."

"Yeah, I know."

Scott slapped together a ham sandwich. "You finished with the mustard? Thanks. When Meg comes down, let's ask her how she got so wet."

David layered cheddar cheese slices on the ham. He stopped. "You suspect something unusual happened?"

"I don't know. Seems odd. And odd bothers me."

"How about a beer?" David strolled toward the butler's pantry.

"Sure." Scott emptied half of the sack of chips on his plate, inched the chair backwards, and sat.

David returned to the kitchen. "Odd isn't good these days." He popped the caps on the two bottles and handed Scott the beer. "Hopefully, it's nothing."

"Yeah." Scott couldn't explain his concern about the rain incident.

* * * *

3:00 p.m. Thursday, December 24

Meg woke from her nap and found that typical of Texas weather, the sun had come out. She found her sister curled up in the living room with a book. Kathy and her family had avoided the worst of the downpour by going in the giant, new building, which housed the snakes. The kids had enjoyed themselves, and when they came out, jumped in every puddle they found. They were tucked up in their beds napping.

Meg stopped in the den where Scott and David sat glued to an action flick on the TV.

"Going for a run, guys. See you later."

"Hey, hold on." David jumped off the sofa, grabbed an arm, and reeled her into the den. "Come and sit down a minute."

"No, I need a long run. Y'all enjoy the movie. We'll visit after."

Scott took her other arm, and the two men positioned themselves on either side and pulled her down on the sofa. What-the-hey?

Scott paused the movie. "Your mother told us you came home completely soaked."

"What happened?" David asked.

Damn, guess she'd have to tell them now. She'd always planned to share with them, but she wanted to run now. Standing proved difficult since the men didn't release her arms.

"Okay, okay. I give. I'll tell you." They let go. She rose, and filled them in about her encounter in the parking lot with the man she suspected was the blackmailer.

"You got out of the car and went after him? Alone?" Scott's tone grated on her nerves.

"Are you nuts?" David's tone left no doubt what his opinion of her actions was.

"No, I'm not nuts, as you nicely phrased the question, but I saw an opportunity and wasn't about to let it go. Neither of you would've done anything different. I'm sorry he got away. Now, I'm leaving." She moved toward the door.

"I don't want you to go alone." Scott followed her and grabbed her hand.

"I'm going for a run." She glanced at his hand holding hers. "I'm a cop." She yanked and he released his hold. "I can take care of myself. If I stumble into something over my head, my cell's in my pocket. Keep an eye out for Dad. See you two later."

She set out by herself, her cell phone tucked securely in her jacket pocket. Despite the bright sunlight, a chill remained in the air, keeping most people indoors. Two hardy souls walked their dogs. Meg made a concentrated effort to avoid the puddles on the sidewalks. After the first ten minutes, she drove herself to increase the speed, barely slowing at street corners. The cold air stung her nose and her eyes. She loved running—the competition with herself, the wind rushing by her ears, the slap of her shoes on the pavement, the sense of well-being, of strength the activity gave her.

Traffic by a church slowed her progress. Couldn't be late enough for any services yet. The hands on her watch declared four-thirty. Wow. When she got in her zone, she lost track of the hour. She'd gone farther and longer than she'd intended. If she took the direct route, she'd reach home by five. She hadn't noticed any old maroon sedans, but she admitted she hadn't been paying close attention. Her brother and Scott wouldn't be happy about how oblivious she'd been. Not particularly smart of her, given the circumstances.

To make up for the lapse, she kept her eyes open for anyone appearing remotely suspicious. Clearly, she wasn't as "fine, just fine," as she wanted Grace Patterson to believe. Her lack of attention was un-cop-like enough to be scary. Meg promised herself to snap into the program. She loved her job and wanted to return whole, healthy, and healed.

Scott's face flashed in her mind. The attraction for him had to be an aberration because of the near death experiences. Nothing more. They'd go back to their jobs and lives in Atlanta and Los Angeles. Fifteen minutes from home, a movement to her left caught her attention. A car slid close to the curb, trolling at her pace. Her heartbeat stuttered. Had the blackmailer tracked her down? She glanced over, relief and disappointment flooded her system. Scott, not the blackmailer.

"Hop in." His voice left no room for argument.

She jogged to the stopped car, her heart pumping like she'd been in a marathon and not a simple run through the neighborhood.

Scott's sudden appearance had a powerful effect on her. No one else ever had.

"Please." He opened the passenger door from the inside.

And she gave in, just like that.

CHAPTER NINE

6:30 p.m. Thursday, December 24

The wipers easily skimmed the light snow from Chuck's windshield. Two cars left the Bourland's driveway one right after the other. Where were they going? He followed them at a leisurely pace. After a while, they maneuvered into a large parking lot. Arlington Heights Methodist Church. Bells pealed the carol "Silent Night." Of course, the Christmas Eve service.

Ellie Bourland in her full-length mink coat hung onto Joe's arm as they made their way across the street. Their steps left prints in the dusting of snow. The sister and her husband each carried a kid. Finally, Chuck saw Meg. Her long black hair curled out from a hat worn low over her forehead.

Her brother, David, the Usurper, and the guy with the cane walked on either side of her. Why'd she let the cripple guy near her? She couldn't find him hot.

Should he take advantage of the hour or so the family would stay at church, go back to the house, and look for a way in? He wanted to lie down on Meg's bed and imagine them getting it on in Dad's house. Thinking about her made him stiff. Maybe they forgot to set the security system in their rush to leave.

Probably hadn't, but be worth checking. The key he'd picked up from the hook in the kitchen during the party assured him about entering. If they'd set the alarm, he wouldn't go in. He wasn't stupid.

Chuck eased the car into traffic and away from the church. He had to give this a shot.

Outside lights focused on the trees and porch. A few gleamed from within. He drove past the house, took the corner and the next. Then he parked. He crept up the street behind the house and ducked through a hedge at the back of the property. These houses sat on large lots with nothing behind them, except the street.

Chuck made his way around to the front to check on the alarm. He peeked through one of the glass panels on either side of the door. His lucky day. A solid green light shown from the pad.

A sharp thorn scratched his cheek as he wormed his way back through the shrubbery. Peeking through the windows of the garden room, his breath hitched as he considered the possibility of going up to Meg's room. He slipped the key from his pocket. It lay warm against his cold hand. A chuckle escaped as he unlocked the door. A single tone chimed confirming the family had forgotten to arm the system. The chuckle became a full belly laugh.

He walked through the house hardly using the flashlight he'd brought with him and keeping close to walls. His family had left lights burning, as if they intended to welcome him. His family. The living room had family pictures filling the shelves. In the dining room, a large painting with the whole family hung on one wall. His face should be in the frame with them.

He moved toward the stairs. Anticipation of what he'd find and do in Meg's room caused his blood to rush and his breathing to increase. He stood on the landing and looked around. Which was hers? On this floor or the one above? He went up the second flight of stairs. No, this is where the sister with the husband and kids hung out. On one of the beds a small, pink sock monkey lay. Cute. He tossed it in the air as he went back down one flight. He wished he'd be able to see their reaction when they found the stuffed toy and realized someone had breached their sanctuary.

In a room on the backside of the house, he found a man's clothes hanging in the closet. David's or the cripple? Chuck moved to the dresser. More family pictures. Dear sweet Ellie could've put them in all of the rooms. Hard to tell whose this was.

Chuck crossed the hall and entered a room on the front of the house. He flashed a beam into the desk drawer and rummaged around in the papers. A plane ticket to LA for Scott McClaine. He slept in here, and the first one had been David's. Seeing nothing else of interest, he hurried on to the next. His hand paused over the knob. His stomach clenched with the possibilities. Meg's room? He turned the handle, pushed in the door, and squeezed through a small opening. He closed the door behind him.

A scent he recognized from the party wrapped around him causing an instant hard-on. Definitely Meg's. The full moon shining through the two front windows provided enough light for him to see without flipping a switch. After glancing around, he yanked open a door. The closet. Fumbling through he found the slinky red dress she'd worn when he'd been here for the party. He ran his hand across the front then slipped his fingers inside the opening. Her breasts had been bare. He imagined touching her nipples. His breath grew short while he rubbed his crotch before he hung up the dress.

He moved to the bureau. One dresser drawer held pajamas and socks. Another had, oh yeah, panties and bras. He picked up one of each as souvenirs. He enjoyed being in Meg's room in this house which should be his, but he couldn't stay. Not the right time for a face to face. Yet. The pink monkey stayed on her dresser where he'd set it when he first entered. His gift to her.

Something else to do before he left. He returned to David's room and removed a picture of the entire family from the frame. If not for Ellie, he'd be living this life. Chuck gouged out her face. His message to them he could do anything he wanted.

* * * *

9:45 p.m. Thursday, December 24

"Kids tucked in, Kathy?" Meg popped bottle caps and offered a beer to her sister.

"Yeah." She downed a gulp and let out a long sigh. "Thanks. Each year they've gotten more and more excited. It's like they can't shut off. Hand me another one, Meg. Ron and I talked about turning in soon. The urchins will be awake at the crack of dawn."

"Are you going up?" Their mother joined them in the kitchen and placed an arm around each of her daughters' waists.

"Yes. Katie and Ronny will wake before any of us are ready."

"I'm looking forward to tomorrow morning with the kids. Christmas is always best with small children around."

Kathy hugged her mom and Meg before heading to the stairs carrying the two bottles of beer.

"Can I get you anything, dear?"

"No thanks, Mom."

"Then I'm going to my room to finish my book. Dad's retreated to the study, and the guys are in the den with one of those awful action movies." Her grin belied her shudder.

"I enjoyed going to church with you this evening, Mom."

"Me too. You all lead busy, important lives, Meg. While we're proud of what you do, we worry, and we miss you. It's been wonderful for all three of you to be home for Christmas."

Meg slid an arm around her mother. "I love you. I'll head up pretty quick myself."

"I love you, too." Her mother rested her palm on Meg's cheek. "You know that, don't you?"

Meg nodded over the lump in her throat and the sudden burning in her eyes.

"See you in the morning." Ellie strolled from the kitchen, a book in one hand, carrying a glass of wine in the other.

Meg stopped by the den. "I'm turning in."

"Now?" Scott stood when she entered. It seemed not to bother him as much as when he'd first arrived. She'd grown up with people behaving the way he did, and men who didn't disappointed her. Scott and she weren't dating by any means, but she liked his innate politeness.

"Kathy reminded me the kids will start the day with the first crow of the roosters. I'll see you guys in the morning."

David got off the sofa and kissed her on the cheek. "Try not to worry about anything, sis. We'll figure out this mess."

Meg smiled, wandered into the hall, and up the stairs. After entering her room, she threw her purse on the bed, leaned against the door, closed her eyes, and puffed out her cheeks with a big breath of air. The scrunchy holding her ponytail came out with another long sigh. What a day.

Shaking her hair released tension. She flung the fuzzy elastic circle toward the dresser. A flash of pink caught her attention. Katie's pink sock monkey sat propped in front of the mirror. How'd this end up here? She pivoted making a complete and slow circle taking in her room. A bureau draw stood half-open. She had been in a big hurry to leave her room, but this went against her habit of neatness. Before shoving the drawer closed, her hands stilled. Huh. Her panties and bras weren't paired up with their mates. Did Kathy come in to borrow lingerie? But she'd have told me. Damn. What was going on here?

The idea someone had been in her room crashed in on Meg. Her heartbeat ricocheted in her chest. She spun around then stood perfectly still scanning the space. No one in sight. Without making a sound, she lifted her purse from the bed and slid her hand inside. Thank God, she'd located her father's revolver and stashed it in her purse. She palmed the weapon, the metal comforting. A quick gulp of air before she glanced under the bed. Nothing. The closet?

The door stood cracked. Damn. She grasped the gun, her finger along the barrel. Electricity spiked along her arms. In one quick motion she yanked open the door. The light clicked on. No one. Her breath whooshed out. Damn. Had she been imagining everything?

She licked her lips and looked more closely. The red dress used to hang at the rear of the closet not the front, because she intended on leaving the outfit here when she went back to Atlanta.

It looked rumpled. Her fingertips skimmed the front, touching little snags right across the bodice. She swiveled around from the closet, and her gaze lighted again on the pink monkey. "Oh, my God, the kids." She flew out of her room and tore up the stairs two at a time. How could she explain her sudden appearance to Kathy? It didn't matter. The kids' safety was most important.

The large third floor room resembled a dormitory with lots of beds and several sliding walls. Meg barely knocked before she burst through the door. Kathy and Ron were propped in their bed watching a wall mounted TV.

"Meg?" Kathy jerked to attention. "What's going on?"

"Nothing, just checking. We forgot to put the security system on before we left tonight." She hurried toward where the kids slept, stuck her head around the partition, stepped in, and squatted to look under the beds without waking them.

By then, both Kathy and Ron had followed her. "Are you carrying your gun?" her sister whispered.

"Dad's. It's best to be armed if you meet up with a burglar." Meg tried to laugh off her behavior. "Just us paranoid police types. Been in the bathroom since you came upstairs?"

"Yeah. It's fine, but you're scaring us, Meg," her brother-in-law said.

Meg never made eye contact with him or her sister. "It's

nothing. Me being super-cautious. Heard a story about break-ins in the neighborhood. During the holidays, we can't be too careful." She moved to the entrance. "Lock this, will you, Ron?"

He slid an arm around his wife's waist and nodded. "Sure."

Meg heard the click after the door shut. She'd face questions in the morning, but too bad. She hadn't been willing to take a chance with her niece and nephew. She tore down the stairs, the gun hanging from her hand, not ready to stuff it in the waistband of her pants. The importance of finding David and Scott sent her straight to the den. First, they'd secure the house then they'd talk about the way she'd found her bedroom. She fought her gag reflex at the idea someone had been in their house.

"You need more quality time with big brother?" David glanced up when she entered and then tuned back in to the TV.

Meg licked her lips and tried to make her voice work. Scott got off the sofa and came to her. He nodded at her hand. "Playing Annie Oakley?"

"What?" David joined Scott by her side.

She let out the breath she didn't realize she'd been holding. "I'm afraid we had a break-in while we were at church. I'll explain later. Right now, let's make sure everything's okay on this floor. I checked on Kathy's family. They're safe"

"So something's not right on the second." Scott stated more than questioned.

She nodded.

"What about Dad?" David asked after they reached the front

hall.

"He's probably in his study. You stay here." Without knocking, Meg opened the door and stuck in her head. "Hey, Dad. You need anything?"

"No, thanks, Meg. Thanks for asking. I'll be up for a while longer."

"Okay." She shut the door and reported to the men. "Alone. Let's finish securing the downstairs rooms."

After going over the entire first floor, Meg set the alarm.

"We didn't find anything out of order, Meg. What set this search in process?" Her brother's eyebrows drew together.

She hated to take them upstairs, but they needed to see with their own eyes. "Follow me."

Her brother and Scott stood outside her door, waiting for a direction from her. She sidestepped to give them clearance. "After you." The two men made the space she'd always thought large seem small. How to explain about the drawer of panties? Easier to do without Scott here, but he was here.

"Tell us what you noticed when you entered?" Scott asked.

"Katie's sock monkey sat on the dresser." She focused on their images in the mirror. Then she faced them. "When I turned I noticed a partly opened bureau drawer." She gripped her hands together before saying, "It was the under-ware drawer, and the items were all messed up."

"How could you tell?"

A logical question coming from her oddly messy brother.

"Because, David, unlike you, I keep them stacked neatly together." She gritted her teeth, not wanting to say more with Scott here.

"Oh, I remember, you have matching sets."

Heat warmed Meg's cheeks. Great, David, thanks for sharing.

"What did you do next, Meg?" Scott's narrowed lips opened just enough to push through the words.

"Got Dad's gun and checked under the bed and in the closet. Let me show you this. She opened the closet. "I'd left this dress hanging at the back. Now, it's front and center, and the once smooth material is snagged."

Scott's jaw muscle began a dance, bunching and releasing. "Anything gone?"

"I don't know." She slid the offending drawer out farther and fiddled with the contents for a time. "Damn." Turning back to them, the heat travelled from her cheeks all the way across her chest. "There's a set missing."

"Crap," her brother muttered.

"Yeah." She nodded. "Then I made a beeline upstairs to make sure everyone was okay."

"How'd you explain being the gun-toting aunt?" Scott's tone was light, but his hands had kept up a steady clenching motion, matching the movement in his jaw.

"Played it off as me being a paranoid cop. I told Kathy and Ron I'd heard rumors of break-ins in our neighborhood, and we hadn't put the alarm on when we left for church."

"Did she buy the story?"

"Well, the last part was true. How careless of us. Guys, we should check your rooms, too."

They followed her out.

Scot stepped into his room for a quick look around. "Mine's fine,"

David entered his room. "God damn it to hell. Take a look," David pulled them in.

Meg and Scott rushed toward David. His tone more than his words alerted them to something bad.

"Oh, my God." Meg's hand covered her mouth. In place of her mother's face in the family picture on the dresser, a gaping hole screamed at them. Meg's stomach cramped with shooting pains. This was worse than what she'd found in her room. She literally bent over to catch a breath, like when she'd been four or five and stood too close to her brother playing baseball. His bat hit her in the stomach on the back swing and knocked the breath out of her. She staggered, and Scott caught her.

* * * *

He looked between her and the man he'd always considered as more like a brother than his partner. Appearing punch drunk, both David and Meg needed Scott's sound thinking right now. Despite anger, which raged through his body at someone daring to harass Meg this way, Scott stepped up for them. "Okay, let's regroup and figure out what we've got and what our next steps are."

Meg paced unable to settle anywhere. David sat on the edge of a chair. Scott remained standing. "Number one. We've had a home invasion. We've got to report this to the police, regardless of what Joe wants."

Neither of the siblings spoke, and Scott went on. "The monkey indicates he went upstairs to the third floor and into both of your rooms. We didn't find evidence of him being anywhere else, but he certainly could've been." He forced his hands to relax, but the attack on this family tied him into a thousand knots. "Number two. Do we assume it's our guy, Coffey?"

"Yeah." Meg nodded, paused in her pacing, and then moved again. "The business with my dress and under-ware is consistent with the feeling I got from what he wrote."

"Messing with Mom's picture also ties in with all the stuff about family and how he thinks he, or someone he knows, should be a part of the family." David rubbed a hand across his forehead.

"We've got to call the police. You are all in danger." Scott stood in front of Meg, forcing her to stop.

"Not everyone. Maybe he's only interested in Mom and me. Her picture with the face torn out suggests he's short on control." Meg angled around Scott. Her short steps carried her quickly back across the rug. "Damn him. Why is he picking on Mom?"

"The notes suggest he believes he is your father's son. Stands to reason he doesn't like Joe's wife." Meg seemed to be worried only for her mother. Well, she could worry about her mother, but SWAT team be damned, Scott would be concerned about Meg. If Scott got his hands on the son-of-bitch making the threats, he'd make him sorry for messing with this family.

Meg pounded on her head with both hands. "Think. Why can't I figure out what to do?"

Scott intercepted her arms and held them down to her side. "It's okay. I'm here. I'll help." He met her eyes full of questions, slid his hands up to her shoulders, and gave them a comforting squeeze. He'd like to do more, but David sat right there, and she wouldn't want more from him anyway.

With reluctance, he guided Meg into another chair. "I've stated my opinion already. Let's take the monkey with us and tell Joe about the dress, how the items in your drawer were disturbed, and are missing. If this doesn't convince him to call the cops—I mean there's been a home invasion. Any sane person calls the cops in these circumstances."

The brother and sister stared at each other. What would they decide? Not his family. Not his call to make.

"He's right, David."

"Yeah, I know. Tonight, huh?"

"Better to push through now. And we should probably tell Kathy to take her family and go home right after lunch tomorrow."

Meg ran her hand through her hair.

"How will you convince her to do something so out of the ordinary?" her brother asked.

"I already told her I was worried someone had broken in, and we're worried about the kids' safety. She and Ron don't take any chances with them."

"Okay."

"Scott, can you go down and make sure Dad doesn't leave."

"Sure." Scott took two steps when David's words stopped him.

"I can still do the stairs faster than you." David rose and clapped him on the shoulder. "I'll take care of Dad." He dashed through the bedroom door.

Damn, Scott hated David being right. Much improved from when he'd first arrived, stairs would always challenge him. He looked at Meg who sat with her legs drawn up in front of her, resting her head on top of her knees. He squeezed her shoulder attempting to give comfort. He wanted to pull her into his arms.

"It'll be all right, Meg."

She raised a hand to his. "Thanks for being here for us, Scott. The way David and I are acting, you'd think we were brain dead and never guess we're cops."

Meg shot off the chair and threw her arms around him, pressing her entire body against his. He staggered to keep his balance then moved in close. God, this was better than he'd imagined. He wanted to hold her a long time. His hands rested at her waist, but he resisted letting them wander. The desire to shift them up her torso, close to her breasts, almost overpowered him.

But this wasn't about sex. It would never be about sex with Meg. She sought comfort, and he was just lucky to be the one to come to her aid. Her crooked smile earlier had torn at his heart. Her bravery about this crazy dude attacking her family touched him. He'd be a fool to let himself believe this was any more than her gratitude.

"Oh, my God." She sprang back. He reluctantly dropped his arms. Her face took on a rosy glow.

* * * *

"I'm sorry, Scott. I don't know what came over me. Did I hurt you?" Talk about being out of your ever-loving mind. Way to handle the tension. Throw yourself at the man. If he were at all interested, he'd respond some way. His hands had barely made contact.

"I'm okay. You've been through a lot and deserve to let off steam. I'm here for you Meg. You and David. You'll come through this."

"I hope so." After a moment, she forced a smile. "You're right. We'll plow through this, and somehow the family will survive. Damn, I'm an idiot. I never checked in Mom and Dad's room. What if he's up there now?" Scott stared at her a frown knitting his brows. He moved toward the door.

"Wait. You can't blunder into the room. Let me check out the situation." She didn't look forward to this, and Scott's face showed his doubt at her decision. He opened his mouth, but she cut him off.

"Get out of my way." She stalked out and down the hall toward the back of the house.

"Wait." Scott's hand grabbed her. "You can't go in alone."

"I'm sorry, Scott, but I am. If she wakes, it will be hard enough explaining why I'm there. You being along will complicate the situation more. But I have to check." She withdrew her father's weapon from the waistband at the small of her back. "Now move."

She scrambled toward her parents' room, holding the gun at the ready. Scott followed more slowly and took up a position to the side of the entrance. His hands clasped his cane like a bat. Thank God, Mother kept the house in such good repair. When Meg twisted the door-knob, no squeak assailed their ears.

She slithered through the opening and stopped to let her eyes adjust to the dimness. A nightlight glowed softly giving out a false sense of safety. She made her way to the bathroom. A light came on when she opened the closet door. All appeared normal. Meg took her first relieved breath and backed toward the door.

"Meg, honey, what's the matter?"

Her mother's whisper stopped her. "Sorry, Mom. Tried not to disturb you. I needed a bandage for a hangnail I couldn't make stop bleeding. Go back to sleep. Sorry I bothered you."

"You're never a bother, dear."

Meg stepped into the hall and nodded to Scott. "She's okay. Let's meet up with David and take on Dad. We've got to find the bastard who's messing with the family and stop him."

CHAPTER TEN

11:00 p.m. Thursday, December 24

Meg knocked once and blew into the study without waiting for her father to say anything. His desires were immaterial at this point. Tonight they'd talk.

Joe smiled when he first saw her, but his eyebrows veered down when David and Scott followed her inside. When Scott closed the door, her father rose.

"What's going on?"

"We need to talk, Dad." She used, as her brother called it, her no nonsense-SWAT tone.

"It's Christmas Eve. Can't whatever this is wait until we finish the celebrations?"

With her brother on her right and Scott on her left, Meg stood in front of her father's desk. She'd do whatever needed to keep her family safe, including angering her father further. In one hand, she held the sock monkey. In the other, she clasped the letters. David held the photo. Dad couldn't back them all down, not with the evidence they'd present to him.

"I'm sorry, but we've been trying to talk to you for days. Maybe if we'd been able to, what happened tonight wouldn't have."

"What are you talking about, little girl?"

She gritted her teeth. Her father went for the jugular. But she wasn't a little girl, and she knew what she was doing.

"Dad, someone got in the house tonight."

"What? Couldn't be. Nothing's been disturbed." He was like a locomotive, getting the steam up to flatten out a mountain. "And if someone had broken in, the alarm would've gone off. We'd have been notified by the company. You must be mistaken. Now the three of you, please leave." He stood rigid, daring them to defy him.

Meg stepped closer. She dropped the toy on his desk.

"What's this?" Her father's nostrils flared, a vein beat in his forehead.

"Katie's sock monkey. I found it on the dresser in my bedroom."

His eyebrows shot up, and he looked from her to Scott and David, as if the words she'd spoken didn't compute.

"There's more. One of Meg's dresses had been disturbed," Scott added.

"A bra and panties set is missing from my lingerie drawer."

"And this is what I found in my room." David shoved the picture next to the monkey.

Meg's father aged in front of her eyes. His face whitened. To say the starch went out of him was a massive understatement. He collapsed into his chair. The animal-like moan escaping from his mouth contained such agony Meg's legs trembled with the effort to hold her body upright. If someone had plunged a knife into her belly, the pain couldn't hurt any greater.

"Joe, we've got to stop this man before he physically hurts someone in your family."

Scott's low voice got her father's attention when she and David couldn't. Dad slowly raised his head. His lips tightened into a straight line. The grooves in his face had deepened since they'd entered his study and David had shown him the picture. A trick of shadow? Meg couldn't be sure.

"Ellie, Ellie." He picked up the picture, and a finger tenderly touched the mutilated figure of his wife. He glanced up at them, but spoke to Scott. "Since you saved David's life, you're a part of us, now. You may wish you weren't." He reached into the bottom drawer and lifted out a bottle of whiskey. "Anyone like a drink before we begin?" He held out the container.

Meg shook her head once and fought to keep her chin from trembling. This was her father. A strong man she'd looked up to her whole life. A man she'd measured others by and often found them wanting. This transformation devastated her, cutting sharp stabs through her middle.

"You better pull up chairs. This may take a while." He belted back a shot and poured another one.

If Meg hadn't already found him drunk after the Christmas party, she'd figure she was hallucinating. As far as she knew, her father seldom drank. Yet here he was downing the liquor like orange juice. She perched on the leather love seat next to David. Scott settled into the armchair.

"The grandkids are okay? I assume you determined that after finding Katie's monkey."

"Yeah, we did. First thing. We also checked out the rest of the house. Evidence indicates he'd gone in David's room, mine, and up on the third floor. Kathy should take her family and go home after lunch tomorrow. If anything else happens, we don't want the kids around."

"Does Kathy know anything about what's going on?" Her father took a sip of the amber liquid, his hand remarkably steady.

"Hell, Dad. We don't know, not exactly anyway." David's shout forced him from the sofa, and he circled around behind.

Her brother's outburst surprised her. He normally stayed calm in a crises the way she did. But dealing with this crises in the family was beyond normal.

"How do you want to do this? Where do I start?" His gaze traveled to each of them, stopping on Meg.

She ran a hand around the top of her turtleneck, trying to loosen the tension pinching like two vices clamped on her shoulders. "We'll tell you what we've surmised. You correct us and fill the blanks."

"You start, Meg. You suspected something before the rest of us." David returned to the couch and crossed one long leg over the other. His foot jiggled back and forth.

Meg told her father about finding the first letter. She reminded him of her attempt to talk to him with David. "Then we had the awful incident with you the night of the Christmas party. Damn, Dad, at first, we feared you'd had a heart attack. I've never been more scared in this house than I was then. The idea this maniac had the kids—." She stopped and drew in a shaky breath. "Not something I want to experience again." She leaned forward. "We've seen all the letters now. Four of them, right?"

"Yes."

"He probably followed Meg one night." Scott stabbed the floor with his cane as if trying to make the point with her father.

"We think we've identified him." David's foot wiggled at a faster rate.

"He came to the house during the party." Meg plodded on. She rolled her head trying to release the explosion of pain. "He worked for the catering company. Scott and I found out his name but not his address."

"He's tall and gangly with bushy long brown hair and bushy mustache and eyebrows. Do you remember seeing a server who fit the description?" David put his foot down and his knee took up the motion. "I talked with him. He followed Meg around all night giving her fresh glasses of wine."

Her father dropped his head into his hands. After a moment, he sat up again. "He's the one who handed me the fourth letter."

"At this point, Joe, it's prudent to assume none of you is safe." Scott stood. "He accessed the house, apparently with a key since we saw no evidence of a physical break-in. You must keep the security system on when home and not just when you're gone. Change the locks ASAP." Scott flattened both hands on the desk. "And, Joe, you've got to report this to the police. For some reason, he's fixated on Ellie and Meg."

"Why, Dad?" David asked.

"Is it imperative for you to know why?" the older man asked.

"Sometimes identifying 'the why' helps us find dick-heads like him," Scott said.

"He's blackmailed you, Dad." David leaned forward. "His actions threaten Mom and Meg. You've got to go to the police at whatever personal cost. Tell us what's behind this. We'll help, but we can't without cooperation."

Of course, with or without their father's cooperation, they'd find a way to stop this assault on her family.

Dad stood and began wandering around his study, the whiskey glass in his hand. He didn't look at them. "Ellie and I had been married less than a year when I had an affair."

Meg simultaneously drew in a sharp breath and took hold of David's hand in a death grip. In her peripheral vision, she caught Scott dropping into the wingback chair.

"I was stupid, got involved with my secretary. The liaison didn't last long before I realized what an ass I was being."

Meg had heard people speak from this kind of black despair when tragedy invaded their lives. Her father's voice had the same lost sound, and she ached for the pain they were putting him through, but lives were at stake.

"Her name was Peggy Coffee." His father went on relentlessly building the case against himself.

"The name in the blackmail notes." David said.

"Ellie found out after I'd broken off the relationship. It was a difficult time for us. But after a while, she forgave me and took me back." He faced them, his voice firm. "I've never looked at another woman in all the years since. You can count on that. I love your mother with all my heart. I won't let anything hurt her or destroy our marriage."

Meg studied her father. The picture of the honorable man tilted on its ear. Somehow, her parents had been able to move past the situation. In one sense, it was their business not hers or David's.

Meg asked the question her brother might be squeamish about.

"Dad, is it possible Peggy Coffee had your child?"

"If so, then she never told me. I found her another job, and she started the next day. I never saw or heard from her again. We were together over a month. Are you asking if we used any sort of protection? No, we didn't."

"So, the son the letters reference could be yours?" David asked in a strained tone.

Meg's hand ached from how hard David squeezed.

"Yes, it's possible." Dad dropped into his desk chair as if the admission had cost him.

David crossed and uncrossed his legs. "So the guy is older than me by six months or a year."

"Yes, if he exists. For us, you were a product of your mother's and my reconciliation and all the more wanted and loved."

The tremble in their father's voice dug into her heart, and David blinked as if to keep moisture from his eyes.

"Why didn't you go directly to the police when you got the first letter, Dad?" Meg slid her hand from David's. She massaged it to get the circulation going. David didn't seem to notice.

"Ellie and I made a good life together. I didn't want to remind her of those times. I figured I'd pay the five thousand and never hear anything more. He made no mention of a child in the October note. He only wrote about the affair with Peggy."

"And once you'd paid the first time, you were hooked," Scott said.

Joe nodded at Scott then faced Meg and her brother. "I'm sorry I hurt you both. Obviously, my preference was for no one else to know about my infidelity. Ellie and I made our peace. We've gone on with our lives."

"Anything else we should know?" Meg dreaded the answer.

A long breath of air exploded from her father. "I've already answered the last letter."

"You sent him the money he asked for?" David sprang from the love seat. "Dad, you've sent him twenty-five thousand dollars. Can you afford that?"

"Yes, I can, but I didn't meet his demands this time."

"Have you decided to call in the police?" Scott asked,

His low tone calmed Meg in the midst of chaos. Her head whirled with all they'd learned and apparently, they had more to face.

"What did you say to him?" she asked.

Her father reached into his center desk drawer. "I made a copy." Scott stepped forward and took the paper Joe held in his hand.

"Read the letter out loud," her brother directed.

Scott's deep voice read:

Dear Chuck,

So far as I know, I have no other son but David
Bourland. For me to send more money, I need proof
what you suggest is true. I'll pay for a paternity test. I'll
meet you to work out the details.

Call me on my cell, 817-555-4268. You should receive
this Saturday. I expect to hear from you no later than
Sunday. If not, I'll do as my children urge and report
the matter to the police.

Joe Bourland.

"Dad, surely you didn't mean to meet this guy alone? He could kill you." Meg stormed around to her father's side. Her hands tingled with the urge to shake him for his lack of care for his safety.

"But setting up a meet is good, Meg," Scott said. "We talked about catching him this way. Joe can select the location in an out of the way place, where it will be safer to grab him. A lot of traffic goes in and out of the post office. Not the best place to take him."

"Too many opportunities to hurt innocent bystanders. You're right." Meg rubbed her father's back. "Dad, let us help with this. We're all experienced. We'll put a plan together, and when he calls, you tell him to meet you where we've decided."

"Thank you, Meg. I hate that I've had a hand in this man touching our lives. Your life." His lips thinned. "But as long as there's a possibility this man's my son, I can't turn him in. The question of paternity must be resolved. If he's my son, I'll find him the help he needs—a psychiatrist, a lawyer, whatever. I won't give him a free pass for what he's done, but if he's my son, I'll have to help with his rehabilitation."

Meg walked away from her father, rubbing her head, which threatened to explode at any minute. They had time to come up with a plan. Tomorrow was Christmas Day, and she prayed nothing would happen then. Kathy and her family had to go home. Her heart lurched. Damn. She stopped pacing. "Should we send Mom away, too? I mean he's clearly unhinged where she's concerned. Even if he is your son, we can't take any chances of him hurting her."

Scott's hand on her shoulder soothed her. She hadn't been aware of him coming near. No one else had this kind of effect on her. "How about if Kathy asks Mom to go back to Oklahoma with them?" she asked.

"Must you to tell Kathy anything?" Her father's anguish roughened his voice.

"If you can figure out a way to do it, Meg, getting your mother out of here is a good idea." Scott stood near. She'd never needed grounding before from anyone, but she'd never dealt with a problem close to home either. She prayed she'd develop her edge again when they got this situation handled, and she returned to Atlanta. Atlanta. Her life in the city seemed a lifetime ago. On another planet.

For twenty minutes, they batted around various scenarios of how to set up the meeting with Chuck. Where to stage it, how important was getting Ellie out of the way, what story they could concoct for Kathy so she'd ask her mother to go home with them. Around and around.

"Stop. Stop," Meg yelled. With less heat, she repeated, "Just stop." Everyone stared at her. Her father rose from behind the desk, walked to her, and put his arm around her shoulder.

"I hate what I've put you through. We take actions when we're young without thinking of the consequences many years down the pike. I'm sorry."

"Dad, we're all exhausted. Those precious little munchkins upstairs will be down earlier than any of us will be happy about to check out what Santa brought them."

"Meg's right, Dad. We have tomorrow afternoon to work out the details for dealing with Chuck. Let's call it a night."

"What about Ellie," Scott reminded them. "Sending her with Kathy makes sense."

"I want Ellie to be safe, Scott, but I don't see any story convincing her to leave Meg and David. We don't see them as often as we'd like and considering the recent trauma you've both experienced...no, it's not happening." Joe ran a hand through his hair. "We're proud of what you do, and the majority of the time, we've been able to keep the dangerous aspects of your jobs relegated to the back of our minds. These close calls brought the danger all to the forefront."

"Okay," Meg heaved a huge sigh. "Mom stays, but she's never alone." Meg looked at her brother and Scott. "One of us must always be with her." The hall clock chimed "Midnight. Merry Christmas, everyone."

* * * *

1 a.m. Friday, December 25

As exhausted as she was, Meg struggled to fall asleep. She must have because she jerked awake, her brain flooded with fuzzy images of her and Scott making love as if they'd never have another chance to. She ached for him. For the sexual release he'd give her, the comfort, and the grounding. He was solid. Nothing bad could happen when he was around. The psychologists would suggest that because Scott had saved her brother's life she trusted him to handle anything. Maybe so. But right now her body cried out for his, to be touched, kissed, and sheltered in his arms.

Great, Meg. Lusting after a man who exhibits remarkable restraint around you. Those two times when they'd looked at each other were all she had to pin her hopes on. Before they left, she'd gut up and make the first move. If he wasn't interested in her, she'd move on with her life, but not knowing would haunt her forever. She'd struggle to recognize other options should they appear. Meg didn't expect happily ever after. She'd long ago recognized that wasn't in the cards for her. But someone to share life with on occasion would be…well, she had to make an attempt with Scott.

CHAPTER ELEVEN

10:30 a.m. Friday, December 25

Meg smiled at Katie and Ronny still sitting on the floor in front of the living room Christmas tree, engrossed in their new toys. She drew Kathy aside. "Let's go for a walk."

"What? Sure. Build up an appetite for Mom and Maria's lunch." She patted Ron on the shoulder to claim his attention. "Meg and I are stepping out for a walk, hon. In fifteen minutes, put the kids down for a nap before we eat. Otherwise their little heads may crash into their plates."

Ron smiled and reached out and patted her behind. "You guys take off. Bundle up, though. I've heard it's only thirty degrees out."

"Yes, sir, Daddy." She dropped a kiss on top of his head.

Meg loved the relationship her sister and brother-in-law enjoyed. They seemed to equally share responsibilities, but either one would do more than their part whenever the other needed. Meg tugged her coat on over the cardigan, which hid her father's gun stuck in the waistband of her jeans. One part of her wanted to refuse the necessity of the weapon. Christmas Day, and she was home with her family, but she was a smart cop. She'd seen too many dangerous situations erupt in perfectly normal families.

When they stepped on the porch, her gaze scanned the street and neighborhood for the older model maroon car. Nothing. "Let's go." She trotted left from the house, down the sidewalk at a fast clip.

Her breath frosted in front of her mouth and boots crunched in the snow. The smell of fireplaces burning against the cold warmed her.

"Okay, sis, what was going on last night? You scared the hell out of me showing up in our rooms holding a gun."

Meg told Kathy in the sketchiest terms about the blackmail. "It seems likely someone got into the house last night." She left out the details about her panty and bra set or their mother's picture. "We'd like you to take your family and go home today after we finish lunch."

Kathy stared at her as if Meg had lost her mind.

"Who's 'we', and what do you expect me to tell Mother?"

"David, Dad, Scott, and me."

"Scott? He saved David's life, but it's strange he has any say at all in this. Except—"

"Except?"

"He certainly seems interested in you, Meg."

"Oh, no. We're all sort of family to him. Mom officially adopted him. We had the ceremony and everything." Damn, butterflies swirled in her stomach. Stupid wishful thinking.

"Well, he sure doesn't look at the rest of us the way I've seen him look at you." Kathy touched Meg's face.

"What?"

"My big, bold sister has extra pink in her cheeks. My sister who never blushes at anything."

"It's the cold wind," Meg claimed and trudged on.

"Yeah, right. Are you interested in him, Meg? Because if you are, you should go after him. The fact he walks with a cane can't bother you."

"No, of course not. He's smart, kind, and I admit he sets my hormones clamoring. But, Kathy, he's never given me the slightest hint—"

"Give, big sister." She took Meg's arm and forced her to stop. "What are you thinking about right now?"

"Twice, when we've looked at each other...I don't know. Something sparked in his eyes. Of course, maybe my imagination was running overtime."

"Is Scott's cane possibly holding him back. Physically, he'll never be the person he was when he and David worked together. A major change in ability can put a big dent in a man's ego, and here you are this big, tough SWAT team member. Maybe he's afraid you'll reject him."

"God, he thinks I'm shallow?" Meg went back to walking, but at a slower pace.

"Men's egos. They don't operate the way we do. Okay, you've got my advice. What you do with my words of wisdom is up to you.

"On the earlier subject, what do we tell, Mom? She'll wonder why I'd leave when I can stay here with you and David. We're down here, or Mom and Dad come up to OK City once a month. But you guys aren't here as often or as much as we'd like."

"Maybe an emergency can come up at work."

"On Christmas Day?"

"Make up a crisis calling Ron to work tomorrow then. Leaving this afternoon gives him a chance to rest before going in to the office. Maybe someone is suing the company. I'm sorry. I've got no good ideas, for you, Kathy." They walked in silence for a minute or more.

"We'll feel better to get you guys out of here. We'll have four fewer people for us to keep up with and to be a target." As soon as the words left her mouth, Meg regretted her slip.

Kathy came to a complete stand still and grabbed Meg's arm, pulling them to face. "This is more serious than you want me to know, isn't it?"

Meg nodded.

"Okay. I'll talk with Ron, and we'll announce at lunch we're leaving early. The kids will pitch a fit. They love to come down here, and they've had fun with their uncle and aunt." They reversed their steps toward the house.

"At dinner, I'll promise to come home more and up to Oklahoma City to visit you guys, too. I'll redirect Mom. I promise. Okay?"

Kathy nodded once. "Let's go home, I'm freezing."

Meg had continued to keep an eye open but never saw the maroon car. A couple of kids had come out to ride new bikes. She suspected they were visiting grandparents. Only two of the houses on their block had sold to younger families. Communities changed, and this one would, too. Her job had taught her to be flexible, to be able to go with the flow.

In her personal life, she liked stability. From her stable upbringing, one might conclude she'd jump at the possibility for changes. Contrary to the theory, she found she was comfortable with the status quo.

Divorce wasn't in her vocabulary, and she'd never have left her fiancé had they married and later had problems. Loyalty had prevented her from allowing feelings for anyone else to develop. Not to mention she considered herself a blind idiot to miss what was going on. What brought the old relationship to mind right now? Scott's face took shape in the vapor before her.

* * * *

1:30 p.m. Friday, December 25

Chuck studied the pictures now spread out on the table in his small apartment.

Daddy Dearest.

David, The Usurper.

Ellie, The Thief.

She'd stolen a father from him and a husband from his mom. With a marker, he slashed a big black X over the older woman's face. She had to pay. He shoved the photos away to make room for those he'd taken of Meg, The Beautiful. He'd been saving them, having picked up the package late yesterday afternoon. They were his reward. His Christmas Day present to himself.

He studied the shot of her in the running shorts he'd taken when he followed her. And here was one taken in the pizza place. A profile, but she'd looked at him that night. Really seen him. Her gaze had locked with his. She wanted him then. He got the message.

And the best one of all. Meg, gorgeous and sexy in the red

dress at the party. His heart raced when he realized how close he'd come to being caught taking those pictures. He ran his fingers over her breasts in the photos the way he'd done when he'd been in her room and touched the silky material. His cock throbbed at the memory, as if she was with him. Soon they'd be together.

After he got rid of Ellie, they'd welcome him into the family. The real first-born son. The rightful heir. Oh, he'd share with David, because he wasn't responsible for his mother being a thief. With one hand, Chuck fingered the pictures of Meg in red silk. She'd welcome him into her bed, and he'd drill her whenever he wanted. She'd never look at anyone else. Certainly not her brother's gimp partner. Chuck's anger blazed at the idea of someone other than him being with Meg. He'd make him pay like Ellie.

* * * *

3:30 p.m. Friday, December 25

"Ellie, I'm sorry about breaking up the holiday." Ron took the brunt of the hard feelings. His expression showed how much he hated deceiving his mother-in-law. They had a great relationship. Meg was sure her mother would forgive him.

"I promise to come back in two months and stay with you guys, Kathy," Meg said. "I haven't gotten enough of my niece and nephew." She ruffled the curls on each head, and they each grabbed one of her legs. "Mom, don't hold it against Ron. Sometimes work takes precedence over family." Meg hauled Ronnie up and placed him on her shoulders. She spoke over his squeals. "It's awful when this happens, but we can't always control events."

Meg came home more than David did, because family was important. She'd always feared David kept himself at arm's length, because in his eyes he'd failed at making a family of his own. When his wife left him for another man, he'd been devastated. He'd buried himself with work to get through. Easy to do as a cop. The behavior became habit by the time the crutch wasn't needed anymore.

"I'll carry out this bag." Scott's voice brought her back to the present. He picked up one of the smaller suitcases and went toward the porch.

Meg realized he'd taken up the role of family for her brother. And probably David for Scott, after his family and fiancée were tragically and needlessly killed. Had to be worse situation for him than the loss she'd suffered with Jerry, who was in a dangerous business. Scott's family had been in their car, minding their own business, when the drunk driver crossed the center stripe and slammed into their car.

Her sister interrupted Meg's thoughts to pull her aside. Meg set Ronnie on his feet and he dashed off. Kathy hugged Meg close and whispered in her ear, "You swear you'll be careful. I'll beat you up if anything happens to you." Kathy hid her genuine concern behind the familiar teasing.

"Like you could, little sister." Meg forced a smile. "Don't worry, we'll be fine." From her lips to God's ears. After all, they had three top cops. Scott wasn't a hundred percent, but his instincts were great—she needed to shut off all other thoughts of the man. No place for anything else now. Focus on finding the blackmailer and holding him accountable for his actions with as little hurt to her family as possible.

Her resilient niece and nephew hopped around hugging each adult, giving and getting special attention. They'd adopted Scott. Upset at lunch when they'd found out they weren't staying, they were now excited to go home and show their friends the toys Santa had brought. They couldn't stop talking about Meg's plans to come visit them. The children made her promise to sleep in their rooms. Kathy and Ron had a huge home, with plenty of space for Meg without her staying in the kids' rooms, but Meg agreed, hoping she could make the leave taking easier.

Finally, after last hugs and kisses, the Hibbler car filled with family and presents dove away. Ellie brushed at a tear, but not before Meg's father noticed. He put an arm around her mother's shoulder and drew her close.

"We'll be going up in a couple of weeks, Ellie, and then they'll make another trip down here. We see them more than many of our friends do their grandchildren who live on the other side of the country." He ushered her from the porch back inside, letting the rest of them fend for themselves. "Oklahoma's not as bad as Wyoming where the Jim and Sue's grandkids are."

"Hey, Mom, let's work on the puzzle the kids got you. I bet I can put it together faster than you."

"Oh, no you won't, David Bourland." His mother scooted past him and scurried toward the garden room. "I bet I find the first two pieces and put them together before you sit down." Her laughter floated behind her.

"My money's on you, Ellie. Sorry, son." Her father patted David's shoulder and followed his wife. Her brother shrugged and trailed his parents.

Meg wondered about her parents' relationship. They'd always seemed loving. Some of her friends' parents never touched each other whenever anyone else was around. Hers had always been demonstrative, holding hands when they were out walking.

Maybe time had come to follow her sister and Julie's advice about her brother's former partner. Julie had promised to put the key under the mat of her guesthouse, and she'd told Meg they were spending the afternoon at her in-law's house. David would be at home to keep an eye on their parents. Okay, gut up and take your shot. If nothing comes of the attempt, at least you'll know.

She found Scott in the kitchen hunting for food. "Hi."

He jumped, but avoided the top of the refrigerator, unlike when he'd first arrived.

"Sorry, didn't mean to startle you."

"No problem this time." He faced her. "Where's David?"

"He and Mom are still dueling over puzzle pieces."

"Want something to eat?"

You. Probably not the best way to start out. She ran a tongue over her dry lips, took a deep breath, and blurted out, "Would you like to go for a drive with me?"

His eyebrows rose. "Sure. Any place particular?"

"How about we drive around to see if we stumble on the

maroon car?" Lame, but she hoped the excuse worked to convince him to leave the house.

"You wanna go?" She held her breath, afraid to look at him. When he didn't speak, she glanced up, and they made the connection they had twice before. Her stomach nosed dived to her toes. Was she certain she wanted to start this?

"Good idea, Meg. Maybe we'll get lucky."

Damn, she hoped so. "Let me stick my head in the den to tell David then we can leave."

"I'll grab our coats."

"Thanks," she said. Scott walked from the kitchen. He must be glad about how much better he'd gotten using his cane. He made good time. Not like when he'd first arrived, struggling for his balance all the time.

"David." Her brother looked up from a puzzle piece he was trying to make fit in an awkward space."

"What?"

"Scott and I are gonna take the car and drive around for a while." She walked over by her mother. "You finding more pieces than he is, Mom?"

"Bless his heart. He tries, Meg."

"I'll be right back, Mom." David followed Meg out of the den.

"We're hoping to spot the maroon sedan, David. You okay to keep an eye on the parentals?"

"Sure. Not a bad idea. Maybe you'll get lucky."

The phrase again. She hoped she wasn't blushing. "See you

later."

"Okay." David ambled back toward the den.

She hurried to meet Scott in the front hallway, touching her cheek to check on the blush, she'd suspected had popped out at her brother words. Not much heat if any. Deep breaths helped calm her heartbeat threatening to kick into overdrive with anticipation.

* * * *

4:30 p.m. Friday, December 25

Meg had driven around for thirty minutes with both Scott and her keeping watch for anything remotely like the maroon car. "Maybe this is foolish." While spotting the car had been the secondary reason to come out with Scott, the possibility existed they'd stumble on something. The sweaty palms in her gloves, and the grip on the steering wheel said her primary focus was Scott. She must've taken leave of her senses.

"No, this is a good idea. Besides, we're doing something."

"As opposed to waiting, which we do a lot in SWAT. Wait for the warrant to come in. Wait for the suspect to arrive. Sometimes it feels like forever. I've never been good at that part of the job." She cast a sidewise glance his direction. "I'm much more impatient and inclined to make something happen in my own time." She had his full attention.

"What are we talking about here?"

"Going after whatever—or whoever I want." Hard to be plainer about her intentions. When they got close to the back of Julie's guesthouse Meg slowed the car.

"I can't imagine you've ever wanted someone who didn't fall all over themselves to please you." His hand rubbed down his left leg. A muscle jumped in his jaw.

"Guess we're about to find out how true that is then." She paused, let out a breath. "I know a place." She tapped her gloved fingers on the steering wheel and made the turn into the driveway, stopped the car, and removed the keys from the ignition. Despite her best efforts, her heartbeat had accelerated more. Any faster and Meg was sure the organ would fly right out of her chest. She'd never been this scared of a situation in her life.

She shifted in the seat to face Scott. Two quick, deep breaths like she did before serving a volleyball, and she took her shot. "This is my friend Julie's guest house. She and her family are at the in-laws. The key is under a mat. Julie gave me permission to use the cottage whenever we like. Are you interested in going in?"

Scott's eyebrows drew down in confusion. Hadn't she made herself plain enough?

"Meg, are…do you mean?" He rubbed one hand down his face. The other kept massaging his left leg. "You talking about…us?" He gestured between them. "To…?"

"Yes." Still he didn't say anything. Damn, she'd made a fool of herself. She'd misread those three looks. "I'm sorry." She jammed the keys in the ignition and twisted. "Forget I said anything."

Before she let go of the keys to reach for the gearshift, Scott's hand came over hers. He shut off the engine. "I'm the one to apologize. Sorry for being slow on the uptake. A beautiful woman hasn't offered me what you did in a long time. Frankly, you blew me away." He reached a hand and caressed her cheek.

Meg pressed into his touch. He put both hands on her face and leaned in toward her, placing soft kisses everywhere but her mouth. Then his tongue softly explored the outline of her lips before drawing her closer, pressing his lips to hers gently at first then with more pressure. His kiss shot fire racing along her veins pooling as molten lava in her lower regions. She pressed her legs together to calm the sensations. And they'd only kissed.

He moved back, ran a thumb over her lips. "Let's go check out your friend's guest house."

She let out the breath she'd been holding and opened her car door.

They made their way to the front of the small house. Scott's hand rested low on her back the way Meg had always seen her father walk with her mother. Hang on there. This is not a forever thing, just a short-lived tryst. Couldn't be anything else. She'd be satisfied with the encounter with Scott, however short the duration, even if her heart took a beating.

"Certainly private," he muttered.

They walked around to the front of the cottage. Meg bent down to find the key hidden under the mat.

It had a note attached.

"What's it say?" Scott slid his arm around her waist and held her close.

Meg opened the card and read,

> *"Remember the security code is 1, 7, 8, 2.*
> *Turn up the heat to take the chill off.*
> *Light the fire both in the grate and—"*

She stopped. "That's all." She stuffed the note in her coat pocket. Meg expected they'd light the fire between them if the kiss they'd shared was any indication, and she hadn't read this man wrong. She stepped away from him. "Ready?

"Oh, yeah. I'll take care of the door. You do the alarm code."

After turning the key, Scott swung it wide. She stripped off her gloves and punched in the numbers for the security system. Meg couldn't remember when she'd last been in what used to be the maid's quarters. They'd obviously remodeled since then. Dark hard wood floors gleamed in the living area. Scott used the long lighter lying on top of the mantle and the gas burst into flames in the fireplace.

"Care to look around?" she asked.

He ran a finger along her jaw. His touch weakened her knees.

He stepped closer then removed her coat and slung it over the end of a loveseat covered in chintz, which faced the fireplace. She pulled off the gloves and dropped them on one of two chairs, which flanked the sofa. He slid his hands from her shoulders down to her fingers and then back up to massage her shoulders. "I'm only interested in finding the bedroom."

"Oh." Her heart jumped into her throat.

"Unless you want me to pull you down right here in front of the fireplace?"

"This way."

He dropped his jacket next to hers. She led him through the kitchen then toward the back of the little house, and past an impressive bathroom. Her mind skipped ahead filled with exciting images of what they might do to each other in there.

* * * *

Scott took no notice of the room decorations. His entire focus on the bed. He forgot to breathe. Was she going through with this? He'd been with lots of women over the years, but none made him crazy with desire the way Meg did. Sleeping in the room next to hers, his dreams had continued to rate triple X.

Waiting to find out what sex with her would be like—well tense didn't begin to describe his reaction. She must be able to hear the noise from his galloping heart.

Meg stood as if unsure what to do next. If she was truly willing, Scott had the next steps figured out. He didn't understand why she offered, but he wasn't throwing away this opportunity. He reached out a hand and took hers, pulling her to him in another kiss, sending his heart into overdrive. After a few moments, he moved back and then he never took his gaze from hers while he unbuttoned her blue flannel shirt, matching the exact color of her eyes. He loved the way her breath hitched up when he ran a finger across the swell of one breast and then the other. He leaned in to sample her neck and ear then across to those tantalizing lips for another kiss before he eased down to tease her nipples through the lacy beige bra.

Her hands had been still by her side, but now she raised his sweater and worked her own brand of magic on his nipples. He moaned when they pebbled beneath her touch.

"Damn. Did I hurt you? Let me take this off so I can see." The sweater hit the ground, and her hand with the gentlest caress imaginable moved across his wounds.

"I'll only hurt if you stop." He moved both of her palms to his chest. "There. Good for now, but I've other places for those hands."

She laughed. "Well, me, too." She slid one hand down his belly straight to his crotch and pressed against his engorged shaft.

"Oh, yeah, but let's hold off for a while. I want to make this last a long time—for both of us." He slid her shirt off and reached around to unhook her bra, dropping it to join the other clothes on the floor. Then he moved in closer. Her arms slid around his back, and her breasts flattened against his chest. "God, you feel good." He breathed deeply pulling in her scent.

He attempted to free her hair from the band holding the ponytail.

"Ow." She laughed. "Let me."

Her fingers meshed with his and then her hair billowed down and around her shoulders. His hands dived in. He'd wanted to run his fingers through her hair forever. When she dropped her head to the side in an open invitation, he nuzzled her neck.

His brain compressed to mush, except for one small section, marveling at his good fortune. Here he was making love to this woman he'd wanted since he first laid eyes on her. He'd been convinced hell would freeze over before he'd be in the position of sliding the zipper down her jeans and pulling them off her incredible body. But that's exactly what he did. His gaze wandered up her great legs, muscled, and strong.

Scott gently nudged Meg backward across the bed and levered himself over her. The pain from his leg caught him off guard, and he must've drawn in a quick breath.

"Are you all right?" Meg scooted away.

"I'm fine." No way, he wasn't going through with this. Damn. Another pain shot through his leg. He shifted more of his weight onto his other side. Better. "We'll be fine."

"Can I do anything to help?"

"Yeah, lie back and let me make love to you."

She did, and he did.

* * * *

5:45 p.m. Friday, December 25

"Are you okay?" Scott wasn't sure when he'd be able to move, and he feared he might be crushing her. She'd yelled loudly when she'd come. Made him feel, well, like a stud. He smiled and planted more kisses along her neck. "Are you?"

"Oh, God, yeah. I'm past okay. I didn't hurt you, did I?" She wiggled a hand up between them.

She'd been gentle with his wounds. And when she'd been on top and placed soft little kisses there, Scott had nearly melted into the bed. He rolled, and they lay facing each other, careful to keep his left leg on top. He needed to look into her eyes to make sure she was all right. The sex had been phenomenal. Best Christmas present he'd ever received.

Meg's eyes deepened to navy, her lips spread in a small grin. He trailed a finger down her arm then moved to where her waist nipped in. He continued down her hip, and lightly touched the area over her pelvic bone. She twitched, and her breathing grew shallow.

Scott leaned in, and with his lips feathering hers, spoke, "Let me catch my breath, and we can do that again." Until the words left his mouth, he hadn't realized how much he wanted a repeat performance. He'd expected once to assuage his hunger for her, but quite the opposite happened.

Meg rolled onto her back, both arms over her head. She stretched like a well-fed cat. God, she was in great shape. His gaze slid over her from the tip of her head to her feet. He loved she didn't hide from him. Of course, he'd already touched, kissed, and licked every single inch of her body.

"Nothing, I'd like better, but what time is it?" She propped herself over his chest, careful to not put weight on his wounds.

The fingers of one hand played with the hairs of his chest, lightly touching his nipples. Oh, yeah, he wanted to do this again. Reluctantly, he shifted to read the hands on the bedside clock. "Five-forty-five."

"We can grab a quick shower before going home. Can't have them wondering what happened to us." She slid off the bed and walked bare-naked toward the bathroom. "Well, are you coming?"

"Oh, yeah." He limped his way behind her.

"The hot steam will help relax the muscles." She twisted the handles and quickly the stall filled with white mist. She stepped in, and again Scott followed.

"Not sure this will work out the stiffness," he mumbled.

"Oh?" She turned, and her gaze drifted down past his chest. "Oh."

His cock stood at attention, not as if they'd just had the best sex of his life. Yes, this was the first time in a while, but the woman played a more important role than the long dry spell.

"I believe I can take care of this for you." Meg went down on her knees in front of him. Water cascaded on top of her head as she glanced up, as if she needed to assure herself of his reaction. Scott leaned back against the cold tile to keep his balance when she took his shaft completely into her warm, wet mouth, her tongue playing with him. His hips thrust into her. She took his ass in both her hands. The feeling was beyond anything to describe. Bells clanged, whistles shrieked, sirens squealed, and drums pounded. The vibrations expanded throughout his whole being.

When he came to himself, Meg had a bar of soap in her hand running it down her leg.

"Here, let me."

"No time now. I'll have to rush to dry my hair before we go home."

She was probably right. How would they explain her wet hair? They also needed to take another stab at locating the guy playing havoc with her family's life. "Chuck, too, huh?"

"Yeah. Then supper with the family." She threw a glance over her shoulder at him. Her turquoise eyes went a deeper color. "But I look forward to us to doing this again."

"That's the second best news I've heard all day."

"Really? What was the first?"

"You knew a place."

CHAPTER TWELVE

6:45 p.m. Friday, December 25

Scott road shotgun while Meg drove. What was the old expression? If he felt any better, there'd be two of him? It sure applied now. Meg had been a generous and passionate lover. He had no clue where their liaison might lead. Not a one. He figured to stick around for the ride as long as she'd let him. For some reason he and Meg had a connection.

The black haired beauty cleared her voice, pulling him from his erotic daydreams.

"I'm sure it's not necessary for me to say this, but I learned a long time ago the mistake of assuming everyone was on the same page with an issue."

He glanced over at her. "What's up?" Her hands clenched and released on the steering wheel.

"You understand we shouldn't let on to the family how we spent our afternoon?"

She kept her gaze on the road, never making eye contact with him.

"What do you expect I'm going to do? March in beating my chest like a stupid cave man, boasting of my conquest?"

"No, of course not, but don't drop a hint to David, and certainly not my parents." Color scaled her cheeks.

"Meg, we didn't do anything wrong, but this can be our little secret if you want. Your family seems to have a lot of those." He looked at the window and fumed. Had he completely misread the signs? Meg appeared to have had as great an experience as he. Had she merely been releasing tension in what had degenerated into a stressful holiday?

How stupid he was. From the beginning, he'd accepted she was out of his league. Who wanted to be saddled with a cripple? How had she suckered him into this deal anyway? He rubbed the area between his eyes where stress sent the beginning pings of pain like tiny hailstones hitting on the roof. Admitting the truth of what had transpired between them made him want to puke.

He'd wanted her and convinced himself she felt something for him. Had this been a sick way of thanking him for saving her brother's life?

"Hell." The word exploded.

"What's the matter? Are you hurting? I worried I was rushing you. Your body wasn't ready for this yet."

"Great. Just great. This was a pity-fuck, wasn't it?"

Meg careened into the driveway of her parents' home. "What insanity are you talking?" She slammed the car into park before they'd stopped moving. The suddenness jerked them against their seatbelts.

"You heard me. This was a twisted way of thanking me for saving David's life. Well, you're welcome, Ms. Bourland. Be happy to service you anytime you want to say thanks." His good leg rammed against the door, and he clambered out.

The car rocked from the force of Meg shutting the door. She made for the front entrance before he'd progressed much up the walk. When he reached the porch, Meg had disappeared inside.

"Hey, Scott." Ellie stood in the entry hall. "Glad y'all are back. We've got the left-overs laid out and can warm up anything you want." She paced toward the kitchen.

"Where's Meg?" Scott wanted to finish the fight. They couldn't leave their relationship the way it was. How awkward it'd be around the family.

"She zipped up to her room to freshen up before eating, but said to go ahead."

Ellie's comment about freshening up reminded him of hot sweaty sex with the woman's daughter. Hell, if he didn't feel warmth spreading across his cheeks. He yanked his gaze from the stairs and focused on Ellie. "Thanks. A turkey sandwich will be fine. Don't heat anything for me."

"Good. Well, let's go into the dining room, before David and his father inhale what's left of the bird." She laughed at her own joke, slipped her arm through the crook of his, and they made their way toward the laughter pouring from the dining room.

* * * *

Meg used every ounce of willpower not to slam her bedroom door. God, the stupid bastard her brother worked with. She stomped across the front of her room, looked outside, but rage clouded her vision, and she saw nothing. She couldn't believe what he'd said. How blind could the man be? She'd made a fool of herself.

Meg tugged open a dresser drawer and grabbed her running clothes. Dropped what she'd been wearing on the floor. The outdoorsy scent she associated with Scott filled her nose and sent warmth rushing to her nether regions like a tidal wave. Not okay. So not okay.

Where were her tennis shoes? She yanked hard enough she nearly broke the laces. As soon as they were on, she headed for the door, but then stopped. Mad she was, stupid she wasn't. She stuffed her dad's gun in a jacket pocket, bolted from the room, and tore down the stairs. She didn't stop to speak to anyone in the dining room. She swallowed convulsively. The idea of food nauseated her.

The door open alarm dinged as she left the house at the same time the clock in the front entry chimed once at seven-fifteen. She desperately needed to put space between her and the handsome former LA cop. What had she been thinking to have sex with him? She'd pursued him.

Whose brilliant idea was this anyway? Oh, yeah. Julie and Kathy both advocated for Meg going after him. Thanks a lot, ladies. Super results this. A flutter down low in her gut reminded Meg if she were honest with herself, the liaison had more than one commendable outcome.

* * * *

8:15 p.m. Friday, December 25

Scott wiped tears from his eyes, caused by how much he'd laughed at Ellie's story about the girls dressing up their big brother in heels and make-up when they'd been barely out of pre-school.

"You'll never let me forget this." David took a long pull from his beer.

"No. And you can be thankful I'm not on the force anymore, because this would be the first story I'd tell when we go back to LA. You've got pictures of this, Ellie?"

"Of course. I'm pretty certain I can put my hands on them without too much trouble."

"Don't hurry on my account, Mom." David said, laughing himself.

When she rose, the men got up, too. "I'll be right back."

"Y'all will excuse me? I'm going to my study." Joe hurried from the room, probably uncomfortable without Ellie to act as a buffer.

"So how'd you and Meg do this afternoon?" David slouched back in his chair.

How could Scott respond to the question? Did David suspect something had gone on between him and Meg? Deciding to go with a surface response Scott said, "We didn't find anything like his car."

"You must've worn her out, man. I've never known her to skip a meal."

Damn. Scott couldn't sit alone with Meg's brother a second longer. "Tell Ellie I'll be back." He rose and walked from the room, much more in control than when he'd first arrived. His comfort with the cane had increased, as had his balance. He'd made progress. Considering his extra-curricular activities this afternoon, it was a near miracle he got around at all.

Driven by a burning need to talk with Meg, Scott climbed the stairs. They needed to reach a working relationship. He tapped and waited then pressed his ear to the door. No sounds. He rapped briskly and called her name. Nothing. His hand twisted the knob, and the door swung open. She wasn't there. The clothes she'd been wearing lay on the floor as if she'd changed quickly. The open drawer held workout clothes. God, did she go for a run by herself? His hands clenched, and he hobbled down the stairs in record time. He ran into Ellie on her way into the dining room. "Have you seen Meg?"

She stopped, and her eyebrows drew together at the briskness of his tone. "Meg went upstairs when y'all returned from the drive. Did you check there?"

"Yeah, but I didn't find her."

"Probably gone for a run then. Come look at these."

He followed her into the dining room and forced himself to look at the pictures she spread across the table. Come on, hurry up, Ellie. Meg was outside alone in the dark, and his worry for her shot his heart rate into the ozone.

"Okay, gentlemen, I'm leaving you alone to peruse these at your leisure. I've started another book, and the handsome hero longs for me to get to know him better." She laughed then swished out of the dining room.

"Meg went for a run by herself." Scott wasted no time, sharing his concern with David.

"What? Why?"

"I'm not sure. We had an argument, and she went upstairs in a huff." Scott had trouble catching his breath. "Meg shouldn't be out by herself when Chuck is still in the wind. Would she deliberately put herself at risk to catch the guy?" She'd been steaming when she entered the house, and Scott's responsibility zinged his gut and dried his mouth.

"Yeah, she might. I'll call her cell."

Scott waited holding his breath.

Nothing. Went to voicemail. Let's eliminate the possibility of her being here. I'll double check upstairs. You take care of down here."

Scott kicked himself as he searched the ground floor. He knocked on the study door and stuck his head around the corner.

"Joe, you want any coffee?" Meg wasn't there.

"No thanks, Scott."

Scott nodded and closed the door. He jammed the tip of his cane on the floor. What a jerk he'd been.

He met David at the foot of the stairs. "Did you find her up there?"

David shook his head. "Her slacks, sweater and shoes were lying on the floor. Her running shoes were missing from the closet. She's obviously gone for a run. It's what she does to control her anger."

Scott nodded. "My fault. I'll go after her. You stay here with your folks."

"Yeah, we can't trust Mom is safe just because it's Christmas Day."

"We don't know what the bastard has in mind. If we both left and something bad happened, you'd never forgive yourself." A little melodramatic, but he wanted to find Meg, and he wanted to be alone with her when he did. Besides, this guy was pretty far out there. No way to predict his behavior.

"Get on outa here. I'll keep an eye on Mom. Call me when you locate Meg."

Scott struggled into his jacket and grabbed the keys before charging out the front door. His hand firmly grasped his cane, which he'd use as weapon if he needed one. He should've checked with someone if Meg took a particular route when she ran. He had a fifty-fifty shot of picking the correct direction. He bore left and drove faster than the speed limit. He'd deal with a ticket if he got one. Right now, he had to find Meg.

* * * *

8:45 p.m. Friday, December 25

Stupid, stupid, stupid. The words resounded to the slap of her feet hitting the sidewalk. She'd been running for at least fifteen minutes now, full out, and hadn't taken time to warm up. She'd probably pay for the omission with cramps later tonight, but she couldn't stand being in the house one minute more. Putting space between her and Scott had been the only thing she'd cared about. She couldn't remember being this mad at another human being or at herself in a long time.

He insulted her. She'd gone to bed with this jerk, because he wildly attracted her. Obviously, he didn't know her at all. He'd accused her of sleeping with him to say thanks for saving David's life. The words he'd used to describe what they did this afternoon caused tears to slide down her face. She brushed angrily at them.

She was upset about Dad and his infidelity, but that was long ago, and he and Mom had managed a great life together despite her husband's straying. Meg was mad for allowing herself to care and for letting Scott's words hurt her. She'd had to leave, but she should've told someone what she was up to. No good reason to scare them if they went to look and didn't find her.

While she'd brought a weapon, she hadn't grabbed her cell. Stupid all right, and the guys would give her hell about her careless behavior. Rightfully so, she grudgingly admitted. Slap, slap, slap. If she ran fast enough she'd outrun the pain. A car drove up alongside hers, and the door flew open. Scott piled out and yanked Meg into his arms.

"What are you doing here?" Meg stepped away from him.

"Get in the goddamned car."

"Don't talk to me like I'm twelve." Nevertheless, Meg climbed in and yanked out the ponytail holder to relieve the pain, which had ratcheted up in the last few moments.

"David and I were worried about you being out by yourself. Have you lost your mind? Please tell me you at least brought Joe's gun." Scott's voice held more than a hint of anger.

Holding her hands out, she welcomed the warm air from the car heater. "Yes."

"What about your cell? We called, but you didn't answer.

That's when we freaked."

He was right. She'd screwed up. Not something to be proud of, nor something she'd ever done working a case in Atlanta.

"Did you?"

Scott's relentless attitude said he wasn't quitting until he got his answer. She might as well fess up and take her medicine. No point dragging out the inquisition longer.

"No, I did not bring my cell. I brought the gun, but I should've told someone where I was going. I acted stupidly. There, are you satisfied?"

The air rushed out of his body like a deflating balloon. She came close to laughing. He'd built himself up to give her hell, and when she confessed, she left him with nothing to say. Clearly this situation with her father, and she admitted her over the top reaction to her brother's partner, had unhinged something in her controlled and logical mind. No other explanation existed for her earlier behavior with Scott or running out of the house afterwards.

"We need to talk about this afternoon." He shifted in the seat to face her.

"No, we do not."

"Meg."

"No, now drive."

Scott slapped his palm on the steering wheel and then started the car. The silence carried them to the street where her parents lived. Damn if she'd break the impasse.

"Okay. Let's talk about plans for keeping everyone safe. We

should all stay in this evening and tomorrow to narrow the window of access for Chuck to you and Ellie. The next couple of days should change the situation, and your family can return to normal." Scott stopped the car in the driveway behind David's rented Escalade.

"Scott, you better rethink the idea of everybody being locked in." She swiveled her body towards his. "Tomorrow is the day after Christmas, the biggest shopping day in the year. Mother never misses, and when I'm home, I go, too."

"Well, maybe David can go with her, and I'll stay here with you and Joe. Both of you can't go out with only David or me. Someone should stay with your father, though he's not the primary target here. The only way this can work is—"

"Good luck dragging David on a shopping trip with Mom. This I've gotta see." She jumped out of car. Scott followed her. "Why can't you remember I'm a trained SWAT officer and can take care of myself?"

"Sure, like you did this evening."

Best not to respond. Besides, she'd already agreed she'd acted stupidly. "You cut our resources if you don't plan to use my expertise to find this guy."

* * * *

11:30 a.m. Saturday, December 26

Scott shook his head. Meg had been right about her mother, and in the end, all five of them had gone shopping. Joe had been easy to convince of the wisdom of going along. He'd do anything to protect his wife from something he believed might harm her. Including paying blackmail. Scott hoped the love Ellie and Joe shared could stand up to the new evidence of his infidelity, in the form of whoever the presumed son was. If indeed, the DNA testing proved Joe was the father.

Standing on the sidewalk of the upscale, U-shaped shopping center its trees draped in sparkling lights, Scott guarded the front door to Shelley's Shelves. The plan had been for David to go in with the family and for him and Meg to stick to Ellie's side.

Scott hooked the top button on his heavy jacket and eased down a hat he'd borrowed from Joe to cover his ears. The blustery north wind blew through everything in its path. The crowds were crazy. Cars honked and drivers shot the finger at people not moving fast enough. So much for the Christmas spirit.

"We've got to go to Target next." Ellie's eyes flashed with the excitement of the chase when she joined him on the sidewalk. "Are you sure you men want to continue on? Meg and I can leave you off at home before we go there."

"They're having a good time. Aren't you, guys?" Meg attempted to squash Ellie's idea about separating.

"But Target will be jam packed," her mother insisted.

"More than this?" Scott gaze traveled down the sidewalks. How would they keep up with the two women in a larger store with more shoppers around?

"Oh my, yes. I always pick up wrapping paper and gifts for next year during this sale."

"And then forget where you put them." Joe's smile said

everything about how he adored his wife. "Maybe if I'm along, I'll be able to help you remember what you've bought and where you stash the loot."

"Good idea, dear. We should've come up with this before."

The decision made, they all climbed into the Escalade and plowed into the scary traffic.

By common consent, Scott stayed outside again, and the others went in. The crowded aisles were difficult for him to maneuver through with his cane. He eyed each person entering the store. Tons of people hustled by—teenagers, mothers with babies in strollers and toddlers clinging to their hands, people old enough to be grandparents, wealthy as well as folks needing to stretch a dime. He'd never gone shopping on the day after Christmas before, and damned if he ever would again. This was beyond crazy.

In front of him, two preteen kids in shoes with rollers glided through the crowd. A stroller tipped at an alarming angle. The startled young mother screamed, and Scott jumped to help. His muscles strained as he righted the contraption on its four wheels. The strapped in baby wouldn't have fallen out but could've been hurt.

"Thank you so much. Jessica could've been hurt. I don't know why those kids are allowed to wear those stupid shoes in crowded spaces." The mother, obviously rattled, thanked Scott profusely and then moved in to the store.

He picked up his cane and returned to his position. The hairs on the back of his neck stood on end. He glanced around. His eerie sixth sense seldom failed him. It's why he'd been able to save David. Scott palmed his cell phone to check on the folks inside.

"David, you guys all together?" he asked as soon as his former partner answered.

"I'm with Dad in the hardware section. Meg's with Mom, wandering through children's toys. Everything all right?"

"Probably, but we had a disturbance at the entrance, and someone could've slipped by. I'd be happier if you and Joe rejoined the women."

"Sure. You stay there. If someone nabs one of them, they'd have to go out your way."

"Got it." Scott's stomach lurched at the idea of someone grabbing Meg. Never mind her ability to deal with tough situations. "Tell me when you're together again." He disconnected. What if someone stabbed her in an attempt to take Ellie? His hands went cold and not from the temperature. They were all crazy. Why had he agreed for everyone to come out this way? They were daring Coffey or whoever to take a crack at them.

Scott paced, his gaze darting among the crowds of people for anyone remotely resembling Coffey. Now he had to keep an eye on both the exit and the entrance. Why didn't David call back? What kept them?

His phone played Elvis' *Jail House Rock*. "Talk to me."

"We're all together."

Scott let out a breath he'd unconsciously held and leaned against the building, his gaze still scanning the crowds. "Good. How much longer do you think?" They couldn't leave fast enough for him.

"Mom's talking about lunch now."

Lord. "What about leftovers at the house?"

"Maybe Meg can convince her, but she's a pretty stubborn lady."

"So I've noticed." Probably where Meg got her attitude, too. "I'm at the front door. Head this way as soon as you can."

"Will do. Miraculously, we've found a short checkout line."

Ten minutes later, David showed up with his corralled family, everyone with sacks in hand.

"You drive, David and I'll give directions," Ellie said in her take-charge voice, sounding a lot like her daughter. She climbed into the front passenger seat.

Scott looked at David.

He shrugged and closed his mother's door. "She parlayed a deal. In exchange for shortening the shopping trip, we've agreed to stop for lunch at her favorite little Italian restaurant not far from our house."

"After you, Meg." Joe held the door for his daughter to climb into the center seat.

Scott shook his head and climbed in on the other side. What a mess. Getting them all home and safely secured behind locked doors with the security system on couldn't happen soon enough for him.

Despite her father being there, Scott fought the urge to physically check to make sure Meg was all right. She'd hate his behavior. He didn't want to trigger one of her blow ups because in her mind he was being overly protective. While his head understood

Meg could take care of herself, his gut had a belief system all its own, and insisted on parking in the back of his throat.

What an idiot to care for her. Especially, when she pitied him. She'd become furious when he'd accused her, but still he faced facts better than most. If once, he might've been considered a catch, he'd fallen from that spot now. His head ached from the stress of wanting more than was possible from the woman with the blue-green eyes. Add the stink they were dealing with because of her father's thoughtless infidelity all those years ago, and no wonder the top of his head threatened to blow off.

David jockeyed the car into a small parking area in what clearly at one time had been a house, now morphed into a small business.

"You will love this place, Scott." Ellie got out and walked toward the entrance. "Neither you nor David have eaten here, Meg. Nina's only opened three months ago, but she's received rave notices...."

Scott zoned out as Ellie ran on. Let's eat and get everyone home. Home? Well, it wasn't his, though Ellie had adopted him. If Scott were picking a new family, he'd select this group of people for whom the word "home" was important. They'd do anything to keep it intact.

His parents had been like the Bourlands. They'd completely welcomed Tricia, his fiancée, from the moment he'd introduced her, as if they picked up something right away he'd been slower to recognize. Still, after all these years, Scott feared involvement with a woman and the ultimate loss of her. He had to leave Fort Worth and put space between him and Meg. He tread a fine line with her. The desire she aroused in him with a mere look or the proximity of her hand, heated his blood and his imagination.

Nothing would develop between them, despite their one incredible encounter. She lived in Atlanta, and from everything he'd learned, she loved her job. Her bosses loved her and wanted her to come back. Scott's life was in LA doing…what? He had no clue.

After they'd made love, she'd asked him to keep what had happed between the two of them a secret, not the action of a person who hoped they had any future. Not a good idea to focus on their shared afternoon of passion while hanging out in the restaurant with her family. The ache of his growing arousal made sitting uncomfortable, but standing wasn't an option.

The meal went on forever. When it looked like they were about to leave, Scott stifled a groan of frustration when the owner scooted up an extra chair, made nice, and insisted they share another bottle of wine, one of her favorites. Ellie was more than a tad tipsy as was Joe. When they finally got home around three-thirty, they'd gone upstairs to sleep off the wine Meg begged for a run, and David had gone with her, while Scott held down the fort.

* * * *

5 p.m. Saturday, December 26

"You two were gone longer than I expected." Scott couldn't keep the tone of criticism from his voice. He rose, but resisted the impulse to move close to Meg to make sure she was in one piece.

"Sorry. We should've called." David dropped exhaustedly onto the large wingback chair in the den. "Meg wanted us to extend the run. We included the post office, hanging around the vicinity for a while. Nothing happening."

"Then we stopped by the new market for soft drinks." Meg sat on the arm of the sofa. "Sipped while we walked around. We fit in, even for such a trendy area. No calls yet?"

"Nothing. Your folks napped for about an hour. Ellie's in the living room reading. She said we were on our own for supper with yesterday's left overs, and it was every man for himself."

"And Dad?" David asked.

"He's working in the study."

She nodded. "Thanks for the run, David. The exercise helps me deal with the stress, but I'm stinky now, so I'm going up for shower." Meg rose.

"You said it. I didn't." David grinned at his sister. She made a face then hurried out. He wheeled from her and stopped staring at Scott. "You okay, man?"

"Yeah. I'm fine, just fine."

"That's what Meg always says when she's not. Are the two of you making nice with each other now?" David propped his feet on the coffee table in the den.

"What do you mean?"

"Answering a question with a question, Buddy. Nice technique. Remember, I taught you that one. But I'll tell you why I asked. A zing of electricity hangs in the air whenever you two are near each other. It's the weirdest thing. At first, I figured I was imagining something, but then I decided you didn't like each other. Let me tell you I'd hate if you didn't like each other. What gives?"

Scott stood, walked a couple of steps toward the kitchen, stopped, and shuffled around. He shoved his hands in his pockets. "We don't dislike each other, David. Meg asked me not to say anything, but since you've picked up on the vibe, I'll be honest with you."

"Yeah? I'm waiting."

"I'm…attracted to her."

"What? As in you 'like' each other?" David leaned forward, finger quoting.

Scott nodded. "Yeah. At least I like her, though I'll never be good enough for her."

"What kind of talk is that? Crap, I'll tell you."

"Get real, David. Your sister is SWAT. She'd never tie herself up with a cripple and shouldn't."

"Did she tell you about her fiancé?"

"Yeah, killed in the line of duty. Pretty rotten."

"Scott, man. I'm not sure what to say here." David ran a hand through his hair. "I don't want either of you to get hurt. Is this a short term fling, or does a possibility exist of something more permanent developing?"

Scott shrugged. "It's not much of anything right now."

"Not being in law enforcement anymore is a plus for you. After her fiancé's death, Meg vowed not to become involved with a cop again. She never has."

"I'm gonna drive around for a while, look for our guy, since you and Meg didn't catch sight of him. He's got to pick up the letter sometime. If Ellie hadn't had us shopping and eating all day, we'd probably have nailed him. You keep an eye on our charges?"

"Sure. Something else. Despite being partners forever, you hurt my sister, and I will you deal with you."

* * * *

6:30 p.m. Saturday, December 26

Chuck rushed from the post office and hopped into the beige car, as nondescript as any he'd been able to find. He couldn't even remember what make it was. The letter had arrived. He'd grabbed it from the post office box and darted to his car. His heart raced as he tore into the letter. The slender envelope wasn't fat enough to contain five thousand dollars much less ten. His hand shook making the single sheet flutter and fall to the car floor. He fumbled around for the page, his fingers shaking. Finally, he read.

> *Dear Chuck,*
>
> *So far as I know, I have no other son but David Bourland...*
>
> *I need proof what you suggest is true. I'll pay for a paternity test....report the matter to the police.*

Shit. Who is he to threaten me? Chuck threw the letter on the seat and punched his foot on the accelerator. His goal, the little house as quick as possible. By the time he reached the driveway, he'd calmed a little. A paternity test, huh? Not a bad idea. Afterwards, Joe wouldn't be able to deny him. Instead of several thousand dollars, Chuck would be entitled to one quarter of all Joe had. Maybe more, because Joe needed to make up for the years he'd done nothing for his first-born.

Chuck popped the top on a can of beer and opened a bag of chips. Yeah, maybe he'd meet his daddy to set up the test. How long before they'd get the results? Afterwards, Joe would invite him to move in with them. Living right there, it'd be easy to make Ellie, The Thief, disappear and easier to move on Meg, The Beautiful.

Would they do it right on her bed? His breathing speeded up. Sweat ran down his back. His cock twitched. His desire to stick his pecker into Meg grew more intense with each passing day.

His hand itched to pick up the phone and call his daddy, but he steeled himself to wait. He'd been doing a lot of waiting, ever since his mom got sick and told him about his father. When she died, he decided to act. The waiting was over. Tomorrow he'd call and set up a time and place for the meeting. He'd use a quick turnaround to keep Joe from pulling a double cross.

Where to meet? The Burger Shack on the corner of Camp Bowie and Montgomery? Yeah. Joe wouldn't take a chance and try anything with kids around. If problems occurred, Montgomery to I-30 made for a quick escape route. He polished off the beer and sailed the can through the air landing it in the trashcan with a satisfying crash. He opened another one. Soon he'd be able to drink the best beer around, not this cheap shit.

He got up, found the pictures of his family, the ones he'd taken

over several days and spread them on the table. With a red pen, he
drew a red line circling Ellie's throat. No more than she deserved for
killing Mama. After a moment, he laid Ellie aside and picked up one
of Meg in the red Christmas party dress. He ran his fingers across the
top of her breasts. The rounded mounds winking out at him from the
pieces of silk called to him. She'd wanted him to notice her. And he
had. Not long now, Meg. Not long at all.

* * * *

1 a.m. Saturday, December 26

Meg tossed and turned, unable to find release in sleep. Twice
she'd drifted off. The first time she woke with terror swamping her.
Coffey had taken her niece and nephew and buried them in the back
yard. Then he dragged her screaming mother, who morphed into
Meg, down the stairs, a large knife in his hand, blood streaming from
a slice to her jugular. Meg's hand touched the rapid pulse in her neck,
expecting the trickle of warm red liquid.

The second dream left her upset, too, but in a different way.
Scott and she were in bed making love. Then he disappeared. She
missed his touch, even if only in the dream.

Given his perception she'd slept with him out of pity, what kind
of a jerk did that make her? They had to talk. She should've agreed
when he wanted to in the car. She'd convince him he was wrong
about her.

Could she go to him now?

Should she go to him?

She climbed from the bed. The hard wood floor chilled her bare feet as she paced the room. Her skin tingled, remembering his touch.

What would happen with her father and Chuck? Who knew what to expect at any time? Every moment of life was a cherished gift. Her fiancé killed. Her team member Hank shot down in front of her. Scott's family taken in a heartbeat by a drunk driver. David nearly killed if not for Scott's quick action and willingness to sacrifice himself for his partner. In this life, one should take nothing for granted. She and Scott had connected on an elemental level. Meg wanted to experience those feelings again before she died.

Without giving herself a chance to second-guess her decision, she opened the door and moved into the hall dimly lit by moonlight coming through the window. Skeleton like shadows from the branches of the bare trees outside showed up on the walls. The wooden floor under the runner creaked as it always did. She stopped in front of Scott's room. Her fingers rapped around the metal doorknob, cold to her touch. A shiver ran down her arms. She remembered bringing Scott soup the day he'd arrived. Talk about a lifetime ago. From the first, she'd fought the instant attraction for him.

Was she doing this or denying herself? She twisted the knob, but it slid from her fingers as the door opened in without her exerting any pressure. Scott stood inside the open door frame, shirtless, but in pajama bottoms.

"I hoped the noise was you."

"I needed to talk with you. I'm not like you said. I didn't sleep with you out of pity or to say thanks for saving David." Her whispered words came out in a rush. "How could you think something so awful?" She ran fingers through her hair.

His hand wrapped around hers, drew her further into his room, and closed the door.

"At this moment I don't care why you did, or why you've shown up here now. I'm glad you have." His mouth descended on hers, and she opened to him. His tongue plundered and took, and she reveled in his power. She gave back equally, straining to be closer, her fingers scoring his back. He maneuvered her backwards toward the bed.

"I'm not able to carry you," he mumbled against her neck.

"It's okay."

"You smell good. It's what I noticed first about you at the airport." He lifted the hem of shirt up over her head. "Let me look at you." His gaze caressed her body. "Gorgeous."

His hands reached for her, cupping her breasts, which sprang to life, the nipples growing hard and aching for his mouth. She drew him down with her on the bed.

"Make love to me, Scott. Make me feel alive." She arched into the stiff bulge resting against her mound. If she rocked too many times against his already hard erection, she was afraid she'd come right then. This man tumbled her inside out. She reached to remove her panties, but his hand stopped her.

"Let me." He grabbed hold of the top with his teeth and inched them down, making frequent stops along the way to kiss and take tiny bites. Then with a yank, the panties were gone. His teeth nibbled on her clit then his tongue plunged into her core. She bucked against him, crying for release, but he backed off. "Scott, please." He turned her on completely. She craved him and how he lit up her body. He'd be sorry he teased.

Meg rolled and slid Scott's pajama bottoms off, stopping to place kisses on the scar on his leg, moving upwards to circle his fully aroused flesh with her tongue—Scott's turn to beg.

"God, woman, what you do to me."

She leaned forward to kiss the scars on his chest and his fingers found her nipples, rubbing the tips with his thumbs. Her heart pounded like a thousand drums. She drew back to give more attention to his swollen and throbbing shaft. The smooth, silky steel excited her. She ached to get him inside of her. Scott flipped her around and went back to nuzzling and nibbling. Then all her focus centered on her own needs as he slipped two fingers inside her warmth and circled her nub with his tongue. Meg arched against him, the pressure building like a volcano about to explode. Her panting increased until dark circles surrounded her vision. Passing out was a definite possibility.

"Come for me, Meg. Let go and come."

And she did.

Afterwards, she lay splayed on his bed, relaxed and replete, moving an impossible task. She ran a hand down his cheek, across his chest, lightly touching his nipples, which responded by hardening as he gasped. Her hand slid farther down his body to his full, throbbing erection, which jumped. She touched the moisture on its tip. Scott stretched across her. She registered the drawer opening and closing and the sound of paper tearing.

"Let me." She took the condom from his hand and slid it on. He positioned himself over her still swollen, sensitive skin, and with one thrust entered. She arched into him, taking him further. He pulled out.

His withdrawal left her feeling cold and alone. But not for long. Scott plunged back in. His rocking motion began to take her up again. She gasped, meeting him thrust for thrust. He swallowed her moans, and in a burst of blackness followed by stars, her insides squeezed around him as she came again, and he exploded inside her.

Meg floated in a safe place. Pictures danced behind her closed eyes. Gauzy drapes blew lightly in the wind. Water splashed into a pool. Everywhere a warm, sunny haze shown on lush green grass and trees. Must be heaven rocked in the comfort of Scott's arms as she was. Their bodies still connected, as if they'd never separate. She forced her eyes open to find Scott studying her face.
"Are you all right?" He touched a tear with his fingertip.

"Better than." She brushed at her other eye. "You're an extraordinary lover."

The word slipped from her lips without her control. They weren't lovers. They'd been having fantastic sexual intercourse. Meg admitted to herself it felt like more.

Scott took her chin in his hand and made her look at him. "This wasn't just sex, Meg. We made love."

CHAPTER THIRTEEN

2:00 p.m. Sunday, December 27

The waiting was getting to them all, Scott included. They still hadn't heard anything from Coffey. The strain was beginning to show. Working on a large puzzle earlier Joe had snapped at David, and Ellie, not understanding, intervened to keep the peace.

"Hey, your mother sent me to find you." Scott said. Meg paced around the garden room, making circles. She whirled at the sound of his voice. Her nerves must be stretched like a tug of war rope.

"Lunch is ready." Scott said.

"I'm not coming."

"What?"

"I'm not hungry, thanks. I lose my appetite when someone betrays me."

"Betrayed? What are you talking about?" He started toward her. Meg moved to put the wicker love seat between them.

"We had an agreement. We weren't going to tell anybody about our...our..."

"Relationship is the word you're searching for." Scott shoved one hand in his pocket and leaned on his cane.

"No, we don't have a relationship. We particularly agreed we wouldn't. Don't you remember? After we..." She dropped her voice into a whisper, "had sex the first time, you agreed we wouldn't tell anyone."

"Well." Scott rubbed a hand across the top of his head and down to his neck. "I didn't tell anyone. Why are you upset?"

She glared at him, both hands fisted at her waist. "David spoke to me about *us*. If you didn't tell him, how did he find out?"

"Oh. He asked me point-blank about what he called the 'zing of electricity' he feels anytime we're together. Meg, he's been my partner for too many years to lie to him. Can we continue this another time? Ellie will wonder if we don't show up pretty quick."

"We don't have anything else to say to each other. I understand the partner thing, Scott, but trust is important to me, and you told me you wouldn't say anything. Whatever we had…going on is over. As soon as you talked to David, you put an end to…whatever it was. Now, let's eat lunch with the family." She stalked past him.

"Hell." Scott followed along more slowly. What had she expected him to do? Lie to David? He couldn't. While she may have started by feeling sorry for him, it had grown deeper. Hadn't it? If she had feelings for him, he wasn't letting her go. They'd work something out.

* * * *

3:30 p.m. Sunday, December 27

Scott couldn't remember a more uncomfortable time. Finally, the meal ended. The tension thick enough, Ellie had sensed the unrest and tried to figure out what was wrong. David kept cutting sharp glances his way. Meg never looked at, nor said anything to David or him. And everyone but Ellie waited. They'd not discussed what they'd do if the call came with her around.

"Mom, let me help you with the dishes." Meg rose and gathered up plates. Ellie followed suit.

"You gentlemen can retire to the smokin' room. Maybe you'll be less on edge," Ellie teased in an ultra-southern accent with a slight giggle following the words. She stopped on her way out, faced back to them, and spoke in her regular voice. "But Joe, you know I don't like that nonsense inside, and if you insist, then you must stay in the study and use the expensive air filter we installed." Then she breezed through the door.

"She's got a good idea, Dad. Let's go. If he calls, Mom won't be around to hear." The three men left for the study.

The old-fashioned Tiffany lamp hanging over Joe's desk spotlighted his cell phone lying in the middle. Scott went to the bay window, leaned around the Christmas tree, and looked out. No cars drove slowly by. None parked near. He swiveled around, facing into the room.

Joe sat behind his desk. David slouched in the wingback chair with one leg thrown over an arm. The jiggling foot defied the relaxed position. Scott couldn't bear the idea of sitting. Every nerve ending screamed. Besides the stress of all they were dealing with because of Joe's blackmailer, Meg's blowup had him on edge. He had to go back to the gym. His modified workout routine would help.

The ticking of the clock on a bookshelf pounded through the silence of the room. Scott made his way over to the unit. Something must be wrong. He hadn't noticed the annoying sound other times he'd been in this room, nor when they'd first come in this afternoon.

Now at close to four, the relentless ticking made his head scream, like an ice pick driving into his brain.

The Eyes of Texas sang from Joe's phone. David stood and Scott moved closer.

"Remember, Joe, you tell him where we decided to meet." Scott leaned forward. "Got it? Joe nodded once. "Hello?"

Noise from the phone broke the silence, but Scott couldn't distinguish the words."

"But I—" Joe held the cell away from his ear. "He's gone."

"Him?" David asked

"What'd he say?" Scott rubbed his temples where the pounding grew worse.

"To meet him in ten minutes at the Burger Shack at the corner of Camp Bowie and Montgomery. He said come alone. He'd be watching, and if I weren't then he wouldn't meet."

"Dad, I can't let you go alone." David moved next to his father's chair and rested a hand on his shoulder. "It's not happening. What if this were all a ruse, someone cooked up to take an easy shot at you?"

"If he wants to be a part of this family, killing me won't accomplish what he wants, son." Joe stood and walked around the other side of the desk. "You understand, don't you, Scott?"

"Yes, but I get where David's coming from. The man might be completely unhinged. What makes logical sense to us doesn't necessarily to Chuck. I agree with David on this. We'll follow along."

"Then for God's sake, make sure he doesn't see you." Joe rushed into the hall, took his coat from the closet, and dashed through the house toward the garage.

Scott and David grabbed their coats and followed. Meg and Ellie were both in the kitchen. Meg's eyebrows rose when they trouped in.

"Heading out on an errand, dear. Be back after a while." Joe pecked Ellie on the cheek.

"What?" She stepped away from the sink, her hands incased in long rubber gloves.

Scott resisted the urge to hug Meg. Her body stiffened as he approached, apparently, still bent out of shape with him. Something he had to work on, but not right now. David leaned down and whispered something in her ear, and then he and Scott reversed direction for the front door.

Joe backed out of the garage before David had climbed into the driver's seat of the large SUV he'd rented or Scott closed the passenger side door.

"What's the plan?" Scott looked at his partner. Lines around his eyes and from his nose to the corners of his mouth had grown more pronounced, clear signs of the stress he was under.

"We'll follow Dad there, but park a block away and walk toward the Burger Shack. I'll watch the front entrance. You take the back."

"What if he's already there? Do we let Joe go in?"

"Guess so. Don't like doing business this way, but.... "

"Me either, but he's an adult, David. Aside from trying to commit him or arrest him, how we can stop him? In this country, everybody's entitled to make stupid mistakes." Scott's gut tightened as he considered the consequences of Joe's "stupid mistake."

They took their positions, Joe entered, and they waited. This brought back memories of various stakeouts he and David had done together over the years. The times they waited back at the station for others to send info they needed for a case. God, he hated waiting. How long would this take? Assuming Chuck had arrived, the meeting should be brief.

Scott grabbed his phone at the first notes of *Jail House Rock*. "Yeah?"

"It's off. Dad called me. Either Chuck made us, or he's testing Dad. At any rate, he'll call Dad Monday. Let's go home."

* * * *

4:30 p.m. Sunday, December 27

"Good heavens, Meg. Can't you light somewhere?"

Her mother's words cut through the mush in Meg's mind. She'd tried to act like nothing was going on. Pacing the house, repeatedly checking the windows, doors, and the alarm system helped her work off nervous energy. Ultimately, if her behavior made Mom suspicious, Dad and David wouldn't be happy with her.

"Sorry." Meg flopped on the sofa in the den. She'd used great creativity to entice Mom to come back here. She'd wanted to sit in the living room. The tree took up a lot of space, but if someone wanted to take a pot shot, the front window provided too much exposure. Meg's stomach clenched at the mere idea of thinking those words in connection with the woman sitting next to her. Being proactive was always best in these situations.

"Don't you want to watch this show on HGTV?"

"Yeah, sure, I do. I've been thinking of redoing the condo, and I saw this advertisement about how to make small spaces seem larger." Did her mother believe her?

"So far, you've hardly seen any of the program."

"You tell me what I missed when it's over, okay?"

"Have you done anything to the condo since we visited last year?"

Meg rubbed both hands over her face, looked at her mother, and admitted the truth. "It's the same. Plain white walls and drapes with the beige Berber carpet."

"Honey, I hate to tell you, but it's pretty boring, and you're not a boring person." She laughed. "Now pay attention here. They've got good ideas." She patted Meg's thigh and tuned back into the show.

Meg took hold of her mother's hand. She'd make more of an effort to come home to visit with her parents. A time would come when they wouldn't be here. Meg's stomach roiled, and her throat tightened at what the loss would mean. Not only to her, but to David, and Kathy. And the grandkids. Gosh, they loved Mimi and Pop-Pop. Please, God, let them be around for a long, long time.

The pinging of the alarm system interrupted her prayer and jacked up her heartbeat. She hopped off the sofa. "Back in a minute, Mom." She bee-lined to the front of the house, sure the men had arrived, but when she got out of her mother's sight line, she pulled her father's gun from the small of her back where a loose denim shirt hid it.

"It's us." Her brother's voice had a calming effect, but she kept the gun out, in case Coffey had somehow overpowered them. Not at all likely, by any stretch of the imagination, but Meg had long ago learned not to take any situation for granted.

"What happened?" With the three men in sight, she returned the weapon to her waistband and studied them. She wanted answers and try as she might, she couldn't read their expressions.

"Where's your Mom?"

"In the den. Tell me, Dad. You can't imagine what I went through waiting here, knowing only you were on the way to meet Coffey." Nerves drawn to the shredding point resulted in her sharp tone.

"I'm going to Ellie, Meg. David, you and Scott fill her in." Her father hung his jacket, patted her on the shoulder, and left.

"So. Talk." Meg planted her fists on her hips, not budging until she got answers.

"It's kind of anti-climactic, Meg."

Scott's voice still had the power to make her middle grow warm. How sick to react this way under the circumstances. She looked away from him to her brother. "Tell me."

"He didn't show up. Something spooked him. The message he gave Dad on the phone was he'd be in contact tomorrow sometime."

"This is so wrong. We've got to make Dad go to the police. Did his phone number register?"

"Nope. Probably a throw-a-way."

"He's playing with us, dragging us around by a chain, and I don't like this." She dropped on to the entryway bench, her head in her hands.

"We can still go with Dad." David put his hand on her shoulder. "Or we can ignore his wishes and talk to the police ourselves. What do you think, Scott?"

Meg looked up. Scott leaned against the wall, the wheels visibly turning. He must be trying out a couple of scenarios, because he didn't respond for several moments.

"As long as we can keep your mother and Meg safe—"

Meg sprang to her feet.

He raised his hands. "I know, I know, you can handle yourself." Scott spoke quickly before she jumped down his throat. "I get it—to continue, while we're reasonably certain we can keep them safe we play along a while longer. That's our best shot at keeping the story quiet. If Coffey or someone else turns out to be Joe's son, all bets are off."

CHAPTER FOURTEEN

10:30 a.m. Monday, December 28

"Why are you giving me these?" Joe glared at the two cards Scott held out to him.

"You need the address of the lab where the DNA test is done," he said. "It's on South Hulen Street. One card is for Coffey."

"I know, I know, Meg gave me these when we set up the first meet."

Despite the seriousness of the situation, Scott smothered a laugh when Meg rolled her eyes at her father. Joe huffed, and shoved them into his pocket.

"Go there directly after the meeting at the Coffee Shoppe. And make sure Chuck understands since you're paying, the results will be sent to you," David said.

"I appreciate your concern, David, about me seeing Coffey alone." Joe rested a hand on his son's shoulder.

The grooves around Joe's mouth had deepened. Hell, he had to share their concerns. If they messed up the second meeting, Chuck had threatened to go directly to the press. Then Ellie would find out. Exactly what Joe wanted to avoid. Could they keep Ellie safe? Joe wouldn't take a chance with her life, but then the blackmailer shouldn't have gotten in the house Christmas Eve, either.

"Remember to call Scott before you exit the car. Leave the phone on and in your pocket, so it can pick up a lot of the conversation."

David talked to his dad like he was two.

"I've got it." Joe paced behind the desk in his study then lifted his shirtsleeve, glanced at his watch. He'd repeated the action less than five minutes ago. He slammed his hand on the back of his chair. "God, this waiting is killing me."

"What are you waiting for, dear?" Ellie stepped inside the room. "What are you all doing in here? Come on back to the den. We can watch a movie or play trivial pursuit. We haven't had a battle yet this holiday." She looked at each of them.

No one spoke for a moment then Meg seemed to snap out of her trance. "Uh, well, we…We're chatting. Right, guys?"

Joe nodded.

"Yeah, Mom." David added.

"Trivial Pursuit sounds fun to me." Meg linked an arm with her mother's. "Come on." She expertly maneuvered Ellie out of the study and toward the back of the house.

Joe let out a long breath of air. "Meg's good, isn't she?"

"Yeah, but if she's stuck here taking care of Mom again, I can guarantee we'll never hear the end of her griping." David dropped onto the sofa, a rueful smile curving one side of his mouth. "She's used to being on the front line."

"So when you go back there to play the game with Ellie, what do you tell her about where Joe and I are?" Scott looked at David then at Joe.

"Tell her…tell her I've gone down to city hall. She'll be mad, but nothing else comes to mind."

David nodded. "I'd say you went for a walk to stretch your leg, Scott, but if she notices the car is gone, she'll only raise more questions."

"Tell her I went for a drive to think about my future." Scott rubbed a hand along the back of his neck. He hated to share the idea, but he'd have to face the subject sometime. Ellie would buy the excuse.

"Good. Dad, don't confront him about the break-in," David said.

"How do I not call him out on Ellie's picture?" Joe's hands shook with what looked like his desire to wrap them around the man's throat. "He claims to be my son? No son of mine would ever threaten my Ellie. Not without consequences."

"We don't know how he'd react to a direct accusation about his actions, Joe. You've got to back off a couple of notches," Scott glanced at David. His father's control stretched to near breaking.

"Otherwise, we won't let you go, Dad," David added.

Joe's hands clenched twice then he relaxed them. "Okay."

Scott looked at his watch. "So you ready to head out?"

"Yeah." Joe's cheek muscle bunched.

"Joe?" Scott met David's gaze again. Were they making a mistake sending Joe out? He had to hold his emotions in check, or he'd mess up the meeting.

"Uh, yeah, I'm ready." Joe moved into the hall and took his coat from the closet.

"Remember to call—"

"I got it, David." Nerves shot his voice up in volume. "I'll call Scott's cell phone before I go into the Coffee Shoppe, and I'll leave it on." He ran a hand down his face. "Sorry about the attitude. Guess I'm more uptight than I realized."

David grabbed him in a bear hug. "It's okay." He stepped back and squeezed his shoulders. "You'll be fine."

Because earlier David had moved Joe's car out of the garage he walked out the front door, but he stopped on the porch and glanced back at Scott and David. Joe nodded once, jogged off toward his car, and climbed in. Scott grabbed his jacket and followed.

* * * *

11:10 a.m. Monday, December 28

Chuck sat in the corner of the Coffee Shoppe, a cup of joe steaming in front of him. Ha! A cup of joe. Joe Bourland would stand in front of him soon, and Chuck would make him steam. He'd arrived early, but at five minutes before the appointed time, his daddy walked through the front door of the shop. He stopped in the entrance and scanned the room. Spotting Chuck, Joe made directly for him.

They must look more alike than Chuck realized for Joe to recognize him right off after only seeing him only at the party. People like his daddy never saw servers. Yeah, must be the family resemblance. Without giving it a thought, a smile spread across Chuck's face.

"I'm Joe Bourland. Are you Chuck Coffee?"

No returning smile from Daddy, but Chuck nodded. "Have a

seat."

Joe sat and slid a card across the table.

"What's this?" Chuck didn't pick it up.

"It's the name and address of the lab where the DNA testing is done. I assume you'd like to move on this quickly and settle the question."

Chuck picked it up and read. The place wasn't far.

"Because I'm paying, the report will come to me," Joe said.

"That's not gonna work. How can I be sure you'll be honest with me?"

"I'll give you a copy of the paper work. What else do you want from me?"

"What's mine." He clenched his hand into a fist, crushing the card.

"Well, let's start the process to determine if what you claim is true."

Heat flooded Chuck's face, and his heart rate accelerated. This stupid man called him a liar. Worse, he called Mama a liar. If no one had been in the store, Chuck would've slugged him. In fact, the idea of beating the shit out of the man who should've taken care of him and Mama looked better all the time. When Chuck proved she didn't lie, he'd take the results of the test and cram them down his daddy's throat. Bourland wouldn't doubt anymore.

"If the report declares you to be my son, I'll do right by you." Joe shoved back the chair. "Follow me to the lab." He stalked from the store.

Chuck hurried to keep up with the older man who got into a car and switched on the ignition before Chuck even pulled open his door. He stayed right on his tail, making sure his old man didn't try anything cute. Chuck continually checked his right, left and rearview mirrors, assured him no family cars followed. Good thing. If they were stupid enough to try something– well, he had something else in mind for them.

He followed Joe into the lot by the lab and parked next to his car.

They filled out a bunch of papers, and the actual testing was over quick enough. He couldn't tell if the attendant recognized the mayor of Fort Worth or not. She didn't make any comment about it one way or the other. Chuck didn't want the information leaking out before he was ready. He'd already pictured a big media event where Joe had to acknowledge him as his firstborn son.

"When do the results come in?" Chuck asked.

"In two to three days, Mr. Coffee. Mr. Bourland, you'll receive the report in the mail."

"Thanks." Joe whirled about and barreled through the exit doors.

Chuck rushed through door of the lab after him. The two men stood in the parking lot.

"Give me a phone number where I can reach you," Joe demanded. "When the report arrives, I'll call you."

"No. I'll call you and come over when you've got the confirmation." Chuck's breath billowed out in front of him in the cold air. He was close. He tasted the first possibility of success.

Joe's face whitened. "No, not the house."

"Why not?" Chuck grabbed Joe by the upper arm. "You said when you got the proof I'm your son, you'd do what's right. You smoke screening me?"

Joe's face grew red, glared at Chuck, and shook his head.

"At some point, you must introduce me to the lovely wife, daughter, and your other son. Let's do it right off the bat."

Despite Joe's attempt to yank his arm away, Chuck held on. "So what're you gonna do? I can come home with you right now, and we can start those introductions, or—" He released his grasp on the older man. He'd show him who was in charge. "Tell you what. I'll play nice, and we'll wait for the report."

Joe nodded. Chuck brushed down the front of his father's coat. "Okay, easy right? I'll call in a couple of days." He waved, leaving Joe standing in parking lot of the lab and deliberately took a route by the Bourland house, the home soon to be his. A smile spread across his face followed by laughter. He slowed the car to extend his enjoyment. Yes, he'd be moving home in a couple of days. He'd sit on the front porch and shoot the finger at all those big shots living in the neighborhood.

Where would he sleep? McClaine's room. Meg would stay in Fort Worth and not return to Atlanta. David would head back to LA, and before too long, Ellie, The Thief, would die. Later Joe would. He and Meg, The Beautiful, would live in the house all by themselves.

After Chuck gained his inheritance, he'd never worry about

working another day in his life. Meg would take care of him, cook, and service him whenever he wanted her, too. Chuck looked up. While he'd been caught up in his plans, he'd arrived at his shitty rental house. The next couple of days couldn't go fast enough for him.

* * * *

12 noon Monday, December 28

Meg's cell sounded, and she jumped up from the kitchen table where David, their mother, and she dueled over Trivial Pursuit.

"Excuse me a minute. I need to take this." A monitor would show her heartbeat bouncing all over. Was her father okay? She walked through the kitchen heading for the front living room, as far away from her mother as possible.

"What happened?"

"Your father's fine, Meg."

He answered her unasked question. She stopped walking, bent over with relief, letting a long breath of worry pour out. "Okay. Good. Where are you? Where's Dad?"

"We're still in the parking lot of the lab. I waited to join Joe until Chuck left. Chuck never saw me."

Meg straightened. "Thank you, Scott. Y'all returning now? We need to see you. Both of you."

"Be right there."

Meg disconnected. She hadn't realized until the words left her mouth how worried she'd been about not only her father, but Scott as well. He wasn't physically a hundred percent. If the deal went bad, needing hand-to-hand, he could've been badly hurt. Of course, the cane was useful in such a situation. But her family was already responsible for enough of Scott's pain and loss.

"Meg?" Her mother's voice preceded her into the hall. "Everything okay? You've been gone quite a while."

"Sure, Mom. Sorry. My boss in Atlanta checking on how I'm doing. I told him he needed me come back and help run things." Damn, the lie came easily to her lips. She never lied. Growing up in her family telling the truth was the expected behavior.

"Well, of course, he does, dear. He's quite lucky you work for him." She slipped an arm through Meg's. "I wish you'd consider moving home. Not to our house, of course, but to Fort Worth." She sighed and raised a hand. "I know, I know. You love Atlanta, but I don't get to see you as much as I'd like."

Meg hugged her mother close. "I'll do better about coming home more often. I promise." And that was the truth.

"All right." Her mother let out an elaborate sigh. "If it's the best you can do. Let's find the fixings for lunch. Maria will start back tomorrow." She pushed open the door to the kitchen.

"What's keeping you?" David hadn't waited for them. The center island covered with everything necessary for a sandwich lunch.

"Every man for himself, huh?" His gaze collided with hers. Questions everywhere.

Meg nodded the best she could do to let him know his father and Scott were okay.

"You got it, sis. Mom's tough competition and my brain worked up a powerful hunger."

Any nerves her brother had showed up in his ability to eat mammoth amounts of food during stressful times. Judging from the size of the two sandwiches he worked on, his insides were tied into giant knots.

"Right. David, I thought I'd heard all the reasons for your appetite." Meg and her brother kept up a steady stream of quips and jabs all the while waiting for their father and Scott's return. At the sound of the garage door opening followed by the door alarm, they both jumped. Meg spilled her iced tea.

"What's the matter with you two? It better be your father, and I'm giving him a piece of my mind for going into the office today. I never heard where Scott got off to."

"Hopefully, he'll be back shortly, too, Mom." Meg wanted to see them for herself and couldn't keep the long sigh from escaping when her father along with Scott joined the group.

"Save anything for us, hon?" Dad dropped a kiss on her mother's cheek.

"Don't think you're pushing me off with a mere peck, Joe Bourland. What do you mean sneaking off to the office? You didn't have the gumption to come tell me yourself. Sent poor David with the message."

"Guess I'm fixing my own lunch?"

"Yes, you are. Teach you to try stealth stuff on me."

Meg loved the sparing between her parents. Her mother's eyes twinkled, and her mouth quirked up on one side. Her father's smile didn't quite reach his eyes, but he did a good job pulling off his part of the game. Meg always hoped for the same kind of relationship herself, but it wasn't meant to be. A shame.

They were such great grandparents, lavishing their attention on Kathy's kids. She and David had been losers on that front.

She glanced to her left when Scott's hand rested on her thigh. He'd slid into the chair next to hers. She should've yanked her leg away, but the look in his eyes warmed places she didn't want warmed with the whole family gathered around the table. Especially when she was furious with the man.

"I'm still voting for supper out tonight. Any takers?" David took a huge bit of his sandwich.

"We're eating a late lunch, and here you are planning supper," her mother chided him.

"I'd like to take you all out to eat." Scott removed his hand from her thigh. "My treat, to say thanks for all the hospitality."

Meg's leg grew cold at the loss of Scott's touch.

"Not necessary," her mother said.

"I know, but I want to do this."

"Let the man be, Ellie." Joe patted her hand. "It's what you'd expect of David if the situation were reversed."

Her father certainly had skills to maneuver around her mother. Before this was over, he'd need every one of his tricks. Meg hoped they didn't end up there.

"Oh, well, when you put it that way. Thank you, Scott. We

accept."

Meg was in a difficult spot with Scott. They shared nothing except a strong case of lust. She couldn't have a relationship with someone who didn't keep his mouth shut when he'd told her he would. Trust and honesty were everything. Except, of course, she'd lied brazenly to her mother earlier.

"How about we check out a tourist spot or two after supper, Scott?" Jeez, couldn't she remember for ten seconds she was mad at him?

"I'm cutting out on you, Meg. You're on your own. I'll ride to supper with the parentals, and you guys go by yourselves." David took a swallow of iced tea.

"Sounds fun. Would this include that large bar I've heard about in the Northside?" Scott popped a chip in his mouth.

"Absolutely."

"David should've taken you the first time you came to town. You can't come to Fort Worth and not go to the world's largest honky tonk." A laugh bubbled out. "I'm beginning to sound like Mom. We've always teased her she was the city's best tour guide." The family launched into story after story of Ellie's escapades. They all did a great job of acting. No one observing would recognize everyone's stress. Everyone's but Ellie.

* * * *

10:30 p.m. Monday, December 28

Dinner at the small Italian Restaurant had gone on forever. A small pain began to beat in Scott's temple. The strain of the uncertainty was catching up with him.

"Aren't you surprised?" Ellie asked him when they first settled into their booth. "Who'd guess you'd find this charming spot in the basement of this strip shopping center. It's been here over 40 years."

"I remember these cozy booths and the checkered table cloths since high school." Meg studied the writing on the walls.

"I remember closing these doors for a little privacy with the girls." David laughed and swung one of the booth doors closed and then open.

"Oh, look." Meg pointed to a set of initials. "Those are mine."

"Who do the others belong to?" Scott asked.

David leaned across Scott. "Oh that's her high school boyfriend, the first serious relationship. We should add our initials tonight. Everyone who eats here does." They grabbed pens and scribbled on the walls and doors.

"This has always been one of my favorite places." Ellie said, humming along with the servers who sang Broadway show songs and old standards. Laughter and wine flowed. It was as if everyone determined to put worry out of his mind for the night. Ellie needed the assistance of Dad and David on either side of her to climb the steep stairs. Scott took longer to make the trip than he did with the ones at the Bourlands.

They said their goodbyes in the restaurant parking lot.

Meg tossed him the car keys. "I should've passed on the last glass of wine. I'll give you directions to the world's largest honky tonk."

Scott tossed the keys in the air. "At your service, ma'am." He opened the door for her, walked around to the driver side, stashed his cane in the back, and then climbed in. "Which way?"

"Straight east on I 30 to downtown then turn left on North Main. It's in the Stockyards."

"Do you plan to stay long?" Scott maneuvered around the courthouse and headed north.

"No. We don't have to go at all if you're tired. I'm sorry. I should've thought." Her hands twisted in her lap, but stilled at his touch.

"I'm glad we're going, but I'm afraid I'll disappoint you if you're expecting me to dance. Even before the accident, dancing wasn't in my skill set."

She laughed. "Interesting description." They drove in silence for the rest of the trip. "The parking lot is on the right up ahead."

He maneuvered into a slot next to a large black truck.

"Come on. We'll find us a few real cowboys, but mostly they'll be the drugstore kind."

Scott followed her in subconsciously glad for the cane. If anyone got out of line, he figured it'd make a good weapon.

"Beer?" Scott gestured toward the bar.

"Yeah. Thanks."

They each carried one to a table. Couples crowded the dance floor. Too bad he wasn't into dancing, it'd give him a good excuse to pull her into his arms. Lots of guys checked Meg out. A well-built cowboy dressed all in black stopped at their table and tipped his hat.

"Care to dance, ma'am?"

"Dan Campbell, when did you learn to dance?" She stood and hugged the man then stepped back. "Dan, this is Scott McClaine, my brother's partner from LA."

Scott struggled up from the table, and they exchanged handshakes, glad to find he was taller than the other man who, judging from his grip must work out.

"Dan and I met on the force here. He used to be on horse patrol."

"Still am. Best of both worlds. Wouldn't do anything else. I've learned to two-step if you'd care to try me out, and if you don't mind?" He glanced at Scott's cane leaning against the table.

"No, of course not." He smiled at Meg. "Go on, have fun. I'll be right here." He settled down in the chair.

"Okay. Be right back."

The smile Meg gave Dan when she took his hand kicked Scott in the gut. His gaze never left the two as they traveled around the crowded dance floor. She looked good with the handsome cowboy cop. Her dark hair flowed around her shoulders. The black jeans cupped her rear. He smothered the long sigh and grabbed for his beer, glad she enjoyed herself, but he wished he'd been the one to put the smile on her face.

She didn't say anything after Dan returned her to the table. The band began a slow waltz. Scott didn't know how he'd manage this, but he'd give it a hell of a good try. He stood and held out his hand. "You game?" And the smile he'd wanted to see directed at him was.

"With you? Sure."

He let out the breath he'd taken when she swirled into his arms. They moved around the dance floor with care. Probably not a pretty sight. He didn't mind, because he held Meg and it felt right, fueling a tiny flame of hope, they could work something out between them.

* * * *

12:30 a.m. Tuesday, December 29

Scott pulled into the Bourland's driveway, cut the lights, and before he could climb out, she'd come around to lend him assistance. It galled him to be slow and not be able to help her. Dancing with her was like a dream. But dreams end. He wished they'd never made love. Leaving in a week would be tough, but he had to. Marty Smith gave him a glimmer of life without serving on a police force. If a chance for Scott at doing something like that existed, it lay in LA where all his contacts were. He'd need time, energy, and focus, but the possibility for life after the LA PD existed. Meg's world was in Atlanta. Maybe if—when he got his life together—no, by then she'd have gone on with her life. Their timing was off. They stepped through the front entrance.

"You have a good time?"

"Mom. Are you waiting up?" She glanced at Scott, an expression of horror on her face.

"No, of course, not, dear. I was reading in the living room and heard you drive up." She eyed Scott. "Did you like our world famous honky tonk?"

"Well, it's big." Big bar. Big cop who danced with Meg a

couple of times. Big, strong, and capable. Scott danced with her but not capably. "Thanks for taking me, Meg. I'm turning in. Good night, Ellie. See you in the morning." When this mess with Coffey got resolved, Scott was out of here. He couldn't leave Meg and David alone before then. Walking away from her was gonna tear out his guts.

CHAPTER FIFTEEN

10:30 a.m. Wednesday, December 30

Scott read his partner's expression before David disconnected from his call.

"I can't extend my vacation," he said.

Meg rubbed her brother's shoulder and rested her head on his arm.

"The whole past week the boss tried to work out a deal for me to stay longer, but the typical holiday crazies are worse than usual. They're calling in everyone."

Scott's heart clenched. The call back didn't include him, because he couldn't help them. Hell. Couldn't be fixed.

He forced his attention in another direction. David must be nearly crazy at the idea of leaving with his father's situation still up in the air. With David's departure, Scott lost the buffer between him and Meg.

He'd pass for being bipolar the way he went from depression to euphoria about their relationship and then back to having no hope whatsoever. His whole life had been knocked on end. He drew in a long breath, held on then let it slowly out. However stressful this was, he wouldn't desert his friends.

"I'll stay until we get this settled. You head on to LA." What he wouldn't give to be able to go back healthy and whole to his job.

Anything.

But his partner's life.

"Thanks, man." David said.

"We'll manage, and we'll keep you up to speed on what's happening here." Meg hugged David then stepped away. "Want me to tell the folks?"

"Yeah, please. I'll pack then I'll stop to say my goodbyes. Can you give me a hand, Scott?"

"Sure." What's this about? David didn't need help to get ready to leave. "What's up?" Scott went right to the point when they reached David's bedroom. "This isn't about packing."

A crooked smile flashed across his face. "Nah. You'd do this without me asking, but take care of my family for me. Don't let Meg run you off on some wild hair. She can be stubborn. Don't sell her short either. She's tough but keep an eye on her. Sometimes she thinks she's superwoman."

"I gotcha covered." Scott laughed. "And I swing a mean cane." He vowed to manage the balancing act between keeping Meg safe and convincing her she was in charge while resisting his lust for her body. Shouldn't be too difficult, right? This operation couldn't end soon enough for him. "We'll keep you in the loop. You're a button away."

"Thanks." David bumped fists with Scott then hauled his bag off the bed. "I better go face the music. Mom's gonna be pissed. I let her assume I'd be here until Meg left. This won't be fun."

Scott followed his partner into the den. Former partner, he corrected himself. Guess he'd never let the title go.

"David, didn't I hear you were going to be here through New Year's?" Ellie asked as soon as they entered.

Meg carried out the dirty work.

"I never said, Mom, but I promise not to wait as long before I come home again. Dad, you two plan a trip out there. It's been a while since you last let me show you the sunny California beaches." He clapped his father on the back.

"You're right, son. Maybe this spring sometime. What do you think, Ellie?"

She swallowed, stood straighter, and hugged David. "Sounds fine. We haven't been out in years. We'll absolutely plan a vacation there."

"Give you a chance to see Scott again, too."

"We certainly like that idea. How about it, Meg? Can you schedule to go with us?"

"We'll see, Mom. Sounds fun."

Was she trying to appease her mother, or did she plan to come to California? A bubble of optimism insisted anything was possible. Scout would love to show her around LA. He'd suggest a couple of days in the wine country, with a stay in the B & B their captain always raved about. A picture of Meg sitting across the table from him on the restaurant balcony, her hair blowing in a soft breeze, flashed across his heated brain. Her low cut top showing the curve of her incredible breasts. In one hand, she held a glass of deep red wine, which matched the color of her lips. Her other hand reached for his—

"What?" The punch on his arm jerked him from his

woolgathering.

"Scott."

Boy, he was in a bad way with Meg.

"Will you stay here while I take David to the airport?"

From Meg's expression he'd better wake up and tune in to the program. "Sure."

"Scott, how long since you've gone to the gym?" Ellie took his arm. "You could fit in a good workout before Meg returns from the airport."

Great, not what they wanted at all. It'd be her and Joe here by themselves. "You know, Ellie, I'd like to challenge you to a game of Trivial Pursuit. I'm certain I can take you." He caught the smiles of relief Meg and David exchanged. They'd told him how Ellie prided herself on being the master at the game.

"It's your funeral, Scott, but I'll give you a shot if you insist. Goodbye, David. Humor me and call when you reach your apartment." She hugged him.

David kissed her on the top of her head then swung his father into an embrace.

"Thanks, son."

"Sure, Dad. Keep me posted. Let's go, sis. The boss won't be happy if I miss the plane."

* * * *

4:30 p.m. Wednesday, December 30

Scott slid his car along the curb and stopped in front of the large white house. The lights blazed from all the windows. He sat for a minute and gazed at the beautiful home and neighborhood. Fort Worth was a good town. Had David's friend been right? Should Scott consider relocating here to work with him in his security business?

Meg handled parent duty while Scott went to the gym where he'd run into Marty Smith again. They'd talked for about twenty minutes. The man invited him to stop by the office to learn more about what the company did.

Scott climbed out of the rental. Marty's interest in him stroked Scott's ego, but leave LA and move to Fort Worth? How often would he run into the Bourlands? Even if Meg didn't come home often, this being her hometown complicated the decision about moving here. Damned if he wasn't beginning to believe there'd be life for him after the LAPD.

He unlocked the front door, went in, and after shutting it off, reset the alarm.

"Scott?" Meg walked in to the entryway hall.

"Yeah." Would he ever get over the rush of desire like a gas well blowing to take her in his arms whenever he saw her after a separation? He'd been gone just over three hours. His knuckles whitened around his cane. "Anything happen while I was at the gym? Mail come?"

"No mail, but our friend called. Mom wasn't around. Dad answered his phone in the study and explained the results weren't in yet."

"Maybe tomorrow then."

"How did the workout go?"

"Interesting. Thanks for holding the fort."

"I've got another meeting with the psychologist tomorrow at ten-thirty."

"I'll take guard duty."

* * * *

11:00 a.m. Thursday, December 31

"Bourland."

Chuck gripped the cell hard enough to make his fingers ached. "So, Daddy, did you pick up the mail? I saw the truck stop by."

No sound from the other end.

"Daddy, what's the matter? You all choked up with the emotion of realizing you have another son?"

"I'd like to show you the results of the tests. How about we meet again at the same coffee shop on Camp Bowie Boulevard?"

"I'd rather come to our house, but okay. Be there in ten minutes." Chuck disconnected and fingered the keys in his pockets before he tore outside. He drove like a bat out of hell. Was Bourland trying to put something over here? Chuck should've insisted Daddy invite his son to the house. His house. He needed to pick out which room he wanted. The tests would prove he was Bourland's son. They had to. Momma wouldn't lie. He'd play along for a while. The man was his father no matter what the goddamned report said.

Chuck bought his tall coffee, added cream, and carried the cup to a table in the corner and settled in minutes before Daddy entered. He came directly over and took the chair across from Chuck.

"Where's the report?" Chuck stretched out his hand.

Joe reached in his jacket pocket and removed a single sheet. Chuck yanked it from him, tearing a small piece. "Shit."

"That's your copy."

Chuck's gaze traveled over the paper. Where was the word "positive?" The nurse who'd done the test explained to him what the report would say to show the man was his father. Where was it? Stupid form. Should be easier to read.

"The answer is on the bottom left. The results are negative. You're not my son."

There. Chuck found the word. Negative. "No. That can't be. Momma always told the truth." He glared at the man across the table. "You screwed with the report."

"No, I did not. I don't know why Peggy told you I was your father. I'm sure she had her reasons. But I'm not." He planted his hands on the table and leaned closer to Chuck. "You listen to me." His voice a harsh whisper. "You're damn lucky I haven't gone to the police about this. But it's over. We'll call it even.

"I paid for a mistake in my younger years, and you got fifteen thousand dollars for doing nothing. Take the money and stay out of my life. I won't turn you in to the cops. You leave me and my family alone. Understand? Don't come anywhere near us. If I you do, I will call the police." Bourland stood, shoved his chair in, and stalked from the store.

Chuck looked down at the paper he'd crumpled in his hand while the old man had raved on. A mistake? *Daddy called his time with Momma and making me a mistake.* Well, Daddy would discover what a mistake he'd made. Time to collect on the payment. The payment came in the form of Ellie Bourland's life.

* * * *

11:40 a.m. Thursday, December 31

"After studying my dreams, I concluded I've got the hots for my brother's former partner." Meg looked across at the counselor. Meg didn't plan to talk about this subject, but here she was. Her crossed leg jiggled. "The couple of times we've made love have been awesome. He thinks I feel sorry for him. I only *condescended* to sex with him to thank him for saving David's life. Somehow he thinks walking around with a cane emasculates him, and I couldn't possibly find him attractive."

"But you do? Find him attractive, I mean?" Grace asked.

"God, yes. It's stupid, but from the moment I saw him when David and I picked him up at the airport, my hormones went on red alert. And in all honesty, he wasn't looking his best then, but something about his eyes, his scruffy beard. I helped him out of the car when we got to the house, he lost his balance, and we fell. He was on top. I was hooked."

She crossed her other leg, but the jiggling continued. She and David shared the family trait handed down from Dad. Fortunately, for them both, they controlled the impulse while working.

"And aren't you grateful to him for what he'd done for your brother?"

"Well, of course. The whole family is." A short laugh burst out. "We warned him we'd gush all over him. My mother adopted him the third night after he arrived. Big ceremony at the dining room table."

"You're sure your feelings are more than gratitude, Meg?"

"Yeah, but nothing I do seems to matter. I've practically drooled all over him and pretty much made a fool of myself. Whenever I'm convinced I've made progress on convincing him, he backslides."

Meg uncrossed her legs, planted her feet firmly on the floor, and leaned forward. "Well, I wouldn't get involved with an alcoholic who didn't recognize his problem. As far as I'm concerned, it's over. I wish him well, but I can't fix what's wrong inside his head."

The counselor nodded. "Impressive, Meg. Susan said you could look at yourself objectively." Grace's pencil scratched the paper as she made notes.

"And so you know I know. It wasn't my fault Hank got killed. The bastard who shot him is responsible. I'm still working on convincing my brother he wasn't the reason Scott got hurt. David's not there, yet, but I'll reach him."

"I'll write Susan and tell her, in my opinion you're ready to go back to work. Of course, you'll need to meet with her so she can sign off on you. But I'm impressed with your work."

"You've been helpful. I confess I didn't put much faith in either of you."

Grace smiled and stood. "I hope to see you when you come back to town. Maybe grab a coffee?"

Meg nodded. "I'd like to, Grace. Thanks." She walked toward the door. "Thanks for seeing me during the holidays." She stopped and reached out a hand to the counselor. "Happy New Year."

"You, too." Grace held the door and Meg marched through, standing taller than when she'd entered. Joy was not too large a word for Meg's excitement about her freedom to return to work. The day appeared to be brighter than before. The cold not as chilling. Meg's laughter bubbled from deep inside. Now if they could get through this business with Coffey.

* * * *

12:15 p.m. Thursday, December 31

Meg parked on the street. Scott's car was in the driveway. Her parents must be home then. The mail should've arrived by now. She scrambled out of the car and into the house as fast as possible. She rushed through the front door, cut off the alarm, and reset the system, but didn't pause to pull off her coat, before she knocked once on her father's study door, and went in.

"Dad?"

He stood behind his desk, his cell phone in his hand. He held it out to her without saying a word. She advanced on shaky legs, holding her breath. Her gaze flew over the face of the device. She read the message out-loud.

"Not related." Her hand stole to her chest as if she'd be able to still the flutter there.

"I texted David just now and wanted to tell you as soon as you returned."

She hugged him. "To say the information is a relief is the understatement of the year." She stepped back. "When are you telling

Chuck?"

"I already have."

"What? Did Scott go with you?"

"No, I left him here with your mother."

She ran a hand behind her neck. Damn. "So how did he react to hearing the results?"

"Angry, of course." Her father dropped into his desk chair. "This meant his mother lied to him. I told him if I caught him hanging around any of us I'd go to the police."

"Good for you, Dad. I'm glad this is over. Promise if anything like this ever happens again, you call the police first and then David and me."

"Yes, little girl."

He smiled at her. Such a different situation than when he last used the phrase with her.

"I'm sorry I caused you all such grief, Meg."

"Crap happens, Dad. We'll make it through. Our family is strong. Does Scott know?"

"No. I snuck out of the house. He and Ellie were engaged in a Trivial Pursuit battle to end all battles. It seemed best to leave them there."

"Since this worked out all right, Dad, I won't read you the riot act." She pointed a finger at him. "But you didn't follow the game plan."

"I'll try to do better. You bring Scott up to speed? I want to visit with your mother for a while." He left the study.

Meg drew in the first healthy breath of air since she'd heard of the blackmail. Damn. Thank God, this was over. She dropped her coat, gloves, and purse on the entryway bench before going in search of Scott. She smiled. Would he still be in the sunroom or have migrated to the kitchen after her mother left? She'd bet in the kitchen. She stepped through the door and stopped. "Maria." They'd forgotten she'd be back at work today. Meg hugged the woman. "How was your Christmas?"

"Bueno, muy bueno."

"Glad to hear that. Hey, Scott."

He nodded.

"I've got everything ready for supper, Meg." Maria slid a large dish into the refrigerator. "Your mother needs to put the casserole in the oven for about 40 minutes, and I've left sandwiches for lunch whenever you're ready for them. I'll be leaving soon."

"Of course. Thanks. Scott, tell me about the Trivial Pursuit game you and Mom were playing." Lame, but she hoped he'd take the hint to leave the kitchen so she could talk with him.

For a moment, his head cocked to the side then he stood. "Sure. Come on back. You won't believe the score."

Meg walked with him to the garden room, where she settled into one of the chairs. Relief left her simultaneously weak and light like a hot air balloon floating over the Trinity River. She reported what she'd learned from her father. "Isn't this great news?"

"Yeah. I'm happy for you." He dropped into the wicker chair next to hers. "Guess it's good I'm no longer a cop if Joe was able to sneak out the way he did."

"Oh, Scott." Meg leaned over and rested her hand on his knee. "You were keeping an eye on Mom. That's what we all wanted you to do and we're grateful for."

Scott stood.

"Where are you going?"

"Upstairs to pack. I'll try for a space available on the first flight heading west."

Meg clamped her hands together in her lap. Her stomach hurt like she'd been slugged. Did he hate being here so much? It never occurred to her he'd leave right away.

His gaze met hers for a minute then moved away. "I told David I'd stay until we finished with this. We have now. I'm returning to LA to find out if there's anything there for me."

"I'm sure you'll find something perfect." If the ache in her middle got any bigger, Meg was afraid she'd throw up. She gritted her teeth for a moment. "Thanks for everything you've done to help with the blackmail situation. I'm sorry you got dragged into it."

"No sweat. This won't take me long." He walked out of the room, his cane making a tapping noise on the hardwoods.

Meg sat with her uncomfortable thoughts. Damn, she'd miss the infuriating man. Well, buckle up, woman. He's got his life, and you've got yours. This was a nice interlude, but now it's over. The door chime beeped, she hopped up, and flew toward the entrance. Surely, he wouldn't leave without saying goodbye. The hallway was empty and when she looked out, she saw her father's car backing out of the driveway. Where was he going? Thumping sounds swiveled her around. Scott, a bag in one hand and his cane in the other, came down the stairs without as much hobble as when she'd first seen him. He'd made good progress in the two weeks he'd been here. Put on weight, grown stronger, and stolen her heart. Damn.

"You were quick. Can I run you to the airport?"

"No thanks. I'm going to drop the rental off there."

"Of course. I don't know what I was thinking?" Actually, she did. Searching for any way to extend her time with the man. "You'll always be welcome here, Scott. Mom, Dad, me, we're all grateful to you for what you sacrificed for David."

"Yeah, I know. You've made your appreciation clear." He glanced away. "I said goodbye to Ellie before I came back down."

Meg shifted her weight from one foot to the other. Did she kiss him or shake hands? What was appropriate in this situation?

He answered the question for her by setting his bag down and pulling her into his arms for a hard swift kiss. Her stomach plummeted to the floor. He shoved her away.

"Take care of yourself, Meg."

"You, too, Scott." He seemed not fazed by the embrace while her legs literally shook. This was like being back in junior high school. He waved once and stalked through the front door. She followed. Scott's rental rolled out of the driveway and down the street. Her breathing hitched while she stood in the open doorway until Scott was out of sight, and then she went back inside, and leaned against the closed the door for several minutes. Now to find a way to go on with life.

"I thought you'd never shut the door."

Her mother's voice carried from the stairway. Good grief, did she see Scott kiss her?

"Were you trying to help out our energy stock by warming up the outside?"

Meg met her mother at the bottom of the stairs. "No, sorry. I saw Dad drive off. Where was he going?" Meg slid an arm around her mother, and they walked toward the living room.

"He went downtown. Last minute details he wanted to check on for the city New Year's Eve celebration." Her mother sat on the love seat. "I'm sorry for Scott to leave. You, too?"

Meg nodded.

"I expected he'd stay through tonight. Nothing worked out between you two?"

"Huh uh." Meg let out a long gust of air. She'd breathe through the pain.

"The kiss in the hall gave me the impression perhaps…"

Her mother had seen them. "No, Mom, just a good bye kiss." Meg's fingers lightly touched her lips.

"Maybe if you both hadn't so caught up in all this blackmail goings on, you'd have been able to spend more time with each other and—"

"What? What are you talking about?" Meg rubbed both hands down her thighs.

"You look dreadfully confused, Meg. Your father told me the

whole business before he left for the office."

"He told you?" Well, damn, a whole bunch of this had all been about keeping Mom in the dark.

"Yes. He groveled appropriately, but I sent him off, because I'm furious and hurt."

"Mom, there's never been anyone else. Dad worships you." Meg dropped down beside her mother on the loveseat.

"Yes, I know. As I do him. I was hurt because he acted as if I was shallow and would've fallen apart if something reminded me about what he did. And because you, David and Scott knew—Kathy too?"

"She only knows someone was blackmailing Dad. We couldn't take a chance of them being here when we didn't know what Chuck might do."

"I'm glad they left. But I am not happy with you for leaving me in the dark."

"But, Mom…Dad was trying…I'm sorry. I didn't know what to do."

"Let me tell you something else, young woman, because I volunteer, keep the family running, and haven't worked for pay doesn't mean I don't have a head on my shoulders."

Meg slid an arm around her mother's shoulders. "Oh, Mom. We all take you for granted, but it's because you make everything you do look easy. Not because you're ditsy. What word do they use for brunettes, anyway?"

"There isn't one, dear, because we're not fluff. We're made of sterner stuff. As Joe is in the process of learning."

Meg hugged her again then squirmed. "What's this?" Her hand fished around underneath her rear then came forward. "It's Scott's money clip. It must've dropped out of his pocket. I'll call him. Maybe I can put it in the mail for him." Meg rose. "Maria's left sandwich fixings for lunch. Everything's ready for supper. We can pop the casserole in the oven for supper."

"You call Scott while I set out the lunch. All this intrigue has made me hungry."

Meg followed her mother into the front hall. "I want one with mustard, please."

"Of course you do, dear." The door between dining room and kitchen swung closed behind her.

Meg punched up Scott's number. Took a deep breath. How would he react to her calling him right after he'd left? Only one way to find out. She pressed the button on her phone. The tone and the front doorbell rang at the same time. Maybe he realized he'd forgotten the clip and returned. She flung open the door. "Forget—" Her stomach dropped to the floor, like when the Giant at Six Flags sailed over the top of the highest point of the track. Everything fell away underneath her. Chuck Coffey "What do you want?"

"Not very friendly, Meg. Here I am in the neighborhood. Figured it was time to stop by to see how everyone was doing. Invite me in."

"No. I understand my father is finished with you. You should leave. Now." Meg shouldered the door to close it, but his foot blocked the motion. "You're not being smart. Back off. You're not welcome in this house." She clenched her hand on the door. What did he want?

"Well, if you're going be like that." Chuck made as if to leave, but without warning shoved the door, knocking Meg back.

Her head cracked against the wall. Stars danced in the blackness. She shook herself to bring the world into focus. Mom was alone in the kitchen. Meg had to make him leave the house. She could do this. This was what she did in her job. Talk suspects out to end a hostage situation. Not all the time, but the different team members took turns doing all of the jobs. The situation wasn't exactly the same, but she had a few strategies to try. Wish she'd been more hospitable when she first saw him standing there, but she wasn't expecting him at all.

"Did I hurt you, Meg? I didn't mean to hurt you." His tone sounded surprisingly sincere, despite the gun he now held in his right hand.

"I'm okay. Not your fault. I slipped." Better. "Chuck, why don't we sit on the front porch for a while. You can tell me something about yourself. And you can put the weapon away." Meg gestured toward the gun as she stepped toward him and the door.

"No. Not outside. I need to be inside. Ellie's here, isn't she? Her car is here. Joe's is gone. And the gimp is gone. I watched them both drive off."

Damn, this wasn't good. Should she holler at Mom to run out the back? Could she make a grab for Dad's gun in her purse lying on the bench?

CHAPTER SIXTEEN

1:00 p.m. Thursday, December 31

Chills ran down Scott's spine and along every extremity, frozen by the ice flowing through his veins at the voice coming through his phone. He'd picked up when he saw Meg's name, but she didn't respond. Coffey's voice filled Scott's car, and he fought the urge to throw up. What the hell was he doing at the house? Nothing good for sure.

Scott checked the rearview mirror and hung a U-turn in the middle of the street. He took the chance of losing the connection with Meg, put her on hold, and called 911. Scott gave his police identification information to the operator.

"There's a hostage situation at the Mayor's residence. Send squad cars to 903 Rivercrest Drive. Chuck Coffee is holding one or more people." Scott hoped he was wrong, but it was more than a possibility. And too damned bad if this meant the adultery story got out. He couldn't take a chance with the lives of Meg and her mother.

"And how do you know that, sir?"

"The mayor's daughter called me, and I heard the guy push his way in."

"Is he armed?"

"Yes, he is." He had to presume the worst. Fear grew like a volcano bubbling up from his gut, nearly choking him.

"Stay on the line, sir."

Like hell. Scott disconnected and flipped back to Meg. He couldn't understand the voices as clearly as before. Maybe she slid the phone in her pocket. He stomped his foot on the accelerator hard enough the power of the car speeding forward forced him back against the seat. Thank God he hadn't reached the freeway before she called. Still, he couldn't drive to the house fast enough. He flew through the second yellow light.

* * * *

1:10 p.m. Thursday, December 31

"Chuck, I'd like to go for a drive with you. Let's go to your place, or we can stop by the pizza restaurant. Was it you there the other evening?"

"You noticed me then. Did you like what you saw, Meg?" He stepped into her space.

With every bit of her willpower, Meg forced herself to nod and stand still while Chuck ran the tip of the gun from her shoulder down to her elbow then back up. Her fingers tingled with the urge to take him down. Only one thing stopped her. If Chuck got the better of her, no one stood between him and her mother.

He ran a hand down her other arm. "I want you. We can finally be together. You'll like what we do."

"Great we didn't end up being related then, isn't it?" Meg stepped toward him, praying the gun didn't accidentally go off. *Please stay in the kitchen, Mom.* If Meg could force him to back up, then she'd make an opportunity to push him through the entrance.

"You're my half-sister, Meg. It's not like full. I couldn't do it to you, if we were full, but we're only half."

Dear God, didn't he understand the DNA report? Confront or not? Maybe not yet. "Chuck, how about the drive we talked about?"

"No. Let's go up to your room?"

He rubbed his hand across her breasts. She swallowed a ball of disgust and resisted her instincts to fight him. She had a better chance of safely disarming him if she played along. If Mom weren't home, this would go down differently. Her teeth clenched and released. She gulped a big breath of air. She'd do this.

"Well, we can go upstairs after a while, but I'd love to go for a drive with you first. Okay?" When she stepped closer to him, his cigarette and alcohol breath hit her in the face, and she struggled not to draw back. She took one of his hands in hers, rubbing her thumb across the back and moved toward him again. He shuffled backwards. One more step and she'd shove him out the entrance.

"Nah." He put on the breaks. "I want to go upstairs with you." He slammed the door.

The chime sounded.

"You said you'd go upstairs with me."

"Sure, Chuck. If you want to." She'd pretend she needed her purse then she'd find an opportunity to grab her father's gun. She backed toward the stairs and the bench. Before she got within reach, he jerked her to a stop.

"Wait, I gotta see Ellie first."

"Why? Let's you and me get it on. Upstairs, remember?" The weedling tone gagged her, but she'd do anything to keep him away from—

"Meg, who was at the door?" Her mother walked into the entry hall and stopped. "We have company?" Her eyebrows rose.

"Mrs. Ellie, I been looking for you." He pointed the weapon at her.

Meg's stomach lurched at the sight of a gun aimed at her mother. "Mom, go into the garden room while I talk with Chuck." Thank God. Her mother pivoted in one quick movement and did exactly as Meg told her. Maybe she recognized his name from what Dad told her.

"Chuck, remember we're going upstairs. Don't you want to anymore?" Meg reached a hand toward him. He swung around wildly, and his gun hit her on the side of her face. Stars circled the dark recesses of her brain, like in the old comics. She staggered toward Chuck. *Mom, please, press the silent emergency alert.*

"I'm sorry, Meg. I didn't mean to hurt you." Chuck caught her close and kept her from hitting the ground. "Oh, Meggy, we'll have such fun. After I finish with Ellie."

Meg used every ounce of self-control not to pull away, praying her mother had reached the garden room.

"Where is she?"

Chuck's focus bounced like a tennis ball, ricocheting from Meg back to the direction her mother had scurried.

"Ellie. The Thief," he yelled then spun on his heel and hauled Meg with him toward the back of the house.

God, he was insane. Meg dragged her feet. Chuck had the gun

in his right hand and his left around her neck. She considered moves to use to get out of the hold, but with her mother in the house, she hesitated to use them. The longer Meg stalled, the more time she gave her mother to escape through the back door.

"Ellie," Chuck bellowed like a wounded animal, continuing to drag Meg with him. "Stop"

Damn, Mom didn't make it all the way. With one hand on the outside door, she glanced back over her shoulder. Fear for her daughter etched on her face.

* * * *

1:20 p.m. Thursday, December 31

Scott pounded his hand on the steering wheel and slammed on the breaks at a stop light, barely avoided running into another car, and then barreled through. A gunshot echoed through the phone and sent Scott's heart into his throat where it parked. "Please, God, let Meg be all right." He whispered the words repeatedly as if by doing so, he'd make them true.

* * * *

1:21 p.m. Thursday, December 31

"You bastard." Meg broke away and ran across the room. "Mom. Mom. Hang on." Meg knelt beside her mother lying on the floor. Blood seeped from a wound in her side.

"Get away from her."

Chuck's voice barely registered as Meg's heartbeat skittered out of rhythm. She yanked a table runner, sending the flowers and vase flying. The crystal broke into a thousand pieces, but Meg didn't pause. She, folded the cloth, and pressed it against the wound. "Can you hold this, Mom?"

"I pushed the alarm, Meg." The words were soft and breathy.

"You did good." Her mother's moan tore at Meg's heart when she settled her more comfortably on the floor.

"I told you, leave her alone." Chuck yanked Meg by the hair and dragged her from her mother's side.

"Let go of me." She reached her hands back to his trying to lessen the pain.

"She must die." Then he let go and caressed Meg's head. "Don't you see that?"

On all fours, where he'd dropped her, Meg glanced up and looked in his eyes, Fear clawed at her heart. Chuck's eyes held no emotion. They were dead and dark. Damn-it. He would not hurt her mother again. She reached deep inside her gut and her mind for her training and experience. Stay calm. Use a soft low voice. "Tell me why, Chuck? What's she ever done to you?" Keep him talking and get his gun.

"It's because of her, my mom was alone. Joe would've stayed with Mom accept for this bitch." He swung back to her mother.

Okay, not the results she looked for. She wanted Chuck to focus on something else. Again, Meg moved and positioned her body between him and her mother. God. Mom's lost color. Surely someone heard the gun shot and called the police. Did she really push the panic button like she said? *Please, God, we need some backup here.*

Chuck paced the room, swinging the weapon wildly. What she wouldn't give to curl her fingers around the butt of her father's gun.

Little chance of that with it tucked away in her purse in the front hall.

"We'd have had money. Mom would've worn warm clothes, and when she got sick, we'd have gotten her the best medical care."

"Chuck, Chuck." Meg wanted to move his attention off Mom, but she wanted to be close if he started firing again. Her mother's occasional moan cut a sharp pain through Meg's gut.

"Chuck." She practically yelled his name

He angled his head as if seeing her for the first time.

"Where is Mrs. Coffee now? We can provide her with the medical help she needs." To Meg's great amazement, Chuck's face scrunched up, his chin quivered, and tears fell.

"She's dead. She's dead." Great bellowing wails came from the man, the gun hanging at his side."

Meg moved then, but words came from her Mom at the same time.

"I'm sorry for you, honey."

It seemed her soft voice penetrated the chaos in Chuck's mind, and he looked up.

"It's terrible to lose your mother. I remember. At first, it's like there's a big gaping hole on the inside, and you don't have a clue how to fill it."

"Stay back." He yelled at Meg, while leveling the gun at her mother.

Meg stopped then glanced back at her mother whose face was now white as the wicker furniture in the garden room. She had to do something soon, or she was afraid she'd lose her mother, too.

* * * *

1:25 p.m. Thursday, December 31

Scott parked a couple of houses down from the Bourland's and lumbered out, leaving the door standing open. No patrol cars or SWAT nearby. He made fast progress with his cane and hobbled around the right side of the house, barely scrunching through the thick bushes to the back yard. The large back windows of the garden room let him in on a scary scene.

Coffey paced furiously across the room. Meg stood with her back to the windows. No sign of Ellie. Not good. With the cane through a belt loop, he used his arms to pull along the ground on his belly past those widows. If Coffey looked at the wrong time, it'd all be over.

Scott's side handled the action pretty well, but his leg hurt like a son-of-bitch. A tree reached its branches past David's room. If Scott could climb up the tree, and if they'd left the window unlocked, he'd be in. Yeah, hot shot, and what do you do against Chuck's gun? Scott had no clue, but he was determined to make the effort.

He grabbed hold of one of several low branches and swung up. Halfway up, Scott paused to check his cane was secure where he'd hooked it into his belt loop. He breathed through the pain ripping his leg apart. Tree climbing not recommended therapy. He lumbered on then swung himself onto the roof jutting out below the window. Despite the cold temperatures, sweat ran down his face and soaked the shirt under his jacket.

Thank you, God. The window slid up without making the

slightest hiss. Like many people, the Bourlands failed to install security system in their upstairs widows, believing the height protected them. Lucky for him. He pushed his cane in, balanced on his good leg and then hoisted the weak one through the opening. He lugged the rest of his body inside, landing with a soft thump. He lay still, listening for any response to his entrance. Nothing. After keeping to the edges in David's room, Scott continued the strategy in the hall, hoping squeaks were limited to the middle, more-used part of the floor.

Straining his ears, he eased down the stairs. Low voices indicated people were still located at the back of the house. What he'd give for a gun, but the cane would suffice. Scott moved his position and peered into the room. Ah, hell. Ellie lay on the floor against the far wall, blood seeping through something pressed against her side. Chuck faced away from the doorway behind which Scott hid. Meg hadn't caught sight of him yet. Probably good. Less chance of her inadvertently alerting Chuck. Scott figured surprise was his best weapon.

"Hello. This is Sgt. Jim Hastings with the Fort Worth Police Department." SWAT had arrived. None too soon in Scott's mind.

"Mr. Chuck Coffee, I'm calling you on the house phone. Please pick up."

The voice echoed with a hollow, tinny sound coming through amplifiers on the bullhorn. Scott didn't care how this worked out as long as Meg wasn't hurt in the process, and Ellie survived her wound.

"Chuck." Meg spoke in a soft and low voice. "Chuck, when

they call, you need to answer."

Chuck paced the room. Was he planning to escape out the back way? Scott hoped the SWAT team got hold of Joe and gained knowledge of the house's layout.

The shrill ring of the phone sent electricity flowing through Scott's system. After the fourth ring, the answering machine kicked in.

"This is the Borland's. Please leave a message." Ellie's recorded voice filled the room followed by the officer's voice.

"Chuck, I'd like to talk with you. Let's see if I can help you work this out. If you don't talk, I can't help." Click. The machine shut off.

"They'll call back, Chuck. If you're not going to answer, let me," Meg said.

Ring. Ring. Ring. Ring. "This is the Bourland's. Please leave a message." Ellie's voice followed by Sgt. Hasting's again speaking faster. "Chuck, please pick up. Let's try to resolve this situation. Chuck, tell me what's troubling you. We can work—" Click.

When the phone rang again and Ellie's voice came into the room from the machine, Chuck lost control.

"No, no. Stop. Stop it." Then he leveled the gun at Ellie. "Shut up. Shut up."

Meg stepped between the gun and her mother. "Chuck, take it easy. They just want to talk with you."

"Get out of my way, or I'll shoot you, too."

I can't wait. Scott lunged into the room. A noise must've

caught Chuck's attention. He twisted sideways, and Scott quickly brought his raised cane solidly down on Chuck's wrist with all his strength. Coffey's scream and the explosion from the gun happened at the same time, followed closely by the weapon hitting the floor. Meg dived for the gun as Scott swung at Chuck's head. Sounds of the front door breaking in came as a canister crashed through one of the back windows. Tear gas swirled. Scott's eyes watered. SWAT members wearing masks broke through the back door.

Was Meg hurt? Scott tried to make his way to her, but a cop grabbed him. In the confusion and coughing, Chuck snuck over to Ellie's side and kicked her. Her screams rang above the bedlam.

"Your fault. Your fault."

"Stop or I'll shoot." A cop's voice loud over the chaos.

"You killed Mama," Chuck yelled and kicked at Ellie again.

One shot and Chuck dropped.

The EMT's swarmed around Ellie. What happened to Meg?

* * * *

1:40 p.m. Thursday, December 31

Meg opened her eyes to blue skies. Where was she? Tree branches towered overhead. Chills ran through her body. She reached for her coat.

"Meg, it's over, you'll be all right." Scott's voice soothed her unspoken worry. What happened? Reality overwhelmed her. "Mom." Meg tried to sit up, but Scott's hand on her shoulder settled her. He pressed a blanket up to her chin. Blanket?

"The EMT's are treating Ellie. She'll recover. Joe rode in the ambulance with her."

"Good, good." She tried to raise a hand to her aching head. Why did it hurt?

"A bullet grazed you."

Had she voiced the question? Maybe. Unless he'd taken to reading her mind.

"My fault. When I hit Coffey's wrist, the gun fired. The ambulance for you is pulling up now. I've called David, and he's hopping on the next plane here."

Meg reached for his hand on her shoulder. "Thank you." Her eyelids closed, but she forced them open. They batted twice before she managed another word. "Coffey?"

"He's dead."

She nodded. "Thank you, Scott. You saved us. Again." She closed her eyes.

* * * *

3:30 p.m. Thursday, December 31

"Hey, sleepy head. I was beginning to worry. Doc said you shouldn't be out more than twenty or thirty minutes."

Meg's gaze circled the room to find the source of the comforting tones. Scott. She gestured, and he came closer. He looked worse for wear himself, scruffy shirt with torn pants and a bandage on the side of his face. She raised her arm and touched his cheek.

"It's nothing." He took her hand. "I lost a battle with a branch when I climbed the tree outside David's room."

"You climbed...?" Her voice faded. "Water...please."

"Here you go." Scott held a plastic cup with a straw for her. "Your brother will be in tomorrow morning early. I'll pick him up."

She frowned, but at the movement, a pain split her forehead. Her hand stretched toward the spot to investigate, but Scott again caught hold.

"Don't. You'll be sore for a while. A doctor put in a couple of stitches. You have a slight concussion."

"Mom?"

"She's in surgery, but expected out soon. Joe got a mid-operation report and she's doing fine. The bullet didn't hit anything vital. More of a flesh wound, but it bled like a son of a bitch. He wanted to check on you, but worried about leaving the surgery waiting room and missing updates on Ellie. I told him I'd stay here and fill you in on everything."

"When can I go home?"

"You can leave the hospital this evening, probably before supper. Meg, the house is a crime scene. You won't be able to enter for several days. I've booked rooms for us at the downtown Hilton. Your father suggested the location because he'd be close to both the hospital and the office."

"Clothes?"

"When you and I leave here, we'll go by, and an officer will go in the house with us while we pick out what the three of you'll want to take with you for a couple of days. Joe also asked me call to cancel their participation in the city's New Year's Eve party."

"The non-alcoholic, family friendly New Year's party. They'll be sorry to miss."

"His secretary had already seen a news report when I called and was relieved to hear Ellie was alive. She said the TV segment she saw wasn't clear."

"A good woman. Mary will take care of things. You?"

"My bag's still in my car."

"You were leaving." Her hand lifted to her forehead again then dropped. "Sorry, Scott. Not much of a New Year's Eve."

* * * *

5:30 p.m. Thursday, December 31

"Okay. This certainly puts a different prospective on what I do every day. After we stop the bad guy and rescue the people, they're left to deal with this chaos to put their lives back together." Meg's gaze took in the blood spatter across the floor and on the back of the sofa in the garden room. A chill slithered up her spine when she stopped near the spot her mother fell when the lunatic shot her. How close Meg came to losing her.

"You up to this?" Scott rubbed her neck. "I can gather whatever you need if you give me some instructions."

"I can manage. I'll call Birchman-Means to put us on their cleaning schedule as soon as the police release the crime scene." Damn. She referred to her family home as a crime scene. The pain in her gut spoke of what a big deal it was. She dragged in a deep breath and stood straighter. "Mom can't see her home this way."

"Is the company you mentioned equipped for this kind of clean up?"

"They're supposed to be the best. Guess we'll find out. Come on." She marched toward the stairs.

* * * *

6:00 p.m. Thursday, December 31

Scott drove under the portico of the Hilton. They left Meg's mother's bag in the car and rode the elevator to the fourth floor. Right after the bellman left them in the large room, Meg's legs crumpled beneath her. Scott caught her and lowered her to the small sofa.

"What can I get you?"

"I'm starving. Missed lunch."

"Me, too. I planned to grab something at the airport to take on the plane."

"Didn't make it there, did you?" She reached a hand to him and eased him down next to her. "You've been a real friend through all of this."

"If you start to thank me again, I may whop you with my cane."

She laughed. Then winced. "I'll keep the warning in mind, especially since I've seen how accomplished you are. Can we eat in here? I want to see Mom tonight, and I'm afraid two trips will wipe me out."

"No problem. Can you manage a shower? You need to clear out all the tear gas from your hair and off your skin."

"Sounds wonderful. You order." She rose. Before she could grab her bag, Scott settled it on the bed. She lifted out her robe, undies, and make-up kit. "I'd like grilled chicken, baked potato with lots of butter, and salad," she threw over her shoulder on the way to the bathroom.

Scott stood next to the table in front of the window facing toward the convention center. Meg was grateful to him. She expressed the sentiment in many ways and often. At one point, sex had burned hotter than a fired pistol between them. He'd about stopped breathing when she took out the pink bra and panties from her case. Were those and the robe all she was going wear while she ate?

The sounds from the shower of water cascading over Meg' naked body nearly drove him over the edge. Food. Order supper. Keep busy. After calling room service, he picked up the security card for Meg's room, and walked to his own on the other side of her father's. Scott showered quickly, put on a fresh shirt and pants, and returned before she'd finished cleaning up. The sounds of the hair dryer told Scott she'd be out soon.

A knock was accompanied by, "Room service."

Scott peered through the peephole before he swung open the door. The aroma of the grilled chicken and the steak he'd ordered made his mouth water and his stomach growl. The server set everything on the table in front of the window. He exited at the same time the bathroom door opened. Scott nearly choked at the site of the woman standing there. Long hair swung around her shoulders. A light colored, silky-looking robe covered her beautiful body.

"Dinner smells great."

"You certainly do." The words were out, but he wanted to pull them back. He didn't need to complicate the situation more than it already was.

"Thank you. Shall we eat?"

Pink color flooded chalky, white cheeks. The trauma left its mark on her.

"You've changed." Meg glanced at him and away.

Scott held a chair for her. Which smelled better, the scent wafting up from her or the food before them? He moved around the table and took his place.

"Yeah. I went to my room and showered while you did." He struggled to keep his gaze from the cleavage at the opening of the robe. Did she have no idea about her effect on him? The bra she put on must be made of thin material. Her nipples played peek-a-boo with him. Somehow, he carried on a conversation as if they sat together in a hotel room every day with her barely clothed. He wolfed down the steak and French fries.

"We can stop at the hospital after I throw on some clothes." She slid her plate back with its half-eaten meal and walked across the room.

Damned if she didn't drop the robe across the bed, grab jeans from the bag and wriggle into them on as if he weren't sitting there. And yes, the bra was thin lace. He tried to control his breathing, but he huffed like a steam engine.

"Are you okay?" She cocked her head at him.

No expression on her face, as if she was little miss innocent. Did she think he was made of stone? Next she took a white shirt from the bag, slipped one arm in then the other, and never took her gaze from his while she worked on the buttons. He took two involuntary steps toward her before her words stopped him.

"Can you help me with my jacket?"

Scott's hands shook while he held the material. Before he moved away, Meg turned in his arms. Her body nudged his. His cock jumped to a dance of anticipation.

"Are you ready?" she asked.

Hell, yes he was ready. He grasped her shoulders and lifted her up on her toes. His lips seared across hers. When she gasped and opened hers, he plundered, breathing with her. He set her away from him, but held on until she got her balance. "Are you?" He held an arm toward the door.

She stared glassy eyed at him, drew in a deep breath, nodded, and then walked away. Scott yanked his jacket off a chair and followed. What possessed him? A crazy man followed Meg down the hall toward the elevator. They didn't say anything while they waited. When the door closed behind them. She stepped close to him.

"More."

She put both hands around his neck and drew his head near. Their lips locked, Scott backed her against the wall, and ground his erection against her. He wanted to be inside, and the stupid jeans blocked him.

"Ahem."

Hell. They'd reached the ground floor, the door had opened, and neither of them noticed.

"Looks like you're going the wrong way, folks. The rooms are upstairs." The guy chuckled as he waited for them to exit.

Scott stepped carefully away from Meg. She didn't look embarrassed, as he might've expected her to be.

She smiled, exited the elevator, and with a long, purposeful stride made for the revolving doors.

* * * *

7:00 p.m. Thursday, December 31

"Hey, Dad." Meg entered the room first.

Scott set her mother's suitcase down in the corner by the closet.

"How's Mom doing?" Meg kissed her father on the cheek, and rubbed the back of his neck.

"She's doing great. They moved her out of recovery and to this room sooner than they expected. Hey, Scott." Joe extended his hand. "How's this one doing?" he nodded toward Meg.

"She's doing well, too." Scott hoped his true thoughts didn't show. She was hot. No way to keep her flame from engulfing him. If he didn't recover, it'd be worth the pain.

Ellie's eyelids fluttered. "Joe?" She reached for him.

"I'm here. Right here and I always will be. Meg and Scott stopped by."

Ellie held out the other hand, and Meg took it in both of hers, leaned over and kissed her mother's forehead. "Hey. Dad's telling me you're a real trooper, doing better than anyone could've expected."

"That's what…we Bourlands do." Her raspy voice was softer than usual. "Water…please?"

"Ice chips are what the doctor ordered." Joe reached for the cup and spoon on the tray. "Here you go."

"Better. What happened to your head, Meg?"

"It's nothing. A small nick."

Ellie nodded then her gaze traveled to Scott. A smile spread across her face. "Too bad I've already…adopted you. Like to repeat…the ceremony." She dropped Meg's hand and gestured him to her side. When he got there, she took his in a surprisingly strong grip. "You're making a habit of saving members of our family. Grateful."

"My pleasure, Ellie. Glad you're recovering well."

"Anything you ever need from us, you speak up, Scott," Joe added.

Scott nodded, but he only wanted their daughter. While the heat was intense between them, how much did it have to do with the near death experiences she kept encountering? After a dangerous assignment, the sex was off the charts, but she needed normality in her life to figure out what she felt, if anything.

He needed to discover where his life was going now he wasn't a cop anymore. He couldn't ask her to be a part of his life when he didn't know where he'd end up. Be a part of his life? What the hell? After David arrived, Scott would take off. As long as he was helpful, he'd stay, but it was past time for him to get out of Fort Worth.

"I'm sleeping here tonight, Meg," her father said.

"Dad, are you sure you'll be comfortable?"

"Make him go, Meg," Her mother's soft voice insisted.

"This is not up for discussion, Ellie. I've already dozed once in the big recliner there. I'd never sleep at the hotel for worrying about you. Scott, y'all go on. Bring my bag tomorrow morning when you come back."

"Okay." Scott gulped. Joe wouldn't be in the room between him and Meg tonight.

"I love you, Mom. Do what Dad and the doctors say."

Ellie nodded. "I will. Want them to release me to go home."

"Glad you stopped by, Meg, but the doctors insist no long visits and you need to rest, too. Scott, take her back to the hotel and insist she go to bed," Joe said.

For a moment, Scott couldn't find his voice, finally he strangled out. "Sure."

* * * *

8:00 p.m. Thursday, December 31

"I'm afraid Mom will be ready to come home before the house is ready for her." Meg looked at Scott as they rode up in the elevator. "No telling how long before the police will release it, and then the cleaning company has to come in. If the hospital lets Mom leave Monday, where will she go?"

"If she has to join Joe here at the hotel for several days, it won't be all bad. Gives her longer to deal with all of this turmoil." The doors slid open, and they walked down the hall.

"You're probably right. They seemed okay, didn't you think? I mean together?"

"They've been married a long time. I imagine they've learned skills for dealing with the bad stuff."

He slid her key card in the slot. Would he stay with her if she asked? She shifted in the open door to face him. The worst to happen is he'd say no, and he might say yes. *Come on, Meg. Go for it.*

"You like to come in for a while?"

"I'd better pass. It's been hectic around here. You need to rest. The next several days will be a challenge. There'll be more questions. The story will hit the newspaper."

"I suppose you're right. In the morning then." She closed the door. His footsteps trailed away. Over after all. He'd only wanted a roll in the hay and wasn't interested in long term. She'd made a fool of herself. Better than if she hadn't tried.

What she'd give for a drink right now to help dull the hurt, but the doctor nixed the idea for a couple of days. Her head ached. Her gut passed for a pretzel. Her heart mangled. At least Coffey was out of the picture, and she hadn't been the one to kill him.

She took a tank top and leggings from the suitcase. Tomorrow was soon enough to put clothes in drawers. A housekeeper left the covers turned down. After changing, she flipped off the lamp and fell into bed. Her body ached for Scott's touch, for the comfort of his body curved around hers, for a repeat of the mind-blowing sex they shared. She'd be a long time recovering from this loss.

* * * *

2:30 a.m. Friday, January 1

Meg's eyes blinked a couple of times. Where was she?

Chuck Coffey chased her and her mother. Gun shots. Her mother fell. Then the blackmailer turned the gun on Scott and fired. Scott tumbled to the ground. Blood flowed from a dozen wounds on his torso. Meg tried to stop the bleeding, but he'd been hit too many times. Gasping for breath, she crawled to the bathroom and wrenched on the faucets. The water touched her skin, and she snapped to reality.

No blood covered her hands. A dream. She leaned her head against the wall. Just a dream. Only a dream. She pulled in several deep breaths and let them slowly out. With a cold, wet washcloth she wiped the sweat off her face and dragged in three more deep breaths.

Fearing a repetition if she returned to bed, she turned the TV volume to low and curled up on the couch. Surely, her life would improve. Focus on the positive. Everybody important to her was alive. Still, what a way to spend New Year's.

* * * *

8:30 a.m. Friday, January 1

What is the noise? It's the holidays. Why can't Mom let me sleep? Meg sat straight up on the couch. What was she doing here? Pounding came not just from her head. On stumbling feet, she made her way in the dimness, flipped the lock, and opened the door. Scott stood in front of her fully dressed.

"Thank God."

His gaze dropped down to her toes and back up. She stood in the open door in her tank top and leggings.

"What?" She moved behind the door, and he took her stance as an invitation to enter. Not what she'd intended.

"I called on the cell several times, and you didn't answer. Not the room phone either. I was scared out of my wits." Scott paced across the room and back to her. "You okay?"

Meg kept her hands behind her, twisted in a knot to keep from tearing the shirt from his body to search for the bullet wounds. The dream consumed her. "Yes. Guess I didn't sleep well." She ran a hand through her hair. "What time is it?"

"Just after eight-thirty. But the police expect us for a ten-thirty appointment, and you wanted to check on Ellie first and take Joe's bag to him." Scott paced, never settling on a single piece of furniture. His cane made no sound on the carpet. "I'll fix the coffee and you dress."

The heat seared Meg's face. Scott couldn't stand to see her like this. Pull yourself together, woman. There's nothing here for you. Move on with your life. "I'll be ready in ten." She grabbed clothes and flew to the bathroom. When she came out, the distinctive aroma of coffee filled the room. She swigged down a couple of sips and then with the to-go cup in one hand lit out for the door, assuming he'd follow.

* * * *

3:50 p.m. Tuesday, January 5

Somehow, they'd gotten through several agonizing days. David arrived and took the room across from Scott. Meg was grateful for the buffer her brother provided. The police released the house Monday morning, miracles happened, and Birchman-Means came out the same afternoon. The company spokesman wasn't certain when the family would be able to move back to the house.

Her father's press conference would begin in ten minutes.

They'd all be standing by his side. Her mother browbeat the doctors to spring her from the hospital. Mom was amazing, the strongest of any of them.

Scott would be nearby and wield his cane if necessary to insure they got safely away. They'd all talked about it, and her father was adamant to come clean about what happened. Kathy came down to check how her mother was, but because of the kids, went back to her family in Oklahoma.

They'd decided to hold the news conference in front of their house with remnants of crime scene tape visible. The media vans had already gathered when the family arrived in the limo. Dad insisted on using one to keep everyone together. His solicitous behavior toward her mother made, Meg blink away tears. They'd serve no purpose. She and David stood on either side of Mom and behind their father when he took the microphone.

"My fellow citizens, I come before you today to clear the air about activities when I was   a young man. Activities with repercussions into the present day. Shortly after I married this wonderful woman standing behind me, I had an affair. I broke it off. Mrs. Bourland suspected, and I confessed. By the grace of God, she took me back, and we've been blessed with a good marriage ever since.

"In October I received the first of four blackmail letters. The writer threatened to go to my wife and force her to relive the details of my infidelity. In an effort to shield her, my family, and because of my pride, I paid the money. That wasn't the end. Later notes stated he'd send the story to the newspaper.

"Ultimately, I paid money to silence a man who believed he was my son. DNA proved otherwise, but he wasn't able to accept the fact and came after my family in our home. He injured my wife, Ellie, in the attack. Thanks to the work our good friend Scott McClaine, our capable Fort Worth Police Department, and my daughter Meg…."

Her father's throat worked as if he fought off tears.

"The incident was resolved, resulting in the unfortunate loss of the blackmailer's life. I provided the police with the blackmail letters, my responses to the suspect, our cell phone information, and all of the statements from our providers.

"I apologize to the citizens of Fort Worth. More important, I apologize to my wife Ellie. My actions put her life in danger."

Her mother stepped forward and slid her arm through her husband's. He glanced at her then cleared his throat. "My daughter's as well. I'm sorry for the loss of life, but I'm grateful my family has been spared.

'I've submitted my resignation to the City Manager and the Mayor Pro-Tem of the Fort Worth City Council to be effective today. Thank you for the honor of serving in this position for 16 years. I will take no questions." He turned, and holding Ellie's arm, they walked from the front porch. Meg and David followed. The reporters shot questions at all of them at a deafening level and at the rate of machine gun fire. Scott and the police shielded the family as they made their way to the limo.

They all rode back to the hotel, but the crazy media people followed them.

"Dad, you should go away for a while to give the story time to die down." Meg took note of the tight grasp her parents held on each other. "What do you say, guys?" She sought her brother and Scott's support.

"She's right," Scott nodded. "Give them time, Joe, and the next new story will pop out and wipe you off the front page of the paper and the off the Internet."

"It's the way the media works, Mom. The sooner you can leave the better." David smiled at his folks.

"What about the house?" her mother asked.

"This will give the cleaning company more time to finish their work." Meg patted her mother's arm. "Maria can come in and put on any finishing touches, and when you come back, it'll be like new."

"Where do you want to go, Ellie? I'll take you any place."

"How about Hawaii?" Meg suggested. "You all loved the place when Kathy and Ron got married there, and you always wanted to go back. This may the perfect time."

"How about it, Ellie? What do you say?" Joe persisted.

Her mother kissed her father on his cheek. "Aloha."

* * * *

8:30 p.m. Tuesday, January 5

Meg set her half-empty wine glass on the table in the hotel's restaurant. The family, including Scott, spent the rest of the afternoon after the press conference working on travel arrangements for everyone. Unfortunately, no seats were available until the following Sunday.

"You know, Mom, if there'd been seats on an earlier plane, you'd be leaving with only the clothes on your back," Meg said. "We'd never get you packed to leave much before Friday anyway. You'll only be here an extra two days."

"But dear, I remember we don't need much in the way of clothes for the islands." Her mother sipped her wine, a twinkle in her eye.

Meg laughed. "True, but Kathy's coming down tomorrow, and we can take a couple of days to make sure you and Dad have everything you need."

"Oh, I can hear the drain on our bank account," her father moaned. The guys laughed.

"Sweetie, you're in no position to complain."

Tension circled the table in the silence.

"You are quite correct, Ellie. Forgive me. Her father picked up her mother's hand and kissed the knuckles.

Meg held her breath, waiting for the response.

"But of course, Joe." Her mother leaned over and kissed her husband's cheek.

A sigh passed her lips, and Meg smiled at her brother. Somehow, her parents would be all right.

"I'm sorry you and Scott can't stay longer, David," her mother said.

"Gotta go back to work, Mom, and Scott needs to meet with his therapists in L.A. Our flights are early in the morning. We'll say our good-byes tonight. You able to look after these two, Meg?" David dug into the steak he'd ordered.

Blood red. Meg couldn't stand to look and focused on her tilapia. "Sure, Kathy arrives tomorrow and, we'll go shop for beach clothes and items for the house. When Mom and Dad return from Hawaii, everything will be ready for them."

Keeping up a steady stream of chatter seemed to put a buffer in place between her and her feelings for Scott. They'd not had any time to talk because someone was always around. She couldn't drive him to the airport tomorrow because he had the damned rental to return. Her leg jiggled under the table, and Meg fought to keep her hands still.

"Which hotel do you have reservation with on Kawai, Ellie? Scott asked.

The center of his T-bone glistened pink. Made much more sense to Meg.

"We're not in a hotel. We're renting a house, which belongs to one of Joe's friends. They frequently lease it for weddings, but nothing was booked for the next several weeks.

"Near a beach?" Scott asked.

"Actually, right on the beach. It's a gorgeous place," Joe said.

"Meg, show him the pictures we found on the website," her mother said. "I'm sure Scott would enjoy them."

Scott's gaze touched hers and bounced away. "Sure. I'd like to see'em."

Meg's stomach knotted. "I'll show you when we go upstairs." Maybe she'd take the opportunity to talk about them. If the term applied.

The leisurely meal finally ended. The hour struck ten when they stopped outside her parents' room.

"David, you must do a better job of coming to visit, now promise." Her mom kissed him on the cheek.

"Yes, ma'am. I promise. Can you stay out of trouble, Dad, until you reach Hawaii?" David hugged his father.

"Your mother is keeping me on a pretty short leash for a time, right dear?" His smile indicated his contentment with her plan.

"You've got that right. This will be the first vacation in years he hasn't taken work along with us. I expect to have your undivided attention, Joe." Everyone chuckled then Joe patted Scott on the arm.

"If you don't find something you like out there, consider coming back here. I'm sure we can find you something." Joe shook Scott's hand. "You know how we feel about you, son."

"Of course he does. After all, we adopted him." Ellie hugged Scott and dragged his head down to kiss his cheek. "You take care and keep in touch." She kissed Meg. "We'll see you for breakfast?"

"Sure, Mom. About nine-ish?"

"Okay. We'll make our shopping plans, and be ready to go when Kathy arrives."

"Sounds good." Her parents went into their room. Meg glanced at her brother and Scott then away. Now what?

"I'm hitting the hay. I'll meet you in front of the hotel at 6:30

Scott, and we'll return our cars before heading back to the land of warm. Meg, take care of the parentals. Glad Kathy can come down to help."

"Yeah." She hugged him. "I worry about you. Be safe."

"Sure, pigtails. Always. You, too. Scott take a minute and look at those pictures. They'll make you consider changing your plans to fly out with my folks." He laughed and moseyed down the hall to his room across from Scott's.

"You don't have to come in because everyone is telling you, but the pictures are beautiful." Her breath stopped while she waited for his response.

He nodded. "I don't want to disappoint the family."

She let out her breath, dropped the card in the slot, an opened the door for Scott to enter.

"I've never been to Hawaii, but others sure talk about how beautiful the beaches are there. I never had enough vacation to make the flight seem worthwhile."

"I've only been once for Kathy's wedding." Meg walked to her laptop on the desk and flipped the top open. "Have a seat. I'll take a moment to pull up the web site" For whatever reason, her fingers refused to follow her brain's commands. When Scott finished with the pictures, he'd walk out. She'd only see him occasionally if he came back with David for a visit when she happened to be home.

"Having trouble?" He walked up right behind her and leaned over her shoulder.

Finally the pictures. With him standing close, she had a great deal of trouble focusing on anything but him.

"Nope. Got them." Meg hopped up and made room for him at the desk. Now, she leaned over his shoulder, drawing in his wonderful male scent. Whatever aftershave he wore punched all her buttons.

"Wow." He whistled. "The back of the house, huh?"

"Yep."

"Some view. The lawn is lush. Is the beach beyond the small stone wall?"

"Yeah. The reviews we've read say you can walk on the beach for about a mile."

"You afraid they'll stay? Great weather year-round. None of this 30 degrees with a wind chill of 15 we've experienced while I've been here."

"I suppose it's possible. Dad will have to find something to do. He's always been super busy with oil and gas work and then politics. His schedule has been booked. It will be different now."

"You worried about him?" Scott swung around in the chair. His gaze pinned her.

"Yeah." She struggled to keep her hands from clasping together. "Wouldn't you be?"

"Big changes staring them in the face."

"And for you."

He nodded, his lips making a firm line. He stood. "I better head out. I'm glad your folks can take off for a while. Thanks for showing me the pictures."

"Sure." Meg stepped back and shoved her hands in the pockets of her slacks. She wouldn't reach out for him first. But damn, she wanted to.

"Meg." He glanced down. His hands fisted at his side. "If things were different...."

"What? If things were different, what?" Her feet moved closer to him, as if they had a mind of their own. "Please, Scott."

He shook his head and reached for his cane, which he'd left against the desk. "But they aren't." His fingers whitened when he grasped the stick. "I'm glad Kathy is coming down to help with your parents." He walked to the door, opened it, and stood for a minute before glancing over his shoulder. "Take care. Meg. Find a good man whose worthy of your love." The door closed soundly behind him.

"But I did." The words fell softly like her tears.

CHAPTER SEVENTEEN

8:30 a.m. Monday, March 8

Scott cut into the sizzling ham steak on his plate. David and he must've eating a zillion breakfasts in the small coffee shop. This morning, the aroma ramped up his hunger more than usual. He tore into the steak and eggs. Then burned his tongue with the hot coffee. Damn.

"Make sure you check out the Texas Coffee Shop in Fort Worth. It's good for lunch and breakfast." David took a bite of pancake, dripping with syrup. "Their pie's great too." He set his fork on his plate, looked down then up. "Man, I can't get over you moving to my hometown."

"It's your fault. You introduced me to Marty."

"And he recognized a good deal when he saw one. Took longer for you to cave than I expected." David spread jelly on his biscuit. "I don't mind taking the blame, but man, how am I going to manage without you around to harass?"

"You'll be busy, and you'll hardly notice I'm not here. I like Logan. She'll be a good for you."

"I don't know. Never worked with a female partner before."

"Treat her like she's one of your sisters." Scott grinned at David. A good looking woman, Jennifer Logan wasn't as tall as Meg or Kathy, but she was strong. She'd taken out a guy in the gym who out-weighed her by at least fifty pounds. He liked the way she stood up to David when they got into an argument over procedure at dinner one night. In the end, they'd called the battle a draw, but Scott admired her. The development of David and Jennifer's relationship would be interesting to follow.

"Speaking of my sisters—"

"Is Meg all right?" Scott's gut clenched. She was the one reason he'd hesitated about taking the job with Marty's company. Finally, he'd decided the chances of them running into each other were slim. She lived in Atlanta, and except for coming home for Christmas, he figured she'd be too busy to make the trip during the rest of the year.

"Yeah. She's fine. Kathy told me she'd been seeing an Atlanta lawyer."

"Oh." Scott shoved his half-eaten meal away. Wasn't as appetizing as when he took his first bite. Given her history he should be happy she'd found someone. "A lawyer, huh?"

"Yeah, a high-powered dude with lots of money."

Scott struggled to form words over whatever had taken a strangle hold of his throat. "Good for her."

"I kind of hoped you two had worked out whatever your differences were. What happened?"

"Nothing to work out, David."

"Oh?"

"Your imagination, my friend. Thanks for putting me up last night. I should've gotten rid of more stuff. The movers took longer loading up the truck than I thought."

"No sweat, man. Not a good idea to start on the long haul in the dark anyway. Glad you decided to stop one night on your trip. I've never understood the crazies who drive straight through. Accident waiting to happen." He concentrated on eating, powering through the meal, as if it might be his last then asked, "When do you start work officially?"

"Next Monday. I've got a reservation at a residential hotel until I can find something more permanent." Scott pushed away from the table and David and he both stood. "Guess it's time." He grabbed David and slapped him a couple of times on the back. "You take care of yourself, man, and give Jennifer a chance, okay?"

"Sure. Keep me posted on how the new job goes." David left money on the table for the meal, and they walked outside to the parking lot. "Make sure you stop by to visit with Mom and Dad after you arrive. If you don't, I'll be in the doghouse, for sure."

Scott climbed into his large SUV and started the engine then lowered the window. "Take care, buddy." He bumped fists with David one last time then drove out of the parking lot and hit the road heading east.

* * * *

11:00 p.m. Wednesday April 21

Scott settled into his Fort Worth apartment down on West 7th Street. Lots of restaurants, bars, shops, and a movie theater were within easy walking distance. His place was only ten minutes from Marty Smith Security in one direction and the Bourland house in another.

He fell into the routine of stopping by their house once a week. They'd eat one of Maria or Ellie's great suppers, or he'd take them out. Ellie reminded him she'd been serious about the adoption, and a good son stopped by at least once a week. With none of their kids in town and his parents gone, they filled a void in each other's lives.

Joe hadn't seemed his usual self, tonight. In fact, he'd excused herself and gone up to bed early. The family experienced a rough time last winter. Only natural sometimes everything would weigh on him. Scott and Ellie worked on a 1000 piece puzzle set up in the garden room. They'd made enough changes no remnants from the shooting remained. It was just a pleasant room.

"This has been harder for Joe than either of us expected. He'd played the politics game for a long time, and he's lost without it," Ellie said.

"You can help him find other interests," Scott encouraged.

"Yes, but he has to try some things before he can find one or two of those he wants to focus on."

"Knowing you, I'd guess you suggested some activities, right?"

Ellie nodded. "Of course. Dancing lessons, a foreign language course, cooking classes. Nothing has caught his fancy. I dragged him up to the gym with me, but he didn't want to go when I went. He doesn't go on his own either."

"The membership at the club has been a nice perk of working for Marty's firm. I'll ask Joe to go with me."

"Would you, Scott? I'm sure he'd enjoy that."

"Don't give up, Ellie. We'll blast him out of the house and back into the world again."

"I'm glad you're here, Scott. I'm getting a glass of wine. Would you like a beer?" Ellie rose and sauntered toward the kitchen.

"Be nice." He followed her.

"What do you love best about the business?" She walked in from the butler's pantry with the drinks. "This okay? She indicated the kitchen table.

"Sure." He held her chair without any twinges then dropped down next to her. Scott swigged from the long necked bottle. The cold sting hit his throat. "Good stuff. What do I like best? When Marty and I sit down to brainstorm strategies for making a home or business safe... those are the best times. Each location has its own unique features. I loved being a cop, Ellie, but I never guessed the pleasure of being proactive. Helping people protect themselves before bad stuff happens is a nice change. It's makes for a positive way to live life."

Ellie reached across and patted his hand. "You haven't met any interesting females, yet?"

Scott stalled with a couple of swallows of beer. What could he say? Ellie's beautiful daughter was the only female to interest him. But she lived in Atlanta. "Huh-uh. But I've been pretty busy settling in."

Ellie didn't say anything, but her eyebrows rose, and she stared him down until he shifted his gaze. "Listen, Ellie, great supper as always, and we made some good progress on the puzzle."

Ellie laughed. "I'm pretty darn good, if I do say so."

He stood then crossed the kitchen and set his empty beer bottle in the sink. "I'm heading out. Have an early meeting with a potential new client."

"Good luck with the presentation." They made their way to the entryway.

He gave her a hug at the front door. "Next weekend is my treat. We'll be going out."

"If you learned to cook, Scott—really cook—maybe you'd find an interesting female who'd like to help."

"Yeah, well. We'll see." He kissed her on the cheek. "I'll come by about 6:30 Friday to pick up you two."

"See you then. Have a good week."

The door closed, and he ambled to his car through balmy late spring night air. All considered, he was a fortunate guy to have such a great job and friends like the Bourlands. Scott would never be a hundred percent physically, but he was useful, doing important work.

* * * *

10:30 a.m. Thursday, April 22

The early morning meeting went well, and Scott flipped through pages of the blueprints for Smithson's, a high-end decorating company only blocks from where he lived. They were relocating after being broken into at their former site and losing merchandise. They were adamant about making sure they had all the bells and whistles to protect their stock and employees.

Scott's phone buzzed, and he answered with only half his mind on the call while he studied the plans on his desk.

"Scott—"

"Hey, David. How's it—

"Mom called me. Dad has possibly had a heart attack. Can you meet them at the emergency room of Harris Methodist downtown?"

Scott clenched the cell in his hand. "Of course. I'll call you after I find out what's what." Adrenalin spiked. Damn, how life changed in an instant from being content to full-blown fear for his adopted family. He called Marty, explained the circumstances, grabbed his cane, and made his way from the office as fast as he was able.

He GPSed the hospital location and made a quick trip to the emergency room. "Ellie." She sat straight backed in a chair staring at the double closed doors. She glanced up and some of the stiffening went out of her. Her hand fluttered in his direction. He hurried across the floor and took hold with both of his. "How's he doing?" Scott sat down next to her, rubbing her hand.

"I'm glad you came, Scott. They've got Joe in the back and won't let me be with him. Can they do that?"

The change in the woman from the one Scott had eaten supper and worked the puzzle with last night stunned Scott. All through Christmas except for when she'd been in the hospital after Coffey shot her, she'd been the stereotypical matriarch of a proud family. While Joe seemed to rule the roost, she'd been the one in command. Now, her face was white and drawn. Hard to find the same person in her.

"When they've made him comfortable, I'm sure they'll let you go back."

"How did you know to come here?" Ellie glanced in his direction then back to the doors.

"David called me. Did you let the girls know?"

"I didn't want to worry them until we have a clear understanding of the situation."

"You've got strong kids, Ellie, like their mom. They'd want to know and to come home. Provide them some lead time to make arrangements."

"I'm not thinking real clearly, I guess."

Fwoosh. A tall, blond man much too young to be a doctor stepped through the double doors. "Mrs. Bourland?"

"Here." Ellie rose, her back again ram-rod straight, but her fingers clutched Scott's hand.

"Mrs. Bourland, I'm Dr. Hancock. Would you take a seat?" His gaze moved to Scott who stood next to Ellie.

"He's family. You can speak freely in front of him."

Scott's heart swelled at Ellie's trust in him. He took a deep breath and forced his attention to the doctor's voice.

"Mr. Bourland is stabilized, but I'm admitting him for tests. It's possible he has an arterial blockage. If that's all we've got, the balloon procedure is routine, and afterwards we'll get him home within a couple of days. Would you like to see him, now?"

"Oh, yes. Thank you, Doctor." Ellie stopped before following. "Scott, will you let David and the girls' know?"

"Sure. You check on Joe." Ellie followed the young doctor

through the double swinging doors. Scott couldn't begin to imagine how she felt. Caring about another person caused a lot of pain. Well, maybe he could. Pictures of Coffey holding a gun on Meg when she got between him and her mother flashed across Scott's mind. Yeah, caring about another person hurt like hell.

Scott took his cell from his pocket and called David with the latest.

David's breath whooshed out. "Okay, we can deal. Let me tell you, man, my head went right to the dark side imagining Dad dead, and the funeral—not a good place to be. How's Mom holding up?"

"Pale when I got here, but the doctor's report on Joe put color back in her face."

"As independent as Mom is, we've always worried about her if Dad went first. He's everything to her, and she to him." David drew in another ragged breath and then let it out. "Well, I guess we got the full picture with the blackmail. He went to such extremes to protect her."

"Ellie's a strong woman."

"More than Dad gave her credit for. Speaking of strong women. I called the sisters. Kathy's leaving this afternoon to drive down."

"She bringing the kids?" Ronny in a setting supposed to be quiet and peaceful? Probably not happening.

"Nah, they've got a young woman who comes in and stays whenever she and or Ron take off. Lucy will pick up the slack while Kathy's down there."

Scott nodded and said, "Sounds like a good plan."

"Yeah. Ronny's a great kid, but we recognize he's something of a terror, and the hospital is not the place for him." David laughed.

"What about Meg?" Seeing her again would be rough, especially if she brought the lawyer with her.

"She's got an early flight tomorrow morning. Can you pick her up? I won't be in until close to noon. Kathy will want to be at the hospital with Mom."

"No sweat." He rubbed his damp palm on his pants leg.

"Thanks for stepping in, Scott. You are a life-saver. Again. I'll contact you with flight information for both of us."

"Hang in there. Joe will be okay." Scott disconnected.

"Scott."

He turned. Ellie stood in the middle of the half-opened doors.

"Yes, what is it?"

"Joe wants to see you."

"Me?"

"Come on." She waved for him to hurry, then grabbed Scott's arm and rushed him through the doors before they closed. They passed several of the separate patient cubicles. Ellie stopped and moved aside a curtain. "Joe, here's Scott."

"Hey, Joe." Scott forced a smile for the man with the pale face he'd grown to care for.

Joe reached a hand out, and Scott moved closer.

"Ellie, grab a cup of coffee and leave us alone, please."

"We all know who the boss is in this family, so I'll go quietly, but I'll be back." She hugged Scott and then stepped outside the curtain.

He couldn't imagine what Joe had to talk with him about, but anything Joe wanted, Scott would give.

"You're looking good, Joe."

"I look like hell, but they seem certain they can fix me up. Pull up a chair."

"That's what I hear." Scott stuck his cane in the corner, sank into a chair, and leaned forward to make sure he heard everything Joe said. His voice wasn't near as forceful as usual. "Can I do anything for you? I've talked with David, and he spoke with Meg and Kathy. She'll be in later today, and she's not bringing the kids." Despite efforts, his smile snuck out and Joe's matched his.

"My grandson's not on the recommended list for sick rooms?"

"Nope, he isn't."

His smile faded. "Which leads me to the reason I asked you back here. I want you to look after Ellie for me, even after the kids arrive. If the procedure doesn't go…doesn't go as hoped… well, they'll be dealing with their own pain."

"Of course, Joe. You don't have to say anything. You can count on me to help Ellie and your kids."

"Good." Joe nodded once. "Now to begin with, Ellie doesn't need to spend the night here. She'll want to, and I'd prefer her at home in our bed getting a good rest."

"I'll do what I can, Joe, but she's a pretty stubborn lady."

"You'll think of something." He sighed and his eyes closed, but popped open when Ellie came through the curtains.

"Are you guys finished?"

"Yes, Ellie we are. Here's the deal. You can hang out here with me this afternoon, but Scott is taking you home this evening. You sleep in our bed tonight."

"Not happening, Joe Bourland. I'll be right here by your side." Her fists sat on her hips and she planted her feet apart, ready for a fight. Joe cast a quick glance in Scott's direction, and he straightened and cleared his throat.

"Ellie, you want to do everything to make sure Joe's surgery goes well, right?"

"Of course I do."

"Well, don't give him anything else to worry about. If you insist on staying here tonight and tomorrow, he'll worry about you and not rest the way he needs. You don't want that."

Her face fell, and her hands dropped to her side. "Well, no, of course not."

"You stay here even after Kathy arrives, but then I'll take you home. Sound okay?"

Ellie walked close to Joe's bed and leaned over to brush at his hair. She stared at him for a moment. "Are you sure this is what you want, Joe?"

He patted her hand. "Yes, Ellie. I'll rest better knowing you're safe at home."

Ellie kissed him on the forehead. "All right then."

* * * *

6:30 p.m. Thursday, April 22

Scott unlocked the office door and went inside. He'd left in such a hurry this morning he forgot to slip the Smithson's file now lying in the center of his desk into his brief case. He picked up the manila folder and started out when his cell buzzed.

"Scott."

"How are you doing, David?"

"I'd be lots better if I were already home, but I'm thankful you're there. I've got travel info for both me and Meg. I'll text you when we disconnect."

"Great. Your mom's in the car now. I stopped by the office to pick up a file, but then I'm taking her home. Maria's got supper ready for us."

"Mom's going home? Frankly, I'm amazed. Figured she'd insist on staying at the hospital with Dad, and then we'd worry about her, too."

"Joe wanted her to, and when I explained he'd worry less with her at home, she reluctantly agreed. Kathy's arrival helped my argument since she stayed with Joe."

"Is Dad going to be all right?"

"The young doctor is impressive, David, and despite Joe's age, this is pretty routine surgery."

"It's just…"

"You're not here. I understand. I'll meet you and Meg tomorrow at the airport."

"Okay. Thanks for stepping in, man."

"Sure, no sweat." After severing the connection, Scott locked up his office and headed back to the car. He didn't like leaving Ellie alone too long. A person's imagination could play a number on you, while you waited and couldn't do anything about a situation.

Scott climbed behind the wheel. "Okay, Ellie, let's take you home."

"I hate how we're interfering with your work, Scott." Ellie's hands twisted in her lap and her normally neat haircut suggested a bird's nest.

"You're not. I'd left this file and wanted to study it tonight or tomorrow sometime. What's Maria planned for supper?" Scott maneuvered through traffic.

"It doesn't matter. I won't be able to eat." Ellie fiddled with a sleeve then straightened a collar that wasn't awry.

"No choice there, Ellie. Joe tasked me with making sure you eat a nourishing supper and a get good night's sleep. It's important to keep up your strength for when he comes home."

Her gaze locked with his. She nodded. "You're right. I know you're right." After a moment, she ran a hand through her hair, patting it back into a semblance of order. She straightened in the car seat, appearing to grow taller.

"We're here, Ellie." Scott rolled into the driveway of the three-story home.

"Yes, we are." She strode toward the porch as if she didn't carry the burden of an ill spouse on her shoulders. "Let's find out what Maria has for us." She looked back at him and waited for Scott to catch up then slipped her hand through his arm. "No more feeling sorry for myself. I'm an incredibly fortunate woman. Joe will make it through the procedure. We'll all get through this and be stronger for the experience."

Ellie squeezed his arm with more strength than he imagined her having.

She smiled. "Maria, we're home."

* * * *

8:30 p.m. Thursday, April 22

"I'm relieved Kathy came down. Knowing she's been with Joe this evening helped." Ellie sat in the den with a glass of white wine before her on the coffee table. "What time will she get home?"

"I expect the nurses will kick her out around nine." Scott's swallow of beer that tingled his throat.

"You've told me, but I don't remember when Meg's plane lands."

"Ten-thirty." Scott's stomach literally turned a summersault at the idea of seeing her.

Ellie took a deep drink of her wine then blew out a breath. "It's time."

"I'm sorry? For what?" Scott asked.

"Have you and Meg talked since you both left in January?"

Her blue eyes, so like her daughter's, starred at Scott unblinking. Her lips pressed together in a straight line.

"David keeps me up to speed about his sisters' lives, and you've talked about them both at our weekly suppers, but no, I haven't talked with her personally." Scott searched Ellie's face for a clue as to what was on her mind.

"You see, Scott, when one experiences a surprise like Joe and I did with his heart, a person stops taking so much for granted. Perhaps we don't have the time we expected to let matters work out in their own way. Perhaps a nudge in the right direction is necessary."

"Let me tell you, Ellie, I'm confused. What are you talking about? Despite what happened to Joe, you're both in reasonably good health."

"Yes, but—Scott, do you remember me introducing you to some lovely younger women at the Christmas party?"

Was she up to her matchmaking tricks again? "Yes."

"Did you notice I never introduced you to women after the party? And since you moved here I haven't once tried once to hook you up with anyone"

He shook his head, puzzled.

"Did you wonder why?"

"Ellie, you don't have to apologize for not arranging my social life, if that's what's bothering you."

"I didn't keep putting you in contact with women, because Meg asked me not to."

"I'm sorry." Scott repeated again. "I must've misunderstood." He raised the beer bottle, took a sip of beer, and replayed Ellie's words in his head. "Meg asked you to stop?"

"Yes."

He set the bottle on the table. "Why?"

"Goodness, Scott." She huffed. "For a smart man, you're being dense. She likes you."

Emotion heated his face. He stood, grabbed his cane, and walked several steps away from Ellie. While sex with Meg had been every bit a wow as he'd expected, a relationship with her never had a chance. He was a cripple, and she was this wonder-woman type character. If he stupidly came to have feelings for Meg and got hurt, that was his own damn fault.

"Say something for heaven's sake."

He didn't turn, but spit the words out, "She wanted to thank me for saving David and helping with the blackmail incident." He swallowed and faced Ellie. "Meg pitied me because I'd gotten hurt. That's all."

"I hope you're not this blind in your work, Scott. Meg cares for you. She hoped you'd get over your hang-up with the stick." Ellie gestured to the cane in his hand. Scott studied Ellie, a strong woman, every bit as sturdy and resourceful as the other members of her family.

"Meg's a member of a SWAT team, Ellie. I understand how strong, how fit she is." He paced the den. His cane made slight tapping noises on the hardwood floors. "I'll never be as physically capable as I once was. I've accepted the consequences of the gunfight. Meg deserves a man who's able to keep up with her, to be as good as she is."

"An awful lot of pity coming from you, Scott."

"So what's with this lawyer David told me about? Thought they were in love."

Ellie's eyebrows rose. She looked away then after a moment, she met his gaze. "He's a friend of Meg's, and they went out once. Kathy let on to David more was going on between them. She was less than truthful with him, and the ruse worked in a way. David passed on the false info to you. Meg has no idea we hatched the plan."

Ellie crossed to Scott and rested a hand on his arm. "I'm sorry. I admit not our best thinking. I'd have bet money you cared about her. I believed you'd fight for her when you got wind of what was brewing. You're not taking the bait crushed me."

Scott dropped onto the sofa and ran a hand through his hair.

Ellie let out a long sigh. "I apologize for putting you on the spot this way, Scott, but I wanted to be honest with you. Meg has no idea about us planning to catch you. Please don't hold my actions against her when you see her. Or will you cut us all off because of our foolishness?"

Scott laughed. At first, only a small chuckle tricked out, but then grew into big, deep down belly whoops forcing him off the sofa. When he finally caught his breath, he brushed tears from his eyes, walked over to Ellie and kissed her on both cheeks. "You're really something, Ellie Bourland."

"Joe tells me that often." She smiled.

Ellie and Joe managed to climb over some tough mountains. Maybe she was right. Maybe Meg's heart could find a place for his less than perfect self the way her mother did with Joe. Scott breathed a small prayer. Time for him to gut up and find out.

CHAPTER EIGHTEEN

10:15 a.m. Friday, April 23

Meg tightened her seatbelt as the plane neared DFW. A
tailwind drove them ahead of their ten-thirty arrival time, which was
good news because thunderstorms were forecast for later in the day.
Her stomach, which already had its own storm brewing, flipped like a
Mexican jumping bean from the moment last night when Kathy
relayed the information Scott would meet the plane.

"Maybe this will turn out to be one of those blessings in
disguise, Meg. Give you and Scott another chance."

"I don't think so, Kathy. If he'd been interested, he'd have
called or sent an email."

"So no contact between the two of you since you left in
January?"

"I sent a card congratulating him on his new job."

"Well, something, I guess. You didn't hear from him
afterward?"

"No." She had hoped, small as the gesture was, a line of
communication would open.

"Maybe he didn't receive the card."

"I didn't get it back. Give me a break, Kathy. The guy's not
interested." Meg had brought the conversation to a quick end.

She glanced out her window to the Dallas skyline. When she
leaned forward across the large man sitting in the aisle seat next to

her, the outlines of the Fort Worth were visible through the window on the other side of the plane. Thank God, the family would all be together for Dad's routine procedure. It didn't matter for all the doctors to talk about how routine the surgery was. When a parent was involved, it ceased to be routine.

While the plane made its approach, her stomach clenched, as nervous with the upcoming landing as the idea of returning to Fort Worth permanently. Kathy believed one of them needed to be nearer to their parents. She didn't understand the consequences of what she was asking of her sister.

Meg gritted her teeth, clenched her hands on the armrests, and braced her feet on the floor. She hated landings. Stupid really. She'd made it through the worst of the flight. Moving back home would eliminate all the plane trips, but it wasn't a good enough reason to do something as drastic. Now her father's heart attack and what it fore-shadowed? Something else again. Clearly, this required more soul searching.

Meg disembarked along with all the other passengers. First, she stopped in the restroom. Not being the best of flyers she stayed seated for the whole flight. The idea of walking around suspended at 36,000 miles above the earth made her a tad crazy. She glanced at her reflection in the mirror, added blush, touched up her lipstick, and adjusted her ponytail. Put a smile on her face and act like seeing him was no big deal. Yeah, right.

She made her way down the concourse and went through to the unsecured area and the baggage claim. None of these people looked familiar from her flight. The flight attendant had rattled off letters and gate numbers, but being caught up in surviving the landing, Meg didn't hear which was hers. She scanned the area. Ah. The guy she'd sat next to, and the woman with the baby who'd amazingly slept the majority of the trip stood in next group of passengers. The carousel carrying their bags started with a couple of beeps.

A man walked up and hugged the woman with the baby. He raised the child up over his head, and she giggled. Someone bumped against Meg, pushing through to grab his suitcase. Her deep maroon colored bag topped the carrousel and serpentined in her direction. She stepped forward, but before she grabbed hold of the handle, a voice stopped her.

"Here, let me help you."

"Oh, Scott, hi."

"Hello, Meg."

If his smile was a reflection of the one spreading across her face, she must look like a real goof. But right at the moment, Meg didn't care.

"I'm your ride. Did anyone tell you?"

"Yes. Kathy last night."

"I hope it's okay."

"Sure. Thanks." God, she'd reverted to her middle school persona with a crush on the class president who'd condescended to notice her.

Scott took the handle on the bag. "This all you brought?"

"Yeah, and my carry on. Let me." She reached for the rolling bag.

"No, I'm fine. Let's go." He rolled her bag in one hand and held his cane in the other.

Meg devoured him with her eyes. What a difference in how he looked now compared to when she met him at the airport in December. He'd filled out and aside from the small limp and the cane, no one would ever guess how close to death he'd been.

His whiskers weren't scruffy the way they'd been earlier either, but a full beard encased his cheeks. Handsome didn't begin to describe him, and Meg scolded her hormones for jumping around. He wasn't here for her but for the family. If he'd been interested, he'd have called her sometime in the intervening months.

By the time they got in his SUV, Meg decided the silence had gone on long enough. "How do you like living here? Did my card congratulating you on your new position arrive?" Direct. Best to tackle this issue before the rest of the family was around.

"Yeah, I did. Appreciated the thought. I love the job."

"Good. I'm glad."

She clamped her hands together to keep from reaching for him and planting a big one smack on his lips. Not recommended behavior in the crazy traffic at the airport or on the freeway. Not to mention, she had no clue what his reaction would be.

"Marty Smith is a great boss. We take a proactive approach, helping our clients learn what they can do to improve their personal or business safety. It's a nice change from coming along after all hell breaks out."

"Sounds like you've found your niche. Marty's lucky you've gone to work with him." She licked her lips. Now what? "How are Mom and Dad doing?"

"Ellie is a wonderful woman." A smile tipped up the corner of his mouth. "We've had some interesting conversations."

"Oh? What about?"

"We'll deal with that later."

Cryptic, but all right, she'd wait. "What about Dad?"

"He's stabilized with surgery scheduled for tomorrow at two in the afternoon. The doctors promise a full recovery."

"I can't wait to see him for myself."

"Lady, I'm doing the speed limit here, do you mind?"

Meg laughed. How could she mind when she'd spend longer with Scott?

* * * *

11:30 a.m. Friday, April 23

"Ellie, I've got something for you." Scott held open the front door to the Bourland house, and Meg brushed by him.

"Mom." She scooted down the hall toward the den. "Mom."

"Here, I am, Meg." Her mother came from the direction of the kitchen, drying her hands on a dishtowel.

"How's Dad?" Meg asked.

Her mother's arms encircled Meg. "I'm glad you got here safely, dear. He's fussing about being in the hospital, and not as in control of his life as he likes to be."

Meg stepped backward. "How are you holding up?"

"We're all doing okay, given the circumstances, which could've been considerably worse. It's helped having Scott here." She glanced around and stretched out a hand to him. He covered the ground between them in long strides, hampered only a little by the limp and cane.

"When Kathy arrived yesterday afternoon, we were able to convince Ellie to come home to rest," he said.

"Your father insisted I stay here last night. I was mad, but afraid to yell and upset him, endangering his health more. Kathy is there now. I waited for you to land before returning to the hospital."

"Let me run my bag upstairs, and I'll be ready."

"I'll take it, Meg. You can both go on."

"You'll bring David straight to the hospital, Scott?"

"Yes, ma'am."

Her mother flashed her smile at Scott. "Have you taken care of the other little piece of business?"

"Tomorrow, after Joe's surgery."

Her lips thinned. "But, Scott, I wanted to know the deed was taken care of.

"It will be Ellie, trust me. But not until we've all made it through the surgery."

"What in the world are you two talking about?" Meg stared at Scott, bemused. He seemed much more at ease with himself than when she'd last seen him.

"It's nothing, Meg, dear. Don't concern yourself, and apparently, I don't have to either."

Did she wink at Scott? What was going on between these two? Meg's gaze moved to Scott again, but jerked back to her mother when she spoke.

"Let's go, dear." Her mother handed the towel to Scott, picked up her purse from the hall bench, and made for the garage on quick feet. Meg hurried to catch up to her.

"What in the world were you and Scott talking about, Mom?"

"Nothing to worry your head about. Now pretend you're not in law enforcement, I'm making tracks for the hospital and don't promise to observe the speed limits."

Meg chuckled. "Nothing new there."

Fortunately, they passed no police cars, because a cop would've flashed her over for sure. Meg bit her tongue to keep from saying anything.

Her mother smiled at the nurses and attendants, calling some of them by name, as she and Meg went down the hall toward her father's room. A door ahead of them on the right opened and Kathy stepped out. A smile lit up her face as she spied them walking toward her.

"Hey, Meg. Glad you're here."

Her sister's embrace brought comfort. "Me, too, you. How's he doing?"

"Why don't you see for yourself?" Kathy held open the door.

Meg's throat tightened into a ball, and swallowing hurt. Dammed if she'd let the tears burning her eyes slide and worry her father. She swiped at her eyes before stepping inside.

He opened his eyes. "How are you, Dad? Understand the doctor is doing a little procedure tomorrow, huh." She slid a chair up close to his bed and enfolded one of his hands in both of hers.

"Hey, darlin', I must've dozed off. Where's Kathy?"

"She's outside with Mom. Do you hurt or need anything?"

"No. They're treating me well. Don't worry, Meg. Normally, this would be an outpatient procedure, but though I hate to admit it, the years are beginning to creep up. The worst part, from what I've heard, is lying on my back and not moving my legs for four hours after the surgery."

Meg smiled. "Yeah, that'd be tough."

"It probably wasn't necessary for you and David to come home, but I'm glad you're here. Maybe the four of you can keep Ellie from going crazy."

Four? He'd included Scott in the family count. "I'm sure she's worried, Dad. Regardless of how routine the procedure is."

The door opened and Kathy and her mother came in, who went right to her father's side and picked up his other hand.

"Nice for both girls to be home at the same time, isn't it, Joe?" her mother said.

Her father nodded and smiled.

"If you promise no more heart attacks, we...I...promise to come more often," Meg fought tears again.

"What a deal. I agree." He smiled, but the effort seemed to take a lot out of him.

"Listen, Mom," Kathy put a hand on her mother's shoulder.

"Why don't you and I go home for a while and leave Meg with Dad?"

"I'll keep an eye on him," Meg said.

"Scott will bring David up here after picking him up from the airport. Sound, okay Joe?" Her mother leaned over, kissed his cheek, and brushed at his hair.

"Fine. Y'all go. Meg will keep me company."

* * * *

8:30 p.m. Friday, April 23

"Do you understand what you're asking of me Kathy?" A sharp pain shot from Meg's gut straight up through her middle to her chest. It took all her control to keep her hands by her side and not throw something at her siblings.

"But, Meg, honey. You agreed to talk about having someone keep a close eye on Mom and Dad, right?" Kathy asked.

"I agree we need to consider alternatives for our parents, Kathy, but is it a forgone conclusion I'll have to be the one to turn my life upside down? My life's in Atlanta. You're much closer."

"But Ron's job is in Oklahoma City. The company's headquarters is there. If he wants to continue to move up, he has to stay there. I'm willing to come down every weekend, but what about checking on them during the week?"

Meg shot a glance in her brother's direction. "So is this what you think, too, David?"

David nodded. "One of us needs to do this, Meg. You and I don't have a family. Kathy does."

Another black mark against her for not marrying and having children. Damn. "What are the possibilities of us splitting the time?" She faced David.

"Come on, Meg. You're smarter than that. Then we'd both be out of a job."

Meg paced. "I don't know if I can do this, guys." Age wise, Meg was still eligible to apply with the FWPD, but the department would require her to go through the entire application procedure, train with the new and younger recruits. She'd be a beat cop again. Physically, she was up to the challenge, but she didn't want to do that at this point in her life.

She scrubbed her hands down her thighs. "What's fair about me having to give up what I've gained? What I do is as important as what David does." The words tumbled out and lay between her and her siblings.

"Yes, of course, Meg, but consider for a minute. Mom would prefer you or Kathy," David said. "I can't be the one to fill this role."

"It has be you or me," Kathy said.

"What about home health care? People can come in and provide 24-hour care when it becomes necessary."

Kathy crossed the room and took Meg's hand. "You've said, in your experience, this only works well, if a family member is around who can drop in unexpectedly. Please tell me, you'll at least consider the possibility."

Meg's gaze traveled between Kathy and David. She dragged in a deep breath. "I'll consider it, but no promises."

* * * *

2:45 p.m. Saturday, April 24

Meg's mother paced the waiting room. All four of them took a stab at enticing her to sit down or go to the cafeteria for coffee. None had been successful. Mom kept up her steady trek back and forth, back and forth. Finally, they gave up and alternated walking with her. Scott had the job now.

Scott. When she returned to Atlanta, would she be able to forget him? The lawyer hadn't worked, but maybe someone else— She jerked her attention from her sore heart to the waiting room. The reality for the family, with her parents both being in their seventies, was they'd ultimately need more help. Yes, Maria came in every day, but her age was an issue, too. Meg stepped up next to Scott and took his place with her mother. He squeezed her shoulder before turning away. She grasped her mother's hand, taking and giving comfort.

The hospital waiting area faded again while she chewed on their problems. Scott lived and worked here now with his own life. Still she couldn't impose on him. Had her parents talked about the possibility of moving to a retirement facility? New and better ones had been built in recent years with all kinds of services and accommodations. Kathy hadn't mentioned hearing anything about those options when she dropped the bomb on Meg to consider moving home. Past time for a family council meeting, one including their parents.

"Mrs. Bourland." Dr. Hancock walked through the door and straight toward Mom.

Everyone who'd been sitting rose. David moved to Mom's other side.

"Mr. Bourland came through the surgery like a trouper."

"Thank God and thank you, doctor." Her mother's breath blew out in a whoosh, as if she'd been holding it the entire time of her husband's surgery.

"He'll be in recovery for a while, but I'm sure you'll be happier once you see him. Let's limit the visitors for now." He glanced at everyone standing around. "After we move him to his room, you'll be more free to see him, but don't stay long or tire him out. Come with me, Mrs. Bourland." He led Mom out of the waiting room.

"Thank God," Kathy said, hugging Meg.

David and Scott did the guy hug with the shoulder bump and hand slaps on the back. When they all got home, Meg would raise the issue with David and Kathy about retirement facilities. Mom would stay at the hospital for a time, giving them an opportunity. After talking with each other, they'd discuss options with their parents. Not an easy task, but definitely time to tackle the subject. Meg crossed her fingers the others would relent, and she'd be off the hook about leaving Atlanta to move to Fort Worth.

* * * *

4 p.m. Saturday, April 24

Meg relaxed against the car seat. What a relief it was to see her father. Hearing the doctor's words had been great, but she needed to confirm for herself her father was all right. Literally, her shoulders loosened. Meg glanced to her left at the man driving, and the cold in her heart made her shiver. The realization they hadn't worked out issues between them washed over her. She struggled to breathe. She kept her gaze on him lapping up mental pictures to take with her when she left.

The discussion with her siblings last night about what to do with their parents had been difficult and emotional. Everyone still looked to her to move back to Fort Worth. What was best for everyone? She didn't know.

"Scott, you missed a turn. We're the next street over." Meg glanced over her shoulder at the street, which led to the family home.

He kept driving and didn't say anything.

Her heart thudded against her ribs when he veered into the driveway for Julie's guesthouse. She sat, unable to force her arms and legs to work. Scott opened her door and held out a hand. When she placed hers in his, warm fingers curled around her hand and a tiny ray of hope zinged through her middle.

They'd reached the front door of Julie's guesthouse before Meg found her voice. "We can't just walk in here. What if they've got company staying?"

Scott deftly unlocked the door. "I've talked with Julie." He stepped across the entrance and deactivated the code. "They don't." He looked Meg up and down. "Are you coming in or staying out there?"

She entered. "With Julie? I've barely spoken to her since I got home to update her about Dad. When did you?" She beat back desire all too ready to spring into a fire of passion. Her heart about flew right out of her chest. If she misinterpreted Scott's actions here, the disappointment would crush her.

"Don't you wonder why I needed to borrow her little house?" Scott moved a step closer to her. Despite herself, Meg backed up.

"Yes." Meg held her breath.

"Come with me." He took her hand and led her to the love seat.

She perched on the edge next to him, one hand rubbing her jeans-clad thigh.

"Your mother wanted me to talk with you about something before your father's surgery. I insisted we wait until we found out how he came through. He did great. So it's time." He leaned forward and took both of her hands.

Her hands felt so at home within his, but her nerves stretched out like taffy. The problem was if you pulled too far, the sugary mess tore a part. "What is it?" She'd be a candidate for a heart attack, if he left her hanging in limbo any longer. "Tell me."

He drew her to him and kissed her like a long lost lover stunned to find the other alive. Meg's arms stole around his shoulders, returning his embrace with all of her pent up emotions. His tongue dueled with hers, and hers fought back. They breathed the same air, drinking each other in. God, she loved this man. Meg jerked away from him. "Stop." She couldn't do this and pretend it didn't mean anything. Her palms pressed against his chest. She wouldn't play the game.

Scott didn't let go of her. "Did you ask Ellie to stop introducing women to me?"

His question threw her. "What?"

"At the Christmas party Ellie made a point to introduce me to several available women. She never did again. She told me she quit, because you asked her to quit. Did you?"

Meg nibbled her lower lip. Damn. Heat rushed from her neck up her face. She looked down. "What was Mom thinking to tell you?"

"You didn't answer my question. Did you ask her to stop?"

Meg didn't meet his gaze, nodded, and fought the tremble threatening to take over her chin.

"I'm glad you did."

"You are?" She glanced up.

"Yep." He dropped his forehead on hers. "I'll always be grateful to your Mom for kicking me in the butt. I've been a blind jackass where you're concerned. I'm sorry I accused you of having sex with me out of pity or to say thanks."

Meg's heart came close to bursting out of her chest. Blood rushed through her veins like an overflowing river. She reached a hesitant hand to his cheek. "You told me once it wasn't just sex—"

"We made love," Scott completed the sentence. "I hope for lots of repeat performances for many, many years to come."

Meg drew in a quick gasp of air, and tears welled when he moved his mouth to kiss the palm of her hand. The tears spilled over, and Scott's thumb wiped them away.

"I love you, Meg. Tell me Ellie was correct, and you care about me, too."

The expression of hope and doubt mixed on Scott's face shattered Meg's fears. She placed both hands on his face and drew him toward her, saying everything in her heart with a kiss. She moved an inch away. "I more than care for you. I'm mad about you, you crazy man. I almost died when you accused me of feeling pity for you. It was like you'd stabbed me."

Scott set her away from him. "I'm sorry, sweetheart. I've been a jerk, but will you marry me anyway?"

"Are you sure? Because when I say yes, you'll be stuck with me for a long, long time. Like Mom and Dad."

"Works for me. Was that you saying yes?"

She nodded. "Uh huh."

"Thank you, God, and thank you, Ellie Bourland. What do you say to us sealing the deal?" Scott nibbled her neck. "The bedroom calls with fond memories of our experiences together in there."

Meg took his hand and tugged him off the loveseat. "In case I wasn't clear, I love you Scott. Let's see how many ways can I show you?" She slid her arm around his waist, rested her head on his shoulder, and they walked together toward the room in which they'd first made love. Happiness like she'd never imagined painted the small bungalow in rosy hues.

* * * *

6:45 p.m. Saturday, April 24

"Mom, is Dad awake?" Meg whispered when she stuck her head around the door of her father's hospital room. She could hardly wait to tell her parents about Scott.

"I am." He shoved himself up on the pillows.

"The procedure went well, Dad."

"So I've been told. Interesting experience. I wasn't completely out and watching the balloon open the artery for the blood to flow…it was like seeing a flower bloom in a fast action documentary on the Discovery Channel."

"Really?" Meg cut her gaze between her mother and Scott. Her father wasn't usually poetic. Must be a result of the drugs in his system.

"Scott, I'm glad to see you, dear." Her mother kissed his cheek. Scott smiled at her and winked.

"You both look—dare I say 'happy'?" Her mother's gaze nailed each of them. "Anything you want to share?"

"Well, we do have news." Meg reached behind for Scott. His fingers wrapped around hers made her believe everything was possible.

"Meg's agreed to marry me."

Scott's voice filled her with such emotion—love, pride, and unbelievable joy. She had to fight to keep a tear from falling. How silly. She'd never been one of those women, crying when she was happy.

"Congratulations. I couldn't be more pleased." Her father struggled to reach a hand toward Scott who moved quickly to clasp it in his own.

"It's about time." Mom seemed to puff up like a peacock. "Heart attacks sometimes come with a silver lining."

"Mom?"

"Ellie, what are you talking about?" Her father's voice not forceful as usual.

"If the attack hadn't occurred, Joe, the urgency I felt to speak up might've been less. But you did and I did. Now look at the wonderful results." She spread her arms to encompass them. "Come here, Scott, and kiss your future mother-in-law."

"More than happy to." He moved closer to her and placed a kiss on her forehead and an arm around her shoulders.

"Tell us all the plans. How soon? Where will you live? Our house is large enough you can certainly move in with us while you look for a place of your own."

Oh, my God. Meg hadn't considered the practical part of her and Scott sharing their lives. Clearly, she needed to spend effort on the subject. Right now, she couldn't put together a single phrase to respond to her mother's questions.

* * * *

"Ellie, we don't have all the answers yet, and we don't want to tire Joe out." Scott slid an arm around Meg's waist and pulled her close. Her eyes were wide. Her brows arched all the way up as if she were afraid. "We've got plenty of time for all of the planning when Joe's on his feet and back home. Which is where I'm taking you're lovely daughter right this minute before she passes out from hunger. Ellie, let us know what time for David or me to come get you."

"No need. I'm staying the night." She said.

"No, you're not." Joe argued.

"You two settle the question between you. We'll give you a little privacy, so you can. See you tomorrow, Joe. Call if you need me, Ellie." Scott patted her on the shoulder and hustled Meg out of the room.

Neither spoke until they were seated in his car."

"Thanks for getting us out of there."

Meg's voice held a tentative sound with a small catch in her throat.

"You looked shell-shocked from your mother's questions. We'll find the answers to those and others. Together. We don't have to decide them right this minute."

Meg nodded, and Scott decided to give her space. He drove in silence. He hadn't focused on the issue of where they'd live. He assumed she'd move to Fort Worth because of his new job here. He was unfair to ask her to give up the SWAT position she'd worked hard to attain. If she moved here, would she expect to return to the FWPD? She'd probably start at the bottom. But what kind of a marriage could they have if she lived in Atlanta, and he lived in Fort Worth?

Before he realized how much time passed, he reached the Bourland home and pulled into the driveway. He used a large umbrella to shelter up the sidewalk. Neither of them had spoken a word for the whole trip from the hospital. Maybe not so good. He propped the umbrella on the porch and reached for the door handle. Meg stopped when they stepped up on the porch. He reached for the door handle, but Meg took his arm and kept him from going in.

"Thought you were starving?"

"I am, but I've got to clarify something before we face more of the family."

Hell. She can't back out. Would she insist on staying in Atlanta? He wasn't losing her. No matter what actions were necessary.

"Meg. I can move—"

"Listen to me, Scott." She grabbed hold of the lapels of his jacket and made him stand directly in front of her. "I don't care when we marry, as long as it's soon. I don't care where we marry, so long as we do."

Her palm caressed the whiskers covering his cheek. He couldn't resist her touch, and angled his head to kiss her palm. He stopped and gazed into her eyes, not sure where she was going. "I'm not about to argue with a quick wedding."

"I'm moving home. To Fort Worth."

"I hate for you to. You've worked the job in Atlanta much longer than I have the one here. We'll work something out."

"I know. I've already given this thought."

"You have?"

"Kathy suggested one of us should live in town. Mom and Dad will be slowing down, needing us more."

"So why does it have to be you? How can I ask you to give up what you've earned in Atlanta?"

"First question. Ron's job ties Kathy's family to Oklahoma City. David's in Los Angeles. Leaves me. Second question. You're not asking me."

"I'm here now, Meg. I can help look after your parents."

Meg drew his head down and softly kissed his lips. "I know you can. I'm grateful you're willing, because even with me moving here, it'll take lots of back-up from you. I'll be pretty swamped with jumping through the hoops to get back on the force—"

"Why don't I move to Atlanta?"

"Oh, Scott. Thank you." Both arms went around him.

She practically squeezed the breath out of him. One strong woman was his Meg, in many ways.

"It means everything to me you'd offer to give up your job, but it's only been a short while you've settled here with Marty's firm. I don't know how we can make a go of a real marriage with half a country between us."

"I don't know either, but you humble me Meg. I'll never be deserving—"

"Don't you go there, mister." Her finger rammed him in the chest. "No one's allowed to say bad stuff about you, especially not you, understand?"

"I understand I'm the luckiest man alive, and I will spend the rest of my life making sure you never regret for a moment making this decision." He set his cane against a porch chair, hauled her close, and pressed his lips to hers. His hands slid inside her jacket and under her sweater. He needed to feel her skin. She quivered at his touch. He loved her so much his heart might explode. Lightening flashed behind his closed eyes followed by fireworks.

When he finally backed away they were both breathless, and Meg's cheeks were pink. "Shall we go in now? Thought you were hungry?" he asked again.

"I am. I suspected you were, too." She squeezed his rear.

Fire shot straight to Scott's groin.

"Let's grab something to eat then we'll take care of the other hunger." She spun out of his arms and scampered through the front door. "Hey, Kathy, David, we've got news."

Scott followed his bride-to-be into the house. He stopped her, placed one hand behind her head, an arm around her waist, and proceeded to kiss them both breathless.

"What's the news?" Kathy asked, coming into the front hall.

"Hey, what's all the shouting about?" David's voice followed on top of his sisters. "Oh. Well, I'm not blind." He patted Scott on the shoulder. "Looks like you worked things out between you."

"Tell us." Kathy clapped her hands together.

"Scott asked me to marry him."

Meg's smile stole his heart, as if it didn't already belong to her. Breathless from their kissing, her voice stirred Scott. Somehow, he gathered his wits and settled to earth. Her siblings deserved an announcement, and he and Meg needed to hear their good wishes.

"And she said yes." He planted a quick kiss on her forehead then released her for a hug from her sister.

"Do Mom and Dad know?" Kathy stood with one arm draped around Meg's shoulder.

"We came straight from the hospital," Scott answered.

"Come here, brother. Let me welcome you to the family."
Kathy hugged him and kissed his cheek.

"I guess Mom started something when she adopted you, huh?"
David hugged his sister. "Happy for you, Meg."

"Y'all are okay with us?" Meg asked.

"Would it matter if we weren't?" Kathy punched Meg's arm.

"Truth be told? No, but I'm glad everyone is happy."

"Where are y'all going to live?" Kathy asked, her eyebrows
drawn together.

"Here. I'm moving home to Fort Worth."

"Getting back on the force?" David glanced between Meg and
Scott.

"Yeah, but I'm going to set my sights on being a detective this
go around."

"Good plan. Safer," Scott said.

Meg put her hands on her hips.

"I take back those words," Scott raised both hands in front of
him. "I've learned my lesson. You can do anything you set your mind
to."

"Maria's left her enchiladas, and I was just about to take them
out of the oven." Kathy said. "Let's eat."

The sisters, arms entwined, ambled toward the kitchen.

Scott's stomach growled. Maria's food was always excellent.
But right now his smile and attention focused solely on the beautiful

woman walking in front of him. As if she sensed his gaze, Meg glanced over her shoulder and winked. She loved him.

The End

ABOUT THE AUTHOR

Marsha R. West, a retired elementary school principal, is also a former school board member and theatre arts teacher. She writes Romance, Suspense, and Second Chances. Experience Required. Marsha lives in Texas with her supportive lawyer husband. Their two daughters presented them with three delightful grandchildren who live nearby. A new dog, Charley, a Chihuahua/Jack Russell Terrier mix came to live with them in November.

MuseItUp Publishing e-released her first book, VERMONT ESCAPE in July 2013 and her second book, TRUTH BE TOLD, in May 2014. In the Fall of 2014, Marsha formed MRW Press LLC to provide a print version of her books. VERMONT ESCAPE, TRUTH BE TOLD, and SECOND ACT, Book 1 of the Second Chances Series are all available now. SECOND ACT follows up with a secondary character from VERMONT ESCAPE and begins a four-part series.

She expects to publish the second book in the series, ACT OF TRUST, in early Fall 2015.

If you enjoy TRUTH BE TOLD, please tell your friends and post a review on Amazon, B & N, or Goodreads.

You can contact her at marsha@marsharwest.com and at her web site http://www.marsharwest.com. She'd love to hear from you.

SECOND ACT

BOOK 1 OF THE SECOND CHANCES SERIES

ADDIE'S STORY

♦

CHAPTER ONE

Monday, September 24

"You promised this wouldn't happen again, Clay." Addison Greer glared at the man sitting across from her in her Cowtown Theatre office, the pitch of her voice higher than she intended. She hated confrontations, but those red numbers marching across the spreadsheets covering her desk made her stomach roil and her hands shake.

"Yeah, I know, Addison. I needed more wood than I'd anticipated. After we put the first set together, it didn't work out, and we had to start over. It wasn't my fault." His leg draped over the arm of the chair as if he had no worries, but his voice had taken on the whiny tone that sent Addie's blood pressure into the stratosphere.

Her fingers tightened around the marker she'd used to highlight the deficits. "No? Then whose? Going over budget isn't an option, Clay. The theatre can't survive this way, and since you can't change, you won't make it here either." Addison hated to put it that way, but damn, she'd been plenty patient with Clay Bennett, the theatre's artistic director.

"What do you mean, *I won't make it.* Are you threatening my job?" He set both feet solidly on the floor, jutted out his chin, and clenched his hands on the arms of the chair.

Good thing she wasn't alone in the building with him. She suspected he'd like to take a swing at her. The first show of the fall season closed last night, and crewmembers were working all over the place disassembling the set, cleaning the costumes, and evaluating make-up needs.

"That's exactly what I mean, Clay." The steel in her voice was unmistakable. She had to make him understand. "We had full houses during the run of the show, but we didn't make enough to pay for the production. You have failed consistently to bring in shows on or under budget. I won't let you continue to drown us in red ink."

She shoved the pages on her desk in his direction. He glanced at the sheets and broke into hysterical laughter. Chills scampered down her back like mice escaping a cat. The man was a creative genius and scary as hell right now, but Addie wouldn't cut him any slack on the financial issue. She'd given him enough second chances to last two careers.

"Being executive director doesn't give you the power to fire me, unless you get the support of a supermajority of the board." His lip curled into a sneer that matched his voice. "And you don't have that." He stood up and walked toward the door. His knuckles whitened on the knob before he yanked it open and turned to face her.

"Don't fuck with me, Addison. You'll lose." His whiny tone switched to a menacing one.

Her face warmed with the rush of blood at his language. She stood, met his gaze, and clenched her hands into such tight balls the nails cut into her palms. "You mess with this theatre, and I'll make you sorry, Clay Bennett."

"Everything okay?" Big, burly, redheaded Pete Talmadge stopped outside her office. Despite many years in Texas, his voice still held remnants of his New Jersey upbringing.

Their words had apparently traveled into the hallway. *Not particularly professional, Addie. Nor adult.*

"Everything is fine." She glanced at him then back at her AD. "Clay, I've been clear with you, and this meeting is over."

Clay pushed past the stage manager. His high-pitched laugh sent chills crawling up the back of Addie's head. Her temper, which she hadn't yet fully controlled, sparked. "Damn, damn, damn, damn." The words spewed from her gut. The pain in her middle doubled her over. Confrontations, regardless of how they turned out made her ill. When she lost her temper, she lost self-respect.

Pete stepped in and shut the door behind him. "So, are you auditioning for the part of Henry Higgins in some sort of reverse gender production of *My Fair Lady*? I suppose it might fly here in Fort Worth." He laughed at his joke.

Addie threw her pencil at him. He ducked, and it fell to the floor. "I guess everyone heard us. I hate to air the dirty linen in front of others."

"Yeah, well, don't let him get to you. He's a jackass, and many of us know that," he said in the gravelly voice of a long-time smoker.

"He's right though, Pete." Air rushed out on a long sigh, and she flopped into her swivel chair. "I can't fire him unless I can convince a majority of the board, plus one more, to support the action. He's got at least three members wrapped up in his hip pocket."

"Shannon DeWitt is one of them."

"I've never understood her support of him, so she's a prime target for me to change her mind. She's a smart woman. If I show her the financials from this production and the ones last spring, she'll get why I'm concerned. The numbers don't balance." Addie doodled with a red marker on one of the printouts.

"Who are his other champions?" Pete leaned against the wall, crossed his hands over his chest, and cocked one ankle over the other.

"James Duffy and Linda Alexander."

"Well, we know why he's got Linda in his court." He waggled his eyebrows and twirled an imaginary mustache.

"Pete." She dragged out his name in a scolding tone. "We don't *know* anything about that. It's just nasty speculation on the part of folks who ought to keep their opinions to themselves."

"You're too nice for your own good, Addie. Their relationship is a conflict of interest."

"Suspected relationship and I'm not the morals police. They're consenting adults. Sure makes the situation awkward, though." She rested her head on her hands for a minute before lifting her thick black hair off her neck.

"I'm not blind, and neither is the cast or crew." Pete walked behind her desk and kneaded the tension in her shoulders. "We know what you're dealing with, and most of us are behind you."

His words and touch comforted, but that was all. It would be nice if a spark or zing of some kind enveloped her. A good, strong man, he'd indicated an interest, but she'd been unable to reciprocate beyond an appreciation for his friendship. Maybe she'd never feel that excitement in the belly again. To experience a relationship, you have to trust. Addie wasn't sure she'd ever be able to do that after what her ex had done.

"Mmmm." She shrugged her shoulders into the pressure. Not as good as going in to see Mary Jane for a full body massage, but very nice. "Thanks, Pete, and I appreciate having the staff support." Addie smiled up at him and patted his hand but then her lips drooped. "Who is in the other camp?" She hated to ask but needed to know.

Pete squeezed her shoulders once more and walked toward the door. "Clay snowed a couple of the younger, temporary ensemble members with his experience on Broadway. The permanent staff is with you." Pete leaned down and picked up the yellow pencil from where it had landed. He tossed it to her and touched his hand to his head in a mock salute. "You're welcome." He pushed through the door.

Addie fished in her pocket for her cell and searched for her important numbers. She placed the call to Shannon DeWitt.

* * * *

Wednesday, September 26

"I'm sorry I couldn't come in to see you earlier, Addie." Shannon spoke in low cultured tones. She didn't sound like she'd grown up in Fort Worth, but she had.

"That's alright. I appreciate you squeezing me into your schedule. Can I get you some coffee?" Addie moved to the credenza on the sidewall.

"Sure. Unusually early cold front out there." Shannon loosened her fur coat and sank into the chair in front of the desk while Addison set out the mugs.

"You take this black, don't you?" She poured the coffee.

"Yes, thanks." Shannon smoothed out unnoticeable wrinkles in her mid-calf-length wool skirt. It was the exact shade as her boots.

Addie settled herself in her desk chair, took a quick sip from her mug, savoring the caffeine zing before she leaned forward. "Shannon, you've always done a terrific job on our board. You ask good questions, and you come up with logical suggestions when addressing concerns."

"Thanks. I've enjoyed the work. It's one of my favorite boards to serve on."

"I asked you to stop by so I could go over some of our financial statements with you." Addie pushed up the sleeves of her sweater and laid a spreadsheet on the desk in front of the board member.

"This is about Clay, isn't it?" Using a red shiny nail, Shannon drew the paper closer.

Addie nodded. "He's gone over budget on the last three shows and only broke even for the summer shows. I know you've been one of his supporters. No one can fault the man for the results. The shows have been well received by audiences and the press."

"But your job is to keep us financially solvent." Shannon drew her index finger across the figures before she met Addie's gaze.

"That's right." Addie folded her hands on top of the desk and leaned toward the woman she needed as an ally. "At this point, it won't matter how much we bring in on the fundraiser, we'll be swimming in red ink before the end of the year. I'm talking personally with you and two other board members to make sure you see the financial crises looming."

"At some point, you probably need to look at changing the bylaws, so it doesn't take more than a simple majority of the board to fire the artistic director." Shannon took a sip of the coffee. "Strong. I like it this way."

"In the meantime, all I can do is talk with you three and try to make sure everyone understands the numbers. If I can do that, then I should get the votes."

"Are you sure it's the only way? Can't you give him a second chance?"

"I talked with Clay after the shows last fall, and in the spring he went over budget again. I warned him then. We did better this summer, but now after this first show of the season we're in the red again. We can't have another year like the last one. He's had his share of second chances." Addie unclenched her hands before she gripped her cup and took a swallow of coffee. She had to convince this woman.

"Who approves his spending?"

"Roger Garland, our accountant." Addie set down the mug with care not to spill. "I've told him I want to see every bill before he pays them, but he hasn't always done that. Roger I can fire if he doesn't straighten up." She let out a rueful chuckle. "I don't need the board's approval."

"May I take these reports home and study them, Addie?"

"Of course. Those are your copies."

"I appreciate what we're trying to do here—affordable, high quality theatre." Shannon stood and slipped her arms into the sleeves of her coat. "I'll let you know my decision soon." She walked toward the closed door. "In the meantime, we have the fundraiser, and maybe that will get us over the crises. Thanks for the coffee. I'll be in touch."

Addison dropped her head in her hands.

And that was the board member she had the best chance to sway. Damn, the next two visits would really be tough. She stood and paced toward the windows and stared out at the parking lot with its smattering of cars and trucks. Cold air seemed to seep through. She shivered.

Since Shannon was iffy, she'd have to meet with the other two board members. Might as well go ahead and set up the next appointment. That'd be Linda Alexander, who had tons of money. Addie huffed out a long sigh. She wasn't looking forward to the meeting, because she was relatively certain the rumors about Linda and Clay were correct. It just made everything so awkward. Straightening her shoulders, she walked back to the desk and punched in Linda's number.

"Hey, Linda, it's Addison Greer. I wondered if you have time to come in today or tomorrow. I'd like to talk with you."

"What's it about, Addison? I have tennis this afternoon, a massage in the morning, a facial later tomorrow." Linda's twangy Texas accent grated on Addie more than anyone else's did. "Couldn't we handle whatever it is on the phone?"

Not the kind of conversation Addie wanted to have on the phone. "How about the day after tomorrow. Any time then?"

"Not good either. What's this about?"

Addie gripped the cell so tight her fingers grew numb. "I want to talk with you about our budget." Linda's slight gasp made Addie grit her teeth while she waited for a response.

"Addison, if this concerns the rumors I've heard about your efforts to fire Clay, then we don't need to talk in person. I won't support that action."

"But, Linda—"

"Don't mention it to me again. Good bye." *Click.* The conversation was over.

Well, that was a total bomb. Addie leaned back in her chair, drained. She wasn't up to facing James Duffy right now, even over the phone. Besides, she had a meeting in thirty minutes with the planning committee for the fundraiser. They were holding the dinner in the large, glassed-in lobby, the auction in the theatre itself. For entertainment, the kids in their Children's Theatre and some of the adult ensemble players had prepared several numbers to present on stage.

In years past, they'd brought in a high profile performer and charged a lot for the tickets. As a community theatre, and given the hard economic times, Addie had insisted they change in order to keep ticket prices lower and encourage more people to come. After initially balking, the board had gone along. Now it looked like the numbers were going to prove her right. They'd never sold many more tickets than in the past.

She set a fresh pot of coffee to perking and then pulled out the folders she needed for the planning committee. Even if this shindig were spectacular, the theatre would be financially hurting. As long as Clay held the position of artistic director, Cowtown Theatre remained at risk.

Coming

Fall 2015

ACT OF TRUST

Book 2 in the Second Chances Series

Kate's Story

Since losing her husband on 9/11, **Kate Thompson** has focused on keeping her daughter (now grown) and herself safe. The inheritance of land from her husband's aunt pushes her out of her comfort zone and into the arms of a Maine lawyer.

Environmentalist and lawyer, **Jim Donavan** wants to protect Liddy Thompson's land and keep it from falling into the hands of the developers, but first he has to convince Kate she should hold on to the family land when she doesn't even want to come look at it. However, he's unprepared for the attraction he feels for the Texan.

How will they be able to settle their differences about the land? Will they find who's killed people to stop the deal going through? Or will they break each other's hearts?

www.ingramcontent.com/pod-product-compliance
Lightning Source LLC
Chambersburg PA
CBHW061304170626
46817CB00001B/45